DELTA GREEN:

STRANGE AUTHORITIES

John Scott Tynes

ARC DREAM PUBLISHING • 2012

DEDICATION

For my wife and daughter
and everyone who ever gave me a chance.

Published March 2012 by Arc Dream Publishing
12215 Highway 11, Chelsea, AL 35043, USA
www.arcdream.com
First printing

ISBN 978-0-9853175-1-5 (hardback)
ISBN 978-0-9853175-0-8 (paperback)
ISBN 978-0-9853175-2-2 (ebook)

Printed in the United States of America

CONTENTS

Foreword

I DON'T REMEMBER NOW whether I knew John Scott Tynes (or "Tynes," as I called him, or "Rev," to people who knew him before I did) before I knew *Delta Green*. I met them both around the same time, across a glass darkly, around 1997. Whether it was 1997 or a few years before or a year after either way, it was a pretty great time to drink and talk all night, to write games and ramble around, and to pretend we knew what the future held. We were just like everyone in every independent film you ever hated. We had no budget, but we thought we had a killer script. It was the great age of the slacker, that Generation X version of the Beat. It was a great time to talk nonsense with a straight face. Bliss it was in that decade to be alive; and to have an open bar tab was very heaven.

Delta Green came out of the Nineties, out of what was, in retrospect, America's Indian Summer vacation between the fall of the Wall and the fall of the Towers. It presented a vision of a black-suited conspiracy in league with alien entities that were using the entire U.S. government as their puppets, or perhaps as their host body. Opposing that conspiracy? Our heroes? Not the heroes of previous decades; not lovers, or reporters, or Rambo. No, our heroes were guys in (slightly different) black suits, members of that same federal government, themselves forced to lie and sneak and conspire to defeat a faceless, multi-headed military-industrial-bureaucratic complex in the name of How Things Used To Be. Our enemies weren't Us—this ain't *Pogo*—but they weren't quite Them, either.

This *grand jetée* of navel-gazing paranoia was, to put it mildly, in tune with the Nineties. That decade's zeitgeist perhaps most famously also created *The X-Files*—which debuted a year after the first *Delta Green* scenario saw print, a datum I must have heard Tynes adduce a hundred times in a fugue of irked pride. Like Cody Goodfellow's *Radiant Dawn* (a glorious 1999 Cthulhu Mythos novel of medical horror and technocratic implacability), our fables clung rigorously to the nuts and bolts of the clandestine and the quotidian, like all proper thrillers running just a few weeks ahead of the headlines. And such headlines they were! Why, in the Nineties, conspiracy theorists used to argue about one guy dead in a park, or taped conversations about blowjobs! People hugged themselves to sleep dreaming up conspiracy porn featuring alien autopsies, black helicopters, and shadowy survivalists in the woods somewhere.

Then.

The next decade, everybody—not just the conspiracy theorists—argued about how many secret prisons the federal government should be allowed to run in foreign countries, and whether the president or just the vice president had connived at murdering 2,800 New Yorkers. JFK's former press secretary declared that a missile, not a hijacked airliner, hit the Pentagon. If you wanted conspiracy porn, you had your choice of beheadings or prison experiments, depending on your politics. Surely, the days of *Delta Green* had passed. It was fun while it lasted, like souvenir T-shirts from Roswell or I WANT TO BELIEVE posters.

BUT.

Cthulhu came out of the Twenties, out of what was, in retrospect, America's Spring Break between the trenches and Dachau. You see where I'm going with this; I don't have to spell it out, beat it to death. Pulp begets prophecy. Put simply:

Cthulhu heralded an apocalypse, of madness and destruction and suicide, and then he ushered it in, and he rode it. Somehow Cthulhu survived Hiroshima—and like Lynn Willis' joke says, "now, he's radioactive."

Somehow *Delta Green* survived Abu Ghraib—and now, it's fucking radioactive. Now, we really know what a malevolent conspiracy can do. We've seen its outlines, rising like Surtsey in the Pentagon and in Pakistan. We sense the approach of our own blind idiot god.

John Scott Tynes will show you its face.

Time to get this show on the road. You have no idea the kind of Hell he has prepared for you.

None of us did, back in the Nineties. Before the apocalypse.

Kenneth Hite
Chicago, 2012

The Corn King

Friday, December 24, 1993

DAVID NELLS RAN HIS fingers through his hair, pausing to scratch at his scalp. The NRO had sent over a new batch of satellite images showing a Chinese missile base in Tibet, and he had to prepare a preliminary update for his superiors in the CIA on what appeared to be a new construction project. He'd already worked through dinner. Jill had been pissed when he'd canceled their date a couple hours ago, but Jill was always pissed at him for one reason or another and he'd just hung up on her when she started to yell. Relationships usually bored him quickly, but his thoughtlessness and her temper kept them in a cycle of break-up/make-up that he found invigorating. David suspected that was why they were still together after fifteen months.

The fact that both were Delta Green agents probably had something to do with it, too. The scale of their secret life dwarfed that of their romantic life, putting things in perspective. Or so he liked to say, when he was getting that weary feeling and wanted to pick a fight with Jill.

He took a gulp of coffee laced with bourbon. Just a little. His boss had instituted an unofficial policy for his small analysis team when they had to work late: bourbon after Brokaw. They were all old China hands, marking time until retirement, and regarded the clean-cut academics who staffed the other groups with something approaching contempt. What business did you have analyzing imagery of a country you'd never lived in? David knew it was a ridiculous attitude for his team to hold, given that they spent their time staring at bird's-eye images of silos and structures that could be in Nebraska as easily as China, but like attracted like and everybody needed somebody to look down on.

The phone on his desk buzzed and he picked it up. A delivery at the front desk. He stood and yawned, looking down for a moment at the photos on his desk, taken by a sleepy satellite glimpsing the Earth far below as it drifted through the silent twilight of orbit. Then he wandered off through the halls towards reception to see what the delivery was.

It was a single long-stemmed rose, wrapped with a green bow. Martha had him sign for it. There was no card, but it didn't need one.

David went back to his desk and typed up a brief report on the images; looked like the Chinese were building a new barracks, nothing to wake the president for. He put the images back into their envelope and dropped them and the report into his boss's document safe. Then he got his coat on, picked up the rose, and headed for the door.

"Merry Christmas, Mr. Nells," Martha said politely as he walked by. David grimaced. No wonder Jill was so pissed; he'd forgotten. It was Christmas Eve, 1993.

Jill Sanders sat at the small dinner table in her apartment, picking at a slice of pie. The voice of Billie Holiday filled the room from a boom box. She'd had other music picked out for tonight, but then David Fucking Nells blew her off on Christmas Goddamn Eve so out came Billie, her favorite music for doing a slow burn. As she fiddled with the lemon meringue she'd picked up from the neighborhood bakery, her thoughts were on the diatribe to come, when she'd tell David she was through with him and his bullshit and so on and so forth. They'd had so many arguments that it was getting harder and harder for her to come up with new ways of telling him what a jerk he was—but the challenge only whetted her appetite for conflict. The trouble was that David was a charismatic guy who could be really charming and considerate when he felt like it. Plus he'd almost taken a bullet for her when he didn't have to, and that had to count for something.

Fucker, she thought. No. She'd used that one before.

There was a knock at the door. *Shit!* It had to be David, come to make up, and here she was with her battle plans still sketchy. As she got up and walked to the door she just tried to flow with Billie, confident that she would be ready to tell David a thing or two, at least. She opened the door.

Sure enough, it was him, holding a *rose* for God's sake. "Ratfucker!" she blurted, then saw the green bow around the stem—a DG op signal.

David grinned.

"You have got to be kidding," she managed, totally flummoxed.

"Merry Christmas, kiddo. Get strapped and let's go."

Billie sang on.

As they walked to the car, Jill reluctantly agreed to table their discussion of David's merits and flaws until later. Business came first.

"So where are we going?" she asked once they left the parking lot. "Joe?"

"Nope, Joe's not in on this one." David sounded cheerful, infuriatingly so.

"Where, then?"

"It's time for you to meet the old man. He's leading this op personally."

"I thought Joe *was* the old man."

"All right. We're going to meet the *older* man."

"David, who is this guy?"

"Major General Reginald Fairfield, retired."

"Never heard of him."

"You aren't supposed to. He's the captain of this whole ship of fools. The guy's a fossil, but for some reason he's going out in the field with us. Usually he just pulls our strings."

"So what's the op?"

"Beats me. I called him from a pay phone and he just said to grab someone and come over, on the double."

"And you chose me."

"Hey, you were the one who wanted a date tonight."

"Don't start."

"Fine."

"So where are we going?"

"The Bentson, downtown. He's got a suite."

They drove in silence for a few minutes. It was snowing on the Potomac and the highway was a white snake, ghostly in the dim. Eventually David spoke, hesitantly.

"There's something you should probably know."

"Yeah?"

"Reggie . . . I don't think he's ever worked with a woman before."

"*What?*"

"I mean in the field, you know. On an op. He's kind of old-fashioned."

"You mean he's an asshole."

"Yeah, pretty much."

"Thanks for bringing me along."

"Hey, if you're going to be mad, you might as well be mad

at someone else for a change."

"I've still got plenty of mad left for you."

"Never a dull moment, kiddo."

They reached the Bentson around 11 p.m. and drove into the parking garage. Leaving David's Chrysler behind, the pair walked outside to the front doors and into the lobby. At the front desk, David rang the bell for a clerk. A young man emerged from a doorway. He was impeccably groomed.

"Yes sir?"

"Please ring Mr. Fairfield's room and tell him his guests have arrived."

"Oh, yes. He left a note for you."

"He's not even here?" Jill said, irritated.

"He just left," the clerk said, handing David a small envelope. David and Jill drifted away from the desk while David opened the note.

Outside, it said. *In your car.*

David looked up sharply. Through the front doors he could see his Chrysler, idling in the snowy street outside.

"Oh hell," he muttered.

"David, isn't that your car?"

"Yeah. We're in for it now."

The man in the driver's seat was a vigorous kind of old. Jill guessed he was in his early eighties, observing the hunched shoulders but muscular arms as she climbed into the back seat. David got in the front.

"Fucking amateurs!" the man bellowed. "I could've taken both of you in the goddamn garage."

"Sorry, sir," David said quietly.

Reggie wrenched around to look at Jill and then scowled at David. "What the fuck is *she* doing here?"

"She's my partner, sir. You said to bring someone."

"I didn't say to bring some goddamn broad!"

"Agent Sanders is a capable field operative, sir. I've done three ops with her and she's cool under fire."

"I'm at your service, sir," Jill said diplomatically.

"You couldn't service me with a tire jack, Sanders. Who cuts your checks?"

Jill turned red, though no one noticed in the dim car. "I'm a criminal investigator for the Office of Export Enforcement," she said, straining to keep an even tone.

"What the hell is that?"

"Department of Commerce, sir."

"You're an accountant with a strap-on! Nells, have your brains turned to shit and shot out your ass? We've got serious work to do tonight and I need men I can count on."

"Sir—" David began, but Jill interrupted.

"Shut up, David. Listen, you toothless old fuck, if you don't think I can pull my weight we can step outside and I'll hand you your ass on a platter. It's Christmas Eve and I've got better things to do than get screamed at by some dickless poster child for prostate cancer. So put up or shut up, motherfucker, because I'm not going to tolerate this bullshit for another minute."

David stared straight ahead and tried to pretend he was somewhere else. In the rearview mirror, Jill could see Reggie's eyes, alive with some weird kind of excitement.

"All right. You'll do." Reggie put the car in gear and punched the gas.

Δ

Back on the highway. Back in the snow. Reggie drove like a madman, swerving through traffic to pass car after car, cursing loudly at the other drivers. But for all his seeming recklessness, he kept an iron grip on the wheel and moved the car with a precision Jill could only admire—he drove aggressively, yet he had the confidence to back it up. When she whistled quietly after a particularly dangerous but deft maneuver, Reggie grunted. "Try booting a Willis through the Ardennes at twice this speed and then you'll have something to whistle about, agent." Soon they entered Virginia on I-66, and Reggie seemed to relax a little as the metropolitan traffic thinned out. David eventually worked up the nerve to ask a question.

"Can you brief us now, sir?"

Reggie nodded gravely. "Not much to brief. There's a party tonight on a mountain called High Knob, and we're going to crash it."

"What are our objectives?" Jill asked.

"Shoot anything that moves."

"That's it?"

"Torch whatever's left."

"And then?"

"Go the fuck home and wait for Santa."

David spoke again. "What kind of opposition are we facing?"

"Wetworks death squads. Demons from higher dimensions. Partridge in a pear tree. Fuck if I know."

"Are you sure we have enough agents?"

"I'm sure we have enough bullets. Assuming you and your lady friend can shoot straight. Either of you handle a rifle, or am I hauling my cataracts up a tree to pick off punks at five hundred yards?"

"I'll take sniper," Jill offered.

"Don't shoot me by mistake, you hear? I'll be the screaming bastard with the big balls."

Jill shook her head. "Don't tempt me."

Reggie laughed, then glanced at David. "Nells, bourbon."

"I'm out, sir."

"Don't shit a shitter, boy, I smelled it on your breath when you got in the damn car."

"I left it at the office."

"Give me the goddamn bourbon or I'll turn this car around and make you buy me some."

David grimaced and took a flask out of his coat pocket.

"Mary, Mother of God," Reggie muttered as he took a swig, then held the flask towards the back seat. "You want some of this, agent? I'm slap outta tea and cookies."

Jill took the flask and had a slug, then handed it back to the driver.

"Finish it off, Nells," Reggie said. "That shit stinks like a pig but isn't fit for one. We've got a long way to drive."

THEY REACHED HIGH KNOB a little before midnight, taking a lonely road through the snow flurries. After a few turns, Reggie wheeled the car off into the bushes and got out. David and Jill followed.

They opened the trunk. Inside were several large plastic cases. Reggie removed an M21 sniper rifle and a twenty-round magazine, then handed them to Jill. "Load it," he barked.

Jill put the mag in and chambered a round, then briefly sighted on a tree through the scope. "Ready," she said, slinging it over her shoulder.

Reggie handed her three more magazines, which she stashed in her jacket, then pulled out two AK-47s for himself and David and bags of mags for both. Finally he strapped on a backpack.

"Demolitions," he explained. "Let's go."

For the next eighty minutes they slogged uphill through the trees, Reggie guiding them by compass at brief intervals. It was cold and quiet. No one spoke.

At last they crested a stout rise, crawling up slowly under Reggie's direction. About two hundred yards below was a clearing fed by a dirt road. Three Broncos were parked end to end, blocking the road. About a dozen men in tactical gear loitered near the trucks, setting up some large light sets to illuminate the clearing and running power cables back to the trucks. None of them wore any sort of uniforms or identifying logos, and the trucks were unmarked.

"Cocksuckers," Reggie muttered.

"What now?" David asked.

"You two watch close. I'm going to get down there and set a charge on the outermost truck. We blow that one and it's instant roadblock. Anybody gets too close to me, Sanders picks them off and Nells, you just start spraying so I can get clear. But don't shoot unless you have to—this party hasn't started yet. If we get separated, meet back at the car."

"That's the plan?" Jill asked, incredulous.

"No, that's the clusterfuck. The *plan* is that I'm back in half an hour and nothing happens until the others show up because these jokers aren't going to notice me playing partisan with their truck."

"Ah," she said, not at all relieved.

"Keep sharp," he muttered, and walked off into the trees.

The minutes pulled past slowly. Jill and David kept an eye on the men in the clearing, who finished setting up their lights and now seemed to just be milling around, waiting for something. Jill identified a tall man in an overcoat who seemed to be in charge.

"Who are these people, David?" Jill whispered.

"You know as much as I do. They look like special ops to me."

"Fuck. This is ridiculous."

"Wait—I see him. By the truck."

Jill trained the rifle on the outermost Bronco and spotted Reggie, creeping up in the stark shadows cast by the vehicles and the trees at the edge of the well-lit clearing. She swiveled the rifle slightly, picking out the men closest to the trucks. None noticed Reggie in the darkness. He moved like a cat, surprisingly nimble for his age and weight.

Reggie had spent five minutes in the trees down the road, just catching his breath. He couldn't afford to be wheezing when he went in close. Once he got his breathing down to a quiet pace, he advanced through the snow until he was behind the truck. Then he took an explosive charge out of his pack and quietly stuck it to the undercarriage of the Bronco. He could hear voices and occasional laughter from the armed men nearby, idly waiting for their guests to arrive.

I'll give them something to laugh about, Reggie thought, as he slowly retreated from the clearing and back into the woods.

Δ

"So tell me about this guy."

David chuckled. "Not much to tell. He plays things pretty close to the vest. I know he was the one who reorganized the group after the Joint Chiefs shut us down, and he's been in charge ever since. But he's sort of a big-picture guy. Joe sweats the details. It's gotta be years since he went on an op."

"I wonder why he's out tonight," Jill said thoughtfully as she watched the old man in the distance disappear back into the woods, unnoticed by the men in the clearing. "And why the hell isn't Joe involved?"

"Reggie's a contrary old bastard. He likes to do things his way."

Jill lowered the rifle and sat back to look at David. "So you've been taking lessons from him then?"

He grinned and winked at her. "Does it show?"

Atop the rise again, the old man rejoined his companions. He had spent another few minutes catching his breath in the darkness so his agents wouldn't see him panting. He'd also taken the opportunity to watch them, long enough for him to establish that they were probably lovers. The thought made him frown, but he had more important things to worry about.

They stood up as he approached. "Ready to blow," he said quietly. "Nells, come with me. We're going to halve the distance and spread apart. I want you in that copse over there. I'll be in the rocks on this side." He gestured to the two locations down below.

"Sanders, you keep eyeballing these sad sacks. Sometime soon, they're going to have some guests show up. You'll know them when you see them. Once they arrive, count to thirty and then start shooting. I want you to tag the guests first, then hit the troops. As soon as you fire a shot, I'll blow the truck, then Nells and I open up. Nells, you need to fire a burst, change locations quickly, and fire again. Don't let them spot you. Between the two of us moving around and Sanders picking them off and the truck going up, they'll be shitting themselves in no time. Number one priority is to kill the guests. Once they're dead, do clean-up on the rest. When I fire three single shots, David and I start falling back. I'll move while David fires, then I'll fire and David moves, and we keep alternating until I fire three more shots and that means get the hell out. We meet back at the car no later than two hours after the first shot. Keys are tucked in the driver's sun visor, doors are unlocked. Make your approach carefully in case they've found the car. If anything looks hinky there, ditch your rifles and make your way to the state road we came in on, then get home however you can. Any questions?"

"Yeah, who are these people?" David asked.

"The enemy," Reggie said. "I said any questions, not any stupid questions. Let's go."

"Hold up," Jill said, raising her hand. "What is this, some kind of vendetta? That your ex-wife down there? Far as I can see, you've circumvented the chain of command and pulled us out of our homes to kill a bunch of people who look to be guilty of nothing more than littering. If I'm going to pull this trigger, I want to know what I'm doing it for."

David glanced away, once again wishing he were elsewhere. What little interaction he'd had with Reggie Fairfield in the past told him that the guy was not used to having his orders questioned.

Reggie stared at Jill for a moment, saying nothing but with a deepening frown on his face.

"We're putting our lives on the line, sir," Jill said emphatically, not breaking Reggie's stare. "We deserve to know what's up."

Finally the old man broke the silence. "First off, girly, I'm not circumventing the chain of command. I *am* the goddamn chain of command. You chose to join this organization. That means you do what you're told and you accept it like a good soldier. If you don't trust the people in charge, what the hell are you doing here?"

Jill started to speak, but he cut her off.

"Shut up! I'm not finished. Despite being an insubordinate bitch, you're still one of my people. And you're right. We are risking our lives here tonight. Those people down there don't fuck around, and the bad news is they've got our whole government behind them. So the simple version is this: they're collaborating with the enemy to sell out our country, and tonight we're going to provoke a little diplomatic incident. If we're lucky, their whole project will blow up in their faces."

David looked wary. "But sir, if they're here on behalf of the government . . . isn't this a big risk? For the organization, I mean?"

"Of course it is," Reggie replied confidently. "That's why we have a corn king. Someone to sacrifice for the sake of the harvest."

Jill's brow furrowed and she shook her head. "I don't get it. Who's the corn king?"

Reggie grinned. "I am. Now quit this foolishness and let's go."

Δ

David and Reggie were in their positions in about ten minutes. Jill stayed on the rise and watched the clearing. The next hour passed slowly, but it passed quietly.

When the others arrived, it was almost as if nothing had happened at all.

Jill wondered briefly if she'd fallen asleep for a few minutes. She was looking around, watching the men in the clearing, when she noticed that there were two more people down there, and the man in the overcoat and a couple of the guards were walking over to chat. No one seemed surprised or in a hurry. Where had these two come from?

She cocked her head against the rifle, which she had resting on a bipod, and took a look through the scope. If her finger had been on the trigger she probably would have fired out of shock.

The two new arrivals were not human—close, but not quite. They were short, naked humanoids with indistinguishable round faces and huge, soulful, black eyes.

It's fucking Close Encounters, *she thought. It's fucking* Close Encounters.

She had seen some things in her time with Delta Green—worse things than this, terrifying things of eye and bone and muscle. But none of them had been shaking hands with representatives of the United States government. Jill's orderly understanding of the Way Things Were pirouetted in her mind and folded in on itself, a tesseract of incomprehension. Oh my God, she thought, trying to come to grips with the implications of the meeting in the clearing.

Then she noticed the countdown that was already progressing in the back of her mind, the countdown Reggie had told her to start when she saw the guests arrive: *Eighteen, seventeen, sixteen . . .*

Jill sighted in on one of the visitors and slipped her finger into the trigger guard.

Six, five, four . . .

She was ready. She just hoped Reggie and David were, too.

One . . .

The rifle crack broke the night like a twig. One of the visitors staggered, flesh and fluid spraying in an arc across the smooth white snow. The liquid splashed back almost as far as the thing's first footprints, which seemed to have begun their trek out of thin air.

Good girl, Reggie thought, as he pressed a button and the outermost Bronco exploded in a burst of flame and shrapnel, catching two men in the blast. They were knocked to the ground and lay there, burning, the sounds of fireworks as the bullets in their suits touched off from the flames, riddling their bodies with gaping wounds.

Oh shit, David thought, as he sighted down the barrel of the AK and tracked a line of rounds up the chest of a guy in tac gear, releasing the trigger after the man's head snapped back and the snow behind him was spattered with brains. Then he raised the rifle and dashed off to change position.

Jill swiveled the rifle slightly and caught the other visitor, who was looking at its companion nonplussed as the little figure fell over backwards, like a cartoon character slapped with a two-by-four. *Don't think don't think don't think.* She squeezed the trigger again and the second visitor joined the first in slack-jawed oblivion.

Reggie brought the rifle up to his shoulder and opened fire, targeting a man near the trucks. As he did so, several men began firing into the woods towards where David had been, then spun as the rattle of the second AK drew their attention. Reggie lowered the rifle and hurried laterally through the trees to find fresh cover.

In the clearing, men ran to get behind the trucks once they realized the fire was all coming from the same general direction. Jill picked off a guy who was staggering near the burning truck, evidently stunned from the concussion. She tried to find the man in the overcoat, but he was already out of sight.

David reached a large tree. He was breathing heavily, but he immediately brought up the rifle. The men were behind the surviving trucks now, so he sent a couple of volleys into the tires and engine block of the lead Bronco. A hundred yards to the west, Reggie found his new cover and followed David's lead, working over the last truck with the rest of his magazine. Both men moved off again, swapping mags as they did so, while Jill kept pinging at the trucks to keep the troops down. Her fifth shot caught a careless man in the top of the head, and he fell backwards into a snowbank.

A couple of the men began firing into the woods from the edges of the trucks, more or less shooting blindly. Reggie and David blew through another magazine with several short bursts, disabling the trucks and keeping the targets down. Then Reggie switched to semi-automatic and kicked off three shots in succession. David turned and ran, as Reggie switched back to full auto and let another burst loose. Then it was his turn to run while David fired. They repeated this pattern six times, falling further and further back as Jill kept pinging, until Reggie gave the final signal and they hauled ass. Jill spent another minute firing at the trucks, and then she got up and took off down the back of the rise. The car was well over an hour away.

In the woods, in the dark and the cold, Reggie moved swiftly. He was panting, but this was no time for authoritative decorum. He had to get back to the car, and fast, to protect his people. They had proven themselves tonight, and he wasn't going to let them down.

Some ways off, Jill plunged down the slope, rifle slung, mind reeling. She had joined Delta Green to fight insanity, to destroy things that perverted her sense of order. What she'd seen in the clearing told her that the sense of order she'd been fighting for was a sham, and that the stakes she'd been gambling with were far greater than she'd ever imagined. *He's got to tell me,* she thought to herself. *When this is over he's got to tell me everything.*

Further distant, David marched. Hands on head. A gun pressed against his back.

Reggie got there first, a lifetime of soldiering guiding him back through the woods like a homing missile. He approached the car carefully, spending ten silent minutes sneaking around to make sure the scene was clear. When he was sure that all was well, he took up a good position to watch the road.

Jill arrived twenty minutes later. Reggie heard her coming. Not so loud, he thought. He clicked his tongue a couple times until Jill clued in, and the two hooked up in short order.

"Fucking great," Reggie said, his eyes alive again. "Clockwork."

Jill nodded, a little distant. She had a thousand questions to ask him, but now was not the time.

David arrived not long after. They heard him moving

through the woods a ways off.

"Shit," Reggie muttered.

"What is it?" Jill asked quietly.

"He's not alone."

David emerged onto the open road nearby, hands on his head. The man in the overcoat stood close behind him, a handgun against David's spine.

"Come on out, folks," the man called jovially. "Party's over. Five seconds and I erase this boy."

"Ho!" Reggie called. "We're coming out."

"*What are you doing?*" Jill whispered.

"Follow my lead. He's not going to kill David."

"Why?"

"Shut up and come along."

AS REGGIE AND JILL entered the road, two of the armed troops came out of the trees near David and his captor. Reggie tossed his rifle to the ground and nodded at Jill, who did the same.

"You folks have got some fucking balls," the man with the gun said. "We're gonna go someplace quiet and have us a little chat."

Reggie shook his head slowly. They were all standing close now. "We're not going anywhere. It's not time yet."

"Time for what?" the man said, looking at Reggie guardedly.

"You don't get to kill me yet. It's not harvest time. Tonight we walk away."

"What the hell are you talking about?"

"In the old days, the good old days, people chose a corn king to sacrifice for a better harvest. Until the day came, they couldn't lay a finger on him. He did as he pleased. But on the appointed day, the corn king had to die. The bad news for you is today is not that day. The good news for you is when that day comes, you'll be the one to pull the trigger. See, I'm the corn king."

The man in the overcoat stared at Reggie for a long moment before he finally spoke. "You know, I would say that you are absolutely fucking nuts. But there's really no need to state the obvious."

"You're right about that. Hey, you two," Reggie said, glancing at the men with submachineguns standing a few feet away. "Make your peace with the Lord. Time's almost up."

The men looked levelly at Reggie, barrels fixed on him and Jill. The guy in the overcoat watched, baffled by the proceedings. David stared at Reggie, fear in his eyes.

"The Lord is my shepherd," Reggie said, as he flexed his right wrist and a small pistol ejected into his palm. "I shall not want." He raised the pistol and fired it in the time it takes to blink, tagging one of the men square in the face. The other man squeezed the trigger and blew a burst across Reggie's torso. The old man staggered but still swiveled his arm crisply. There was a crack and a moment later a red welt blossomed in the shooter's forehead. "He makes me lie down in green pastures," Reggie said as the men dropped to the ground.

The man behind David turned his gun at Reggie and pulled the trigger. There was a click. David stiffened.

"Oh look, your gun jammed," Reggie said idly, as he shot the man in the left arm. The man dropped his gun and took a step back, clutching the wound with his right hand and making a sound like a kitten. Reggie walked forward, implacable, pistol trained on his target. David staggered forward, fumbling in his jacket for his sidearm, momentarily forgetting that the men had taken it from him in the woods. Jill hurried to David's side, keeping an eye on the confrontation unfolding before them.

"Tell me your name," Reggie said.

"Adolph Lepus," the man replied through gritted teeth.

"It's a pleasure to meet you, Adolph." He kicked him solid in the crotch. Adolph went down, gasping, on his knees. Reggie put the pistol away and took out a combat knife, then kicked Adolph in the shoulder and sent him falling back into the snow. He knelt down on Adolph's chest with a terrible smile.

"Kevlar," he said cheerfully, thumping his chest with his free hand. "You should try it sometime. Not that I could have died today anyway." He put the knife against the man's throat and his face hardened. "It's the same with you—I wish I could gut you like a goddamn pig, but I can't. Two months from now you're gonna wax me like a Pontiac and there's not a thing I can do to change that. But right now I can at least see that look in your eyes. And enjoy it." He pressed the knife a little harder, and a thin line of blood welled up and ran down Adolph's throat. The man gasped and moaned, hands between his legs.

"I just wanted you to know what it feels like to be under the sacrificial blade. When the harvest comes, you'll remember this night. Fuck, I'll *remind* you. And you'll know the only reason you're still alive is because I let you live. Because all of this was set in stone at the moment the void shat out this ball of dirt."

Adolph's face was covered in sweat. His eyes were huge pools of panic.

"The book of life told me when I was going to die, and it told me that you were going to kill me. The only thing I'm not going to tell you is this, you sack of shit: whether or not I'll take you with me screaming into Hell when it happens."

Reggie pulled the knife away and stuck it back in his jacket. Then he slapped Adolph, hard.

"Think about that two months from now, when you're walking towards my door. Think about that when you see me again, in the moments before my death. Think about that."

He stood up gingerly and turned to his companions. "Get the car started. It's time to go." David and Jill, both still wide-eyed, nodded vaguely and stumbled over to the sedan. Reggie watched them for a moment and then looked back down at Adolph with a terrible grin. He unzipped his jacket, which was riddled with bullet holes, and plucked at the white t-shirt inside that hung loose—loose over his bare, unmarked chest.

"Be seeing you," Reggie said, his words cutting through Adolph like a plow through soil. Then he turned and walked away.

Final Report

Friday, February 25, 1994

Received: from anonx.ywy.ub by anonx.com with SMTP id AA-(5.65C/IDA-1.4.4 for <distrib@anonx.com>); 25 february 1994 21:59:32 -0700
Message id: <19940225--.AA--@anonx.com>
Received: from anonx.ywy.ub by anonx.ywy.ub (IBM VM SMTP V2A2) with BSMTP id--; 25 february 94 00:00:09 CDT
Received: from anonx.ywy.ub (NJE origin dx1@anonx.com) by anonx.ywy.ub (LMAIL V1.2a/1.8a with BSTMP id--; 25 february 1994 00:00:06 -0500
Date: 25 February 1994 00:00:01 -0500
Reply-to: dx1 <dx1@anonx.com>
Sender: dx1 <dx1@anonx.com>
From: dx1 <dx1@anonx.com>
Subject: Final Report
To: dx2 <dx2@anonx.com>
x-uidl: ----------------

Major General Reginald Fairfield, U.S. Army (Ret.)
Final Report
2/25/94

It's been twenty-four years, a month, and two days since the bastards brought us down.

In that time we've come back strong, doing things they couldn't conceive of doing. They think they understand us, those who know we're still around. They think we're cowboys, meddlers . . . They think we're just too pig-headed and selfish and old to let go of what we once were.

They know nothing.

They think they're better than us. Stronger than us. And worst of all, they just plain think they're right. They sit in their offices and debate the Accord with the skinny little fucks from space. They sell out the American dream in exchange for stealth technology and sonic weapons. They betray our highest ideals, our loftiest principles. They've lost sight of who they serve—the people who vote them and their kind into power. They've forgotten why they're in power.

They know nothing.

Every night my teeth rest in a glass and every morning I have a bowel movement and I couldn't even begin to get it up these days. My eyes are hollow and bloodshot and my wife left me fifteen years ago. My children are callow monsters who laugh at me and the ideals I cherish and vote fools into office because they saw them on MTV.

They know nothing.

My generation supposedly saved the world from the forces of darkness. Now everyone thinks that evil died in 1945—or was it 1989? They think that things will never be that bad again. They think the apocalypse, the end of all we hold dear, just isn't going to happen. They abandon the Lord and don't go to church and teach sex in the schools and put filth on the television.

They know nothing.

Evil never dies. Darkness never retreats. In the cracks and the crevices of our society there are monsters undreamed of by the rank and file of humanity. I've been there. I've seen them. They exist in the spaces between things, in the folds of existence where we can't find them. Sometimes they cross over, sometimes they manifest, and all Hell breaks loose. Only this is not Hell, nor Heaven. This is like nothing anyone has ever understood. This is pure evil, pure destruction. This is the apocalypse, and I've been fighting it tooth and nail since 1961. They made me retire in 1970 when Cambodia blew up in their faces and they blamed us, but I didn't stop then and I'm not stopping now. They think I gave it all up that day in the Pentagon when they told me the choice—the only choice—I would be allowed. I took it, and then, like most of us, I made the decision to continue the fight. They thought we were washed up.

They know nothing.

But they know enough. They know how we started—a little slice of the OSS, investigating the Nazis' interest in the occult. They know what we found—how the supernatural was realer than real and more powerful than the A-bomb. They know what we accomplished—three decades spent fighting the monsters wherever they cropped up, three decades that kept the world a saner place. They know what we want—to abolish the accord and send those ET fucks back to wherever they came from.

They know nothing.

Things are different today. There's a whole new generation coming into the ranks, men—and women, for Christ's sake—who are smarter and slicker and tougher than I ever was. We've got it down to a science. Something crops up, phone calls are made, operatives are re-assigned, paperwork is filed, and the darkness gets pushed back for another day. When it's over everyone goes back to their routine and no official records exist to reveal the truth. We travel light, we probe deep, and we strike hard. We're Delta Green, and we may be outlaws and cowboys and fools, but we've kept this green ball of shit safe and sound for longer than most people have been alive. They think we're idiots.

They know nothing. But they know enough.

The Majestic group made the deal. They signed over the constitution to the Greys, those bastards from space—or so they claim—in exchange for technology and information. Majestic thumbs their nose at the Executive Branch and has more security clearances than brains. They call the shots when it comes to the Accord with the Greys, and they dispense the technology breakthroughs and they cover their tracks and they let the aliens do whatever they like to God-fearing U.S. citizens. They're fools. I've seen the Greys for what they really are, and they sure as hell aren't refugees fleeing a sun gone nova. The things that lie behind the Greys are no different from the things I've been fighting on the edges of reality since '61. I couldn't begin to guess what they're really up to, but Majestic couldn't care less. They just want to make deals and cover their ass.

They know nothing. But they know enough.

They know what I've been up to. Finally, after fourteen years, a month, and two days, they've figured it out. The news reached me fifteen minutes ago through six connections and two satellite bounces—the news that they were coming for me. I could give a shit. I've lived life true and full and rich and I've never betrayed my country. I've done my duty and ten times more and I regret nothing. Nothing.

I have, perhaps, another ten minutes before they arrive. They'll come tromping through the snow and put a bullet in my brain. My communications have been "out of order" for hours, all except for the line I laid myself three years ago after hoarding the equipment for twice that time. That's my escape route. A digital relay that will take this letter and the accompanying files and put them in the hands of my successors. A line that our slimy twin DELTA, the Majestic wetworks boys, know nothing of. I've used it five times since I set it up, and it, at least, is secure. It's enough to get this information into the hands of Delta Green. It may be enough to save this planet a few times more.

That's it. My power just died, except for the backup generator I installed in the basement for this room. They're upstairs, tripping my internal alarms. In minutes they'll come through the hidden passage and spread my insides across the wall.

Before they do, they'll have a fight on their hands. I may be eighty, but I'm the toughest goddamn son of a bitch these assholes will ever meet. I'm Delta Green, and I'm not dying alone.

But first, I'm going to hit Send and put this information into the hands of a few people who will carry on the fight. People who will crush the Accord and—when the time comes—who will tell the public about all the lies our government has been force-feeding them since the Roswell saucer crash in 1947. They'll carry on and they'll fight hard and true and maybe they'll leave a better world for their children than the one I'm leaving behind.

Entry One has been breached. Time to get this show on the road. They have no idea the kind of Hell I've prepared for them. May God have mercy on my soul.

(signed)

Major General Reginald Fairfield, U.S. Army (Ret.)

:: transmitted 1323 est 2/25/94::PGP encoding enabled::

<eof>

My Father's Son

Tuesday, September 24, 1996

I'm in this dream, deep down, and there's a baby crying. It's a boy. The scene is murky. I assume it's a hospital, but I'm just grafting assumptions on, limning a shadow with whitewash. It's baffling. The boy is crying. I'm dreaming. "Wake up."

I'm twenty-seven. I've just gotten my master's degree in political science. My dad is there. My mom is there. They've brought their "friends," those three guys that turn up at every big occasion in my life. It's weird. They're like a Greek chorus. They show up, they don't give their names, they offer me homilies about my progress. Around them, my parents are affable but subtly guarded. These men were at my Eagle Scout ceremony, they were at my high school graduation, they were at my bachelor's graduation, they were at my writing award ceremony, and now they're here. My younger sister isn't here today, but I've talked to her about these three men. They never go to her events. Just mine. My parents refuse to discuss this. They just say that the men are people who are interested in my progress, friends of dad's from the State Department. If I press them on this issue, mom starts to cry. Dad says, "See what you've done?"

I'm seventeen. I'm at a party at Doug's house and I'm pretty drunk. Sarah is a senior, a year older than me. She leads me into one of the upstairs bedrooms. We chase out Ricky who is passed out in a corner. Sarah takes my hand and we sit on the bed. I'm nervous, I haven't done this before. She kisses me. It's nice. It's wet. Suddenly she grabs the folds of my shirt and pulls it up over my head and then tosses it in the corner. We're still kissing. Her hands run down my chest, stroke my skin. She rubs me for a moment just above my waist. She stops kissing me and looks down, baffled. She looks back up at me. "Why don't you have a belly button?"

I'm twenty-nine. I'm an agent with the DEA. I'm in Colombia in a personnel carrier full of local troops. A rocket strikes the carrier in front of us; there's a massive explosion. Our vehicle swerves to avoid the flaming wreckage and we go off the road. Inside the carrier, we're falling all over each other. Outside, the carrier is tumbling down a hillside. I hang onto cargo straps as bodies flail around me. The carrier comes to a stop. I shove the door open and climb outside, dizzy and stumbling and spattered with blood from the injuries sustained by the troops during the wreck. A dark shape obscures my vision. "What does the shape look like?"

"What?"

"The shape, the one in your dream. What does it look like?"

"It's not a dream. I was in the DEA."

"Derek, please. I'm familiar with your history. You were never in the DEA. This is just a dream. The drugs are confusing you. What does the shape look like?"

"It looks like my father."

Derek takes a drag on the cigarette. His feet, shod in expensive Italian shoes, are propped irreverently on the conference table. His fingers, carefully manicured, tap on the sides of the cigarette like it was a trumpet. His hair, combed and oiled, is just short enough to be regulation but just styled enough to look out of place in the bureaucracy of the federal government. His teeth are where his skeleton shows through, dead white. When he grins it's as if the skin is gone and there is nothing but his skull before you. He doesn't mean it that way—he's a nice guy. It just happens.

We move slowly over the table, beginning at Derek's end. The table is a modern piece of shit, particle board overlaid with contact paper. You could buy it at an office furniture store for $150. The Pentagon paid $600 for it. Of the additional $450, $100 went to the requisition officer, $100 went to the sales rep, and $250 went to the owner of the vendor. The only thing French about this tacky piece of American crap furniture is that the process it was acquired by was strictly *de rigeur.*

For starters, we see a speckled-green cardstock folder in front of Derek. It's currently closed. Affixed to the cover of the folder is a chalky piece of cardstock with an orange border an inch and a half wide. Repeated at the top and bottom, in large orange sans serif letters, are the words **TOP SECRET**. In the middle, also printed in orange but much smaller, are the words:

> **ALL INDIVIDUALS HANDLING THIS INFORMATION ARE REQUIRED TO PROTECT IT FROM UNAUTHORIZED DISCLOSURE IN THE INTEREST OF THE NATIONAL SECURITY OF THE UNITED STATES.**
>
> **HANDLING, STORAGE, REPRODUCTION AND DISPOSITION OF THE ATTACHED DOCUMENT WILL BE IN ACCORDANCE WITH APPLICABLE EXECUTIVE ORDER(S), STATUTE(S) AND AGENCY IMPLEMENTING REGULATIONS.**
>
> **(This cover sheet is unclassified.)**

Cigarette ash dots the cover sheet.

Moving forward, we pass Charlie. Like Derek, he's in the DEA. Unlike Derek, his feet are on the floor. He has an identical folder and cover sheet in front of him. His copy is open, disgorging an unkempt sheaf of papers, photographs, and charts, amended with various notes he's made.

Beyond Charlie, we pass an expanse of bare table until we reach the end. Seated there is Special Agent Matthew Carpenter, a Deputy Director within the FBI national headquarters in Washington, D.C. Carpenter doesn't have a folder in front of him; he doesn't need it. Its contents have become a catechism for him. He could summarize or repeat verbatim any paragraph on any page within the primary report. As we cease our movement across the length of the table, he speaks. (We are ignoring the two armed guards standing outside in the hall, securing the entrance to this Pentagon briefing room. The incongruous nature of a meeting within the Pentagon chaired by an FBI deputy director and attended by two DEA agents does not concern us; the meeting is, after all, of Delta Green origin.)

"His name is Darryl Montgomery. He's 32, works for NYC gov pulling corpses outta the Hudson. Master's in library science, believe it or not, though he's done jack shit with it. Near as we can tell he's a complete non-entity."

Derek chuckled. "And the punchline is . . . ?"

"The punchline is that an NSC analyst spotted him in three photographs of three apparently unrelated national security incidents in NYC during the past year: an accidental car wreck resulting in the death of a Russian Embassy attaché, a hit by a Jamaican posse on an NSA file clerk deep in debt with a bad coke habit, and the suicide of NYC Deputy Mayor Andrew Smith—his brother is the CIA station chief in Lisbon. There was no connection between these incidents whatsoever until the NSC realized that this guy Darryl was at the scene every time in after-the-fact photographs taken by reporters and investigators. As a result, we can't be sure that he wasn't there from the get-go and maybe had a hand in things. It is the official and classified opinion of the NSC that he's a low-rank schmo in with one of the five families of the east coast La Cosa Nostra, and that they somehow had their hands in each one of these situations. It is my official and top-secret opinion that the NSC is full of shit. They don't know from mobsters; that's my turf. They did know shit far enough from shinola to hand me the investigation, at least. I've got an FBI task force assembled and I've fed them the usual line of bull. You two bright boys are the real investigation."

Charlie stroked his jaw and tried to look thoughtful. He seemed to fail.

Derek looked away from Charlie, took his feet off the desk, and leaned forward. "I've heard the punchline, but I don't get the joke. What makes the investigation of Mister Synchronicity a DG op?"

"All three victims—the attache, the file clerk, and the Deputy Mayor—appear on our routine surveillance roster of known persons frequenting Club Apocalypse."

I'm twenty-three. Lisa and I are in love. We've been dating since we were freshmen. Now we're planning our future, seriously. Graduation is just a few weeks away. I've already applied to grad school for the fall. But Lisa and I have a secret plan. We're going to elope after graduation. I'm not going to grad school. Her dad owns a chain of small bookstores in the northwest. He's going to let us manage one. We're moving to Portland in two months. If it goes well, we'll buy the store from him as soon as we can afford to. We're very happy. This is the life I want to live. I hold her close. "I love you."

I'm eighteen. I'm in the hospital. My parents' three friends are here. I lie on the table while the plastic surgeon works on me. I'm sedated but semi-conscious. The three men are paying for this procedure. I don't understand why. But I'm going along with it just the same. The surgeon is nervous. He's never worked in an Army hospital before, but they wanted it done here instead of his clinic. He's supposed to be very good. The three men are buying me a belly button. "You may feel some discomfort."

I'm thirty-one. I'm in the Library of Congress. Dr. Camp is showing me an old statue. It smells to me of Colombia and what I saw there. There are inscriptions around the base. I can't translate them. He's clucking away about antiquity and legend. I'm nodding, doing my best to keep up. I'm not sure why my boss at the DEA sent me here today; what does this have to do with me? Then Dr. Camp looks at me cannily. "We know what you saw."

I'm twenty-four. Graduation is behind me. I'm wearing the sweater that Lisa gave me for my birthday last week. She says it's chilly in Portland. We're eloping tomorrow. I'm packing up my apartment. There's a knock at the door. I open it. It's the three men, the Greek chorus. They look grave. They say there's been an accident. They say Lisa is in the hospital. They say it looks bad. They say they're very sorry. Then they say that my parents found out about our plans to elope and they are very unhappy. Mom and dad? "No. Your parents."

"What does that mean?"

"I'm adopted."

"That's ridiculous, Derek. You're not adopted."

"I'm adopted."

"Derek, please, I thought we got through this already.

You're not adopted, it's just this idea you've embraced to justify your estrangement from your mother and father."

"You know!"

"What?"

"Even you know! Your behavior is just as institutionalized as the Greek chorus!"

"What do you mean, Derek?"

"Even you, doc. Even you can't refer to my mom and dad as my parents. Because you know they're not."

We begin at the bar. Chet is behind the counter, pouring drinks for an eager clientele. We drift lazily across the ceiling, looking down. The band Charnel Dreams is on stage, making a lot of noise. The crowd is dancing frenetically. Anton Merriweather, the lead singer, is flailing about with the microphone. He's cut himself again with the microphone stand, a clean red line across his bare chest slowly dripping streaks of blood mingled with sweat. We pass Belial, standing idle and looking immaculate all at once. He watches Anton on stage, watches the crowd watching Anton, and keeps a mysterious smile in reserve solely for himself. We drift further, over the heads of moshers, over the small candle-lit tables crowded with the tragically hip, over the uneasy jock lounging against a pillar and trying to fit in, over the high-school Goth poseur here alone on a dare, over the married swingers here for new conquests, over the drunken would-be poet here for inspiration, over the waiter who takes weekend trips to upstate New York with his zoophilic friends to fuck goats, over the twenty-something photocopy-shop clerk who is itching to try watersports, over the black corner-market owner who yells at Koreans, over an aging realtor whose desperate clutch at fame was that she hung out at Warhol's Factory in the early 1970s but never scored a mention in anyone's memoirs, over the reporter for the New York Post who thinks he's scoring a coup by getting in here but doesn't realize that the last of his life-blood will pump out of his veins late tonight in the private club down the spiral staircase from the club proper, over the old man who masturbates on the train every day as it passes by the World Trade Center, over the young couple out on the town and in over their heads, over the guy dealing Aklo, over the girl wearing nothing but wax paper, over the musician tapping his foot to the music in his head, over the web designer who wants to score with the girl in the wax paper, over the janitor from the NY Public Library who is writing a biography of his mother, over the counselor from P.S. 159 whose life is a procrastinated suicide, over the six terminally bland yuppies here because one of their college-age children said she heard it was "a happenin' spot," over the guy who OD'ed on alcohol ten minutes ago but who hasn't been noticed yet except by Belial who finds it amusing that a librarian is still trying to hit on the guy, over the librarian who's still trying to hit on the guy, over the rad dyke who wants to hit on the librarian and wishes that she'd stop hitting on that passed-out drunk, over the crew of crack dealers here to make a bargain with some Russian mafia fuckwits to ace a mutual competitor, over the Metro Vice cops here to get drunk on the house tab and write faked reports on the laudable lack of drug traffic in Club Apocalypse, over poor Darryl Montgomery whispering the secrets of the dead to himself near the entrance, over the two DEA/Delta Green agents just now walking in the front door, and then we come to a stop over their heads as Derek and Charlie both spot Darryl simultaneously and start moving towards him as innocuously as possible and we watch them as they move off into the crowd.

Δ

I'm thirty-three. I've been a Delta Green agent for eighteen months. It's exciting. I feel privy to a world of secrets. I've seen things I never could have imagined. The world isn't the place I was told it was. I'm in San Francisco, staking out an alleged crack house—that's what my report will say. It's not a crack house. It's an abattoir. The walls are lined with human skin. A shelf in the kitchen holds a row of dried genitalia. The bathtub is full of feces. He extracts it from the digestive tracts of his victims. He wants them to be clean. He washes them, inside and out, shampooing hair and organs alike. Purifies them. For the ritual. For the offering. A light goes off. It's time. I sprint across the street, Charlie close behind. I kick in the door. I don't wave my badge. I don't shout a warning. I just shoot the fucker. Charlie slams the door shut behind us. We've just broken a host of procedures and laws—but not in the eyes of Delta Green, who sent us here. Blood and chunks of brain run down the wall behind the dead murderer. We grin. Charlie speaks: "Good shot, cowboy."

I'm nine. I'm playing in a stream near my home. My friend Tim is there. We're skipping stones. An old guy, maybe fifty, with salt-and-pepper hair and a dark suit, steps out of the bushes. He smiles at me. He reaches in his jacket and pulls out a gun. He aims it at me. A shot rings out. There's a hole in the center of the man's forehead. His head snaps back. He drops to his knees. His gun falls into the stream along with streaks of his blood and bits of brain and skull from where the bullet blew out the back of his head. One of my parents' friends, a member of the Greek chorus, is behind me. There is another gun present. He puts his left hand over my eyes and holds me close.

There's another shot. He leads me away from the stream. He takes something from me. I hear two voices behind us. I never see Tim again. The papers say he was kidnapped by a wanted child molester. His blood flows down the stream with the dead man's. The man with his hand over my eyes smells of something which I imagine to be cologne but will much later in life recognize as semen. My right hand is bruised and it smells of something I will recognize much later in life as cordite. "That was a close one, kid. Shame about your friend."

I'm twelve. My parents and I are at the cabin on the lake. The afternoon is spent fishing from the balcony on the second floor over the water. My dad has a beer. He's smiling, a little drunk. My sister is off riding her bike. My mom is reading a magazine. My line jerks. I've got a bite. My dad is excited. He coaches me. I fight the fish. Eventually I win. I reel it up through the air. It's a three-pound bass. I'm ecstatic. My dad hugs me. He looks at my mom. There's a tear in her eye. She lies: "It can always be like this."

I'm thirty-five. I'm in a long corridor underground at Los Alamos. There's a large pane of glass before me. I'm wearing a technician's outfit. The M9 is jammed in under my shirt. Fake identification hangs from my chest. A micro-camera is in my lapel. I'm looking in the window to another room. There's a bed, surrounded by all sorts of equipment. Something is lying in the bed. It's humanoid, built like a short and stocky Graeco-Roman wrestler. Its skin is slick, even in the dry recirculated air. It's sea-green. Its head lolls stupidly to one side. The instruments beep. Its crystalline eyes, which never seem to close, are the most beautiful sight I've ever seen. They've seen all the secrets I've seen a hundred times over and still found them fresh and wondrous. "What is it?"

"I don't know. I'm just here to take photos of it."

"What were you told?"

"Not much. Just that there was a patient in this room and I should photograph him."

"Were you told to record data from the instruments?"

"No. Just pictures."

"What did you do with the pictures?"

"I gave them to you. To Dr. Camp."

"Who was the patient in the bed? Who did you tell about this assignment?"

"I don't know. No one."

"Darryl," Derek says. "We'd like to have a word with you."

Darryl stares at Charlie and Derek stupidly. His face does not lack a certain native intelligence, but he has no idea who these men are or what they want and he cannot help but look confused; he is not a very adaptable human being; he cannot control his reactions. He is the most unwittingly honest man in this room.

"Sure, okay," Darryl says. The three men find a conveniently empty table and sit down. None of them realize, unfortunately, that Belial had the table's previous occupants shooed away a minute ago in anticipation of their need.

"Who do you work for, Darryl?" Charlie asks. "We know what you've been up to."

Darryl looks sheepish. "I work for the City of New York."

"Bullshit," Derek says. He splays out photographs showing Darryl at the scene of the three incidents that drew the NSC's attention. "Some people think you work for the mob. We know better. We think you work for Bobby Hubert—a.k.a. Belial. That's fine. Lots of folks do. What we want to know is, what did Bobby Hubert have to do with these three deaths?"

Darryl looks at the photographs. "I don't know nothing about these things. I was writing down prices."

Derek and Charlie look at each other in practiced fashion. "Prices? What do you mean, Darryl?"

Darryl points generally at the photographs. "Prices. I was writing down prices, see?"

Derek and Charlie look at the photographs. Darryl is in different places in each one, coming and going. But in each, barely glimpsed at the fringes of the photo, there is always a different glass-front store with big price banners in the window: "$1.99!" "HALF PRICE: $2.75" "PICKLES 98¢". Derek and Charlie look at each other, exasperated. Derek seems to do a better job than Charlie.

"Okay, Darryl. You were writing down prices. I can accept that. Who were you writing down prices for?"

"Mister Hubert."

Derek and Charlie both perk up. "Mister Hubert?" Derek says. "You were writing down prices for Mister Hubert? What for?"

Darryl looks back and gives away nothing. "'Cuz he asked me to."

Derek lights a cigarette and looks at Charlie. "Ask a stupid fucking question."

I'm thirty-four. I'm standing in an alleyway in Atlantic City, New Jersey, a few blocks from my hotel. This place makes me fucking sick. The casinos are full of decrepit old wasters. There's no life, no vitality, in these people. There's some pathetic drunken fuck leaning against the wall of the alley, panhandling for slot-machine quarters, trying to take even my vitality.

By morning I'd be just another wrinkled loser in a cripple-walker, betting my Social Security check against a full house. What a piece of shit town this is. I can't stand it anymore—the shit, the degradation, the deception, the lies, it's too fucking much. I take three steps towards this old drunk, clasp my hands on his shoulders with a big shit-eating grin on my face like I'm about to do him the biggest favor in the fucking world, and then I live up to my promise. I do him the biggest fucking favor in the world. I do him—I do him in. I knee him in the crotch, he wheezes out a hot breath of malt liquor and puke, I throw my hands around his throat and smash the back of his head into the brick wall, he goes down like the sack of pathetic shit that he is. He's wheezing. He's lost his breath. I flex my wrist. The combat knife pops into my hand. I shove it into his neck, jerk it roughly to one side. Blood pours down onto his filthy shirt. The swift kill comes courtesy of my DEA training. We weren't trained to shiv bums in particular, but that's what's good about civil-service training: it has uses in such a variety of situations. The corpse falls forward into the trash of the alley. I kick him in the head with a $140 leather wingtip just for spite. I turn around and look out at this loathsome excuse for a city and the hatred I feel for the human race is absolute. "Fuck you all."

I'm fourteen. Amy is thirteen. We're in our special hiding place where the grown-ups never find us. We're the closest of friends. We keep it a secret from everyone. We don't have sex—our friendship and love is too pure for that. We're soul-mates. Years later, my love for Lisa will stand as only a dim shadow of what I had with Amy. On this special afternoon in April, I take a rock and beat Amy's head in. Her brains finally spill out, disgorging all of their bloody secrets into the spring air for me to inhale. I keep smashing the rock down, again and again and again, sucking in the thick and meaty stink of her brains for my own enjoyment. She's long since dead. When I finish, I cum in my pubescent jeans. From the bushes, one of the Greek chorus steps forth. "Don't worry, kid. I'll clean it up. Go home and play."

I'm thirty. I've learned to live a lie. I'm undetectable. I pass among the rest of the bleating herd unseen, unknown. I'm ready. I'm prepared. The rest of my life spreads out before me like the legs of a dead whore. I'm going to fuck this world into the graveyard and keep going until it begs for more. Humans have only one real god: Thanatos. I'm death and I walk among them. They'll fuck me until they bleed to terminal, then wonder what went wrong. I'm *le grand mal* made flesh. "Derek Johnson, DEA. Glad to meet ya, Charlie."

I'm thirty-six. I waxed Amy and Lisa and the pepper-and-salt-haired guy and Tim and the troops in Colombia and so many others. I've escaped detection all this time, even—for three decades—by myself. The Greek chorus sings for me, belting out stanzas of rubber stamps and official denials and altered reports. Even Dr. Camp and his lame excuse for mind control can't stop me. I'm hardcore. I'm unstoppable. I'm your end. I am my father's son. "Who is your parent?"

"You know. Mister State Department. Andy Woodrew."

"He's your father, Derek, but he's not your parent."

"That's right."

"So who is your parent?"

"These drugs you've got me on, all these questions—you're just trying to confuse me, to get the truth out of me."

"That's right. And when I'm done, you won't remember a word of this conversation."

"Good fucking luck, Dr. Camp. Good fucking luck. I didn't

think Delta Green did this to its agents."

"We don't."

Darryl looked around the club nervously. "It's not safe to talk here," he says. In silent agreement, we begin to track away from the threesome at the table, drifting silently across the crowded nightclub. Darryl and the two DEA/DG agents get up and head for an unmarked door at the back of the club. Darryl, for once in his life, leads the way.

The door leads the men onto a landing, from which an ancient and decrepit spiral staircase leads down into the gloom. Darryl starts down without a second thought.

"Hold up," Derek says. Charlie looks at him anxiously. His look is not feigned, for the first time since Derek met him, but Derek doesn't notice.

"Yeah?" says Darryl.

"What's down here?"

"Just a meeting room. We can talk privately. Mister Hubert, he's got people all over the club up there."

"All right," Derek says. "But if we aren't alone, I kill whomever we meet."

Darryl nods anxiously, eager to please. He resumes his descent of the stairs, followed by the two agents. As they descend, a strange smell wafts over them: a musty, decrepit smell, like that of an overburdened crypt, motes of skeleton-dust drifting lazily in the draft. They arrive at a landing, and Darryl gestures toward the door. "We can talk in here."

"Oh we can, can we?" Derek responds. "I'll just see about that."

Derek sidles quietly over to the door. With his gun drawn, he uses his free hand to shove the door open and then jumps inside, crouched very low to duck panic fire from any occupants, his M9 surveying the room, an extension of his eyes and arms. No sound greets him from the gloom.

"Come on," he whispers.

Charlie steps next to him and presses the muzzle of his .44 Desert Eagle to Derek's temple.

"I'm here," Charlie responds grimly. Outside, Darryl scurries up the stairs.

"What the fuck?" Derek says, twitching slightly until Charlie presses the gun tight against his skin once more.

"Just sit tight, motherfucker," Charlie says.

The lights come on.

Stephen Alzis stands in the middle of an empty room.

He regards the two agents for a second, and then approaches them, holding a seemingly ancient bound volume. He walks over slowly, taking in the scene greedily.

"Excellent work, agent. This is the sperm I've been looking for."

The Greek chorus coalesces from nothing. They no longer appear as three individuals; they are interconnected in strange, unwholesome ways that defy terrestrial biology.

Derek flushes. "What the fuck is this?"

"You know what this is, Derek," Alzis says. "It's a homecoming."

"The book!" Charlie blares, with a strength and surety that Derek has not heard in the seven years they've been colleagues. It is suddenly evident to Derek that things have not been what they have seemed for a very long time.

Alzis steps forward and hands the book to Charlie. "A fair swap, I should think. This seed of mine has been wreaking altogether too much havoc in the world of men."

Charlie takes the book and steps back beyond the threshold. "Whatever. The fucker is yours now."

"He always was," Alzis says. "He always was."

Charlie's face pretends to lighten for a moment, the way it has pretended so many things in the last seven years. "Hey—I know this is an irregular request, but this is a pretty irregular fucking situation. Do you mind if I put a bullet in his head?" Behind the cynical, jocular violence of his request lies a coiled snake.

Alzis shakes his head in a bemused fashion. "Do whatever you like, agent. It is irrelevant."

Charlie stares down at Derek with burning eyes, the gun reaching out into Derek's reality like an extension of Charlie's arm. "My real name is Mark. Amy was my sister, you piece of shit." He pulls the trigger.

Derek's brains blow out through his temple. His face hits the wooden floor like a mallet on meat. Charlie/Mark speaks.

"All these years you weren't a DG agent, motherfucker. You were a DG op."

Mark stands stock still for a moment, holding the smoking gun in mid-air with one hand and the weird book with the other. He extends his tongue and licks the blood on his face for a brief moment.

"Glad we could do business, Alzis."

"My pleasure, Agent Darrin. I'm sorry it took so long to make this arrangement."

"Quite all right. Quite all right."

Mark steps backwards slowly, holding his gun out just in case. Alzis stands there in the darkened room as his wayward son's life-blood soaks into the floor and runs down the metal drain put there for occasions like this. The Greek chorus fades into insubstantiality, their reality-buoyancy provided solely by Derek's unconscious guilt-complex and ungrasped magickal potential, and now erased, in death.

Mark follows Darryl Montgomery's recent path up the staircase, incredulous and silent. Arriving at the top floor, Mark sees Darryl get a drink and doesn't care what happens to the man. Mark leaves Club Apocalypse and meets with FBI Deputy Director Matthew Carpenter in an undisclosed location. We are not privy to the contents of their conversation.

Dr. Camp is hard at work. He is preparing an electronic file on DEA Agent Derek Anderson, who could not escape his heritage nor fully assimilate his station in life. "It is of the same small bricks that the greatest and the worst men are made," writes Dr. Camp. He clips this short note to a crumpled piece of writing in Agent Derek Anderson's script, written when he was sixteen but recovered by an FBI forensics team from his mother and father's home when he was thirty-four:

"I AM SORRY AMY. I LOVE YOU. I DID NOT WANT TO HURT YOU. BUT MY FATHER TOLD ME WHAT TO DO."

Dr. Camp puts the note in with the rest of the documents assembled in the speckled-green cardstock folder prepared by Delta Green and prefixed by the chalky white piece of cardstock with an inch-and-a-half wide orange border. Repeated at the top and bottom, in large orange sans serif letters, are the words **TOP SECRET**. In the middle, also printed in orange but much smaller, are the words:

ALL INDIVIDUALS HANDLING THIS INFORMATION ARE REQUIRED TO PROTECT IT FROM UNAUTHORIZED DISCLO-

SURE IN THE INTEREST OF THE NATIONAL SECURITY OF THE UNITED STATES.

HANDLING, STORAGE, REPRODUCTION AND DISPOSITION OF THE ATTACHED DOCUMENT WILL BE IN ACCORDANCE WITH APPLICABLE EXECUTIVE ORDER(S), STATUTE(S) AND AGENCY IMPLEMENTING REGULATIONS.

(This cover sheet is unclassified.)

Cigarette ash dots the cover sheet, until Dr. Camp blows it away.

Dr. Camp files the folder in with the rest of his private files at the Library of Congress. DEA Agent Mark Darrin goes on to his next assignment. DEA agent, human being, and being of something simultaneously greater and lesser than human Derek Anderson ceases to exist. Dr. Camp lights a candle over Derek's file. "In the fires of passion are cold realities cast," Dr. Camp says. He wishes Derek's spirit the best and the worst of luck, and privately wonders which came out on top in the end.

The Dark Above

Friday, February 7, 1997

SHE'S ABOUT TWENTY-FIVE. CAPTAIN Forrest James of the U.S. Navy picked her up at a bar on Lakeview. They're in his hotel room; their clothes are mingling in a pile on the floor. He's in town for a seminar. He's tall, well-built, blond hair going grey. Twenty-plus years in the service have given him a form of confidence, a certain bearing, that some women find very attractive. She certainly did. When she saw him in the bar, she thought of Harrison Ford. She bought him a drink, asked him to dance. Her name is Carly.

"Yes . . . " she breathes. He's kissing her breasts, his breath thick with liquor. "Yes . . . " She barely recalls his name, but he's good-looking. He's got scars on his chest, weird scars, like from an animal attack. She runs her fingers over the scars as he kisses her. "Yes . . . "

Captain James is drunk, wicked-bad drunk, having sex with a woman he doesn't know. It's the only form of intimate relationship he thinks he's capable of anymore. She liked his edginess, his tales of a life in the Navy, his intimations of things he cannot speak of for reasons of national security. He seems like a dangerous man—but a comfortably dangerous man. He does not seem as if he'd hurt her for the world. He seems, rather, so profoundly grateful for her passion, her attraction, that he is like a child. "Yes . . . "

She lies back on the bed, moans, wraps her fingers over the top of his head as he nuzzles at her. Aroused, excited, and rather drunk herself, she draws a pleasured breath. "Kiss me . . . Kiss me . . . "

James kisses her, licks her, presses his face greedily towards her nipples. "Kiss me . . . here . . . " she says.

Carly smoothly guides his yielding head down between her thighs, brings his lips up against her warmth, tenses her legs for the pleasure to come, expectant for his tongue.

James inhales.

The breath chokes in his throat. The smell curdles in his liquored brain. He's on the deck of the sunken *Santa Cruz,* three hundred feet down. It's 1981. The smell—the smell is everywhere, unaccountably permeating his SCUBA gear. The air from his tanks is somehow tainted with the smell of the green, gilled humanoids that are swarming over the rest of the SEAL team. It's sea smell—the sea made choate, made alive, made mad. One of the freakish things lashes out, lacerates his suit, cuts his chest open and bleeding, leaves scars that Carly will stroke sixteen years later just before she wraps his face in her rich scent. His chest flares with remembered pain from the wound, remembered fear.

He obeys his training. He fights back.

The first blow breaks Carly's nose. James roars, inhuman, throws a meaty fist into her gut, cracks two ribs. He brings his hands together into a mallet of flesh, brings it down, causes fractures in her skull, chips teeth, bloodies her lips. She cries out. He hits her again, and again, he's wailing pathetically and he doesn't know why, then he realizes, then he stops. He looks down at the bloody mass of her face, hears her sudden, ragged breathing, her terrible cry of pain and hurt and confusion, and his scream is both drunken and primal—two states connected in ways no psychologist would ever admit, suggesting as they do something of the human condition that is antithetical to modern psychology.

Hotel security finds James on the floor, curled in a fetal position, screaming his throat raw and clutching his chest, while Carly spits up blood and teeth and cries for help.

The landscape is littered with metal barrels. Dozens, hundreds of them. They contain an industrial cleanser, twenty years out of date and fifteen years illegal owing to carcinogens. This place was once a coastal plain, a mile from the shores of northern California. Today, it's a newly inaugurated Superfund site—toxic waste, polluted ground-water, corporate culpability as far as the eye can see.

Shanty shacks line the property. FOST Oil deactivated this site fifteen years ago and left it to rot; squatters, ferried in by the cargo trains of the hobo network, took over the area around the site and no one cared enough to tell them not to, to tell them it wasn't healthy. They were squatters in a remote rural area, far from population centers. They stole from farmers and worked odd jobs to buy milk and beer. No one cared about their little shanty town here at one of the worst toxic waste sites in the state.

Dr. Stephanie Park, an environmental scientist with a year-old doctorate, blinked back tears as she knelt in the clearing rimmed by tents. She looked at the fat orange sun looming low over the settlement.

Some of these squatters had been here for ten years. There were children, little boys and girls not five years old, with deformed features and obvious mental disabilities. *Details* magazine had written up this settlement three years ago, pitching it as a Fuck-the-Government commune for the truly out-of-the-loop. Meanwhile, the squatters drank contaminated water and ate half-tended vegetables from sickly tomato plants and splotchy lettuce patches. Don't even ask about the frogs;

five legs and three eyes were the norm before the local amphibian population died out entirely three years ago, a warning sign those at the scene either didn't notice or didn't care about.

These squatter folk were fucked. Being fucked socioeconomically was one thing; being fucked biochemically was another. Few of them would live another ten years—disenfranchised, they had no real expectation of relief. Their presence here violated so many laws that no useful lawyer would take their case against FOST: how can you sue someone for endangering you when you were present against the law?

The sun was going down on these people's lives. Stephanie looked down at what she held in her arms—an infant born without a skull. She rocked him back and forth, while the half-assed midwife cleaned up the mother and gathered the afterbirth into a bucket. There was no guarantee that the placenta wouldn't end up a meal for visiting raccoons, sending the chemicals of the site yet further into the regional ecosystem. The FOST site was such a fuck-up that there was little point in trying to recover it; Stephanie could only chart the divergence, mark the point where the ecology took this mad path, and hope that maybe the information she collected for her employer, the Environmental Protection Agency, would help someone else.

Stephanie sucked up guilt like a Hoover. She wanted to take every crime committed by her government, her employer, her race, her species, and absorb it into herself. Her capacity for absorbing pain was grossly overestimated. She desperately needed to draw lines, to establish priorities. She could only eat the pain and make it her own.

The infant did not last the night. Stephanie went to bed late, eyes red from crying.

The next morning she was roused from the makeshift EPA

tent to deal with yet another birth, yet another maudlin situation. She got up, still half-dreaming of her old college boyfriend, wondering how she had chosen a path that led through such misery, when she was taken to a ragged tent where a girl scarcely past puberty had given birth during the quiet hours of morning before the sun rose.

She looked at the mother, whose ignorance and ill health were writ large on her face. Stephanie's eyes welled with tears at the thought of another tragedy, another crime laid at the feet of FOST Oil that they would never pay for, when she finally saw the infant.

The large-eyed little boy took short, sharp breaths, like any newborn infant coping with life in a gaseous environment, coping with leaving the liquid womb.

But he was breathing through gills in his neck.

Stephanie staggered back, cried out, blew her nose into a crinkly handkerchief. "Oh God," she cried, first stumbling, then falling back into the reeds, "oh God, no, no, oh God . . . " The young mother beamed with idiot happiness as her little pride and joy flapped his gill slits and processed the unfamiliar air for the first time. Stephanie curled her legs up to her chest and wrapped them with her arms and wished that this damnable current of knowledge had never split her placid sea of ignorance.

If she'd had a gun, she might have killed the child on the spot. Instead, she would begin to love him.

The Washington, D.C., Naval Yard is home to ships, sailors—and academics. The headquarters of the Library of Congress is here, for reasons that no longer matter. Within the administration offices, Dr. Joseph Camp—the leader of Delta Green—

stared at the decrypted email message on his desktop computer. It came from Dr. Stephanie Park of the Environmental Protection Agency.

Dr. Camp drummed his thick fingers on his cluttered desk, stirring tremors in his coffee. Dr. Park was a Delta Green friendly: an ally, a contact, but not someone brought fully into the fold. She was not an agent. She believed that Delta Green was a covert program serving under the Joint Chiefs of Staff. She had no idea that those very officials had disbanded Delta Green in 1970, the year she was born, and that it had operated as an illegal conspiracy ever since.

The thing about covert programs, Dr. Camp reflected, was that they were easy to mimic if you were in the government. All you had to do was feign authority and speak with certainty. Your basic civil servant, when confronted with a presentation of secrecy from someone with security clearances she's never heard of, will believe whatever is said. What is she going to do—ask her boss? "Hey, boss, this guy under the Joint Chiefs of Staff says he's with a covert program and needs my confidential help. Is this for real?" Bam—kiss that promotion goodbye, you stupid shit. There were so many covert programs running in Washington that it was pointless to pursue verification, not to mention that it ran against protocol. The unspoken reality was that anyone with the balls—sorry, the PC term was *brass*—to feign membership in a covert program was probably someone you wanted on your side as you crawled up the wall of seniority. If you were a woman, they might help you hammer through that glass ceiling and, wonder of wonders, might not even ask for sex in return; better than the drill sergeants on the nightly news, at least. *I'm from the government, and I'm here to help. Welcome to the civil service.*

"Dr. Camp?"

Ms. Buie was at his door. A staffer with the library's Federal Research Division, she worked among many scurrying drones collating information requested by other government employees. She was another Delta Green friendly, only barely; she'd never heard of Delta Green, but when Dr. Camp needed a bit of research done after hours or behind closed doors, Ms. Buie helped out. For that spirit of generosity, she was now in the Delta Green database as a friendly; should push come to shove, she would, by default, be one of the many dozens of sacrificial lambs tossed to congressional investigators or wetworks death squads while the real Delta Green covered its tracks and headed for the hills. The organization had one overriding priority that made such casual horrors commonplace: containment. Containment of threat, containment of disaster, containment of knowledge. So it went. Buie was ignorant of the dangers of the waters in which she swam. She was a beautiful woman of fifty-nine, nineteen years younger than Camp, with lush cocoa skin and a smile that crinkled her cheeks in a way that made Camp feel like a spry fifty-five again.

"Yes, Carssandra?"

"You paged me, Dr. Camp?"

"Oh, yes. I've got one of my special requests for you."

Carssandra Buie gave him one of her winning, crinkly smiles. "What do you need, Joe?"

"FOST Oil has a site in northern California near Roscoe that has recently joined the EPA's Superfund list. I'd just like a look at their file, if you can get it for me."

She was quiet for a moment, her face intent. Then she smiled again. "I know someone over there. No problem."

"I won't need it for long. Just need to make some notes."

"I'll get right on it."

Carssandra left. Camp watched her glide down the hall, and sighed.

Then he picked up the phone and began dialing. A lot of numbers were involved. The call went through Delta Green's encryption router, which blocked all known tracers and taps. Forty-five seconds later, he was on the phone with Rear Admiral Harley Patton, the director of the Office of Naval Intelligence.

"Harley? This is Alphonse." Dr. Camp used his Delta Green code name. "I need Agent Darren, pronto." Darren was another Delta Green code name, belonging to one Captain Forrest James, commander of SEAL Team 7 and a Delta Green agent since 1988 whose specialty was a scarce race of primitive, ocean-dwelling humanoids unknown to modern science but apparently antagonistic towards humanity. In decades past, they had attempted interbreeding with humans as a means of asserting power over isolated coastal towns. (Unaccountably, they were genetically and physiologically compatible with humans.) Delta Green's existence could be traced back to a large-scale, successful military operation against these creatures in 1927, at a Massachusetts town called Innsmouth. The government used the Red Scare of the period to cloak the operation, claiming that the town held seditionists and anarchists along the lines of Sacco and Vanzetti; this falsehood concealed a loathsome truth that, it was judged, the public did not need to know. Captain James was one of a handful of currently active Delta Green agents who had faced these creatures directly, and was by far the most experienced: eradicating them seemed to be his personal crusade.

Dr. Camp listened for a few moments to the response to his

request.

"Well, shit."

Dr. Stephanie Park's plane touched down in San Francisco that afternoon. Twenty minutes later, she was in a taxi into the heart of the City on the Bay. When she arrived at the metropolitan jail, she paid the driver and kept the receipt. Taxes.

Inside, she took out the credit card delivered to her with the plane tickets and some odds and ends by courier that morning and posted bail for one Captain Forrest James.

The first few minutes of the car ride passed in silence. Captain James sat in the passenger seat, large and sullen and still hung over. His face was covered in bruises. Even given his condition, he was a handsome man.

Driving the rental car that had been waiting for her at the jail (courtesy of Alphonse), Stephanie hazarded a few glances in Captain James' direction. Finally, tired of waiting for his questions, she spoke.

"I'm not with the ONI, Captain. I'm an investigator with the EPA. I'm here on behalf of Delta Green."

James looked at her and a death-rattle chuckle escaped his throat. "Jumping fuck." His face was expressionless.

"I thought you surrendered without a struggle. Those bruises on your face—did the police do that to you in interrogation?"

James shook his head. "Self-inflicted. I woke up mad and had to hit something. Figured I'd hurt my knuckles less on my face than on the wall."

Stephanie ignored this last comment. She exhaled slowly and spoke the words she'd been rehearsing for the last few miles, and on the plane before that. "Look, I don't know what your story is. I know what you did to that poor woman, and if it wasn't for the fact that your experience is allegedly instrumental in my investigation, I'd have left you there to rot. My intention is to make the most of your insight as quickly as possible and then put you right back in jail where you belong. From what I gather, the Navy isn't going to cut you any slack. Your career in the military is probably over. You're a reverse poster child for the new and improved armed forces, which means that as a drunk and an abuser of women you're going to be sent up the river. Given the classified nature of my investigation, your work with me is not going to help you score any points with your superiors and it certainly won't be admitted as evidence in your trial and therefore will not help to sway a judge. If you don't think you're going to contribute anything meaningful to my work, we can turn around right now and put you back in the hands of the SFPD. This isn't shore leave. It's your call."

James sat quietly for a few heartbeats, then sighed.

"There's only one reason why Delta Green would have popped me free. This has something to do with aquatic humanoids, doesn't it?"

Stephanie stared at the road. "Yes. I've got evidence of probable hybridization among a squatter camp living at a toxic waste site up north."

"Then I'm in. Might as well get a few more notches on my belt before they lock me up."

Stephanie shook her head slowly. She'd been hoping against hope that he'd be antagonistic and would just tell her to take him back to the jail or drop him off at a hotel out of spite. Instead, she was stuck with him.

"All right. The file is on the back seat. We'll be on a plane in forty-five minutes and you can't look at those documents while others are around. Read fast."

By the time the plane lifted off, James was sound asleep. He went under, just like that. He'd long since grown accustomed to grabbing sack time at a moment's notice, in anticipation of hard work and long hours waiting up ahead.

Restless, Stephanie kept glancing at him until she was sure he was asleep. Then she allowed herself a long, lingering gaze. He was handsome, even bruised as he was, but that wasn't the only reason that she allowed herself the indulgence of sustained inspection. He fascinated her. She'd read some of his Delta Green reports before, been impressed by his acuity and competence—and, in the moments where it was least expected, his guarded sensitivity. She found it hard to reconcile the mental picture she'd built up months ago, poring over those files, with the man capable of the savage act he had committed the night before. Who was he, to possess such insight and yet such brutality?

Stephanie forced herself to take her eyes off of him. She adjusted her seat back and looked at the ceiling of the plane. It was loneliness, she told herself; she'd been lonely for some time, her every attention focused on her new career. Last night the man sitting next to her had gotten drunk and horribly beaten a woman almost her age that he'd picked up at a bar. He was a monster, the kind of psychopathic freak that the armed forces seemed to draw out of the woodwork from time to time. That was all. She understood him, and could dismiss him.

Yet still she turned her head, studied his face, until she caught herself doing it and closed her eyes.

Δ

The EPA land rover bucked across the unsteady landscape, wedging its way through the grassy plains. The squatter camp by the FOST site lay somewhere ahead. Captain James flipped through the document folder in silence.

"All right," James said. "I've got the background. I've looked through this six ways from Sunday. There's nothing here for Delta Green; what's the score? Where's your report?"

Stephanie sighed and clutched the wheel. "There's no report. Not yet. I just found the evidence this morning, and it's not guaranteed authentic. I dropped email to Alphonse, and the next thing I knew I was on a plane to pick you up. I guess he was convinced by what little I had to say."

"So what were you doing on the plane down here? Why weren't you writing up a report? For all you know we're gonna get waxed in an ambush at the next turn, and whatever you've seen will die with you. That's not the way we work. Not anymore."

"I'm sorry. I was disoriented. I'm not used to this stuff. I only got Delta Green clearance a few months ago."

James looked at her and whistled slowly. "Okay. I get it. You're not a Delta Green agent, are you?" There *was* no such thing as "Delta Green clearance." Not since the organization was disbanded in 1970. This lady was a friendly, not an agent, and didn't know the score.

Stephanie glared at him as best she could while she drove. "No, I work for the EPA. I told you that already. I'm not employed by Delta Green."

James was quiet. He'd have to be careful. This woman hadn't yet earned agent status, which meant that he couldn't assume much about her knowledge base or her willingness to comply with Delta Green procedures—which, by most standards, were pretty unorthodox. He'd have to play this assignment carefully. Normally, Alphonse would have briefed him going in, but his being in jail made that difficult.

"Okay. No sweat. Just back up and tell me what made you contact Alphonse."

Stephanie exhaled a weary breath, glad to get onto comfortable ground. "These squatters are pretty well inundated with toxins, and they've been here long enough that they've got kids, families. It's a way of life for them.

"This morning, a child was born, a boy. They've got midwives, more or less. The child had gills, and was actively breathing through them—they weren't just for show. His eyes and other characteristics match that of the hybrids."

"Okay. So what do you know about that? Why did you assume it was anything other than a birth defect brought on by the environment?"

"Well, I didn't. Not completely. We can't rule that out as a possibility."

"But . . . "

"But, I got my Delta Green clearance because of a similar case earlier this year. I was investigating reports of toxin contamination in rural Massachusetts, and when I filed my report on genetic defects among the immediate population I was contacted by some Delta Green agents sent by Alphonse. They got me some lab tests I couldn't have gotten normally in that time frame, and a lot of anomalies showed up in the subjects' physiologies that I wouldn't have known to look for. I was with the agents when they went into some of the sea-caves where the subjects were living. They were disenfranchised squatters, much like our current crew—post-hippy, semi-commune, poor as dirt. While we were in the caves, we encountered some of the amphibian humanoids that you seem to know so much about."

James was shaking his head. "Fuck, yeah, okay, I heard about this. I was out of the country when that went down. Otherwise, I would've been there, and you would have been on the first plane back to Washington so we could take care of it properly."

Stephanie felt her hackles rise. "Well, you weren't there now, were you? Two of the three agents died. I got out, along with Agent Garrow. I saw those things. Alphonse showed me some of the files on them; your name was there." She wasn't keen to make compliments, but for some reason she couldn't help herself. She managed to lower her voice into a faint emotionless whisper that gave away more than it concealed. "I've read your work. It's amazing stuff."

"Yeah. Fat lot of good it does anyone. So the infant from this morning looked suspicious?"

Stephanie exhaled. "Yes. I mean, I haven't run any genetic tests yet, but I believe it's the same phenomenon."

"Hah! Yeah, it's a 'phenomenon' all right. Let's see you call it that when it's looking to slip you the big one. It's like the old horror movies: Mars needs women, only it's not Mars. It's the fucking ocean."

Stephanie grew irritable again and drove faster. "Thanks for the insight."

"You're welcome. So what're the chances that what you saw this morning is just a birth defect?"

"Pretty slim. Cases of gill-like slits are recorded, but *functional* gills that can breathe our atmosphere as well as underwater are pretty much unsubstantiated. I think it's hybridization."

"I think you're right. Good thing you were here. This shit doesn't pop up every other Tuesday. Next question: these hybrids usually don't manifest gills and so on until they reach adulthood. Why was this kid different?"

"I don't know. It's possible that the mother is a hybrid also, making the deviant genes more dominant. It's also possible that the toxicity of the site affected the foetus, damaging the human cells and leaving the stronger hybrid cells to develop more rapidly. At this point, there's no telling."

"Okay. Last question: how far now?"

"Not far. Not far at all. But *I've* got a question."

"Hit me."

"Why the secrecy? I mean, I've seen these things. If half of what I've read in the files is true, there's an entire civilization out there, living in the sea. Why don't we know more about them? What have they been doing all this time? Why are they a secret?"

Why indeed, thought James. He could only reply with the unvarnished truth: "You aren't cleared for that information."

Stephanie bristled.

They made the rest of the drive in stony silence. James thought to himself: *I didn't mean that you weren't cleared for that information in terms of status or rank. I meant that you weren't cleared for that information psychologically. No one is. When the time comes, you don't get briefed. You just get fucked. I can no sooner prepare you for that information than I can ask you if you're self-conscious about that mole on your cheek.*

He checked himself.

Now what the fuck made me think about that?

Δ

They arrived at the squatter site scant minutes later. The site consisted of a population of about forty. Maybe half of those were transient; some might stay, some might leave. The other half were hard-core, had been there for a few years or longer, were eking out a subsistence living as best they could. They lived in tents, in shanty shacks, in groves of trees with sheets of rusted tin roofing hung from the branches overhead. It wasn't exactly a utopian community; James thought briefly that it was more like a dystopian community. It looked like at any moment Mad Max might drive up in a souped-up post-apocalypse dune buggy and start bitching about getting some clean H_2O.

Stephanie took a chug from a bottle of Evian spring water. James chuckled.

They parked by the EPA area. Stephanie and her two colleagues had set up on-site, since there was no motel in useful proximity. It was a little unorthodox, she had to concede to herself, but needs must.

Their first stop after checking in was the site of the birth this morning. The mother, one Andrea NMI Cooper, was nursing her newborn boy. The child was pale, green veins showing through fragile flesh. He suckled hungrily. As he drank from her breast, his gills fluttered; he could breathe and swallow at the same time.

"Well," James said. "Would you look at that."

Stephanie crouched down by the mother. "How is he doing?"

The woman smiled. "He's fine. He's beautiful."

"What's his name?" Stephanie asked.

"Jamile," the mother replied. "After his father."

James perked up. "His father? Is he here?"

Andrea Cooper shook her head. "He's not from around here," she said dreamily.

"Where is he?" Stephanie asked.

"He comes sometimes. With the tide. I met him on the beach."

James snorted. "I'll bet."

Stephanie ignored him. "Tell me about him. About the father."

Andrea got a far-away look in her otherwise dull eyes. "He's beautiful. He comes from the sea. He's the son of nature."

"He's not human," Stephanie asked, "is he?"

"That's not important—not nearly as important as his loving soul."

James looked long and hard at the scene, then turned and stalked off towards the EPA tent. Stephanie lingered a few moments longer, then hurried to catch up. She found James at the tent going through a rucksack.

He pulled out a large handgun, a Desert Eagle, and put a magazine into the handle. The gun was one of several things left by the courier that morning.

"What are you doing?" she asked warily.

James worked the action, checked the barrel, nodded with satisfaction. ".44 caliber abortion."

"What!" Stephanie exclaimed. "What the hell do you mean?"

James looked into her eyes with what he hoped was a grim expression. His shell of cold, stern strength was, at times, taxing to maintain. "You made the right call. That kid is a hybrid. We've got to deal with him. Containment. Sanction."

Stephanie shook her head slowly, unbelieving. "That's crazy! You're going to just blow his head off? He's just a baby!"

James closed his eyes for a long moment, taking his time, lowering the sidearm to his waist. "You don't understand."

"The hell I don't! You're going over there to put a bullet in his brain!"

James nodded. "That's right."

"That's ridiculous! He's a living being! He hasn't even had a chance yet!"

Feeling more confident, James looked at her coolly. "He'll grow up like other kids. He'll play Nintendo and throw a baseball. Twenty years from now, he'll feel the call of the sea, the call of his father. He'll change. He'll transform. He'll adapt to a life of water. He'll regard humans as prey, or as a repository for his seed. Next time you see him, he'll be chowing down on a runaway kid from Portland and waving his arms in the air, calling his crazed gods from the sea. They all turn out the same." He started to walk off, towards the young mother and her son.

"No!" Stephanie barked. "You could be wrong! I've seen the files. Maybe he's got the blood in him, and maybe he doesn't. Maybe his father is human, or mostly human. It could just be a genetic situation with no behavioral abnormalities."

"And maybe you feel like sticking with him for the next two decades, making sure that he doesn't grow up to be a murderous bastard, making sure that he isn't raping women like her to make more of his kind? Do you want that responsibility?"

Stephanie was silent for a moment. "It's premature. We need to do tests. This is my investigation, not yours."

James sighed. "All right. Fine. We'll do your tests. Then, when they show what we both know they're gonna show, I'll kill him. I'll make it quick. He won't know what's happening.

But when we confirm he is what he obviously is, there's no way I'm letting him live."

James put the safety on and returned the gun to the rucksack. Then he shook his head and spoke again. For some reason, it was important to him that she understand.

"You think I *like* this? You think I like killing children? I've seen what he'll become. I've seen what he'll do. So have you. Things like him killed those agents you were with in Massachusetts. A cute face and a baby's cry don't make him human." James stalked off into the trees.

Stephanie breathed out slowly, sank to her knees. She was wracked with guilt: this morning when she'd first seen the boy, she'd felt the same way that James felt now. But now was different. Now, as soon as she saw James heading towards the EPA tent and knew what he was thinking, her first reaction was to protect the child. She knew better. But she couldn't turn off her emotions like that. She just couldn't.

She wasn't cleared for this.

The waves rolled onto the shore. The coast here was cliffs and rocks, with occasional short strips of beach in between. To sea, the water stretched lonely to the horizon, bisected the golden disc of the setting sun. A cool, salty sea-breeze whistled through the rocks, made the grass at the edge of the sand rustle.

Stephanie, James, and Andrea Cooper made their way through the grass, down the gentle slope, and towards the sand. Andrea held newborn Jamile in her arms, propped awkwardly against one shoulder. The boy had been crying during the slow walk from the squatter site, but when he got in reach of the sea-breeze, he suddenly grew quiet and content. James noticed. Stephanie didn't.

"Here," Andrea said. "This is where he comes. My man. We're in love."

James rolled his eyes in practiced fashion. Stephanie noticed, as she was intended to. She shot him a sharp look, and followed Andrea down to the small, sandy stretch of beach.

Andrea took a seat on a rock, and began nursing Jamile.

Stephanie paused, looked away to give them a moment of privacy, looked back, and then sat down on the sand beside them. James stood a few feet behind.

"Andrea, how did you meet him? Jamile, I mean. How does he come?"

The girl smiled vacantly. "He comes when the moon is high. I met him late last year. I called him."

"You called him?"

James perked up at this and took the final few steps down to the sand.

"Yes. I called him. I sang his song. Our song. Our song of love."

James knelt down beside Andrea, a look of wariness on his face. "This song. How did you learn it?"

"From Henry, at the camp. He's a wise man. He did my star chart, told me I was special, that I had a soul-mate who lived in the sea. A true son of nature. We belong together."

James' brow furrowed. "Andrea, could you sing us the song?"

"It's too early. He won't be ready to come until a little later."

"I know. But could you just sing it for us? So we can hear it?" His face was, Stephanie thought, surprisingly earnest.

"Okay."

Andrea gathered her thoughts for a moment, then opened

her mouth and began to sing.

The sound was a caress, wordless, an ululating invocation that bespoke all the rich mystery of the sea. It sounded of whale song, of lullaby. It was the most beautiful sound Stephanie and James had ever heard.

James fumbled inside his jacket and turned on his tape recorder.

The song lasted perhaps five minutes. Stephanie and James scanned the surface of the ocean, watched for any sign of an audience. There was none. Finally, Andrea reached the end, the last notes cascading upwards into a plea.

"That's beautiful," Stephanie said. "That's—"

Another voice rose and began to sing, the same song that Andrea had just sung. Only this voice was higher in pitch, a little ragged in tone, and possessed a curious, unsettling quality: it never paused. The voice never took a moment's respite to catch its breath. It just sang and sang without the slightest halt. The effect was beautiful, but subtly eerie—humans are used to hearing pauses in a song.

The singer was the infant boy, Jamile. Less than a day old, and he already knew the song of his father by heart. The effect of the newborn singing was surreal, almost shocking. There was a violence to its strangeness; a lie to its beauty.

James tensed. Perhaps the boy's song would draw the father from the sea early? But no—nothing occurred for the entirety of the song.

Finally, the infant's voice grew still. James turned, ever so slowly in case the boy's father came after all, and then began to stride back towards the camp.

Stephanie hurried after him, leaving Andrea to nurse her son, pleased.

"So?" Stephanie said. "What now?"

"I'm going back. I've got to find this Henry guy and see what the score is."

"I guess we got our test results just now, didn't we?"

James stopped walking. "Yeah. We did. We know what that kid is."

"So why didn't you kill him? Wasn't that what you were all fired up to do?"

James looked away. "I've got to find out what Henry knows. If he knows the score, he might not be alone. If we start taking terminal action now, we could blow everything. It's too soon."

"There's something else. You're waiting for something else."

"Yes."

"The father."

"Yes." *No,* James thought to himself. *I'm waiting for something different. I'm waiting for the moment when what I have to do doesn't come at the expense of your hatred. God help me, I'm waiting.*

"Well, get going then. I'll stay here with her."

James was still looking away. Stephanie touched him lightly on the shoulder. "Okay?"

James turned towards her sharply. His inner shell was in pieces. Their eyes met, and Stephanie saw what he was really waiting for.

"Yeah," he said. "Okay." He walked off.

Stephanie watched him, a hand to her lips, then headed back down the slope to the beach.

Henry lived away from the rest of the squatters, in a makeshift tent of canvas. He was in his eighties, with crinkled, leathery skin and a body hardened by a hard life. His eyes were intelligent, but with a hunted look that James had rarely encountered. Henry was nursing a bottle of muscatel. He hadn't bathed in days or longer. Clots of dirty clothes littered the ground of his living space. Incongruously, a tattered astrological star chart was pinned to one wall of the tent, alongside a torn poster of an eighteenth-century sailing vessel on the high seas.

James came to the opening at the front of the tent. "You Henry?" he asked.

"That's me," the man replied drunkenly. "Come on in, son. Get comfy."

James thought it unlikely he could comply with that last, folksy command, given that the tent reeked of unwashed human. Still, he ducked and entered, then sat cross-legged across from the old man.

"I was just down at the beach with Andrea. We were talking about the father of her child. She said you taught her the song to call him from the water."

"Yep, I did. I did do that."

"How did you know it? What do you know about—about those people, the ones in the water?"

"Oh, I picked it up here and there. You know."

"No, I don't. Tell me."

"It's nothing, fella. Forget about it. Have a drink."

James shook his head, uncomfortable with how welcome the suggestion had struck him. Then he reached out for the bottle anyway and took a long drink.

"It's not nothing, old-timer." He pulled his shirt out and lifted it up, revealing the old scars on his chest. "I know these things. They're not human. They're not kind. They only exist to hurt, to destroy."

Henry took back the bottle of muscatel, had a slug, and laughed. "You're with that nice government lady, aren't you? Seems to me that you folks said those same things about the Indians, way back when."

James felt his face harden. He lowered his shirt. "It's not the same thing."

Henry's glazed eyes regarded James regretfully. He shook his head and looked down at the ground. "No. It's not." He took another drink, then gave James one.

"So what's the story, Henry? The real one?"

Henry sighed. "Well, shit," he said.

"Back thirty-odd years ago, I was a sailor. Worked for merchant ships, small fry. Loved it. Loved the sea.

"One boat, there was this captain, a real drunken bastard. He knew about them things, them folk out of the sea. Had traffic with them. They would scavenge wrecks for him sometimes, sabotage other boats some other times. But he was holding out on them. Seemed he'd promised them his crew someday—us—on account of how they needed a fresh batch of men for something. So finally he gave in, said, 'Okay, you can have my crew. I'll give them a big party on the beach, get them drunk, and you can come in and take them. But I want something in return.' See, they had this jewelry—weird stuff—made of gold and other things. They were gonna bring him a whole big bunch of this stuff to seal the bargain when the trade went down.

"But this captain, he was a real drunken bastard. We knew about those folk, about his dealings with them. He told us the score. We planned an ambush. We'd fake a party, but when they came out of the sea, we'd be ready for them. We'd kill 'em all, and take their gold. When we were docked in Haiti, we got it all ready. The captain passed out guns and knives. We went to the beach late at night and raised a ruckus.

"Of course, the men got into the liquor. By the time those things came, everyone was three sheets to the wind anyway. They were clever. They ambushed *us*. Came by land, by sea, over rocks. Tore into us. Men were dying everywhere. They just tore us right up.

"I saw what was gonna happen. I was sober—had been sober a long time. Back then. As soon as the shit hit the fan I clambered up a bunch of rocks where the captain was hiding. We hid out there while those things killed every man there on the beach. When they were done, they started dragging the bodies out into the surf, and checking around to make sure they got us all.

"That's when I did it. I stood up all of a sudden, hoisted the captain up with me. All them critters looked up at us, and I cut that drunken bastard's throat right on the spot. Kicked him down to the beach below. Then I jumped down, dropped my knife, held up my hands.

"They coulda killed me. But I'd made them happy. Plus, the captain was dead—and they could always use somebody on land to help 'em out. So they let me walk outta there, and said that someday I'd owe them one.

"I came back home, got a job on a railroad, never set foot on a boat again. Never heard from them again till last year, when I started having these dreams."

"So Andrea—that was the one you owed them?"

"Yep. She's a sweet girl. Not right in the head. But she loves her man. She's got a beautiful boy. Hell, maybe her man loves her, too."

"No. He doesn't love her. He doesn't love the boy."

"Well shit, how do you know? Maybe he do! And if not, at least she loves him. Love's worth something, ain't it?" Henry's voice grew plaintive, drunken, and guilty. "Love's worth something, ain't it?"

James rose, standing only halfway up in the confines of the tent, and stepped outside.

He was so tired. So very tired. Tired of all the little corruptions, the little tragedies. Tired of all the misery, all the sorrow. He couldn't think clearly. The muscatel was buzzing in his head. His training would see him through. Delta Green's driving policy was simple, after all.

Containment. Containment of threat, containment of disaster, containment of knowledge.

He crouched and stepped back into the tent. He leaned over and took the bottle of muscatel from Henry, took a long drink. Set the bottle down. Threw a punch into Henry's gut that knocked the wind out of the old man, who fell back wheezing. Grabbed the man's pillow and shoved it down over his face. Held it there. Kneeled on his chest. Stayed put for three full minutes. Until he was dead.

James pulled the pillow off Henry's stricken, still features.

He sat down heavily and picked up the bottle. He drained the rest of it. There was quite a lot. He tossed the bottle to one side. He arranged Henry to look as if he'd been sleeping and died peacefully. No one was going to look at this old bum too closely. He sat back again and watched the dead man's face drunkenly. He put his face in his hands. He wanted to cry. He failed.

He wasn't cleared for this.

On the beach, the sun was gone and the moon was rising

high. Stephanie and Andrea had been talking for what seemed like ages. James had not yet returned, and Stephanie wondered where he was. Andrea talked about her life: the orphanage, the foster parents, the reform school, the arrests, running away from home once, twice, a final time. How she'd read this article in a magazine about a place where you could go when you had no place to go. She'd torn it out, read it again and again, dreamed about it, loved it, loved the idea of it. When she'd run off that final time, eighteen months ago, she'd gone there. To the squatter camp.

Stephanie shook her head, shivered in the cool night sea-breeze. Their lives were so different, but only as different as what you see in a mirror: opposite, but otherwise the same. She'd spent so much time searching, unhappy, trying to find her place in the world, wondering why she was always so miserable, always so full of pain. She put her hand on the girl's knee.

"It's okay; it is. Some of us have to make our own way in life. It's not easy."

Andrea looked her full in the face. "Yeah," she said. "That's right." Her face held something back, some suspicion, or some secret knowledge, that Stephanie could not place. Perhaps this was jailhouse reserve.

Then Jamile began to sing.

It was the song again, his father's song. He started it up all of a sudden, jarring them both, his uneven but unbroken tones rolling out across the beach. His mother joined in, singing in her strong, clear voice that nevertheless had to pause for breath every so often, her very humanity damaging the purity of the song. Jamile's singing betrayed no such fragile allegiances to the human race. He sang—as simple as that.

Stephanie felt a chill go up her back. She shuddered. The

song was just as beautiful as before, heartbreakingly so. But this time there was something else. It was, she decided, a strange potential. A feeling obvious to them all that this time, the song would be answered.

It didn't take long.

He broke the water, a ways out from shore. His head was powerful, thick, set low into his hunched shoulders. He strode forward, his arms and legs massive, his chest a barrel, his whole body ripe to burst with vitality and the savor of the sea.

He was singing.

The voices of the three joined in song, calling higher and louder. The song was so beautiful, the moment so ethereal, so transcendent, that all of Stephanie's suspicions and fears melted away in the rapture of the moment. There was nothing wrong here, nothing unnatural. Everything was right.

Then she saw his eyes.

His crystalline eyes, which never seemed to close, were the most terrifying sight she had ever seen. They'd seen all the secrets of the cosmos a hundred times over and yet he knew his place among those secrets from the very start. His eyes betrayed him: he was the proper product of the universe, whereas humanity was but incidental. His eyes had no emotion, no spirit, no nothing—they were as blank as a starless sky, and just as deep.

Stephanie froze as the man from the sea, the true son of nature, came striding out of the foam with the awful surety of a god. She could not move. She could barely breathe. His gaze held her hypnotized, and then he was standing before her where she sat upon the beach. The song the three sang came to an end, its awesome sense of joy belied by what she saw in his eyes: the song was not meant for the ears of humans and its beauty was an accident; it appealed to a different aesthetic sense altogether, and to that sense it was not beautiful. It was proud and terrible.

She would have sat there, frozen, lost in the trackless wastes of his eyes, but for Andrea's voice.

"Yes," the girl said. "I brought her here for you."

Something large swelled between his legs.

The spell was broken. Stephanie spun, stumbled up, tried to run. A massive webbed claw grabbed her shoulder, dug in, ripped her windbreaker, shoved her down roughly onto the sand. She rolled over, threw a punch, he caught it, held it, swung with his other claw and clouted her in the side of the head. She fell back, stunned. He dropped to his knees, moved the claw that held her to her throat, pinned her; then his other claw grabbed for the waistband of her jeans, while the distended thing between his legs bobbed erect and grotesque in the sea-breeze.

Her hands freed, Stephanie reached in the pocket of her windbreaker and pulled out the taser, another item left by the courier that morning—*was it just that morning?*—and jammed it against the beast's gut.

He croaked, a terrible sound like bones breaking, froze, then fell onto her, dead weight.

Stephanie was pinned. The beast was incredibly dense, three hundred pounds and more. She struggled to get him off of her.

"No!" Andrea cried. Stephanie looked to the girl with relief. Her relief died. Andrea had set Jamile down on the sand and was picking up a large rock. She staggered quickly over to Stephanie, raised the rock, and prepared to smash her face in with it.

A single shot rang out. It struck Andrea in the left side of her chest, spun her to one side, dropped her to the sand, her heart pierced and broken.

Bang, thought James.

He stood perhaps sixty feet away, both arms cocked out steady, the Desert Eagle perched in his hands. He breathed heavily.

The beast atop Stephanie stirred. The taser would have made short work of a human. It only brought the beast down for a few precious moments. As he pushed himself up, groggy, Stephanie scuttled back, out from under his weight, and ran. She ran up the slope, into the grass, straight towards James, who lowered his left arm and gestured to her to come, to run, to run to him. His other arm remained out, trying to get a shot around his fleeing partner in the dim twilight.

The beast had scuttled onto the beach, still weak, and then rose to its feet and started to run away just as James took aim and squeezed the trigger. The slug went wide, drunkenly wide in the dark. James walked forward as fast as he dared, still aiming, trying to get a shot that would count.

Stephanie reached him. He warded her off with his left hand, then brought it up to steady the other. With two hands on the gun, he continued walking forward swiftly, closing the gap.

The beast was running now, crouched more than usual, into the surf.

James fired again. Again. One of the shots punched into the beast's back. The .44 magnum slug carved through the beast's flesh, and blew out the other side. The beast staggered, ducked tighter into itself, arms clutching its chest, up to its knees in water now, pressing on through the surf.

Again. Again. Again. The grouping was tight, the muzzle blazing as fast as James could fire. In the space of a breath, all three shots caught the beast in the back. It staggered, roared, dropped to its knees, fell face down into the shallows.

James ran forward, releasing the magazine and putting another one in its place, the gun held out before him like a flashlight illuminating a violent path. Stephanie ran with him.

They reached the surf. James planted one foot on the beast's back, leaned down swiftly, put a final slug into the back of the beast's head. The sound was like a crab shell bursting in a restaurant.

Stephanie stopped just short of running into him. She put a hand on his shoulder.

James lowered the weapon, then put it back into its holster. His trouser cuffs were soaking wet. He turned to her. They embraced clumsily, revolved slowly in the shallow water.

Stephanie's view danced from the far horizon of the water to the near line of the shore as they turned, she saw Andrea's body atop the rocks and sand.

There was something else—something she didn't see. Because it wasn't there.

She gasped, withdrew from the embrace. "Turn him over!" she cried.

James looked at her dumbly, then leaned over and grabbed the beast's shoulder. He pulled hard, straining against the weight, and flopped the dead thing over onto his back, the crystalline eyes meeting the limitless night sky.

Where the beast had lain, lay Jamile. A hole the size of Stephanie's fist gaped from the back of the boy's head. One of James' shots had blown through the beast's body and struck the infant—the infant cradled in the hunched beast's arms as he fled for the sunless sea.

Jamile was dead. His father was dead. His mother was dead. The path from her discovery to its conclusion was littered with corpses.

Stephanie looked up, into James' eyes. She smelled the wine on his breath. He looked at her, silently pleading for her to understand. The things that separated them were not important—not nearly as important as the possibility of their being together.

Stephanie looked away. To look any longer would be to understand James. To look any longer would be to understand herself. To look any longer would be to understand everything. She looked up into the night sky, into the far stars. The dark above held no secret. It held no hope. It would not help her understand. The cosmos radiated ignorance, and she accepted it greedily, for the alternative was too terrible to contemplate.

James watched her face for a long moment, hoping against hope that she would return his gaze. She did not, could not, dared not. Finally he looked down at the bodies, slick with surf. He crouched slowly, his knees coming to rest on the dead beast's back. He put his face in his hands. He wanted to cry.

He did.

By the time the sun rose, a Delta Green sanitation crew had disposed of all the corpses. When morning stood firm, Stephanie and James got into the land rover and headed for Roscoe. At the small airport, James would board a commuter flight back to San Francisco. An attorney, arranged for informally by Harley Patton of the ONI, awaited his return so they could prepare for the trial. A flock of reporters were waiting, too; in James' absence, his crime had become national news. The novelty of drill sergeants raping female recruits had faded, and a nation hungry for the degradation of its own spirit now turned its attention to this latest pairing of lion and Christian to enter the arena. Across the country, talk-radio hosts invited callers to ring in and express their profound disgust for this man, this Captain Forrest James of the United States Navy, prestigious commander of SEAL Team 7, who was a drunk and a woman-beater and unfit to serve his country or his species.

James listened to one such show on the radio in the land rover, hearing his name dragged through the mud, until Stephanie turned it off. James did not object. It was not because they couldn't bear the senseless rage of the callers; it was because the callers—ignorant and ill-informed though they may be—were to a great extent right, and they both knew it.

At the airport, Stephanie walked with James until they reached the gate from which his plane would depart. They stopped when they could walk no farther. They embraced again, a final time, wordless. Then James turned and walked into the gate to board the plane.

Stephanie watched him go, then began the walk back to the parking lot outside the little terminal. She put her hands in her pockets. They contained a piece of folded paper which had not been present before.

She stopped and took it out. James must have slipped it in there when they embraced. Her mouth was dry. She unfolded the paper and read what he'd written:

You are the rock and I am the wave—and when I touch you, I break.

She folded the paper back up and returned it to her pocket, then resumed her walk to the car, and beyond.

DR. JOSEPH CAMP READ through Dr. Stephanie Park's report

for Delta Green. It was proper, clear, and informative. With it was the cassette tape of the calling song that Captain James had recorded, something that Dr. Camp hoped would have the same effect in other circumstances.

There was something in Park's report, something that Camp couldn't put his finger on. Something between the lines that she hadn't stated flat out.

Carssandra Buie, leaning against the doorway, said, "Knock, knock."

"Oh, hello. What can I do for you?"

"I'm heading to lunch, Dr. Camp. Would you care to join me?"

Dr. Camp looked at the report a final time. Whatever it was that he couldn't quite catch wasn't important—not nearly as important as the prospect of lunch with Carssandra, certainly. "I'd be delighted."

He stood up gracelessly, approached the door a little unsteadily, and then made up for all his infirm years by gallantly offering his arm. She smiled and took it, and they walked pleasantly down the hall.

There are worse things in life, he thought to himself, *than to be in love. Even if it's not returned.*

The Rules of Engagement

Dedication

For Damon, for Kim, and for Mom & Dad,
this valentine of doomed romance.

Then he said, I pray thee therefore, father, that thou wouldest send him to my father's house: For I have five brethren; that he may testify unto them, lest they also come into this place of torment. Abraham saith unto him, They have Moses and the prophets, let them hear them. And he said, Nay, father Abraham: but if one went unto them from the dead, they will repent. And he said unto him, If they hear not Moses and the prophets, neither will they be persuaded, though one rose from the dead.

—The Gospel of Luke 16:27–31

Fiat justitia et pereat mundus.
Let justice be done, though the world perish.

—Ferdinand I, Holy Roman Emperor

Prologue

∞

There's a room as big as all outdoors. I rise from the still body in the bed and stride forward purposefully, embracing my future. As I near the far wall, the plaster ripples and parts like a curtain of obedient water.

Beyond? Beyond is everything. The cosmos in its strange null entirety, the mad planets whirring in space, the expansion and contraction of the universe, the dancers at the soul of time, the lint in the giant's navel.

I step through the wall, and it all starts to happen. This is the end and the beginning.

Chapter One:
The Violet Hour

Sunday, February 14, 1999

Dr. Stephanie Park stepped naked into the clawfooted bathtub and slid slowly into the water. The bathroom was dancing with steam—she'd begun running hot water into the tub half an hour ago, and had opened the drain several times to get the water down to a useful level, since she kept putting off actually getting in. Finally, though, she was in the thick of it. Candles burned on the counter around the sink, sputtering slightly in the damp air. Her cat, Clotho, scratched fitfully at the other side of the door.

It was one o'clock Sunday morning, and Stephanie was about to commit suicide.

She picked up the scalpel from the white plastic soap tray that was clipped to the shower pipe. The surgical steel was damp with humidity. She lowered the scalpel into the warm water to heat it up, so that the surface of her skin, the water, and the cutting tool would all be at roughly the same temperature. When she opened the arteries of her left arm and thighs, she wanted it to feel like she was slicing through butter. Gently, as if to say hello, she stroked her calves with the back of the scalpel, getting used to the motion and the feel of the metal on her skin. It was also a way of saying goodbye.

No more of this shit. No more of this pathetic excuse for a life.

Stephanie was tired of how things were going. She was tired of her work, tired of her parents, tired of her relationships, tired of her pseudo-friends. She was so very tired of it all. She wanted it to stop.

Sitting in the tub, naked, with a brilliantly sharp scalpel clasped in her right hand, Stephanie began to sob. The first shudders came suddenly, haltingly, then were amplified and regulated into a steady motion that shook her body and wrenched her soul. Tears poured from her eyes, running down her face before falling through steam and splashing small into the water of the bath. The hard clench in her guts seemed to well up like bile, but emerged as a voice rather than an eruption of stomach acids; the feeling was the same, however. There were no words. She had run out of words. She had nothing left but a wail of terrible anguish.

The phone rang.

Stephanie sat in the tub and sobbed. The phone rang again. And again. And again. She began to feel slightly ridiculous. Here she was, minutes from death, and the damn phone was ringing.

Fuck it, she thought. *It's not my problem anymore. I don't have any problems anymore.*

The phone stopped ringing and the answering machine picked up. Her own voice came through the bathroom door, muffled: "You've reached Dr. Stephanie Park. Leave your name and number at the tone and I'll get back to you."

Beep.

"Hello. You are cordially invited to a night at the opera." The caller hung up the phone.

Stephanie sat in the tub, frozen by the voice. A long minute went by as her mind raced.

Finally she lifted her right hand up from the water and carefully, almost reverently, laid the scalpel down in the soap holder again. Then she placed her hands on the edges of the tub and lifted herself up from the water. She stepped out onto the cool tile floor and put on her white terrycloth bathrobe, then emerged into the living room. Clotho meowed at her feet and followed her. When Stephanie sat down in the armchair and picked up the phone, Clotho jumped in her lap. Stephanie began scratching the grateful cat's head involuntarily as she dialed a long series of numbers into the headset. By the time she was done, the cat was purring.

The phone rang. There were a series of clicks as the call was switched through encryption routers, then the phone rang some more. Finally someone answered "Hello," with the same voice that she'd just heard on her answering machine.

"This is Agent Terry," she spoke carefully. "I'm accepting your invitation, Alphonse." There was a pause while her voice print was checked.

"Hello, Terry," said the voice finally. It was the voice of an old man, but a vigorous one. "We need you."

Stephanie took a deep breath and let it out. "I'm here. I'm here for you."

The voice chuckled, then spoke. "That's good."

She listened for a while, then soon after went to bed. In the morning she took a taxi from Georgetown to the D.C. airport and boarded a plane. When she left, the tub was full of cold water and the cat's dish was full of food. Dr. Stephanie Park did not die that night.

Special Agent Abraham Mannen of the Federal Bureau of Investigation hustled down the basketball court. Rick Snyder from legal support was in front of him the whole way, bucking and dodging, trying to steal the ball from him. Abe let the ball bounce wild off to one side. Rick lunged for it, but Abe brought it back into the inevitable arc of his long arms and blew past the off-balance Rick, who hit the ground on one hip and cursed. Abe came to the end of the court, the nearest defense ten feet away, and he lifted his tall, athletic frame into a graceful leap up in front of the goal. The ball spun out of his hands, arced narrowly across the backboard, hit the rim, and bounced out and off towards the stands. It landed on a bench and rebounded towards the exit from the gym. Out of bounds.

Abe, having hit the ground before the ball reached the bench, looked and then ducked his head in a silent expression of frustration. That shot was gold, he'd been sure of it. Then bam, out of control and beyond his influence. No score.

"Brick!" Rick called out cheerfully behind him.

Abe leaned forward, resting his hands on his knees, and breathed heavily. *Damnit,* he thought. *I had that bastard and off it went.*

The other players clustered in mid-court. Rick was high-fiving his partners while Abe looked ruefully at his colleagues. "Sorry," he said.

Tom Patterson shrugged. "No sweat, man. We'll get those losers."

The two teams took up positions as Rick sidled up towards the edge of the court with the basketball in his hands. He threw the ball into play.

Tom lunged, leaped, and the ball was his. He rocketed down the court and before Abe could even get his bearings and move in to block the guards, the ball was airborne. Swoop, swish. Through the net. Two points. The team clustered and hooted. Abe gave Tom a high-five, thinking: *This shoulda been mine.* Rick cat-called merrily: "Gonna take it in the shorts this go-round!"

The game ended twenty minutes later, Abe's crew losing

24–28. Legal support prevailed over field agents once again. The running gag was that the lawyers spent most of their billable hours practicing on the court, while the agents were busy doing the will of the people. In truth, the lawyers just spent more off-duty time at the downtown gym—it was a good place for networking with the Milwaukee legal community. Both groups from the city's office of the FBI worked hard days, every day.

Abe came out of the showers and got dry and dressed. *Fucking lawyers win again,* he thought. *They better win for us like this in court.* He slid the Glock 17 into his shoulder holster without thinking twice about it.

The cell phone in his gym bag chirped. Abe answered it and said hello. There was a pause while some distant computer checked his voice print.

"Hello, Agent Thomas. You are cordially invited to a night at the opera."

Abe listened closely. When the call was done, he went home and got some sleep. In the morning, Abraham Mannen was on an early flight out of town.

Vic Winstead—she disliked Victoria or Vicky—sat on the small platform in a corner of the little storefront coffeehouse. She had an acoustic guitar in her lap, and as she exhaled a cloud of cigarette smoke, she wedged the filter end of the cigarette into the neck of the guitar. Through the smoke, she took a last look at the dozen or so people present, none of them particularly there to see her. Some were reading, some were jotting notes onto a pad, and some had stopped talking to their companions just long enough to listen politely to the first few seconds of whatever song she was about to play to open her act. Those folks, she knew, she could write off now; her music wasn't going to change their lives, so it was hardly going to make them stop yakking with their friends.

Vic tapped her right foot on a rung of the stool: *one, two, three . . .*

I didn't know
I didn't know
I didn't know you'd fuck me like that
I didn't know you'd trick me like that
I didn't know
I didn't know you at all

Boom. The talkers went back to talking. Another song that wasn't going to stop anyone in their tracks. She kept on singing, thinking *what the hell, a routine is a routine.* Saturday nights she played at Noise Espresso in the Queen Anne district of Seattle. It wasn't exactly a high-profile gig. Still, she figured she'd have enough material—enough *good* material—for a CD soon, and she could afford to have a run of 500 pressed. She'd send them out to local reviewers, clubs, give them away at gigs, whatever. Vic wasn't exactly in this for a career, but it was something to do with her ample spare time.

She was a park ranger for the National Parks Service, assigned to the Hurricane Ridge Visitor's Center on Washington's Olympic peninsula, a couple hours from Seattle. On her occasional weekends off she'd take the ferry into the city and crash with Sue, her old college friend, and on Friday they'd get drunk and talk and laugh and maybe once in a boozy blue moon they'd fool around a little, but it was just fooling around. Saturday Vic would go to Noise to play and hang out, and Sue would go off with her city friends to the Wild Rose in Capitol Hill, the neighborhood Sue campily referred to as "the *theater* district." Sunday they might see a movie or go to the zoo or just hang around Sue's apartment reading the weeklies, then Vic would pack up her car and take the ferry back out to the peninsula. Sometimes if Sue was dating, she and her girlfriend would leave Vic alone for most of the weekend, and Vic would watch television or take long, long walks down and around Eastlake. There were houseboat communities there on the water, and she couldn't believe that people paid so much money to live in cramped, floating houses that were surrounded by more cramped, floating houses. Maybe there was a song there.

I didn't know what I could do if I had half a mind
I didn't know what to do with the love I did find
I didn't know where to go from where
I didn't know how to who to when to why
I didn't know
I didn't know you and I didn't even try

Vic played on, head nodding in the groove, doing a fifty-minute set before taking a break to scattered applause. She wanted a mocha, but milk was bad for her throat when she was singing so she settled for hot unsweetened tea. Sitting at a table in the back of the room, she stirred the tea absently. Her bag was on the table, a ragamuffin item she'd sewn from cast-off fabric ends. Inside was an address book, pocketbook, hairbrush, Altoids, a small plastic bag full of spiced sunflower seeds for snacking, tampons, tissue paper, a large paperback copy of *The Wind-Up Bird Chronicle* by Haruki Murakami, some aspirin, a pager, a cell phone, and a sturdy Bulgarian knock-off of the

Browning 9mm Hi-Power semi-automatic handgun with a full magazine of thirteen rounds (none in the pipe) and a second magazine of ten rounds loose in the bag. The Washington State Concealed Weapons Permit inside her pocketbook gave her license to carry the weapon almost anywhere she went.

Five years ago, when she'd started at Olymic National Park, she'd never owned a firearm in personal life, let alone carried one concealed to also-ran coffeehouses half-full of zoning slackers. But five years ago she hadn't joined Delta Green.

The cell phone rang. Agent Tonya answered it. In the morning, Sue drove her to the Seattle-Tacoma airport and saw her off, exchanging a hug before Vic Winstead was gone.

THE THREE OF THEM arrived within two hours of each other, congregating in a bar at the Memphis International Airport, down in the southwest corner of Tennessee. This was their third time on an op together, but it was the first time with Stephanie as an actual member of the team—the first two times, she was an advisor.

"So," Abe said. "You guys know anything about our hotel?"

Vic nodded. "Alphonse PGP'd me. Looks like we got our choice of billing: daily or hourly," she joked. PGP was the name of the email encryption software used by Delta Green to keep its internet communications secure. The organization maintained a high degree of paranoia in its tradecraft. Agents were given digital PCS cell phones with aftermarket encryption installed, all DG-related calls were passed through the group's own secure router, and agents routinely swept their living spaces and telephones for clandestine surveillance gear. Delta Green believed that not even the National Security Agency could compromise the group's safeguards, at least under routine circumstances.

Abe chuckled. Stephanie looked nervously around the terminal. They had exited the bar and were heading towards the baggage-claim area. Vic noticed Stephanie's anxious look.

"Don't be so obvious," Vic said, veteran of a thousand movies but only eight ops. "Pretend like you own the place. Quit scoping everyone in sight."

Stephanie looked at her, a bit tired. "Sure thing. Just jumpy."

"Lunch will fix that," Abe said. "This town must be famous for some kind of food. Whatever it is, we'll eat it."

"I'll feel better when I've got my gun again," Stephanie said quietly. "I hate plane rides. Feel so helpless."

Abe and Vic said nothing.

The last time the three of them were together, Stephanie was not a full Delta Green agent. She was a friendly, briefed on certain aspects of Delta Green's mission but unaware of DG's status as an illegal, unauthorized conspiracy within the federal government. That was when Larry was still alive, still a part of Cell T; his code-name had been Agent Tim. Larry, Abe, and Vic were on an op in Baltimore. Stephanie arrived, officially on loan from the EPA to assist with an IRS investigation into corporate malfeasance in the waste-disposal industry. By the time the op was over, Larry was dead and Stephanie was a full agent, one of seventy-eight who comprised the functional entirety of the Delta Green conspiracy. That was three months ago.

At baggage claim, the group picked up their luggage, including their firearms. Airline regulations prohibited the transport of ammunition without special arrangements, and so after conferring with a phone book and a map of Memphis their first stop would be a gun store. By the time their rented minivan was pulling onto I-240, Stephanie had her Ruger P-85 9mm handgun out and was checking the action, visibly relaxed. Vic and Abe looked on, mildly unsettled.

Two hours later, the trio had purchased three hundred rounds of 9mm Parabellum ammunition—there was a reason why they all carried the same caliber handgun—and checked into their lodgings at the Highway Motel, near the intersection of Jackson Avenue and I-240, the beltline that ran around the city. Based in midtown Memphis, they asked the desk clerk for lunch advice and drove out to Payne's—a tasty little joint, it turned out, located in a former gas station—for barbecue sandwiches and planning; as Abe said, this town had to be famous for some kind of food, and barbecue was it. Vic was the senior DG agent of the three, with eight ops under her belt across five years. She conducted the briefing quietly between bites of saucy pork and cole slaw.

"Agent Shasta vanished two weeks ago from his home in Langley, Virginia," she said. "The cops and the CIA, his employer, are conducting investigations, but they don't know what we know—that he was in Memphis for three days last month on a DG op. Since the legit investigations aren't panning out, Alphonse wants us to re-open Shasta's last op and see if there are some leads there. The other members of Cell S are excluded from this op, in case they're already compromised."

"So why was Shasta here in podunkville?" Abe asked. Agent Shasta was Cell T's superior contact in the Delta Green chain of command. DG's cells were arranged in an alphabetic hierarchy, with code names assigned beginning with the letter of the three-person cell. Cell T, therefore, was comprised of Agents Terry, Thomas, and Tonya: Dr. Stephanie Park, Abraham Mannen, and Victoria Winstead, respectively. Agent Udall, of Cell U, reported to Agent Tonya of Cell T. In turn, Tonya reported to Agent Shasta of Cell S. And so on, all the way up to Cell A, headed by Agent Alphonse, the nominal leader of the Delta Green conspiracy, who often circumvented the hierarchy and spoke directly to the cell leaders. Real names were a premium currency, usually traded only within a cell—though Alphonse knew everything.

"His cell was re-investigating a DG op that they ran in Groversville, Tennessee, a couple years ago," Vic replied. "Some sort of alien-abduction deal. The townsfolk apparently cleared out and the land reverted to the state, who eventually sold it to some developers of a planned community, one of those new corporate-managed urban-village deals. Only Cell S couldn't trace the original townsfolk—their records trailed off into nothing. A few weeks ago, Shasta found a Groversville native here in Memphis and brought Cell S to investigate. They wrapped up in a couple days and bailed with nothing. The contact wasn't talking."

"And then Shasta disappeared?" Abe asked.

"Two weeks later," Vic replied. "He left work, went home, and was never seen again. No witnesses. No signs of foul play. No wife, no kids, no gambling debts, no questionable investments, no large cash purchases, no family trouble. He was a loner, except for Delta Green. Someone else did this to him."

Stephanie shook her head. "We all knew Shasta. He wouldn't just vanish, would he? It must be some past op catching up with him."

Abe looked rueful. "Yeah, but which one? He's been an agent for more than a decade and at least half of that was pre-Alphonse, so there's jack-all for records. Any number of fuckos could've popped up and done him in, and that's not including any enemies from his day job. The guy got kicked out of China as a spy back when he was a military attaché in the '80s. I heard he was even in on the Cambodia fiasco in '69. Hell, he once told me his dad was in the Flying Tigers and fought to free Tibet after the war. Shasta had a serious track record, ground up. He could've made enemies from Vietnam onwards. This is a big wishbone we're pulling on."

"I didn't know he was in that deep," Stephanie said thoughtfully. "But he must have done something to trigger this, assuming he just didn't vanish on his own."

"Well, the only recent action we're aware of is his cell's investigation into that Groversville survivor here in Memphis," Vic said, pulling a notepad out of her purse. "That was eight months since his last op. So we'll start with her." She put the fork down and flipped open the pad. "Joan Blackwell, 45, 1281 Stonewall, apartment 23. Rented the place six months ago. Single, no kids. Employed at Federal Express as a package sorter, an entry-level position. No car, takes the bus. No criminal or military record. She's clear with the IRS—tax returns filed all the way back to age nineteen. Service jobs, assistant-manager crap. Krystals, Dairy Queens, Wal-Marts, that sorta stuff."

"All those records could have been faked," Abe said.

"True. She might be a plant," Stephanie added.

Vic nodded. "It's a possibility. But there are property records showing that she owned a doublewide in Groversville for six years. Alphonse even found credit-card records showing her purchases in Groversville from before the original op. If someone set this woman up with a paper trip, they did a really good job."

"So let's go talk to her," Abe said.

"What's our cover?" Vic asked.

The trio sat in silence for a minute and munched on their barbecue.

"We're private investigators doing property research on legal claims related to Groversville," Stephanie said. "We'll say there's a class-action suit from former residents alleging some kind of deception on the part of the company that bought the town."

"Hold on," Abe said. "If she's legit, that's fine. But if she's a plant, she'll know that's bullshit because there wouldn't be any class-action suit for a situation that was faked from the ground up. Far as I understand, not a single Groversville resident has been found except for this lady. Big-time fishy. So fishy the media didn't even blink twice."

"Except for *Phenomen-X,*" Vic snorted.

"Then we're looking for someone," Stephanie replied emphatically. "Ask Alphonse for the name of a Groversville resident—maybe an older one, some old lady whose relatives might be looking for her—and say we're tracking down former residents to find this person."

Vic and Abe nodded. "That could work," Vic said. "We'll need a Memphis P.I. permit in case she checks."

"Call it in to Alphonse now and we'll have it in a day or two," Abe said between mouthfuls of food.

"Okay," Vic said. "We'll proceed as P.I.'s. Maybe we can use the class-action story if we need it. Stephanie, I know you're not a lawyer, but you've done a lot of testifying for the EPA. Can you fake being our attorney with this woman? Bogus or legit, she'll spook better if we have a lawyer."

"Sure," Stephanie answered. "I've got fake ID from Alphonse. I'll get a P.O. box and voice mail first to get the front set up, then get some business cards from a copy shop. I'll make

P.I.-branded dupes under your fake ID's. Memphis Investigative Services or something. We'll be all set."

"All right," Vic said. "We've got our cover. Steph'll get the identity stuff started this afternoon and we should be ready to roll hard by mid-week." Abe and Stephanie nodded during fork-fulls of beans. "In the meantime, let's set up a surveillance on Joan Blackwell. I'll take the afternoon at her house while you two run errands, then you'll split the evening between her work and her home. But first, Steph, you call Fed Ex and ask for Joan. Let's make sure she's still there." Stephanie nodded and headed off to the pay phone by the entrance.

Once Stephanie was gone, Abe looked at Vic candidly. "Do you think she's okay for this? She seems twitchy to me."

Vic looked at Stephanie, who was nearing the front doors and heading for the pay phone. "There's something about her I can't read. I think she's kinda spooky. But that's par for the course. I mean, she and Alphonse both gave us the run-down on her past ops as a friendly, and they didn't sound too rough, though I dunno what was up with her and Agent Darren on that Roscoe op. He got busted around then . . . still, I think she's okay. Just keep an eye on her."

Abe nodded. "Yeah. I hope she works out."

Vic frowned. "If not, we may have to put her down."

Abe sipped his coffee. "She's not a mad dog, Vic."

"Not yet," she replied.

They nibbled on the remains of their food, but neither had much of an appetite now. Stephanie returned after a couple of minutes. Her eyes were bright. "I called Fed Ex. They have no record of a Joan Blackwell ever working for them."

Vic boggled. "You're kidding."

"No. They've got nothing. No such person."

"But Cell S found full confirmation," Abe said. "Up and down the line, she checked out!"

"Not any more," Stephanie said, excited. "I called her home number, just to be thorough. I got some guy named Ray Moore, said he'd had the number for years. Didn't know our Blackwell."

"Damn," Abe said. "If that's all straight, this is a serious plant. Cell S was duped."

"But why?" Stephanie said. "Why would someone have faked this?"

Abe and Vic looked at each other. Finally Vic spoke: "To flush us out. To bring one of us in and tag him, like a migrating goose. That's how they got Shasta."

"A trap?" Stephanie asked.

Vic nodded. "A trap for Delta Green." She glanced at Abe, who nodded worriedly. "The question is, who was the target?"

"What do you mean?" Stephanie asked. "They got Shasta, right?"

"Cell S might have been the target," Vic acknowledged. "But maybe Joan Blackwell was for real, and someone erased her *because* Shasta found her."

"Then what?" Stephanie asked.

"Then now *we're* the target," Vic replied.

None of them knew what to say to that. They sipped their coffee in silence.

Dr. Joseph Camp of the Library of Congress Research Division sat down slowly and somewhat heavily in his living-room armchair. He'd arrived home from a grocery run an hour ago, and had been puttering around in the kitchen when the phone rang.

The milk he'd been heating on the stove for chai had boiled over and then burned. He didn't put his caller on hold until the smoke alarm in the kitchen went off.

His tea ruined, he'd simply settled for a beer and took his chair to await the pizza delivery man. This was no sort of meal for a man of his age and physical condition, but he couldn't be bothered to deal with the mess in the kitchen right now. The smell of scorched milk reminded him of things best not brought to mind. He took a long gulp of beer, set the bottle down, and lit up a Nat Sherman cigarette. Smoke swirled in the air above him as he sat, deep in thought. He was thinking about Agent Shasta.

Dr. Camp was also known as Agent Alphonse, the leader of the Delta Green conspiracy. Sitting in his threadbare tweed suit with a beer in one hand and a cigarette in the other, he looked like nothing more than a tired old pensioner, collecting Social Security and wondering why the kids never called anymore. He sagged in his clothes, his face long, his white goatee—worn to hide a double chin—flecked with moisture from the beer. Reaching deep into himself, Dr. Camp summoned up a gargling cough and spat a wad of phlegm into the ashtray. A small cloud of gray dust rose in a short-lived flurry.

The phone call had been from Agent Tonya in Memphis, calling to report on Cell T's findings in the disappearance of Agent Shasta. The news had been disconcerting. Dr. Camp sat and pondered this mystery, and wondered what to do next. He also wondered, sarcastically, who died and left him in charge. *Oh that's right,* he thought to himself harshly. *Reggie. Reggie Fairfield. Saint Reggie, the martyr to our cause.* Major General Reginald Fairfield, U.S. Army (Retired), had led Delta Green in its illegal incarnation from the day the Joint Chiefs of Staff disbanded the legitimate agency in 1970 to the day that he died: February 25, 1994, murdered in his ancestral cabin in Vermont. The fifth anniversary of that event was a couple weeks away. *I didn't know what a job you had, Reggie, until you were gone. Damn you.*

Dr. Camp finished the beer and the cigarette at about the same time. The pizza arrived, and he made a sorry dinner of it—dipping the ends of the slices in a bowl of non-fat ranch dressing he took from the fridge—while watching CNN. The news was par for the course: government scandals, foreign agitation, on and on. For a man who'd served in WWII and worked in federal service for the fifty years since, the news was old news at best; they just delivered it faster.

Finally he rose and put the leftover pizza in the fridge, using the box it came in. Then he padded in sock feet to the spare bedroom, the one he kept locked with a system that read his body's magnetic field through the key and would not unlock unless it recognized him. A retina scanner would have been simpler, but also too obvious.

Inside was a technological marvel. The room was soundproof and shielded against surveillance via broadcast transmission. The windows were shuttered and the glass dampened to prevent audio surveillance via laser-scanned vibration. The walls, floor, and ceiling were completely lined with two layers of steel separated by a gas. If someone drilled through with a micro-camera or some other device, the gas would be released into the room, triggering a silent chemical alarm. The airtight room's ventilation was piped in from the basement, and passed through a variety of filters and chemical sniffers to detect and block contaminants. The only communication to the outside world was through a digital fiber-optic cable that Dr. Camp had run himself, down through the building's walls, into the basement, out through a storm drain, and eventually into a Department of Works utility tunnel beneath the street, where it was cleverly patched into the phone company's trunk lines through a custom encryption unit. The degree of security was excessive, except for one important and unusual respect: the fact that this cutting-edge installation, which had cost more than four hundred thousand dollars, was in the spare bedroom of Dr. Camp's house—the one whose address appeared in the phone book next to his name for all to see. He figured that if someone got to him, Delta Green was screwed anyway; might as well have the op center be convenient, right? It was, perhaps, the only real piece of recklessness he had left in him. Or so he liked to think.

Reclining into the expensive task chair in the secure room, Dr. Camp tapped on the keyboard of his computer. He accessed Delta Green's database system—it and the group's main encryption routers were stored elsewhere—and pondered various screens full of information. The information concerned the missing Agent Shasta:

> Shasta was born in Taiwan in 1950. During the war, his father served as an Army transport pilot in the Pacific theater; afterwards, he worked for the CIA-owned Civil Air Transport, running airborne smuggling, surveillance, and civilian transportation flights out of Taiwan from 1946 until his death in 1964. Father was a Delta Green friendly and staunch follower of the Dalai Lama, and did personal work on behalf of Tibet against Communist China beginning in 1958. Father died in the 1964 crash of a C-46A transport he was piloting during a Delta Green op intended to assassinate PARIAH.

> Shasta grew into a skilled observer with excellent regional language skills. He was drafted in 1968 and the Army sent him to Vietnam as an interrogator and translator for the Military Assistance Command, Vietnam (MACV). Acting in this capacity, Shasta did some brief work for Marine Colonel Satchel Wade, who later organized the Delta Green operation in pre-invasion Cambodia. In 1970 Shasta testified before the Joint Chiefs of Staff in the secret hearings that shut down Delta Green. Shortly afterwards, Shasta was recruited by the CIA. He has maintained a dual Army/CIA status ever since.
>
> In 1979, he was sent to the new U.S. embassy in Beijing, China, as a military attaché. In 1984 he was recruited by Agent Alphonse—a wartime friend of his father's—into Delta Green, following an assignment to retrieve the *Ghorl Nigräl.* He remained at the embassy until 1986, when Chinese authorities exposed him as a CIA agent and ejected him from the country.
>
> Since his return, he has worked as an intelligence analyst for the CIA's Office of East Asian Analysis, under the Directorate of Intelligence. Today, his work focuses on Chinese dismantling and re-deployment of ICBM launch stations, specifically those formerly or presently located in Tibet. He is unmarried and forty-eight years old. He has participated in thirty ops since his induction into Delta Green.

Dr. Camp read and re-read the profile. He accessed the meager files on Shasta's past ops. Somewhere in there, he hoped, there would be a clue to Agent Shasta's disappearance.

Who would want to kidnap David Foster Nells?

David Foster Nells slept. It was a deep sleep, brought on by medication. When the guard came to wake him, he was slow to rise.

"Get up, Nells. C'mon, get up." The guard shook him, then shook him harder. David mumbled something and began blinking his eyes. As the guard continued to berate him, David's vision came into focus and he looked at his surroundings.

He was in a jail cell—that much was obvious. He was lying on a bunk bed with a thin mattress, a bed suspended from the cinder-block wall by metal brackets. The walls were painted light green, a thick institutional coat. The wall he faced when he raised his head was not a wall, but a network of metal bars with a locking gate set off-center. The gate was closed, and another guard stood outside in a hallway painted the same color as the cell.

David sat up groggily, confused by his surroundings. "What's going on?" he managed to ask.

"Get up. Your lawyer's here. Move, move!" the guard barked angrily.

David swiveled around and got his feet on the floor. He put on an unfamiliar pair of shoes, and then realized he was wearing an orange jumpsuit marked SAVANNAH CITY JAIL. "I don't understand," he said.

"I don't give a shit, asshole. Get up and let's go." He grabbed David beneath the arms and pulled him up until he was standing, then pushed him towards the gate. The guard outside opened it and jerked his head to one side, indicating that David should come out into the hallway. David complied, followed closely by the guard who had awakened him. The gate clanged shut behind them, and the pair led David down the hall.

They entered a small conference room. Inside was a table, four chairs, and a metal cart containing a television atop a VCR.

A security camera was mounted to the ceiling in a corner opposite the door, and a large mirror was set into one wall. Seated at the table was a small man in his thirties, wearing a dark suit. A briefcase sat unopened in front of him.

The guards led David to a point opposite the seated man. They pushed him down into the metal chair and handcuffed his left wrist to the padded arm. From somewhere down the hallway outside came the sound of a telephone ringing and the low murmur of people talking. In the distance, someone was yelling and banging on metal bars, perhaps a prisoner demanding attention. Once David was secured, the guards left and closed the door behind them.

"Hello, David," the seated man said with a high Southern accent. "How are they treating you?"

David looked at him, still bleary and very confused. "What's going on? What is this?"

"I needed to see you, David, because the prosecutor's office has just provided me with a copy of their key evidence. It's not gonna be pleasant, but I want you to watch it. We're going to have to rethink our defense strategy, and there's little time—your trial starts in two weeks. I can ask them for a plea bargain, but given this evidence, I don't think they'll take it."

David's brow furrowed. "What the hell are you talking about?"

"I'll show you," the man said. He leaned over to the metal cart and turned on the television, then pressed a button on the VCR. The word PLAY appeared on the screen in large blocky letters, and then a title card appeared. It bore the logo of the City of Savannah Office of the District Attorney. Beneath the logo it read: "The People vs. David Foster Nells." Below that was a long case number, and the words: "People's Exhibit A." David stared at the screen, baffled.

The card vanished and the picture jumped, then settled into a new image. The footage was clearly shot with a home video camera. It was a static shot, probably from atop a tripod or other level surface, and showed a dignified elderly woman seated at a grand piano in what appeared to be a luxurious parlor. She was playing a piece by Debussy. She looked frequently at the camera to smile and nod.

A man entered the frame behind the woman. He appeared to be in his late forties, in good shape but not overly handsome, with silver hair and a faintly military bearing. He wore dark blue jogging pants and a grey sweatshirt. In one hand he held a crowbar.

The man swung the crowbar and it connected with the woman's head. She let out a sharp cry and hit a wrong note on the piano, then tipped off the stool and fell to the floor. The man stepped over her and brought the crowbar down three times, crushing her skull in full view of the camera while making a strange wailing sound, like a wounded baboon. Blood spattered onto the floor, onto the man's sweatshirt, and into the air. The camera lens was untouched—it was probably twenty to thirty feet away from the events it recorded. The man stood over the dead woman and panted for a moment, then turned and walked out of the frame. Static filled the screen.

David's face was pale. The man in the video was himself. The woman in the video was his mother. The parlor was in his mother's house in Savannah, Georgia. He even knew about the video camera—his mother gave piano recitals at Savannah society functions, and often practiced in front of a video camera so she could critique her posture, attention to the audience, and performance. It was all very familiar, except that David had no recollection of this event whatsoever, or how he had come to be in jail, or who this man was seated across the table from him.

The man leaned forward and turned off the equipment, then settled back in his chair. "As you can see, David, our defense strategy—that you were taking a drive when your mother was murdered—just ain't gonna hold water." He pronounced "water" as "wah-tuh."

David looked at the man in shock. "I don't understand any of this," he said in a strained voice.

"Well you better start figuring it out. A little bird told me they're gonna seek the death penalty. We might get life, but even that's a long shot. They got you dead to rights."

David shook his head slowly, "This . . . this doesn't make any sense."

The man's tone grew heated. "It makes all the sense in the world! You beat your mother to death with a crowbar, and any jury what gets a look at that tape is gonna put paid to your ass! It's over, sir. You're done for."

Tears welled up in David's eyes. "But I didn't do it! I don't know what's going on!"

"You killed your mother, you son of a bitch!" The man was yelling now, his face flush. "You fucking killed her! It's over! It's all over!"

David screamed.

The television shattered. A flash of blue sparks erupted as glass and plastic flew across the room. The man hit the floor, clutching at his bleeding head. David sat there rigid, screaming, with tears running down his face, and the VCR erupted in flames. The smell of burning plastic began to fill the room. There was a sudden sound like a balloon popping, and the man lying on the floor exploded, spraying blood and tissue and fragments of bone all over the room. David was drenched in it, struck by the human shrapnel, and still he screamed, tears streaming over the gore on his cheeks.

On the other side of the mirror, two lab-coated men watched with interest. They stood in a room packed with computers and monitoring equipment that tracked measurements from the environment of the conference room and from microtransmitters implanted in David's body. A thick piece of reinforced plexiglass covered this side of the mirror, bolted into the wall to protect the men and equipment in case the mirror shattered. A door led out to a large, open soundstage, in which stood a freestanding environment consisting of the cell, the hallway, and the conference room. Speakers provided credible background sounds—phones, people talking, an inmate banging on the bars—all of it pre-recorded in a studio within the same facility.

One of the men spoke into a microcassette recorder he held in his left hand. "Stress simulation 10.0 provokes dramatic psychokinetic response, 1532 hours."

The other man picked up a telephone handset and dialed a three-digit number. "It's happened again, Dr. Yrjo. He even killed the lawyer this time . . . yes, our equipment survived. The power sink on the mirror worked perfectly. We've got the measurements of the energy he put into the glass, and they're just incredible."

In the conference room, David screamed and screamed and screamed. Inside his head, his mind screamed louder than his voice ever could.

Interlude: Thirty Six Fifty and a Wake-Up

Monday, June 16, 1997

The court-martial had been brief. Just a formality, really. Captain Forrest James of the United States Navy—captain of the U.S. swim team at the 1968 Summer Olympics, winner of an Olympic Bronze medal, graduate of the U.S. Naval Academy at Annapolis, veteran of three tours of duty in Vietnam, commanding officer of SEAL Team Seven—had pled guilty to charges of Assault and Conduct Unbecoming an Officer. The trial was brief, but loud. The news of this career officer's arrest for the brutal beating of a young civilian woman in a San Francisco hotel room had gone national, the latest in a string of military snafus that had shamed the armed services and focused a spotlight on the behavior of the ranks. The Navy had no intention of letting Captain James off the hook for what its psychologists agreed had been a psychotic episode brought on by post-traumatic stress and alcohol abuse. It helped that he pled guilty, fully owning up to the loss of self-discipline and the addiction to alcohol that had brought about that terrible night, but all the same the brass saw no choice: a punitive discharge and ten years' hard time in the United States Disciplinary Barracks at Fort Leavenworth, Kansas. He was stripped of his rank, pay, and benefits, and that night he put on his uniform for the final time. The MPs at Alameda NAS drove him to Oakland Army Base, where he was led in shackles onto a transport making a routine flight to Fort Leavenworth. At dawn, he reached the walls of the USDB.

Fifty-six, James thought to himself. *That's how old I'll be before I'm standing here outside again.* He shook his head and, for the thousandth time, cursed himself for a damned fool.

The USDB was a huge, imposing compound covering more than twelve acres, encased in walls and under round-the-clock watch from twelve guard towers. Though it consisted of a number of buildings, there was only one that really mattered: the Castle. The Castle was a monstrous old structure of red brick and barred windows at least six stories high. It was built like a wagon wheel, with a central hub surrounded by eight radiating wings of varying lengths.

At the entrance to the compound, the MPs turned James over to four Corrections Specialists in modern Army-standard camouflage BDUs and heavy boots. They had no weapons, but each wore a whistle around his neck to summon backup in case of trouble.

The guards took James and walked him through an arched doorway. They emerged into a long, open concrete yard broken up by several grassy fields. As they marched in unison, they passed a column of guards in riot gear running early-morning drill. Ahead, at the end of the yard, stood the Castle. James squinted in the sun and gazed at his new home, feeling a shadow fall across his spirit. This place, so quiet here in the dawn light, felt like a mausoleum in which he was to be buried alive.

Inside, James began his processing. He was stripped and thoroughly searched, then given a medical check. The guards took his uniform away and returned with the drab apparel of the USDB. These were identical to the Army's old ODs, but they were dyed brown. The only marking on the uniform was his name, on an embroidered patch over one breast pocket: JAMES.

Once he was checked out, dressed, and re-shackled, an officer entered the room and addressed him by rote.

"Welcome to the United States Disciplinary Barracks," he said in a stern, clipped voice. "It is our mission to incarcerate U.S. military prisoners sentenced to long terms of confinement, to conduct correctional and treatment programs to maintain good order and discipline, and to reduce recidivism upon release. Despite your punitive discharge you are still accountable to the Uniform Code of Military Justice. This,"—he whipped a small book out from behind his back and handed it to James—"is your new way of life. *The Manual for the Guidance of Inmates*. Read it, study it, know it, because if you violate it, you will be punished."

The briefing went on for five more minutes.

Wings 3, 4, 6, and 7 of the Castle were used for confining prisoners. You started on the top floor, and if you were a good inmate you could work your way down to the ground, eventually sparing your aging bones the punishing stairwells. New cons started off in maximum custody, with no access to recreational facilities and movement allowed only in shackles under guard. Maximum custody gave you time to sit in your cell and think about what got you here and not much else. Over time and with good behavior you could achieve medium custody, where you would join the general prison population. You could move in groups for work detail and enjoy the weight room, television sets, exercise yard, and a scant few other amenities. There were further custody grades, each allowing more access and freedom, up to the final grade of trustee. Trustees lived in barracks outside the Castle that functioned much like halfway houses, with the freedom to even wear civilian clothes after hours. For James, the grade of trustee was a long, long way away.

With the briefing concluded, James was led to breakfast in an enormous common room. The USDB housed more than a thousand inmates, including twenty women and fifty ex-officers. Enlisted personnel were only taken here if they had sentences longer than five years; otherwise, they did their time at lower-security regional prisons. All officers went to the USDB even if they were only serving a day.

In the cafeteria, James was seated in a section reserved for maximum-custody inmates. They ate in silence, surrounded by the noisier general population, all of them watched closely by numerous guards and video cameras.

After breakfast, the maximum inmates were marched in shackles *en masse* by a group of guards back to their cells. James was in the fourth wing, where most of the ex-officers were kept. At present, however, James was the only ex-officer in maximum custody.

One by one, the cons were locked in their cells. Finally, it was James' turn.

His cell measured just six feet wide by eight feet long by ten feet high, and was fronted by a heavy metal chain-link door. Through the door he saw a cot, a sink, a toilet, a chair, and a small folding desk hinged to the wall.

My new home, James thought, as the guards removed his shackles. A buzzer sounded, the door swung open, and he stepped inside. The door closed behind him and the guards marched away with the rest of the maximums.

James stood still and pale, his mouth dry, looking at the spartan little room. When he went to Vietnam, the soldiers referred to their year-long tour of duty as Three Sixty Five and a Wake-Up, meaning three hundred sixty-five days and then a departure. He'd done three tours there, three years spent hunting guerillas in the Mekong Delta and disrupting NVA infrastructure north of the DMZ and along the Ho Chi Minh Trail. Three years of blood, sweat, and tears. Three years that in retrospect looked like a goddamn cakewalk compared to the time he'd do here, starting right now, right this minute. Ten years' hard time in the Castle.

James lay down on the cot and closed his eyes. He wondered if he could just sleep for the next ten years, a prince in a fairy tale who slept and slept until the miracle came.

Thirty Six Fifty and a Wake-Up, he thought. *Thirty Six Fifty and a Wake-Up.*

Chapter Two: The Awful Daring

Monday, February 15–Tuesday, February 16, 1999

VIC TURNED THE KEY in the lock, then opened the door. Behind the door was an empty area roughly eight feet wide by ten feet deep. She sighed, then turned to Abe and Stephanie behind her.

"Okay, let's have the stuff."

Stephanie handed her a crumpled paper bag. It contained six small boxes of 9mm Parabellum ammunition, totaling three hundred rounds. Vic pulled the boxes out, one by one, and stacked them in a corner. Then she turned back to her compatriots. "Anything else?" she asked.

Stephanie reached into the backpack she had slung over one shoulder and produced six mag lights—heavy-duty flashlights, equally useful at providing illumination or beating someone up. Vic put them into the storage area, then locked the door.

"Oh, wait," Abe said. "I forgot—I brought some pocket lint."

Vic and Stephanie cracked smiles but couldn't muster much enthusiasm for the joke.

Cell T was setting up a Green Box. This was Delta Green's term for a private-storage area used for storing useful supplies. Ideally, each major city had a Green Box where departing agents could drop off valuable resources, which future teams would access as needed. It was sort of a junk stash, a place to leave leftover ammo, flashlights, batteries, or what have you. In practice, only a handful of cities had Green Boxes, and their contents were highly random. Some might have sniper rifles and thermal-neutral suits invisible to infrared cameras; others might have a stale sack of nachos and a corpse sealed in plastic.

You never knew what you'd find—assuming that the city you were in even had one. In the case of Cell T, Memphis had no Green Box. So they set one up. Alphonse would keep the keys and rental agreement, making regular payments and overnighting the keys to future agents' motels before they arrived so they could get equipped.

With the Memphis Green Box enabled—containing three hundred rounds of 9mm Parabellum ammunition and six magnum flashlights—Cell T dropped the keys, fake ID, and rental agreement in the overnight box to Alphonse. They'd set up the fake Memphis Private Investigations firm yesterday afternoon as planned, since they thought they might still need that cover, and booked flights for the next day. Once they arrived in Knoxville, they'd have the keys to the city's Green Box and a fake set of Memphis private-detective permits courtesy of Alphonse coming the day after. Once they had everything they needed, Cell T would take a rental car out to Groversville, in the middle of nowhere, and follow what leads they could find.

Tonight, however, they were in Memphis, with a night to kill before their flight to Knoxville. For security purposes, Vic, Abe, and Stephanie were all in the same motel room; Delta Green agents tended to request a lot of folding cots, since agents who slept alone often suffered for it. They'd flipped coins to see who got the cot, and Stephanie lost. But for now, the trio sat on the two main beds and traded shots of bourbon, having relied on Abe to purchase the liquor for the night.

Vic knocked back a solid shot of booze in one of the motel's dust-covered plastic cups. "So Abe," she said with a smirk, "why don't you tell Stephanie about your first op?"

Abe sighed and swallowed a shot of bourbon. It was a Delta Green tradition to get drunk as hell on the first night of an op, when the risk was usually lowest, and swap stories. "I was in the 'Nam, 1969, and Charlie was everywhere," he began. Vic busted out laughing, and Stephanie snorted liquor out through her nose then began coughing. Both women laughed hysterically—drunkenly, actually. Abe feigned a hurt look. Vic regained her composure and spoke more forcefully.

"Fuck you, Abe, you weren't in fucking Vietnam. Take it from the top," she said.

Abe nodded reverently. "Okay, okay. It was 1995. I was an innocent FBI agent in Milwaukee trying to take down a Chinese heroin posse. All straightforward, totally above board and legit. I'd been married maybe five, six months. Career man. This guy—Shasta—came through the system and recruited my team for an op. No big deal, right? Shit went to hell. Godawful. Bullets everywhere. Made that L.A. *Heat* bank robbery look like squaresville. There wasn't any footage, thank God, or it would've been all over the TV. Full auto, left and right, my partners whipping out twelve-gauge slugs at a moving car—shit, you can't imagine the hell that came down. I never thought I'd be that deaf shy of a *Gwar* concert. Dropped two motherfuckers personally, blew their brainpans all over the street.

"Trouble was, that was the the seventh and eighth times I shot them in the head.

"They had something in their favor. Some kind of protection. My bosses told me I was crazy, said I must have missed them. But the forensics boys told me the straight dope. They *found* all the rounds I'd fired that had 'missed.' They were lying in the middle of the street, flattened. No other obstacle to account for their collapse. Just flattened bullets lying there, like they'd hit an invisible wall and dropped to the ground. I knew something else had gone down. I knew that a whole 'nother career track had just opened up. Alphonse contacted me within a few weeks, and everything changed."

"So you cut your dick off and wore scarves to hide your adam's apple?" Vic said, grinning.

"Fuck you, ya dyke bitch," Abe replied, knocking back another shot of bourbon and grimacing from the burn. He turned to Stephanie. "You better watch out for this rug-muncher, Steph. You'll wake up and find—hey!" Vic had thrown a pillow at him. He caught it and started whacking Vic with it across the gap between the two beds.

"Pillow biter! Pillow biter!" she yelled between blows. Abe relented and laughed, pouring more bourbon once Vic stopped.

"Well," Stephanie said, a little perturbed. "You guys get out much?"

Vic turned serious. "Look, Steph, this is it. From here on out, it's blood and thunder and misery and heartbreak. That's the way it always is. You gotta cut loose at the start and enjoy it while it lasts."

"So what's your story, Steph?" Abe asked. "What's up with Darren, anyway? You two get it on?"

Stephanie took a slow drink of bourbon and stared at the floor. "You know, not everything is funny."

The room got quiet for a moment. Vic broke the silence. "Steph, hon, the truth is that nothing is fuckin' funny. It all sucks, up and down the line. But sometimes you gotta pretend."

"Yeah, okay," Stephanie said. "Okay, I thought that look on Larry's face when they tore his guts out was pretty funny, don't you?" She got up and stormed out of the motel room.

Vic looked at Abe once Stephanie was outside. "I told you she was kinda spooky."

Abe sighed and ran his fingers through his thick red hair. "Shit, it's her first op as a full agent. She can't just up and join the Three Investigators Club right off the bat. It takes time to assimilate. She'll get there."

Vic took another shot of bourbon. "I hate this nickel-and-dime crap you buy. Why do I send you on liquor patrol, anyway?"

"It's my charming smile."

Vic grinned. "Starfucker."

"Gutter mouth," Abe said, pouring more bourbon into his cup.

"Speaking of what a starfucker you are," Vic said, "how's the wife?"

Abe emptied his cup and closed his eyes for a moment while he swallowed. "Well, she's got a label again, finally. She's been humping that tape around for months, and somebody at Virgin finally bit. They're angling for a big comeback story—former teen sensation returns, that kinda crap. First thing they told her is lose twenty pounds."

"I didn't mean her career," Vic said quietly.

"I know. I'm just ducking the issue." Abe refilled his cup yet again. "The truth is, I don't think we've got much left. We don't really talk these days unless it's a fight. I think the writing's on the wall. We're just waiting to see who calls a lawyer first. Carol's already got one for this contract business, so maybe she'll get the ball rolling."

"Well, shit. What about Eric?"

"Hell if I know. Joint custody, if I'm lucky. Visitation rights if I'm not. He's barely two. Probably be better off with her, if this Virgin thing goes big. At least she could really provide for him. I'm lucky to spend less than sixty hours a week at the office, not to mention that I could get my head blown off one of these days."

"I'm sorry, Abe. I shouldn't have asked."

"No, I'm glad you did." He finished his drink and winked at her. "You know, I've always had a thing for musicians."

Vic took another sip, smiling behind the cup.

Outside the motel room, Stephanie leaned against the metal railing and looked out into the deeps of the night. Below her was a swimming pool. There was a good-looking blond guy paddling around, flirting with a dark hispanic woman who was also in the pool. They looked so normal, so real, and so happy; Stephanie hated them from first sight. Who were they to lounge around a motel, enjoying life without any sense of the shitstorm lurking over every horizon?

Stephanie had walked into that shitstorm, willingly, and returned to tell the tale. It wasn't a pretty story, and she wished that she could be in that pool with that guy, laughing and touching each other from time to time, losing the world in a simple caress, denying the inevitable with a look and a smile.

But that was no longer an option, was it? She was up here on the second floor, gazing out at the whole wide world. She could see so much more than they could, that happy, lazy couple down there in the pool. Still, what good was knowledge if it didn't bring happiness? She'd made a decision on the Roscoe op: she'd focus on the immediate problems of human suffering, and steer clear of the big picture, of the big questions. But up here on the second floor, gazing into the night, she saw nothing but big questions.

Somewhere, she knew, Forrest James—Agent Darren—was in a cell at Fort Leavenworth, the military prison in Kansas.

He was the last man to reach inside her, to really give a damn about what she thought and how she felt. When they first met, she thought he was just being an asshole. Once she realized what he was trying to protect her from, she felt a sort of gratitude, mixed with resentment at his belief that she couldn't handle it. Yet when push came to shove, she really couldn't—in the face of the cosmos itself she wilted, retreated back across the line that demarcated reason and sanity. She'd left him alone out there in the cold and dark, at a time when he needed her more than she could then imagine.

She loved him still, with that doomed sort of passion that is no more than half-rooted in reality; James had become for her a sort of fantasy, a phantom protector who would do anything to save her. This phantom didn't watch TV or read books or pass the time in any mundane way; it simply hovered nearby, ready to offer protection at a moment's notice. Yet the reality of the phantom was that he was locked up in Fort Leavenworth for years and years to come. Stephanie was on her own.

Just thinking about these things made her head hurt. She knew she'd been a jerk just now, with Vic and Abe, but she resented their familiarity, their borderline intimacy, and she resented their attempts to get to know her. She just wanted to go to bed and get to work in the morning, when things might make more sense—and when that damned, happy, flirting couple in the pool would be gone.

Finally she turned and went back into the motel room. The lights were off, but Vic and Abe were chatting quietly in the dark, across the space that separated the beds. They stopped talking once Stephanie was inside. She stripped and climbed into the cot, then pulled the covers over her shoulders and eventually went to sleep. She dreamed troubled dreams.

Δ

The following afternoon, Cell T got off the plane in Knoxville. All three were listless and red-eyed from the night before, and they spoke only rarely. Departing the airport in their rental car, they headed straight to a gun store to buy another three hundred rounds of 9mm Parabellum. From there they went to the motel and checked in, where a package from Alphonse was waiting for them. Inside was a key to the Knoxville Green Box. Cell S had set up this box when they'd come back from Groversville a few years earlier; no DG teams had been through this neck of the woods since.

The storage facility was typical of the breed. Cell T drove up in their car, punched in a code at a box by the gate, and then drove into an indoor parking area. From there they took an elevator up to the third floor and found a door marked 323. The key fit smoothly. Inside were two boxes containing a variety of handgun ammunition calibers; three sets of XL cold-weather clothes; an instant camera with six unused packs of ten exposures each; a microcassette recorder and three blank tapes; a half-dozen business cards from Groversville merchants and one from a TV news producer; and a Chamber of Commerce map of Groversville that had obviously been taken from a motel room, with some locations circled and annotated. Cell T took everything except for the clothes and the ammunition.

Returning to their hotel room, Cell T faced the prospect of a twenty-four-hour period of nothing to do. They had to wait in Knoxville until tomorrow, when they'd receive the fake Memphis Private Investigator ID's from Alphonse, along with "something special" he'd promised to include. The three of them sat on the two beds. A cot was once again set up against a wall, though Abe had lost a rock-paper-scissors competition and been assigned to it this time.

"All I'm saying," Abe said, "is that we've never been to Groversville before, and it's a strange situation. As long as we're sitting on our ass, we might as well send a canary into the coal mine, you know?"

Stephanie looked at the business card in her hand again and shook her head. "It's too risky! I can't believe you'd tip off the media before this op even starts."

"First off, *Phenomen-X* hardly qualifies as the media," Abe replied. "Second, those guys have experience in Groversville. They were there during Cell S's original trip. And shit, if we're right about this being some sort of trap, better them than us."

Stephanie turned to Vic. "It's your call, Vic. I don't know these guys. I've never watched their show or seen them work. If you think they could be useful and not screw up the op, then I guess we might as well."

Vic sat in silence for almost a minute. Abe lay back on the bed and folded his arms across his face. Stephanie tapped her foot rhythmically on the floor, softly betraying her anxiety at this discussion. Finally, Vic spoke.

"We'll do it. They've been good lackeys in the past. We might as well turn them loose on this situation. If nothing else, they should serve as a good smokescreen—the bad guys might accept our activity as part of the *Phenomen-X* team's meddling."

Abe sat up, smiling. "You won't regret this. Those guys make great Oswalds."

Stephanie shrugged. "If you think so, Vic, then I'm okay with it. We'll send them in and see what happens." She clearly sounded unconvinced.

Vic took the business card back from Stephanie. Then she picked up the phone and started dialing numbers.

THE FLOOR MANAGER WAS terse. "Would the talking head like some coffee?" David Carmichael, the aging and blandly telegenic host of *Phenomen-X,* bristled. "I have a *fucking name,* goddamnit!" he shouted. "Call me *David,* you cocksucker, or *Mister Carmichael* if you're feeling formal!"

The floor manager paused for a moment, then spoke into his headset mike: "The talking head doesn't want any coffee."

Carmichael grumbled some more, but it was almost time to tape this week's episode of the popular, syndicated, UFO/supernatural "news" show *Phenomen-X*. From their studio in Culver City, California, a staff of two dozen labored to bring the latest and greatest *outré* stories to a credulous public. Ratings were down. There were only so many UFO sightings to go around, and the networks had muscled into the action lately, buying up all the good vid.

The floor manager listened to his headset and then spoke to Carmichael as if he were addressing the Wailing Wall: "Go in five, four, three, two, one . . ."

"Can you handle the truth?" Carmichael said in a pleasantly nondescript voice. "Because we're bringing it to you—right here on *Phenomen-X!*"

"Roll title," said the director in the control room, and the opening montage and credits began. The show was recorded "live to tape," which meant that there was no live audience, but that they produced each episode as if there was one—real time start to finish, hopefully with no need to go back and edit the footage later. Forty-four minutes and ten seconds from now, this week's episode would be over. "Cue talking head," the director said once the intro was done.

"Bigfoot surfaces in Madagascar, and a child's doll turns deadly in Minnesota. But first, Sonja Dewey goes ghost-busting at a hotel in Port Townsend, Washington, in this *Phenomen-X* exclusive. Sonja?" Carmichael's face was a mask of strangely distant enthusiasm. A pre-recorded video of Sonja's report began to play.

In the control room, news director Frank Carincola sat back and watched the episode unfold through his thick bifocals. He had done everything he could up to this point, and now the show was in the hands of the production staff. Tommy Prendergast, an enthusiastic young gofer and general assistant, tapped Carincola on the shoulder. "Uh, you've got a call, sir." Tommy held a cordless phone out to the news director, the smell of deodorant wafting off his portly body like steam from a hot tub. Tommy was, rather unwittingly, the show's target market: an ill-adjusted, socially inept technogeek with a jones for the inexplicable. Carincola gave him a withering look which could be loosely translated as "beat it" and answered the call.

"Yeah?"

"Frank Carincola?" The voice on the phone was digitally processed to disguise its identity.

"Yeah?"

"You know who this is."

"Uh—yeah, I do. This is the group, isn't it?" Carincola said enthusiastically as he fumbled for a pen to take notes. "The group" was his term for the conspiracy that he believed pulled the strings of the federal government, particularly those agencies charged with dealing with extraterrestrials. From time to time, the group would contact him with leads for stories and cryptic clues.

"A couple years ago you went to Groversville, Tennessee, correct?"

"Yeah," Carincola said again, his tone a little muted. "That was me."

"You need to go back to Groversville, Frank. You need to go there tonight. Things have changed there." The voice was electronic and buzzing.

"What?" Carincola bellowed. "What do you mean, changed? It's abandoned!"

"You'll find out," the voice replied. "Just get on a plane. Now. We'll be in touch."

The caller hung up.

Shit, thought Carincola. *Groversville.* His trip to Groversville was his baptism by fire. The other three people on that trip had died soon after of Hantavirus, leaving him alone with the knowledge of what they'd seen. He was a health-food nut and a vegan, and during *Phenomen-X*'s trip to Groversville, Tennessee, to investigate UFO reports, cattle mutilations, and alien abductions, he was the only one to bring his own supply of food and water, just out of habit. The others had eaten locally and drank from the sink faucet, and they all died—at least, that was the connection that Carincola made afterwards. The Groversville trip convinced him that journalism was where he had to be, but it also convinced him that there was more in Heaven and Earth than humans dreamed of, and that under the right (or wrong?) circumstances, Heaven and Earth might conspire to kill good people. Like his fellow staffers who'd bought the farm.

The phone call rattled Carincola to his core. There hadn't been a peep from Groversville since the incidents, and even the diaspora of town residents and the closing of the highway exit to the valley had failed to catch the national media's eye.

The fact that this situation was now coming to light surprised Carincola, but the associated risk did not dissuade him. By midnight, he was on a flight to Knoxville with his star reporter, Sonja Dewey, and his grizzled video-grapher Allen Eddington. They were bringing a lot of gear, but more importantly, they brought enough bottled water and pre-packaged food to last them a week. Sonja and Allen thought he was acting paranoid—that was nothing new, actually—but Carincola laid out the ground rules very clearly: "You eat nothing from there, you drink nothing from there. You assume everyone's out to poison you at every opportunity." His companions nodded mutely and swapped looks as soon as he looked away. Whatever they were heading into, their boss was taking it very, very seriously.

DR. CAMP STOOD IN the breakfast nook off his kitchen, assembling a large cardboard shipping box that he'd be sending counter-to-counter on a plane to Knoxville first thing in the morning. There was a manila folder on the table containing three forged private investigator ID cards, allegedly issued by the city of Memphis. He'd picked them up from his usual forger on the way home from work. They were going into the box, along with some fluid containers that Agent Stan was bringing over sometime this evening. If all went well, Cell T would have the box in their hands tomorrow afternoon.

The fluid was something special. A DG friendly—a microbiologist—had knocked it together for him during the original Groversville op a couple years back. Cell S had found evidence of surgical tampering on some of the residents of the town, surgery that the victims weren't aware of and that didn't bear much resemblance to human medicine or procedures. In all cases, there were no scars. The wounds were closed with a strange substance that the friendly had called "neo-tissue," because it could mimic most any form of human tissue on the fly—skin, muscle, lung, whatever was needed. It allowed surgery without scarring, and in some places the neo-tissue had been used to replace entire organs or limbs with new ones that were superior to the originals. The fluid—a compound called leucopararosaniline—was used in spray bottles. When it came in contact with the substance, a reactive dye in the fluid would turn a bright purple. Sprayed on a human body, or on anything else that contained neo-tissue, it made an obvious identification.

After the op, Cell S kept the concentrated powder that the friendly had supplied. Agent Stan was prepping a few bottles for Dr. Camp to send to Cell T in Knoxville, though Stan didn't know where the material was going, to who, or for what purpose. He and Agent Susan had been kept in the dark about the investigation into Shasta's disappearance.

There was a pounding at the front door. Dr. Camp put down the tape gun he was using to assemble the box and shuffled through the living room to the foyer. He checked through the peephole to verify that it was, indeed, Agent Stan, and was unsettled to see that the man appeared to be crying. Dr. Camp slipped his right hand into the pocket of his housecoat and opened the door with his left.

"Hello, Hank," Dr. Camp said evenly, addressing him by his real name.

Hank Steiner stood on the front steps in an overcoat, holding a rain-spattered cardboard box. His hair was damp from the storm outside, but the tears on his face weren't from the rain. His eyes were red and he was shaking. "Joe," he said, his voice cracking with emotion. "Oh God, Joe, oh Jesus."

Dr. Camp stood to one side and ushered him in. "Get in

out of the rain, Hank. Just set the box down over there." Hank stumbled inside and laid his burden down by the armchair. Dr. Camp closed the door and watched Hank. His right hand remained in his pocket.

"Hank, what's wrong?"

Hank turned around, blubbering. "Ah Jesus, Joe, fuckin' Jesus . . . they did it, they did it to me, oh shit, they did it to me."

"Steady on, Hank. What are you talking about?"

The man was weeping, great shuddering sobs rocking through his body. He said something unintelligible and pulled open his overcoat. Beneath, he had no shirt on.

His chest was stained with purple dye.

Dr. Camp flicked off the safety on the handgun in his pocket. "All right, Hank. I understand. Now listen—are you listening to me?"

Hank nodded and wiped his face, still crying.

"I want you to strip down. We'll get you in the shower, wash off the dye, and then we'll spray you again and see exactly what the situation is. I'll need to take some photographs."

"I was just working with the stuff, you know?" Hank said, shaking, as he pulled off the overcoat. "The concentrate, it's a real fine powder. It was all in the air, you know? Just floating. Then I looked down and saw . . . I saw . . . m-my hand . . ." The overcoat was crumpled to the floor now, and Hank was staring at his right hand. Dr. Camp could see a dim purple discoloration over the man's entire arm.

"Steady on, Hank," Dr. Camp said again. Then he noticed something.

Hank's tears were now running out of his eyes and *up* his face, over his forehead and into the tangle of wet hair on his scalp. Hank started looking up and around, reacting to the odd sensation. Suddenly he understood. "*Oh Jesus, Joe—*"

The first shot struck Hank Steiner in the heart, sending his system into shock. The second punctured his left lung. Blood spattered on the armchair. Hank's eyes were pools of liquid fear.

Dr. Camp lowered the handgun and slowly backed away, tracking Agent Stan as he collapsed to the living-room floor. "Twenty-three skiddoo!" he bellowed. There was a beep. Armored steel shutters slammed down behind all the windows and doors in the small house, and all the lights went on. Hank's right arm liquified as the neo-tissue abandoned its shape, and then blood from the raw stump began to pour onto the carpet. Bloody gashes appeared all over his naked chest as the rest of the neo-tissue liquified, unsealing the invisible surgery scars. His body cavity opened up like an envelope and his innards bulged out. His scalp and the top of his skull dissolved, leaving a mass of hair on the carpet and his pulsing brain exposed to the air. All of the neo-tissue ran together into a blob the size of a large cat. Dr. Camp turned and hustled down the side hall, his heart pumping wildly as he fumbled for his keys with his left hand. Reaching the door to the spare bedroom, he got the keys out and found the one he needed. Down the hall, the blob was rolling across the carpet towards him.

He got the key in the lock, and the pause while the security system verified his identity seemed like an eternity. Then the door opened, he stepped inside, and slammed it shut behind him. A moment later the internal seals kicked in, leaving the room impregnable.

Dr. Camp took two steps forward and grabbed at a chair for support. His breathing was heavy and ragged, and his face was damp with sweat. He set the gun down on the desk.

The secure telephone rang. Dr. Camp fumbled with it for a moment before he got the receiver up to his face. It was Agent Adam, calling about the alarm that Dr. Camp's computer had tripped when he'd spoken the activation phrase.

"It's all right, Adam," he said. "Just had—" He paused for breath. "Just had a bit of excitement here . . . no, I'm okay. But I can't leave this room just yet. Listen, I need you to activate Agent Nancy. Get her handlers to bring her here in a couple hours. The situation should be under control by then. I'll have dinner prepared for her . . . no, you stay there. Just make the arrangements . . . okay . . . exactly. Goodbye."

Dr. Camp hung up the phone and took a deep breath. He spent a few moments reloading his handgun and checking the action, mostly just to calm his nerves—a trick he'd been using since his first days under fire, back in the Second World War. When he had regained his composure, he picked up the phone again and dialed. He didn't have to wait long.

"Good evening, Andrea. This is Alphonse."

HIGHWAY 321 WOUND THROUGH the eastern Tennessee landscape, bracketed by rolling hills, forests, farms, and the Smoky Mountains looming just to the southeast. The sun was obscured by clouds and the air was cold and clammy. It was an ugly morning.

Frank Carincola trembled. He tapped out patterns on the steering wheel as he drove the rental car, and kept pushing his bifocals back up his nose; the sweat on his face let them slide down again within moments.

In the seat next to him, Sonja Dewey had a worried look on her face. She was twenty-four, and *Phenomen-X* was her first job out of college. This was her second season with the show. She was short and slim, with short-cropped black hair and a winning smile that had made her very popular with the viewers. A month ago some forged photos of her head atop a naked woman's body had made the rounds of the internet; she took it as a sign that she'd arrived. She didn't put much stock in the bizarro stories she reported on for the show, but it was a better job than most of her classmates had scored. They were stuck in Small Town, U.S.A., and she at least was on a national program, albeit a syndicated one that usually played in the wee hours.

"So we're almost there?" she asked hesitantly.

"Yeah," Frank replied. "I think the exit used to be just up ahead."

"Used to be?"

"I came back out here four months after the first trip. The exit was closed off. I had to take the next one and backtrack into the valley."

In the back seat, Allen Eddington snored. He was an old-school photojournalist with decades of fieldwork under his belt. He took a bullet in Sarajevo in '94 and decided he was ready to settle down, so he landed the videography gig with *Phenomen-X* and figured he'd take it easy. He was adept at grabbing a few minutes of shut-eye under any circumstances.

They came around a bend and saw a road sign: EXIT 5 TO PROMISE 1 MILE.

"That's the one after Groversville?" Sonja asked.

Frank shrugged. "I guess. I don't remember the name of the town."

"Do you think we'll have any trouble getting into Groversville?"

"I didn't. There were warnings up and the road was blocked, but I just drove around. There was nobody there to stop me. Deserted."

"That's so strange," Sonja said, shaking her head. "I can't believe the whole town just left and nobody noticed."

"Well, the CDC had it locked down for a few weeks and they relocated the county seat. That bullshit Hantavirus outbreak. There were a few stories when the quarantine lifted—the town rebuilding, that kind of crap. Then nada. By the time I came back, everybody'd left and no one gave a damn anymore."

They sat in silence until the exit appeared. Frank signaled and pulled off the highway. The road they entered was narrow two-lane blacktop, recently paved. The growth here was all wild, the winter-bare boughs of trees jabbing chaotically over the road, thatchy skeletons of leafless underbrush blocking the view at ground level. There didn't seem to be any farms or houses here.

The road was even more winding than the highway they'd left behind. Frank tried to keep the car at forty miles an hour, but the frequent sharp curves meant he kept having to punch the brakes. His driving made Sonja tense. To keep their speed up, he was taking the curves pretty wide, banking out into the other lane.

"Easy, Frank," she said. His knuckles were white on the steering wheel. He wasn't bothering with his glasses, now, either; he just tilted his head back a little to keep his sight line through the bifocals clear. "What's wrong, Frank?"

He didn't reply. Instead he kept jerking his head to the right, trying to catch a glimpse of something through the trees outside Sonja's window.

"What is it?"

"Can't be," he muttered between glances.

"What?" Sonja asked again, annoyed now at his behavior. Then she screamed.

It was a white panel van, a big one. The logo on the hood—the front hood, the one pointing straight at them—read FEDERAL EXPRESS. Frank was turned towards the side window. Sonja grabbed the steering wheel and pulled hard to the right. The van veered left. Their car shot off the damp road, missing the van, and jumped a ditch before blowing into the underbrush.

The driver of the van slammed on the brakes and pulled off the road. He jumped out and ran across to where the sedan had left the pavement, swearing to himself, a first-aid kit under one arm.

When he found them, Sonja was on the ground on her hands and knees, shaking. Allen was sitting up in the back seat, yelling curses and rubbing his shoulder. But Frank—Frank was standing on the roof of the sedan, looking off through the branches of the trees.

"You folks okay?" asked the driver, nervously fumbling with the first-aid kit. "Ma'am?"

Sonja looked up and nodded, taking a deep breath. "I think I'm okay. I . . ." Her voice trailed off as Allen got out of the car. "I'm not fucking okay!" he bellowed. "I've got a fucking idiot for a news director! Frank, what the hell were you doing?"

Frank ignored him, intent on whatever he was looking at.

"Frank!" Allen yelled again, mad as hell.

"Frank, what *are* you doing?" Sonja asked quietly, her voice still weak from shock. The driver looked around at the trio, thinking *It wasn't my fault. It really wasn't my fault. Shit! Shit! Shit!*

Frank spun around and looked at the driver. "What's that

town down there?" he asked, pointing through the trees behind him.

The driver wondered if this guy had a concussion. "Uh, that's Promise, sir."

"What the fuck is Promise? There was no goddamn Promise here!"

"No, it's new, sir. Some kinda corporate town. I was just down there making deliveries."

"What *used* to be here?"

"Oh," said the driver, relieved now that the conversation was making more sense. "Groversville. They tore it all down and started building that place. Maybe a year or so ago. Just got up and running a couple months back."

Frank turned away and looked through the trees. He shook his head and muttered something to himself.

Their car had come to a halt on an overgrown ridge, part of the V-shaped rise that defined the small, narrow valley where Groversville had been. It all looked familiar to Frank, but at the same time it was so very new. A town was there, but it wasn't Groversville—not a single building was the same. There were new houses, new businesses, all done in the same old-fashioned architectural style, all planned and executed with precision. It was an idealized replica of turn-of-the-century Americana, sprung up here in the valley like a fertile thought taken root in the rich Tennessee soil.

"Well I'll be a monkey's uncle," Frank said, taking in the sight.

Sonja was standing up slowly, helped by the driver. "You folks want me to call some help?" he asked. Allen and Sonja looked at each other, then at Frank.

"Nope," Frank said. "We'll take it from here."

The driver looked at each of them again briefly, to make sure they weren't dazed or bleeding or just plain ticked off at him. Then he nodded and said, "Okay. Watch those curves, folks. You can't go too fast on the roads 'round here."

"We'll be careful," Sonja said quietly. The driver nodded again and stomped off through the brush, sweating bullets and glad as hell that he wasn't going to get fired over this foolishness.

Allen climbed up on the car and stood alongside Frank. He looked down into the valley below them. "So that's Promise, huh?"

"No," Frank said. "It's Groversville. It's still Groversville."

That afternoon, Abe returned to the Knoxville motel with a large cardboard box he'd picked up at the airport. Alphonse had phoned them that morning—sounding rather haggard, Vic thought—to give them the shipping info and also to inform them that they shouldn't open the box until they called him.

Abe gave the usual knock at the door—the old shave-and-a-haircut—before unlocking it and stepping in. Stephanie and Vic were sitting on one of the beds, drinking coffee and reading the morning paper. "I'm back, ladies," Abe announced grandly. "And I've brought donuts."

Vic winced. "Ew. No bagels, I suppose?"

"Is that supposed to be a joke?" Abe replied with a smile. He tossed the bag of donuts on the bed and closed the door behind him. Stephanie began rummaging in the bag. Abe brought the large box over to the table and took out a pocketknife. He started to cut the tape.

"Whoa!" Vic said. "Hang on. We gotta call Alphonse before you do that."

"Right, right," Abe said. "Maybe he left his dentures inside by mistake."

Vic shot him a snarky look and began dialing on her cell phone. Stephanie munched on a glazed old-fashioned. "I can't believe people actually soak these things in coffee," she said to no one in particular. Abe plopped down in one of the padded chairs next to the table and watched Vic on the phone.

"This is Agent Tonya," she said. "We've got the box . . . okay, just a minute." Vic rummaged in her carry-on bag and pulled out a small speaker unit and some cords. "Alphonse wants this on the speakerphone," she said by way of explanation as she plugged the unit into a wall socket and then into her cordless phone. "Okay, Alphonse, we're all here."

"Good," came the voice over the speaker. "Now first things first. When was the last time any of you saw Agent Shasta? In person, I mean. This is very important."

Vic thought for a moment. "Must have been three months ago, just after the Baltimore op. I made my report to him about Agent Tim's death."

Abe nodded. "Same here, Alphonse. I was with Tonya for that report."

Stephanie continued to eat her donut.

"Agent Terry?" Alphonse said.

Stephanie swallowed and took a sip of coffee. "About three weeks ago."

"*What?*" Vic cried. "What the fuck?"

"Three weeks ago!" Stephanie repeated, angry and defensive. "All right?"

"No, *not* all right," Vic replied. "You see him a week before he disappears and you don't bother to fucking mention it? What is this shit, Steph?"

"Don't call me fucking Steph," she replied quietly. "My name is Stephanie."

"Agent *Terry*," Alphonse emphasized from the speaker. "Tell us about the last time you saw Agent Shasta."

Stephanie sighed. "We were seeing each other, okay? We were dating. Last time I saw him, he broke it off. He dumped me."

"Oh, *Jesus!*" Vic exclaimed. Abe rubbed his forehead and stared at the wall.

"It's not relevant, okay? It's fucking *personal,*" Stephanie shouted. "Don't you think I've gone back over that night over and over since this op started? He didn't say a goddamn thing that had anything to do with him disappearing. It was strictly personal."

They all sat in silence for a moment—Alphonse by proxy—before Abe spoke. "How long had you been dating?"

"Not long," Stephanie replied sullenly. "Maybe three months. It was just a stupid fling."

"What is he, like twice your age?" Vic barked. "Jesus, Terry, I can't believe you didn't tell us."

"It just wasn't any of your business," she replied, almost in a whisper.

Alphonse sighed audibly over the speaker. "All right, calm down. This is something you should have shared with your cell, Terry, but let's move on. You saw him a week before he disappeared. Did he say anything about the op he'd just been on?"

"No," Stephanie said. "I didn't even know he'd been on that op until Vic told me—I mean, Agent Tonya told me—a couple days ago. We didn't talk about Delta Green, ever. That was sort of the point, you know?"

"I see," Alphonse said. "Now I want all three of you to

listen to me very carefully. Are the three of you armed? I mean at this moment, on your person."

"Negatory," Abe said. "I just went to the airport, so I'm not packing."

"I am," Vic said. "Me too," Stephanie chimed in.

Alphonse spoke very slowly and very precisely. "Tonya and Terry, I want you to take your sidearms out and give them to Agent Thomas."

They all looked at each other, befuddled. Vic shrugged and did as Alphonse said. Stephanie complied as well.

"Okay, it's done," Vic affirmed.

"Agent Thomas?" Alphonse said.

"Yeah, I've got both the weapons."

"Good. Take the safety off of one of them and chamber a round."

"Are you serious?"

"I'm very serious, Thomas. Do exactly as I say and be quick about it."

Abe did as he was told. Stephanie and Vic exchanged concerned glances.

"Okay, it's good to go."

"Fine. Now Thomas, remember to do exactly as I say, as soon as I say it."

"All right."

"Thomas, point the gun at Agent Terry. Agent Terry, *do not move.*"

Stephanie blinked as Abe leveled the handgun at her. She sat as still as a statue.

"Agent Tonya, retrieve your firearm and do as Agent Thomas has done."

Vic jumped up and moved across the room to where Abe

was. She took her handgun back from him, turned off the safety, chambered a round, and pointed it at Stephanie grimly.

"Okay," Vic said.

"Very well. Agent Terry, I want you to get up very slowly and lie down with your hands behind your back. If she doesn't comply, shoot her."

The room felt very, very cold. The heater wasn't working well, but that wasn't the only reason. Vic and Abe kept their eyes focused on Stephanie, who looked shellshocked. "Do as he says, Stephanie," Abe said calmly. "It'll be all right." Stephanie got up very slowly and lay down between the two beds, then put her hands behind her back.

"I fervently hope so," Alphonse concurred, not bothering to correct Abe on his error in tradecraft. "Thomas, retrieve your handcuffs and fasten them on Terry's wrists. Do it slowly and watch her closely. *Very* closely."

"Would somebody mind me telling me *what is going on?*" Stephanie said fiercely, blinking back tears as Abe got up and cuffed her wrists. "All done," Abe said hollowly.

"Good. Agent Terry, we have to take some precautions that I'm hoping are absolutely unnecessary. I'll apologize later, because this is going to be very unpleasant, but right now I'm going to have to walk all of you through some important procedures." He went on to give them their instructions.

Listening, Stephanie began to cry. Tears ran down her face. She cried as quietly as she could so as not to move. Vic turned pale, but if she was pale at Alphonse's words, Abe was positively ashen.

"Damn, Alphonse," Abe said, his voice unsteady. "You better know what the hell you're doing."

They got started.

Δ

SONJA INSISTED ON DRIVING the rest of the way into Promise. Seeing how tense she was, Frank eventually relented. Allen stayed out of the argument and whistled softly as he cleaned his fingernails. His shoulder was sore and Sonja was bruised from the belts, but that was the extent of their injuries. The seat belts had protected Sonja and Frank from serious injury, while Allen had merely flopped around in the back seat. All told, Sonja believed they'd been damned lucky. This kicked off another argument with Frank in which he claimed that the driver of the van was really at fault, but she cut him off short and they were back on the road soon enough.

Soon they were coming down the ridge and into the lowland of the valley. Curiously, there was no sign announcing the name of the town or anything else of the sort. There weren't even any advertising billboards in the untended fields outside the town proper. Frank noted that the farms which used to take up the valley and even much of the ridge were gone, the buildings demolished and the ground left to grow wild.

Promise was beautiful—if you wanted to live in an amusement park. The roads were newly paved, the landscaping was perfect, the houses were all aesthetically compatible, and on and on. It really was like being in a theme park's "Old-Tyme U.S.A." attraction, except for the obviously modern elements such as cars and joggers.

The road came to a wrought-iron gate and guardhouse, both styled to match the architecture of the rest of the place. The gate was somewhat symbolic; there was no wall around the town, so it wasn't a huge deterrent if you really wanted to get in. But normal travelers wouldn't be that determined. A guard in a khaki uniform and a straw fedora leaned out the window of the gatehouse and said, "Good afternoon, may I help you?" Sonja recognized his accent. She'd gotten her degree at Boston University, and knew a beaner when she heard one.

"We're here to see Promise," she said. "Can we take a look around?"

"Business or pleasure?" the guard replied, smiling. In the car, Frank began whispering.

"Business," Sonja said, ignoring Frank. "I'm a reporter, and I'm interested in doing a story on community restoration."

The guard chuckled. "Just kidding. Everyone's welcome in Promise. Drive on."

"Thanks!" Sonja called cheerfully as she rolled the window up.

"Damnit, did you have to tell him we were reporters?" Frank asked testily. The gate was swinging open.

"Oh come on," Sonja replied. "Like they won't figure that out in half an hour anyway. We might as well get on their good side while we can." The gate was all the way open, and she drove forward as Frank crossed his arms and looked out his window, ignoring her.

Predictably enough, they were on Main Street, according to the decorative street signs on every corner. Sonja spotted a corner mailbox and realized it didn't have U.S. Post Office markings; instead it read PROMISE POST.

There weren't any power lines or telephone poles, either. Evidently all such utilities were underground. There were street lamps, but they were much shorter, clearly intended for the benefit of pedestrians on the sidewalks, and their styling was once again of that tiresome Old Tyme look so popular with suburban shopping centers. Sonja shook her head. Why would anyone want to live in Squaresville, U.S.A.?

Main Street, it turned out, was the main drag. It was lined with small businesses. Sonja was surprised to see that they were almost all chain franchise stores—she was expecting local outfits by the bushel. But no, it was like every other business strip in the country: McDonald's, Taco Bell, Pizza Hut, 7-11, Exxon, Border's Books, and on and on. The buildings kept the same decor scheme as the rest of the place. If anything, it was impressive just to see this many brand-new corporate stores in what was, frankly, a podunk town. Sonja figured the company that owned the town must be paying for these franchises to be here. There weren't any huge superstores here, but then again a town of twelve hundred people—at least, that was Groversville back before the Hantavirus—couldn't be expected to support quite that much commerce.

Sonja turned off of Main Street and onto Shady Glen Pointe. Rows of houses were here. No two houses were identical, but they were clearly variations on a theme. All sat side-by-side with a reasonable amount of grace and aesthetic appeal, however, and Sonja began to get the feeling that this place had been carefully designed block by block. It was more impressive and less ridiculous than she had first thought. Promise was growing on her, at least a little bit.

Something was bothering her, though. "Frank, didn't you say this was primarily a farming community?"

"Well, a lot of it was agriculture. But the town was the county seat back then, so there were a fair number of service and bureaucratic jobs around, I guess. Still, there used to be farms all over the valley, and now they're gone."

"So where do these people work? Is everyone flipping burgers for everyone else?"

"Sounds like fat-commie utopia," Allen chortled from the back seat.

"I'm serious. Where do these people work for a living?"

"Maybe over there?" Frank said. He pointed out the side window to a large complex on the outskirts of town. It consisted of a campus of six or so sizable buildings, all brand new and, of course, in tune with the rest of the community. A number of large tractor-trailers were parked in one area, backed up to one of the buildings. There were no signs identifying the facility.

"Could be," Sonja said skeptically. "But does that mean that most of the adults work at the same place? I mean, I know this is some kind of company town, but that's just a little weird."

"Welcome to Groversville," Frank said. "The more things change, the more they stay the same."

"Well," Sonja replied, "let's find a local hangout and see what we can learn from the people. A park or something, since we're not allowed to have a cup of coffee," she said sharply, glancing at Frank.

"You want coffee, get back on 321 and we'll find a Stuckey's."

"Stuckey's? What the heck is that?"

Frank looked at her grimly. "You'll find out soon enough. Let me just say this: shot glasses from all fifty states."

Sonja shook her head. They were a long way from California.

CELL T'S MOTEL WAS a Motel 6, part of a chain of low-priced accommodations. It was a two-story building in the shape of an "L" with several dozen guest rooms, all of which opened to the outside. Next door was a Denny's restaurant, open twenty-four hours. There was a covered carport area in front of the lobby, which was decorated in no particular style other than nondescript. A young woman sat in a chair behind the front desk, reading a magazine.

Outside, there were two sets of stairwells that led to the upper floor of rooms, one set at each end of the building. There was guest parking on all sides. At the base of the stairs nearest the lobby there was an alcove marked "Convenience Station," which held an ice machine, a soda machine, and a snack machine with an assortment of potato chips, candy, and chewing gum. Cell T's car was parked near the crook of the "L." It was a 1996 Ford Taurus, obtained from a rental company at Knoxville's McGhee Tyson Airport. The car was a pale green in color.

From the car, the nearest stairwell was at the end opposite the lobby. Up the stairs was room 219, where Cell T was staying. The curtains were drawn on the large window, and the sound of the room's heater drifted out into the chill afternoon.

Inside room 219, there were two full-size beds with dark purple spreads. The walls were covered in a patterned wallpaper, the pattern consisting of light pink crosshatching against a cream background. A nightstand stood between the two beds, on which rested an alarm clock supplied by the motel. Just above the nightstand were two reading lamps, with a central rotating switch. The switch had four positions: both lamps off, left lamp on, right lamp on, both lamps on. Opposite the two beds was a long, low bureau with four drawers, atop which rested a television set. Atop the television set was a guide to cable channels and a stand-up color advertisement for the motel's pay-per-view movie service. In one corner stood a small table and two chairs, with a hooded ceiling lamp hanging down overhead. On the table sat the cardboard shipping box from

Alphonse. It was open. Inside was a manila envelope and two large spray bottles full of a clear liquid. A third spray bottle sat on the table next to the box, though it was only three-quarters full. Next to the third bottle lay Vic and Stephanie's handguns, the safeties engaged. Behind the table was the large air conditioner/heater unit, directly beneath the curtained window.

Abe sat on the bed closest to the window. He'd put his overcoat on because it was cold; it hadn't occurred to him to turn up the heat. Abe was in his early thirties, with thick red hair, green eyes, and pale skin. He was just over six feet in height, with a sturdy build that had a slight tendency towards flab. He dressed conservatively. Back in Milwaukee, he had a son, a car, an office, and a wife, in roughly that order of importance. He'd been married for four years, which it turned out was about two years too long. After the birth of their son, Abe and Carol rapidly lost interest in each other. The stress of having a young child certainly had a lot to do with it, as did their too-small condominium. But in the end, they'd simply married the wrong people, and had yet to deal with that situation. Abe was willing to play the husband for the sake of being the father, but he agonized over the paradox of his regret at marrying Carol and his joy in their young son, Eric. Any chance to leave this problem behind was a welcome one, so he threw himself into his work—and into the occasional opportunities Delta Green sent his way to leave his drably conflicted life behind and enter a world of secrets and danger, where he could be with other people and indeed be another person. One who was confident, decisive, commanding . . . but all of this was getting him nowhere. He simply couldn't bring himself to speak at the moment.

On the opposite bed lay Vic. She was curled up beneath the

bedspread, face buried into the pillows, because she was cold, too. Vic was in her mid-thirties. She was short and slim, with strong legs from the constant hiking her job with the parks service required. She kept her hair dyed strawberry red and cut short for ease on the trail. While she knew Abe considered his life to be somewhat in disarray, hers was the opposite. Everything was slotted away in neat cubbyholes. Everything was figured out. There were no messy contradictions or areas of confusion. Vic had a routine, and she believed in routine. But there were times—times like this—when she allowed that perhaps her life was a little too tidy. She wasn't a very ambitious person, and neither was she a passionate one; even her music had a clinical detachment. Vic felt disconnected from the surging tide of life that others around her seemed to be drenched in. She had tamed the world by casting out everything wild, and she had grown to regret it. Delta Green was her one escape, her one indulgence. She enjoyed copping an attitude, carrying a gun, solving mysteries like some butch Nancy Drew; she was willing to accept the horrors that this work brought to her doorstep as a fair exchange for the mundanities she got to leave behind. Occasionally, that bargain tasted of ashes.

On the floor between the two beds lay a crumpled pile of clothing. They belonged to Stephanie. Abe and Vic had to cut some of them free with a knife because of the handcuffs. Once they'd stripped her, they sprayed her with the liquid from the package, slowly and carefully, because Alphonse had just given them some idea of what they might expect in the worst-case scenario. It had been a taxing and painful ordeal, full of dread over what might happen and guilt over the process, exacerbated by Stephanie's obvious pain and humiliation. It had felt like a violation. It was an exercise of power that neither Abe nor Vic were interested in wielding.

And in the end, it had accomplished nothing. Except, perhaps, to hammer at the fragile trust they had with Stephanie.

By the bed in which Vic lay was the door that led to the bathroom. It was closed. Inside, Stephanie lay in the bathtub. She had the shakes, and the hot water wasn't making them go away. The room smelled of the chemicals that Abe and Vic had doused her with, though she had done her best to wash them away. The memory lingered also, and was the more toxic of the two.

Lying in the water like this, Stephanie could only think of that night just a few days ago when she lay in the bathtub of her apartment and prepared to kill herself. Looking back, Stephanie admitted that perhaps she wouldn't have gone through with it. She'd approached that brink before—three times, in fact, as an adult—and had never done herself physical harm. That night might have been just another false alarm.

The breakup with David—Shasta, the little voice of tradecraft reminded her—hadn't been the main reason. That really had been just a fling, initiated after the Baltimore op. David reminded her a bit of Forrest James—they were the same age—and she was attracted by the depth of his life experience and the warmth of his smile. At first, she couldn't understand how he had gone through life without getting married or finding a long-term love. But it didn't take long for her to find out. David had a lot of surface warmth, but inside he kept himself very, very tightly guarded, and tightly wound. He angered easily, and disliked intimacy. He was fine over dinner at a nice restaurant, but as soon as they got back to his house he was eager to romp in the sack, call it a night, and send her home. When she surprised him on his birthday—he was forty-nine—he accepted the dinner graciously, but then told her that he didn't think they should see each other again "in a romantic capacity." Evidently she'd pushed too far, and now he was pushing her away. He disappeared soon afterward. She was politely questioned by the CIA, but as she had an alibi and no real bitterness towards David, it hadn't gone very far.

No, the reason for her alleged suicide attempt was the same as all the others: a pervasive sense of futility about her life. At times, nothing seemed to matter, and she believed that she might as well just check out of the whole mess.

Stephanie took a deep breath. She was avoiding the present issue, which was the humiliating ordeal she'd just been through. Was this what she'd joined Delta Green for? To be handcuffed, her clothes cut off, and her body doused with God knows what chemicals by people she thought were allies? The obvious discomfort on Vic and Abe's faces was the only mitigating factor. She hadn't even hung around to hear Alphonse's harrumphing, stammering apology and explanation, but had instead run immediately into the bathroom to get clean. She'd never felt so vulnerable, so exposed, so compromised. It was like a sick joke. Part of her bitterly wanted to believe that Abe and Vic were sitting out there now, laughing about her body or planning some other degrading outrage against her, some nightmare of teenage summer camp come mockingly to life. But she didn't really believe those things. They had simply done what they were told, and there were good reasons involved. She was willing to summon up the courage to get past this and focus on the op. She wanted to believe that they were still a team, that Vic and Abe still accepted her, and that she was still willing to accept them. David was missing, and while she might be disappointed with the way things had worked out with him, she still cared for him.

Maybe she couldn't rescue Forrest James, but she was damned if she wasn't going to try and save David.

James. He was never far from her thoughts. In the time since the Roscoe op—while he'd been court-martialed by the Navy and sentenced to ten years in Fort Leavenworth for assault and conduct unbecoming an officer—she had finally crossed that line, the line past which she was willing to accept the horrific for the sake of forestalling the apocalyptic. Some part of her felt guilt at not accepting him and his actions at the time, as if his subsequent incarceration were her fault. But he had chosen that fate before they'd even met. Regardless, they hadn't spoken since.

Stephanie brought her hands up from the warm water of the bath and rubbed her face. She wasn't crying. She'd shed enough tears, and the shakes were gone. It was time to get up and move on. The more time she spent feeling sorry for herself, the less time they had to find David and spare him from whatever fate had befallen him.

She emerged from the bathroom a few minutes later, clean and dressed. Vic and Abe looked up at her furtively.

"Okay, I'm ready," she said. "Let's go."

SONJA HAD PARKED THE rental on the side of the road next to what was clearly the town park. It wasn't very large—half a block wide by a block long—but it was pleasantly landscaped with benches, trees, a fountain, and a few meandering paths. There were also several picnic tables off in one corner, which Sonja noticed were nearest the fast-food restaurants on Main Street. (There were no other kind of restaurants, actually.) There were a dozen or so people in the park, eating or walking or talking or what have you.

Sonja, Frank, and Allen wandered into the park. They approached several people and asked polite questions, but were rebuffed every time with polite excuses. After the fourth person turned them down, they looked around and realized that the park was now empty. Everyone had left, and they were here alone.

"Well fuck a dog," Allen murmured. "They sure high-tailed it away from us."

"Yeah," Frank assented. "Even the ones we didn't approach."

"Even the ones who weren't anywhere near anyone we *did* approach," Sonja observed. "They all just wandered off."

"Wait," Allen interjected. "Here comes someone."

A man had entered the park from the far end. He was of average height and build, with black hair streaked in grey. He wore a heavy, dark suit with a white shirt and no tie, and strode with a confident bearing. Soon he reached them.

"Hello," he called as he walked up. "Welcome to Promise!" He smiled, showing three gold teeth.

"Hello," Sonja responded, stepping forward and holding out her hand. "Nice town you've got here."

The man took her hand and shook it heartily. He continued smiling. The skin of his face was pale and taut, almost like the grafted skin of a burn victim, but it was clear this had been a feature since birth. "Certainly is," he said, his Alabama accent coming through clipped and proud. "Certainly is." He let go of her hand and they all stood there for a moment.

"I'm Marty Trenthem, corporate information officer for Promise Inc.," he said. "I understand you folks are reporters?"

"Yes, sir," Sonja replied. "We're doing a story on community rebuilding."

"Of course you are," Marty said cheerfully. "Well how can I be of service?"

"Well, what is Promise all about? Why the change from Groversville?"

"Ah, Groversville. A fine little place. Fine town. We weren't here then, of course. They had a Hantavirus outbreak. Carried by mice, I think. The Centers for Disease Control had a quarantine, and then the whole valley was seized by the state for public-health reasons. The residents were compensated, of course. Once the crisis was over and they gave the all-clear, we bought the land and started building Promise."

"And Promise is . . . " Sonja asked.

"The wave of the future!" Marty exclaimed. "A planned community, sketched out from the ground up. Owned and managed by Promise Inc. Our residents—most of them old-time Groversville residents, real salt of the earth types you know—don't own their homes or land. Instead, they own stock in Promise, along with very generous long-term leases that are renewed upon their death, so they have something to leave to the kids, you know? But the lease means they don't pay property taxes, the company pays for housing upkeep and renovation, and so on. It's an experiment, a grand experiment, in corporate-assisted community building."

"What about employment?"

"We have an exclusive contract with Message By Mail, the largest direct-mail company in the country. Most of our residents work for MBM, in every conceivable capacity. Administration, marketing, printing, demographics, distribution, you name it. There's a one in six chance that you've gotten something in the mail from MBM—from this very town, in fact—in the last month. Unless you live in the northeast, that is—MBM hasn't gotten a leg up on that neck of the woods."

"Well, that's a fascinating story, Mr. Trenthem."

"Call me Marty," he replied, gold teeth gleaming in the sun.

"We'd like to take a look around some more, if you don't mind. Talk to some of the residents. You know."

"Of course, ma'am. Why don't you follow me in your car over there, and we'll go to the MBM facility. That's also where the town hall is, and you can speak with some workers there as well as some of the administration of our fair town."

Sonja and Frank exchanged looks. Allen looked bored—but he was surreptitiously recording everything on a little Hi-8 camera stuck inside his jacket. He wasn't getting any video, but he hoped the mike would pick up the conversation.

"All right, Marty, that'd be fine," Frank said.

Marty beamed. "Glad to hear it." His eyes slid sideways, then, and focused on something at the near end of the park. He didn't like what he saw.

Sonja and Frank turned around. A green sedan was parked on the street, and three people—two women and a man—were striding quickly towards them.

"Oh dear," Marty said with a mocking tone.

A short woman with bright red hair in a punkish cut—dressed somewhat improbably in a conservative dark suit—was leading the trio, which also consisted of a tall blond woman and a taller, heavyset guy with dark red hair. They reached the group and the short woman spoke. "Who here is from *Phenomen-X?*"

The three TV people looked at each other. Marty whistled softly and stared at the horizon, tapping one foot absently.

"That's us," Frank said. "This gentleman,"—he nodded at

Marty—"was just taking us to town hall."

"That won't be necessary," the woman said. "You're leaving town, now. With us."

"Who the hell are you?"

"We spoke on the phone yesterday. It's time for you to leave."

"You sent us here, for pete's sake!"

"I know. And now I'm sending you back."

Marty broke in, darkly amused in a strange way none of them could place. "Now ma'am, you don't want to go interfering with the press. If these folks want to accompany me to town hall, you shouldn't oughta stop them."

"Back off, goldie. They're coming with us."

"Frank, what the hell is going on?" Sonja asked. "Who are these people?"

"Never mind who we are. Get in your car. Now."

"Hey, lady, we're on a story here," Allen protested.

The woman looked back at her companions. Then all three reached in their jackets and drew handguns.

"Whoa!" Sonja cried.

"Okay, okay!" said Frank, raising his hands slightly. "We'll go, already!"

Marty grinned wide. "It's hardly midnight, Cinderfella. But there you go, turning into a pumpkin."

"Shut the fuck up," the woman replied.

The three reporters began to move towards their car. As they did, Sonja reached into her pocket and pulled out a microcassette recorder. She thrust it towards the tall guy.

"Could I get your name?" she blurted. The man grabbed the recorder with his free hand. He pushed the eject button and dropped the cassette to the ground, then crushed it with his shoe. Then he handed the recorder back to Sonja, smiling pleasantly. "I've always wanted to do that," he said.

Sonja took it back gingerly and placed it in her pocket again, then turned and hurried to the car with Frank and Allen.

BEHIND THEM, MARTY ADDRESSED the trio. "If we want them, we'll get them."

"They aren't worth it," Vic replied. She began to back away, accompanied by Abe and Stephanie.

"You can forget about Mister Nells," Marty said. "He's not here."

The words—and the cruelly confident way he said them—twisted like a knife in Stephanie's guts. She stopped backing up and advanced quickly, gun leveled at Marty's chest. "Where is he?" she demanded, her face flush with sudden fury. "What have you bastards done with him?"

"It's not my job to keep track of Mister Nells," he replied evenly. "It was simply my job to keep him away from here."

Stephanie looked into his eyes for a long moment. Memories of David came cascading down, mingled with the humiliation of the morning and this crystal-perfect thought: *If he's already dead, this bastard is the closest shot at payback I'm gonna get.*

Marty's eyes flicked between Stephanie's face and her gun, a twinge of a smile growing on his lips at her apparent hesitation.

That settled it.

"Fuck you," she said—and then she pulled the trigger. Bang. Bang. Bang. Marty jerked back, stumbled, then hit the ground groaning.

"Shit!" Abe cried. Across the park, the three *Phenomen-X*

staffers broke into a run and piled into their car. They started the engine and burned rubber.

Abe and Vic took off as well, back towards the car. Stephanie lingered for a moment, smelled the cordite and noticed how quiet the world had gotten—she was briefly deafened by the shots—before she, too, turned and ran for the car.

Frank was bearing down on the gate at the edge of town. It was shut. The guard was even now stepping out of the little hut and holding his hand up for them to stop. His other hand rested on the gun hanging from his belt.

"Oh, no—" said Sonja.

Frank floored the gas pedal and wrenched the wheel. They shot off the road and into the front yard of the house nearest the gate, crunching a tricycle under their tires and driving through a bed of azaleas. The guard drew his gun and yelled something as the sedan blew past the side of the gate, then swerved back onto the road and roared for the ridge overlooking the valley.

Sonja took a deep breath, relieved. "So what the hell was all that about? Were those people from that group you keep talking about?"

"I think so," Frank said, focusing on the road, "but I doubt anyone's gonna tell us . . . hey, what the hell was that crap you pulled with the tape recorder?"

"Oh," Sonja said, calmer now that they were outside of town. "A long shot that paid off." She pulled the recorder from her pocket gingerly, grasping the top edge of the unit with just the very tips of her thumb and forefinger. She dangled it in the air and then put it in the glove compartment.

"Yeah, so?" Frank asked.

In the back seat, Allen began laughing. "What's so funny?" said Frank, irritated. "Huh?"

Sonja was beaming. Allen chortled some more, then calmed down. "Dontcha get it?" he asked Frank.

"Get what?"

Allen laughed again, and Sonja whooped. "She got that tall guy's goddamn fingerprints!"

Frank paused, then cracked a huge smile. Sonja grinned back.

"Well all right," he said. "Dinner's on me!"

THREE NRO DELTA AGENTS in suits came into the park at a full run, each brandishing an MP5. They reached the man on the ground who was sitting up and clutching his chest, where he had been shot three times. The Delta Green agents had fled.

"Are you okay, sir?" the lead man asked.

"I'm fine, son, I'm just fine. Bitch had an itchy finger." He stood up slowly and began unbuttoning his shirt, revealing the body armor he wore underneath. He plucked three flattened slugs out of the dense material and put them in his pocket.

"What are your orders, sir?"

"My orders? Don't do a goddamn thing. Let 'em go."

"But sir!"

"I said, let 'em go! If you're gonna flush quail, you gotta get a bird dog. And that bitch just barked."

Chapter Three: The Lady of Situations

Wednesday, February 17, 1999

It was quiet in the car. Cell T had landed at the D.C. airport an hour ago and they were now entering Georgetown *en route* to their meeting with Alphonse. All three were tired and cranky from air travel, and more than a little exhausted after the events of the day. They'd taken the very first flight north out of Knoxville as soon as they'd fled Promise, and their haste meant it took them three wearying connections to get to D.C.

The reporters had gotten away. Vic was supposed to debrief them, but the encounter in the park had thrown their plans to the wind. Under the circumstances, though, she wasn't exactly angry at Stephanie for killing that gold-toothed fuck. He was asking for it—and given the way things had gone, she could even see granting Stephanie a little vengeance. No amount of rationalization, however, could make her feel very good about watching Stephanie gun down an unarmed man. She might not be angry, but she wasn't cheering, either; it was, frankly, a shitty end to a shitty op. There just wasn't any anger in her at this point.

Abe was driving. As he steered them through the night, their faces passingly illuminated by the headlights of oncoming traffic, he bit his lip. The op wasn't going well. All the progress seemed to be happening on Alphonse's end, while they spent several days and thousands of dollars in squandered resources—plane tickets, rental cars, ammunition, motel rooms, the fake P.I. firm—mucking around in Tennessee like a bunch of amateurs. Now they were returning, no doubt to get dressed down by Alphonse. Then there was Stephanie, who had *shot* some mouthy asshole. Admittedly, he was clearly on the inside of whatever they were up against, but that didn't make it acceptable for her to just unload like that. He was disturbed by the ease with which she took a life. Certainly there were some mitigating factors: the events of that morning hadn't left Stephanie in the best state of mind, and there was her relationship with Shasta to consider. No doubt she was looking for a little payback. But *damn* . . . just bang, bang, bang, like that. He wasn't comfortable with the way things were going.

Stephanie sat in the back seat, replaying the scene in the park over and over in her mind. Gold teeth glinting in the sun, the sudden shock in his eyes as she pulled the trigger. She smiled.

THEY ARRIVED AT THE Green Man at 3 a.m. The bar was closed, but Alphonse had told them when they called from the airport that they could come around to the back door. Sure enough, he opened the door just after they knocked—shave-and-a-haircut—and waved them inside. They walked quietly through the small kitchen and emerged into a cozy oak-paneled barroom. A fire was burning in the flagstone fireplace, and several people were already seated and waiting. They'd shoved some rickety tables together to make a rough sort of conference area. Plates and glasses were all over the place, the aftermath of a late dinner. Papers and folders sat in disorderly stacks. Alphonse looked a little drunk.

"Evening," he said to them as they entered the room behind him. "Can I get you a drink?" Alphonse padded over to the bar and started taking down glasses.

"Scotch," Abe said. "Balvenie if they've got it."

"Hard cider," Vic requested.

"Cocoa?" Stephanie asked hesitantly. "With some Bailey's."

"Coming right up," Alphonse said reassuringly. The head of Delta Green liked playing bartender. He nodded towards the group sitting at the tables. "Go ahead and introduce yourselves."

Cell T turned somewhat nervously to address them. Vic gave their code names politely.

In return, they were introduced to Agents Adam, Nancy, Nick, and Nolan. Abe suddenly recognized Adam from the academy at Quantico—he was a Deputy Director for the FBI. Abe stared, agog. Adam winked and placed a finger to his lips.

"Adam was just leaving, actually," Alphonse said from behind the bar as he placed the drinks on a tray. "But he wanted to say a few words to you first. Adam?"

Adam stood up from the table and waved Cell T forward, gesturing to the seats opposite him and Cell N. "I just wanted to ask Agent Terry a question. Terry, can you describe the man you shot in Promise?"

Stephanie had just sat down and now looked up at Adam, a bit uncomfortable. "Well, he was an older man. I'd guess late forties, about the same age as—as Agent Shasta. Caucasian, dark hair going gray, wearing a heavy suit. He had several gold teeth. His accent sounded local."

Adam nodded and folded his arms. "I see. Tell me, did you bring back his severed head?"

Stephanie stared for a moment. "Uh . . . no." Alphonse handed her the cocoa, and she took a nervous gulp.

Adam smiled. "Just kidding. What I mean is that if you didn't, he's probably not dead."

"I shot him three times, sir, center mass. We were as close as you and me, maybe closer. He had a white shirt on under a dark suit, no tie. I couldn't miss."

"I'm sure you didn't. Was there any blood?"

"Well, not that I recall, but we left immediately."

"Have you ever shot someone before, agent?"

"No, sir. I've shot *at* someone before, but—"

"You described his suit as 'bulky,' agent, can you tell me why you think that might be?"

Stephanie paused, then looked down into her cocoa. "I see."

"So the bad news is, I can guarantee you he was wearing body armor, and that means he's not dead. The good news is, if you see him again, nothing would delight me more than if you blew his damn head off."

Stephanie looked up sharply. Vic and Abe—who had been looking elsewhere so they would flinch less when someone started yelling—did the same. "Sir?" Stephanie said.

"I just wish I could've seen the look on that S.O.B.'s face. It must have been priceless." Adam was smiling slightly.

"He did have an air of surprise about him, sir," Stephanie said, smiling a little in return.

"I'm sure he did." Adam dropped the smile. "You got lucky, Terry. You went off half-cocked and shot a man—thought you'd killed him, in fact—because you were having a bad day. We all have bad days. Get used to it. The next time you try to murder some guy who ticks you off, he might *not* just happen to be on our most-wanted list. You got me, agent?"

"Yes sir," Stephanie replied firmly.

"All right. That's all. Except—if you do see him again, don't let him see you first. He won't give you a second chance."

"Yes sir," she said again.

"Good night, agents. Alphonse will take it from here."

"Sir?" Stephanie interjected.

"Yes?"

"What's his name? The man I shot at?"

Adam looked at her for a long moment. "He has so many that frankly, it doesn't matter." He nodded to them sharply and then left the room. Everyone's attention turned to Alphonse.

Alphonse had settled leadenly into a chair at the head of the assembly. He started to speak, then paused and looked around the room. He shook his head. "I can't tell you how many times I've done this." The others looked at him, a little baffled. "Chaired a meeting like this, I mean. A bunch of agents, a hasty meeting room, no real names exchanged, dangerous business ahead. I've been doing this work for fifty years plus, did you know that?" He took a sip of his vodka tonic and shook his head again, looking out the window. "Never seems to get any lighter outside."

Vic sat up a bit. "Sir, first I'd like to apologize for the business with *Phenomen-X*. I should have consulted with you before I brought them in, and I should have debriefed them before they left."

"You're right on both counts," Alphonse responded. "Those people are a valuable resource to us. Regardless, had you consulted with me I would have agreed to bring them in. Events on this end prevented us from looking any further into Promise, but I suspect they would have worked out well."

"You know," Abe cut in, "I feel kinda like we didn't get a chance down there. We'd barely gotten started when you yanked us back. I know you had some problem with Agent Stan, but can you tell us why the hell we're sitting in Georgetown instead of working on the situation in Promise?"

"I'll let Agent Nancy do that, actually," Alphonse said. "She debriefed Agent Stan and has some information for you. But don't worry, Agent Thomas. This op's not over by a damn sight."

Agent Nancy looked up from her notes and began talking. As she did, she struck Vic as being very strange in a way she couldn't put her finger on. Nancy looked like an NFL cheerleader, except for the huge, thick glasses perched on her nose and the too-large sweatshirt she wore to try to hide her attractive figure. When she spoke, her voice had a tone that somehow didn't match her face. It just didn't belong to the young woman sitting there, as if Lauren Bacall was dubbing her voice over a performance by Marilyn Monroe. She spoke with an accent unsettlingly reminiscent of the man with gold teeth.

"In the spring of 1997, Cell S investigated the case of a teenager named Billy Ray Spivey. He was on a multi-state crime spree, and surveillance video showed him committing feats of superhuman strength. Once he was captured, we determined that portions of his body had been replaced with some sort of superior material. It was still biological material, and on first inspection it looked like bone, muscle, skin, and so forth. Closer analysis showed that the material could in fact be any of those things at any moment, or indeed most any other organic substance it chose, and that it seemingly had a will of its own—or at least some set of instincts or instructions. We termed this substance 'neo-tissue,' for lack of a better word.

"Cell S's investigation led to the boy's hometown of Groversville, which had been suffering a rash of UFO sightings and alleged alien abductions. Cell S determined that this neo-tissue was present in large quantities in the town's reservoir, and that the entire population had been infected by it. A DG friendly along for the op died because of such an infection. Within days, whoever was in charge of this situation pulled the plug. The Centers for Disease Control were called in—we still don't know by who—and they quarantined the town. Hantavirus killed a few hundred residents over a period of two weeks. Before Cell S fled the scene, they had a standoff with an armed group of federal agents led by an older man with three gold teeth. He knew Cell S worked for Delta Green. I gather you've met him.

"A month ago, Cell S came to Memphis looking for a Groversville survivor who'd popped up. As you know, they learned nothing useful and returned after three days.

"What we didn't know is that there was no such survivor in the first place. Cell S was ambushed on their first night in Memphis and abducted. They were subjected to surgery, which involved the implantation of neo-tissue, and then they were released with no memory of their abduction. Instead, they remembered nothing but fruitless efforts to interview the survivor."

The members of Cell T looked at each other, surprised at the news. "What was the surgery for?" Stephanie asked.

"Insurance. They wanted to flush Cell S out and program them to report on any further investigations into Groversville—now Promise. Should anything come up, they had instructions on how to contact their handlers and report on what we were doing. They brought them back in a couple weeks later to run some tests. Stan and Susan were released right away. Why they kept Shasta, I have no idea."

Alphonse broke in. "You know we routinely practice a policy of compartmentalization. This is why. I kept the rest of

Cell S out of the investigation of Shasta's disappearance, and it's a damn good thing. So far, not a word has gone up the channel to their handlers. They don't even know that Agent Stan is dead."

"He's dead?" Vic asked, looking right at Agent Nancy. "I thought you debriefed him."

Agent Nancy shifted nervously in her seat and looked at Alphonse, who paused thoughtfully before speaking. "He didn't survive. The neo-tissue fled his system, and had replaced enough crucial elements that he couldn't live without it. It wasn't very pretty."

Stephanie was unsettled. "So you're saying that the last time I saw Shasta, he had already been abducted? He had that stuff in his body?"

"I'm afraid so," Alphonse said.

"Anyway, there's a silver lining to all this," Nancy continued. "Agent Susan is likewise programmed to report should she hear anything about us and Promise. She doesn't know about what's going on. We can feed her whatever scenario we like, and then find out who she reports to. Follow the chain."

"You call that a silver lining?" Vic said forcefully. Nancy was getting under her skin, though she wasn't sure why. "Susan doesn't know she's got some crazy shit in her body, and not only are we not gonna tell her but we're gonna use her as bait? What great fucking news!"

"Calm down, Agent Tonya," Alphonse said quietly.

"I'm not gonna calm down! Can't we cure her or something?"

Nancy sighed. "Maybe. But only if the neo-tissue hasn't replaced anything critical. And only if we can get her into a trauma unit before the stuff bails, because she may be bleeding out when it happens, like Stan. He got shot to hell during the ambush, and they replaced a lot of him with this stuff to cover it up, so when it left him it was a death sentence. Now from what Stan told us, Susan was taken unharmed. Hopefully she'll have pretty minimal infestation."

"Then let's fuckin' do it!"

"We can't," Nancy replied evenly. "Not yet. We can't tip off her handlers until we can track them down. For all we know, removing the neo-tissue could warn them somehow; we don't know this stuff's capabilities. And to top it off, we're not even sure we *can* remove it."

"What do you mean?"

"It's vulnerable, don't get me wrong. Fire, acid, the usual. But chasing it out of a living human isn't going to be easy. We developed a procedure, after Groversville first went down. It's a radical treatment, it's very dangerous—essentially, it's a controlled form of blood poisoning, and if it's not supervised properly, it's fatal. But we haven't had a test on an infected human subject. We haven't had the opportunity until now."

"So we use Susan as a double agent, then hope we get her back so maybe she can survive an experimental treatment that could kill her."

"Bingo."

"This sucks!"

Alphonse coughed, drawing everyone's attention and stopping the conversation short. He lit a cigarette, inhaled, and blew out a smoke ring. Finally, he spoke. "It always does, agent. That's why we're here."

Vic sat back angrily in her chair and finished off her drink. She shook her head. "Another round here, bartender." Then, quietly: "Agent Susan, we hardly knew ya."

Δ

LT. COMMANDER ELIZABETH SEVERS tapped the edge of her desk with a pencil and looked at her appointment book: "Lunch w/Ms. Green 1pm." She'd found the message waiting on her voice mail this morning when she arrived at the Office of Naval Intelligence in Suitland, Maryland, a suburb of Washington, D.C. The ONI was the U.S. Navy's intelligence organization, and Elizabeth spent her days deciphering ELINT data—ELINT meant Electronics Intelligence, and consisted of signals received from radar, satellites, computers, and other sources of real-world data that did not consist of human-to-human communication. She was skilled at turning digitized electromagnetic information into recognizable shapes: submarines, fleet move-ments, and so forth. If people built it and it was in the water someplace, Elizabeth could find it and quote you chapter and verse on its specifications.

Her desk was littered with crossword puzzles. She worked at them constantly, even while on duty. It was calming to decipher information provided in a form that anyone could relate to—everybody knew what "Earth's largest satellite" meant, but few could recognize the sound of a Russian-built twin-screw Kilo-class diesel submarine. Crosswords were her lifeline to the real world, they made her feel that she wasn't quite such a specialist in obscurities. Her customary approach to deciphering a new mass of data was to use her left hand to tap at the keyboard while her right hand held a pen and fidgeted over a crossword. She'd whip her head back and forth, applying a custom signal-processing filter one moment and then agonizing over 12 Across ("21 Jump & 10 Downing") the next. Her co-workers didn't think twice about it anymore, but sometimes visitors gawked; it never occurred to her that her passionate effort to remain connected with the real world just made her look even more disconnected.

Her lunch appointment was in half an hour. She recognized the *modus operandi*: a Delta Green agent was requesting a wetware interface. (That was her usual phrase for meeting someone in person; she really had no idea just how far outside the mainstream she'd gotten.) This was bothering her for some reason, though she wasn't quite sure why. There was the disappearance of David, of course, but if this was about him, wouldn't the meeting be with Alphonse? Of course, "Ms. Green" (or "Mr. Green") was a standard *nom de plume* for the group; she had no idea who it might be, and conceivably Ms. Green could be Andrea of Cell A, coming in place of Alphonse. Presumably, though, Ms. Green was some other agent looking for information on a past Cell S op. Elizabeth shrugged mentally; she'd find out soon enough.

Still, she was unsettled enough—probably because of this David business—that she decided to leave her office early and go see Harley. Rear Admiral Harley Patton was the director of the ONI, and also the man who'd recruited her into Delta Green almost ten years ago, first as a friendly and then, in 1995, as a full agent.

Elizabeth got up from her desk and got her coat and purse. She was thirty-seven, short and stocky, with black hair that framed her fleshy oval face. As she walked out of the office, her heels punched holes through the papers on the floor. She didn't notice.

The floor of Elizabeth's office was littered with dozens of torn-out crossword puzzles. For the last month, she'd been doing them at the rate of almost a hundred a day, zipping through them as fast as she could read in between bouts of signal processing. They accumulated on her desk so fast that she'd taken to tossing them on the floor, where the cleaning staff picked them up and disposed of them every night. A few of her co-workers had made nervous jokes about it, but they hadn't registered with her—this sudden surge of activity was somehow compartmentalized in her mind, and she wasn't even aware that it was going on.

It took her almost ten minutes to reach Harley's office. He was up in administration, away from the analysts' warren where she worked. His secretary, Jacob, smiled when he saw her. "You can go on in. I think the old man's practicing his swing." Elizabeth smiled back and opened the door. *That Jacob is sweet on me*, she thought. *Or as an alternative helix he's sculpted of sugar and meltdowns in the rainbow or through a prism of mitochondria.*

Harley Patton had his feet up on his desk, his arms behind his head, and his eyes focused on the large picture window in the opposite wall. It was mirrored on the outside for security reasons, and dampers at the edges prevented vibration-sensitive lasers from recording conversations held within. "Lizzie!" he exclaimed as she walked in and saluted him. He sat up and returned her salute. "What brings you up to these lofty heights?"

Elizabeth took a seat opposite his desk. "I was just wondering, Harley. I've got a lunch date with Ms. Green today. Do you know anything about that?"

The smile briefly faded from Harley's wrinkled, weathered face. "No, it's news to me, darlin'. I suppose it's about Shasta."

She nodded. "That's my guess, but why Ms. Green then? Wouldn't it be Alphonse?"

Harley shrugged. "Lizzie, I left that game. I'm happy to do

what I can to help out, but it's not much. They got me pretty boxed in here. They hand you a load of security clearances, next thing you know you can't take off your shoe without somebody wanting your sole." He cackled and slapped the desk.

"Harley, you're incorrigible."

"It's the devil in me. Mrs. Patton always said so."

"I'm sure she knew. Well, I'd better get to that lunch date. Sorry to bug ya." She started to get up.

"Hey, wait," Harley blurted. "Siddown."

She did so.

"Listen, I know this Shasta thing is bad news. How ya dealing with it?"

"Just fine, Harley. Comes with the territory."

"Just fine, yeah, I know," he said quietly, drumming his fingers on his desk. "But look. I'm a little worried about you." He paused. "Other people are worried about you. You haven't been yourself lately."

"What do you mean, Harley?"

"I mean, maybe you should take some time off. Hell, you never take a rest from this place. That's my secret—I get outta here every damn chance I get. All those zeroes and ones, hell, it'd crack anyone up."

"I don't understand."

"You know, I asked Alphonse about you and this Shasta business. Because I'm worried about you. He stonewalled me. Hah! Old bastard. He's never forgiven me for letting Darren go down."

"What is this about, Harley?"

He sighed. "You've been acting a little strange lately, darlin'. People notice. It's not good. They come to me and say that

Santa's little helper is maybe stressed out, maybe."

"I love my work, Harley. I work hard. Not everyone understands that."

"Yeah, I know, I know. But . . . darlin', can you tell me about this?" He pulled a folder from a stack on his desk and opened it up. Inside was a ripped-out crossword puzzle, all filled in—but not in English. The puzzle was filled with strange markings, almost like cuneiform.

"I got almost a *thousand* like this. A *thousand.* In just a few weeks. What the hell's up with this?"

Elizabeth sat there quietly, staring at the markings on the puzzle. *Position suborned assault substantiate blanket,* she thought.

"Lizzie? Help me out, here."

"Bury it. Bury it, Harley. Or I tell the press how I slept with you to get into the ONI."

Harley boggled. "Lizzie! What the hell is that talk? We never did no such thing!"

"It doesn't matter, Harley. You're old. You're just marking time here. They'll make you retire, no matter what you say. When the press figures out how Darren was your protegé, they'll torpedo you. You'll be gray and under way, Harley."

"Christ, Lizzie! For the love of Christ, girlie, you're like a daughter to me, how can you say these things?" The old man was distraught.

"I love my work. I want to stay here. Bury it, Harley."

He shook his head, uncomprehending. But finally a small voice emerged from his weary bones.

"Okay."

Elizabeth rose sharply and saluted. He just stared at her. She left the office.

Lunch, she thought. *Digestive enzymes break down organic matter shunt wastes absorb nutrients. Pleasure center indication stimulus derivation glucose-spiked mastication experience.*

"Stick of gum?" she asked Jacob as she took a pack from her purse.

"Nah, I got Altoids," he replied. "How's the old man?"

"Still not getting any," she said cheerfully, putting a piece of gum in her mouth.

"No wonder he's always playing golf."

"Why me?" Stephanie said in the dim barroom. "Vic's the cell leader. She's got the most experience." The expression on Vic's face seemed to suggest that she concurred.

"Because you pulled the trigger," Alphonse said coolly. "They're going to be curious about you. They might even have a grudge. Because of the three of you, you're the most interesting to the people behind Shasta's disappearance."

"So what am I supposed to do?"

"Make her believe you."

Elizabeth exited the ONI building and headed for the nearest intersection. It was around noon, and the sun warmed the busy lunchtime pedestrians as they poured out of office buildings and came blinking into the light. She crossed the street and entered a little park, erected by the Navy. At the entrance was a small memorial to Naval personnel lost in the Cold War. Elizabeth stopped by the memorial and stared at the names on the list. She tapped her foot impatiently.

A blond woman got out of a taxi and walked over to the memorial. She turned to face Elizabeth. "Hi," she said. Elizabeth looked at her. "I'm Ms. Green," the woman explained, and they shook hands. Ms. Green was taller than Elizabeth, quietly attractive with a studious air about her. She wore a dark blue peasant dress with a necklace made of small seashells.

"What is this about?" Elizabeth asked curtly.

"I just need to talk to you," Ms. Green said, a little nervously. "I need some help."

Elizabeth nodded. "Okay. Where to?"

Ms. Green looked around, then gestured at a sandwich stand. "Let's get a bite to eat and go find a bench."

"So where do we meet?" Stephanie asked.

"Meet her in a public space," Alphonse replied. The fire was burning low, and it had gotten quite dark in the barroom. Abe got up to put another log on. "Get a hot dog or something. Stay outside, in the open, away from the street. It doesn't matter if her handlers are eavesdropping. You just want to make sure they can't take you."

Sparks flickered behind the glass screen as Abe moved it back into place. His face was bathed in a warm glow. Agent Nancy and the rest of Cell N sipped at their pints in silence, letting Alphonse do the talking. Vic kept stealing glances at Nancy, vaguely trying to figure her out.

"You think her handlers will be there?"

"Probably not. They've got her programmed, so why bother? But we can't be too careful."

The pair took their sandwiches into the Naval park and found a small picnic table nearby. Ms. Green glanced around for a moment before sitting down. "So you need some help?" Elizabeth asked. "What with?"

Ms. Green looked nervous. "I just got back from Groversville."

"You mean Promise," Elizabeth said, her features hardening.

"Yeah. Promise. I was just there, with my cell. You know. Following up on Shasta."

"Which cell?"

"Oh, right. Cell T. I'm Agent Terry."

"Terry?" Elizabeth asked. "You reported to Shasta?"

"No, I'm not the cell leader."

"But you knew him."

Agent Terry seemed uncomfortable. "Yes."

Elizabeth waited for her to go on.

"Anyway, we met this guy. Older, southern accent. Three gold teeth. I think your cell met him before."

"Sure did. He's a piece of work."

"He's dead," Terry said. "I shot him. Three times."

Elizabeth nonchalantly took a bite of her sandwich and chewed for a moment. "Sounds good to me. What's the trouble?"

"Alphonse yanked me. Said I was out of line, shooting that guy."

"Was he threatening you?"

"No. He just made a crack about Shasta and I lost it."

Elizabeth smiled for the first time during their meeting. "Well. Quite the Lash LaRue, aren't we?"

Agent Terry glowered. "Look, it just happened. And now I'm catching a shitstorm for it."

"So what do you want from me?"

"I think Alphonse is going to call you in soon for an op. I'd really appreciate it if you could put in a good word for me. I want a piece of it."

"What op?"

"NOW THIS IS THE crucial part," Alphonse said, sitting down with a tray of fresh drinks for everyone. "We've got to give them something that's too dramatic for them to ignore. Something that'll throw them for a loop. Something so good that they'll want to do more than just have Susan report by phone. They've got to bring her in for this to work, or we get squat."

"So what's the story?" Vic asked, taking her cider off the tray.

Alphonse snorted. "Something beefy. They'll flip their lids over this one."

"WE'RE GONNA NUKE GROVERSVILLE," Terry said.

"*What?*" Elizabeth was taken aback.

"I don't mean nuke, nuke. We've got some sort of bioweapon against the neo-tissue. We're gonna get a crop duster and just saturate the place. Within a few hours, there won't be a drop of the stuff left alive. Probably be corpses everywhere, too, if the population is infested like before."

"Jesus."

"Yeah, exactly. We're gonna hit town hall while it's going down, blow in and get whatever documentation we can. Names, numbers, the works. A major strike. Enolsis all over again, only whoever has Shasta will be forced to keep it quiet."

Elizabeth sat back, stunned, her sandwich forgotten. "That's insane."

Agent Terry smiled, a trifle scary. "That's why I want in. We're really going to stick it to those bastards, and I don't want to sit on the sidelines. I'm sure you'll be in on it. Payback. I want some, too. Can you help?"

Elizabeth looked at Terry for a long moment. Then she seemed to reach some sort of decision—or at least some sort of terminus. "Of course. I'll insist that you come along."

"Great!" Terry said. "We'll make a good team."

"Of course we will," Elizabeth said blankly. "I need to get back to work. You will excuse me, won't you?

"Sure," Terry replied, still smiling. "Thanks for your time."

"No problem."

Stephanie sat at the picnic table and finished her sandwich as she watched Agent Susan hurry back to her office across the street. Once she was inside, Abe ambled over from where he'd been standing, feeding the pigeons, and sat down across from Stephanie.

"She buy it?" he asked.

"The whole thing," she replied with confidence. "We're in."

"Good work." He glanced down at Elizabeth's barely-touched sandwich.

"I wouldn't eat that," Stephanie advised.

Abe nodded grimly. "Cooties."

Late that afternoon, around four o'clock, Agent Nancy parked her rental sedan just up from the ONI headquarters and started keeping watch. Across the street, Vic nodded to her from a parked car, then turned the key and drove away. Vic and Abe had swapped off keeping watch from lunch until now, just in case, but Cell N was taking over at this point, since it was almost Agent Susan's normal time to leave work. Nancy's partners, Nick and Nolan, were in two other cars a couple blocks away, ready to pull a three-car alternating tail on Susan.

Although Cell N was a functional cell within Delta Green, they didn't see a lot of action. Technically, Nick and Nolan were more Nancy's handlers than her partners, and Nancy's role was generally that of a consultant rather than an active agent. But Alphonse's meticulous policy of compartmentalization meant that since Nancy had come in and learned all about this op, Alphonse would rather use her cell in tandem with Cell T instead of bringing yet another cell into the situation. As it was, Cells N, S, and T were all involved; Alphonse wasn't happy with the size of this op, and he was determined to keep it as tight as could be.

Agent Nancy had two handlers instead of partners because she wasn't human. Not anymore. She used to be Debra Constance, an FBI forensic psychologist, but an unfortunate encounter with an old friend had destroyed her life—and her humanity. He had turned her into a horrific creature with a hunger for human flesh, a monstrous humanoid with hooved feet and terrible jaws, like something from a childhood nightmare. Without Delta Green, she would have gone mad. Instead, she came to study her condition with a clinical fascination, and eventually discovered that she had other abilities besides superhuman strength and a physiological inability to vomit. She could access the memories of corpses whose brains she'd eaten, and even trick those around her into seeing an illusionary body that disguised her own hideous one—as long as the body looked like someone whom she'd devoured, that is.

Delta Green got her a new identity as Jean Qualls, and she had the ultimate makeover: remade from a petite, sharp-nosed woman with curly brown hair to a tall, voluptuous blond woman fifteen years younger. There were even days when she enjoyed her new appearance, but they were outnumbered by the many mirrors she'd smashed and broken in the throes of her ongoing supernatural identity crisis. Debra Constance was dead, after all—dead and buried, since she could never again look like her old self; even her fingerprints were altered beyond recognition by the terrible transformation.

As "Jean Qualls" she attended Debra's funeral, posing as an emotional co-worker. She cried a river, embracing Debra's mom and dad, her ex-husband, and her friends, leaving the funeral party unsettled; her mom later said, unknowing, that it really was like Debra was there to say goodbye to them all. She would never know how right she was.

Jean's unusual situation meant she had no real-world friends outside of Delta Green. In consequence, she spent a great deal of time on the internet, hiding behind yet another false identity. As "Sarah Jackson," who appeared to be posted to the U.S. Embassy in Sri Lanka, she was a frequent contributor to web pages and newsgroups related to her enduring passion, *Star Trek*.

Under her new identity, she was re-employed by the FBI as a consultant. She worked from home in a house paid for by DG, with a handler either present in a spare bedroom or a phone call away, ready to retrieve her strange meals from a morgue run by a DG-friendly when the cravings came—and, secretly, to put her down if she ever lost her hold on her human identity. Jean spent her spare time researching her condition, working with several DG-friendlies to explore what had happened and, maybe, someday find a cure. Meanwhile, Debra Constance/Jean Qualls/Sarah Jackson/Agent Nancy made the best of a very, very bad lot and occasionally had trouble remembering who she was and how she'd come to be in this situation.

Of course, her abilities made her of immense value to Delta

Green. She could change her appearance with a thought (albeit from a limited palette of devoured corpses) and she could read the minds of the dead. She was also incredibly strong and a powerful fighter, though Alphonse was rarely willing to risk his star resource in that way.

Alphonse had summoned Jean the night that Agent Stan had shown up and bled out. Once the scene was secure, Jean had feasted on Stan's brain tissue, perversely grateful for the opportunity to sate her inhuman hunger. From the dead man's memories, she was able to reconstruct the story of the fate that had befallen Cell S, and brief Alphonse on what he needed to know to continue the op. Jean's status was a secret known to few members of Delta Green; Cells S & T had no idea as to her nature or abilities, and Alphonse wanted to keep it that way for as long as he could.

Jean sat in the car, reflecting on her strange, sad lot in life—until Agent Susan emerged from the ONI building. She made a beeline for her car in the staff parking lot and quickly tore out and onto the street. Jean cranked the ignition and followed her, signaling her partners by encrypted cell phone that it was time to move. Soon, three sedans followed Agent Nancy at irregular distances as she drove rapidly towards home.

The principle of the three-car alternating tail was a simple one. With the target identified, three agents in three cars would follow her—but only one would keep her in sight at a time. That "chase" car would keep relatively close, a few cars behind, while the other two would drop back out of sight. At irregular intervals, one of the backup cars would take the chase position, closing in while the former chase car dropped back. (All three stayed in touch via encrypted cell phones.) This cut the chances that the target would make the tail, and even allowed one car to visibly abandon the tail entirely if the target seemed to be suspicious. Under different circumstances, Delta Green might choose to place a microtransmitter on the target car, allowing for simple electronic tailing. But given the evident resources and sophistication of Shasta's kidnappers, Alphonse had ruled against any form of technical surveillance; they'd do it the old-fashioned way.

Agents Nick and Nolan had more experience at this sort of espionage tradecraft than Nancy did; they had formerly worked as field agents for the DEA and the FBI respectively, and tailing was routine to them. Nancy, on the other hand, had been an FBI analyst with little more than basic training in fieldwork, but she understood the principles of the procedure. And unlike her handlers, she could change her appearance in the blink of an eye, cutting the chance of being made down dramatically—as long as no one was looking at her when she made the change.

Twenty-five minutes later, Agent Susan arrived at her condo in the D.C. suburb of Oxon Hill. Her building was well secured, with a gated underground parking garage that required a passcode to access. She pulled into the garage and disappeared from sight, just as Agent Nolan drove by slowly, talking on his cell phone.

"Okay, she's inside."

"Roger that," Abe said quietly, looking through a tiny pair of binoculars. "Nothing doing here for the last hour. Tonya has op control." Abe had driven over to Susan's condo after Vic relieved him at the ONI a few hours earlier. He'd been keeping an eye on the place to see if anyone showed up who might be waiting for Susan, but all the arrivals looked routine. He was sitting in a bagel shop across the street and to the south a few doors, with a clear view of the condo and the parking garage. Vic was out of sight in a bar two blocks away, reading her Murakami novel and listening to the conference call through a small earpiece that ran to the cell phone in her jacket.

Agents Nick and Nancy arrived a few minutes apart, and both found parking spaces a few blocks from the condo. They fed the meters and sat in their cars, listening and waiting. Agent Nolan stayed on the move, driving at normal speeds in irregular patterns through the neighborhood.

Fifteen minutes went by uneventfully. Abe and Vic swapped places, since Abe had been sitting in the bagel shop for quite a while now. Vic chose a street café north of the condo, and once she was seated with her book and a skinny tall half-caf latté, Abe yawned and stretched, then ambled out of the shop with a sack of bagels and headed off down the street towards his car. Nolan parked his car and Nick took up the aimless circling.

Stephanie waited in a motel room, pacing and listening to the conference call. Alphonse had kept her out of the tail so she wouldn't be made by Susan, and it was driving her crazy.

"Heads up," Vic said suddenly. The other five agents on the call perked up. "Dark blue sedan in the waiting zone. Driver plus two, all male, suits, look like pros. The two are getting out. They're at the front door. Reading the roster. Using the intercom. Nick, get over here. This looks good." Agent Nick began driving back towards the condo. The two men stood waiting at the door. Their driver sat in the car, engine running.

"It's Susan!"

Agent Susan came out and spoke briefly with the two men. Then all three got in the car.

Abe, Nancy, and Nolan all started their cars and began pulling out into the streets. Nick was at a stop sign one block down from the condo, watching the blue sedan intently through binoculars. "Roger that. Late-model Ford Taurus, dark blue, Maryland license plate DX9 138. Four occupants including target."

"I'm leaving the café," Vic said. "Nick, you've got op control."

"Roger Tonya," Nick said, putting down the binoculars and moving into the intersection slowly. "They're northbound. I'm on chase. Cell N, fall in behind me. Cell T, get moving northbound but stay clear. Nancy, you're next chase."

The sedan drove north doing thirty. Nick hung four cars back. Nancy and Nolan were about two blocks behind them, while Abe paralleled them a couple blocks over. Vic was still hustling to her car.

The staggered procession continued northbound for six blocks, and then the sedan turned northeast.

"Northeast on Livingston Road. Nancy, you're chase. I'm going north a block and then cutting over to parallel."

"That's towards the beltway," Abe cut in.

"Roger that," Nick replied. "Cell T, I want you at the on-ramps."

"On my way," Abe confirmed, speeding up rapidly.

"Nick, I'm just reaching my car now," Vic said hurriedly as she unlocked the door. "I'll head northwest and get on one exit back."

"Roger. Thomas, hustle."

Abe drove swiftly, moving ahead of the target so he could confirm which direction on the highway the target went. He reached the 495 on-ramps in minutes and pulled into a gas station at the intersection. As he came to a stop he took out his binoculars and started scanning the cars.

"Approaching the beltway," Nancy reported, tailing the sedan from a distance.

"Thomas, you got anything yet?" Nick asked.

Abe whipped the binoculars back and forth. "Nothing . . . still no sign . . ."

"Shit!" Nancy sputtered. "I'm stuck two blocks back, missed the light."

"Thomas, make me happy," Nick said sternly.

Abe continued scanning, then spotted the sedan. "Got them! Eastbound highway lane. They're three cars from the turn."

"Roger," Nick said. "Thomas, you're on chase. Tonya, status?"

"Still heading for the on-ramps down here. I'll get on eastbound and catch up."

"Nick, I'm in the turn lane," Abe said. "Target on the on-ramp. Eastbound confirmed."

"Right behind you, Thomas," Nancy said.

"I'm coming in, too," Nick confirmed. "Nolan, you're next chase."

Soon, all five agents were on the beltway. Vic was unable to catch up—rush-hour traffic slowed things down considerably, keeping her a mile or so behind the pursuit. It also made swapping chase much more difficult; they were only able to do so twice during the drive. Eventually, the target signaled for a turn: exit 16 to Bountin, another suburban community in the wake of D.C.

"Target exiting to Bountin," Nancy said.

"Nancy, skip it and backtrack from the next exit so they don't make you," Nick said. "The rest of you, close in and get off at Bountin. We won't have long to re-establish the tail after

Nancy breaks off."

Nick, Nolan, and Abe were fairly close together, and all exited in sight of each other. Vic was still lagging in rush-hour traffic, and Nancy would have to catch up. They were down to a three-unit tail.

"I'm on chase," Nick said as he came down the on-ramp in the lead. He looked around at the intersection and cursed silently. "Lost them! I'm east. Nolan, you take north and Thomas south." The three headed off rapidly in different directions and looked for the target.

Precious moments ticked by. Finally, Nolan spotted the sedan two blocks ahead.

"Got him on Montgomery, northbound," he reported.

"Roger, you're on chase. Catch-up time, everybody."

Vic neared the exit and turned off, heading northbound from the intersection. Traffic was lighter here and she quickly caught up to Nolan. "I've got visual," she reported.

"Outstanding," Nick said. "You're next chase, Tonya."

Everyone caught up within a few minutes, and once again they had a five-car tail going. The target made several turns, eventually reaching a light-industrial and office area on the outskirts of the suburb. Vic took chase.

"Target turning south on Marginal Way," Vic said. "Dead end! Do not follow, repeat, do not follow."

"Roger," Nick replied. "Tonya, you've got op control."

"Find a place to park or just circle, but stay out of here," Vic said. "Looks like a facility up ahead . . . it's a cul-de-sac. I'm pulling into an office park." She turned the car and came to a stop in a large parking area full of cars. The target was a hundred yards down the street. Vic jumped out and crouched behind the back of the next car, binoculars poking over the trunk. "Confirmed. Target is at a gated entrance. There's a big stone wall encircling what looks to be a large private area. Two security guards at the gate, tan uniforms with black jackets."

"Sign?"

Vic looked for a long moment. "Negative. No markings I can spot, not even a street address. The gate's opening. Target moving forward. I've got two more guards through the gate, waving the car in. Uniforms look like private security, can't make the insignia. I can see a one-story building through the gate, but it's set back at the end of a long drive. Not much cover." The gate closed. "That's it. They're inside."

Nick sighed. "Okay Tonya, stay put. I'm coming over with a camera so we can get a few shots of the entrance. The rest of you hang loose until we're clear. Terry, see if you can get Alphonse online. We need to find out what this place is."

"I'll tell you what it is," Vic said as she peered through the binoculars at the entrance, wondering if Shasta was inside. "It's bad news."

David Foster Nells sat on a concrete bench in an open, grassy area. The air was warm. Breezes carried the smell of wildflowers and the distant noises of traffic. David held a rubber ball in one hand, which he squeezed rhythmically. He was wearing pale yellow silk pajamas with matching slippers, a middle-aged man dressed for bed. On the bench next to him was a paper cup half-full of water. They'd given him his medication a few minutes earlier.

"Hello, son," Andrew Nells said, standing over him. "Are you being a good boy?"

David swung his feet back and forth, hanging off the bench, and shrugged.

"Now come on, son. You know my work takes me away a lot. I need to know—are you being a good boy?"

"I guess so," David said quietly.

His father smiled. "That's my boy." He sat down next to David on the bench.

"Dad?"

"Yes, son?"

"I think mom's been hurt. I think maybe I hurt her."

Andrew laughed and tousled the little boy's hair. "Don't be ridiculous, son. Your mom's just fine."

"But I think I saw it. I saw something in a room . . . it's kind of fuzzy."

"Son, your mom's fine."

"But—"

"Look, David, if you're so worried about your mom, why don't you go see her?"

David cocked his head to one side. "I dunno. I think I have to stay here."

Andrew nodded. "Sure, you have to stay here. But that doesn't mean you can't go see mom."

"It doesn't?"

"Nope! You can see her right now, if you like."

"Okay. But how do I see her?"

"Just make a wish," his father said. "It'll come true."

David closed his eyes and wished as hard as he could.

SARAH NELLS SAT IN the breakfast room of her rambling Savannah mansion, tears running down her graceful face. Her gray hair was unkempt; she hadn't had the spirit to do herself up properly today. David's disappearance was wearing hard on her.

He'd always been a little distant. Andrew's death had left

his son adrift. His father was such a heroic figure, a dashing pilot fighting for a just cause, with the swirl of intrigue around him and his missions. Sarah had certainly fallen for him at first sight, but eventually realized that Andrew loved being a hero more than being a father. It was easy for him to fly in and fly out, his parental responsibilities discharged as quickly and efficiently as an arms drop to the Chinese nationalists. Sarah was left to tend a boy who wanted only to fly at his father's side, fighting the Communists and saving the world. They were awfully big dreams for a little boy, and when Andrew's plane went down, it seemed that he took part of his thirteen-year-old son with him. David lost his sense of romance and adventure, and instead nurtured a cold grudge against those who'd taken his father away.

Since then, David had gone his own way in the world, flying in and out of his mother's life just as his father had. He was punctual with birthday and Christmas gifts, and visited Savannah once a year to see Sarah and his father's relatives. But they rarely talked about anything substantial.

Although Sarah traced her son's distance back to his father, she didn't really feel any bitterness towards poor Andrew. She saved that for Joe Camp, Andrew's Army buddy who was always, maddeningly, two steps ahead of everyone around him and didn't mind letting you know it. Joe worked in intelligence, and she knew that it was Joe who got Andrew his job with Civil Air Transport after the war. Men and their secrets—they were obsessed with intrigue, almost romanced by it. Andrew had fallen for it, had envied Joe's winks and whispers about things he couldn't discuss. Sarah felt it had cost Andrew his life.

As if to compound his crime, Joe Camp seduced her son, as well. David had told her as much, back when he was still posted to China fifteen years ago; it was the last time they had a meaningful conversation. Sarah hadn't heard a word about Joe Camp since Andrew's death, and when David mentioned in passing that "Uncle Joe" had said hello, her blood ran cold. David confessed that he'd been doing some work for the old man as part of his job as a military attaché to the embassy in Beijing. Sarah lost her temper, started crying and shrieking that Joe Camp had taken her Andrew away and he was damned well not going to take her David, too. She'd had a few glasses of wine, just for the holidays, and was perhaps too strident on the subject. David had walked out, yelling that his life was his own. And so it was.

Ever since that day, Sarah lived with the fear that David would be taken away, as his father had before him. No matter the distance between her and her son, Sarah still loved him fiercely and feared for his safety.

Now he was gone, a thousand nightmares come screaming to life. The police were investigating, the CIA was investigating. They claimed to not know what had happened. But the same faceless bastards had told her the same thing when Andrew's plane went down, and she hadn't believed them then, either. They all knew. They just wouldn't tell her. Now, she was sure, she would never see her son again.

She buried her face in her hands and sobbed, hunched over in the chair, orange juice untouched on the breakfast table. Outside a mockingbird sang.

"Mom?"

Sarah shook. The voice came again. "Mom?"

Through her tears, through the tendrils of gray hair that hung down over her eyes, through her fingers, there stood her son. A boy of thirteen.

"Mom? Why are you crying?"

It was David, just as he'd been in 1964. The men had come to the house with the news, and left her to weep for her beautiful young warrior, forever lost in China clouds.

"Mom? Are you okay?"

"Oh, God . . ." Sarah murmured. "Oh, David . . ." She was confused. This was her kitchen in Savannah. She was an old woman, not the young British socialite who'd married a Yank and then lost him. The men from CAT had walked away thirty-five years ago. Or was it thirty-five seconds?

"David," she said, bewildered and dislocated in time and memory. "David, it's your father. He's had an accident." They were the same words she'd spoken then. She didn't know what else to say.

David smiled a boy's confident smile. "I know, mom, it's okay. I know. That was a long time ago." He knelt down before her, took her hands in his. His hands were large, and worn with age. He was tall, with silver hair like her own. He was older now than his father was when he died.

"David?" Her voice broke with emotion. "Is that you?"

He laughed a funny little laugh. "It's me, mom. Are you okay?"

"Oh, David!" she cried, and wrapped her arms around his shoulders, pulling him close. "David, I thought you'd left me, I thought you'd gone away like your father."

"I'm right here, mom. I'm okay."

"But what happened?" she asked, pulling back and touching his face. "Where did you go? They're looking for you!"

"I'm not sure, mom. I don't really understand what's going on. But I wanted to see you. I wanted to know you were okay. I thought—I thought maybe something had happened to you."

"No, no, I'm fine, David. I'm fine, now that you're here. I thought you were gone forever!"

"Forever. That's a funny word."

"What?"

"Mom, I can't stay. I have to go. I just wanted to see you, make sure you were all right."

"But David, wait, you can't go!"

"No, I have to. I can feel it."

"David, please!"

David Nells, age eight, touched his mother's face, then spoke in the sweet little boy's voice that was indelibly etched in her memory.

"I love you, mom."

And then he was gone.

Interlude: Thirty Four Forty Three and a Wake-Up

Friday, January 9, 1998

Ex-Captain Forrest James jogged around the exercise yard, his breath coming out as vapor in the cold Kansas air. He had an hour before dinner.

The day had gone quickly. They all did. It was the nights that lasted forever.

After four months of well-behaved incarceration, James had graduated to medium custody. He was moved to a cell on the fifth floor and allowed to mingle with the other prisoners. He joined the work detail in the woodshop, studying the basics of carpentry. The USDB's sizable workforce trained and worked in a wide variety of occupations, vocational training intended to give them useful job skills upon release. James began in a classroom, then moved to normal work after a few weeks. The prison workers constructed and repaired many products for the military, ranging from replacing zippers on sleeping bags to repairing damaged doors for humvees. In the woodshop, the inmate carpenters made furniture, desk accessories, plaques, and other items, many of them finely crafted, ornate pieces. They made riot batons for units in Germany, plaques for Saudi Arabia, and museum display cabinets for Fort Dodge. The civilian plant manager for the wood shop was a hard-working but affable guy named Clyde. His top crew was engaged in a four-year project to replace the hardwood floors in thirty-seven historical homes within the Fort Leaven-worth Army Base.

Around the exercise yard, inmates did push-ups, played

basketball, or just congregated in groups to shoot the bull. A few eyed James as he jogged past.

James had made a point of keeping his distance from the rank and file. He hung with the other ex-officers, who tended to cluster together anyway and who were housed in the same part of the prison. They ate meals together, watched television together, and exercised together. It wasn't anything official, but you had to associate with somebody or you'd go nuts. The ex-officers had a common bond of duty and experience, and tended to be a cut above the enlisted inmates—or at least, they liked to think so.

As James jogged, he picked out inmates he recognized. There was Eric Reynolds, a Marine private who'd gone AWOL during basic training and stolen a car. He got into a high-speed chase with the cops and slammed into a schoolbus, killing a child. He'd spent six months in the hospital and still had a limp. They'd given him forty years. He was six in. Eric worked in the woodshop with James and had a seemingly endless stream of prison lore, stories handed down from con to con across the generations, stories of deaths, pranks, rapes, escapes, and a thousand other things. He swore he'd write a book someday. On the basketball court, Jake Larson went out for a pass. An Air Force lieutenant, Jake had dealt crystal meth supplied by a civilian buddy from off base. He got eight years, four in, and was active in the prison's underground economy. He dealt in cigarettes, toiletries, and the occasional illicit batch of joy-juice—rough alcohol made from fruit, sugar, and water, stuffed into a plastic bag and allowed to rot and ferment for a few weeks. They called him Jake On The Make. It was clear he had no intention of going straight when he got out; he was too addicted to the art of the deal. Off in a corner, Tommy DeLuca shuffled aimlessly, hands in his pockets, while big Gerald Lewis leaned against a wall nearby, smoking a cigarette. Tommy had been a sergeant in the USMC, caught with his pants down in the company of a fourth-grader. A kiddy-raper, Tommy was low man on the totem pole inside the Castle. He'd been a constant target for harassment in his first few months of medium custody until Gerald turned him and made him his punk; after that, nobody did nothing to Tommy unless they were willing to go toe-to-toe with Gerald, and thus far nobody had.

James shook his head. By definition, the Castle was full of losers and fools, men too stupid or too drunk or too weak to toe the line. Some were victims of their passions, others addicts to vice, and a few were just mean S.O.B.s who cursed the world for birthing them and wanted to make everyone else suffer. They did their time, their varied sentences to pay for their crimes. They worked, they played, they attended endless classes on decision making and personal responsibility and general coping. They watched television, they told jokes, they beat off or played sister for smokes. When they could, they got drunk or high. When they couldn't, they might just break down and read a book. They did whatever they had to do to get by.

James stopped and hunched over, hands on his knees, taking deep, chill breaths, sweat beading on his forehead. His hair was going gray, big time. He'd put on a little weight. He hadn't had a drink or a smoke since he'd been here. Other than that, he didn't feel much different. His life had been a long and lonely one, and that didn't look to be changing. He'd never been married or had a long-term girlfriend. He'd kept his nose to the grindstone and done his duty, drinking himself to sleep in the bad times and laughing with his buddies in the good.

He stood up, still breathing heavy. He decided to head back

to his cell so he could get changed before dinner. As he strode across the yard, he thought of Delta Green.

In 1981 he'd been a Lieutenant Commander with the SEALs. A spy ship, the USS *Santa Cruz*, had gone down in Vietnamese waters. His team went down to recover some sensitive equipment and swam straight into a nightmare. Things came at them out of the darkness, powerful creatures that were built like men but owed their allegiance to some deviant evolutionary track. His men were slaughtered around him, and he was injured. When he made his way back, he concocted a story about Soviet *Spetsnaz* divers and enemy attack subs.

In the years that followed he'd ransacked the Naval archives for other evidence of what he'd seen. His research eventually attracted the attention of a rear admiral named Harley Patton, the director of the Office of Naval Intelligence. Harley was a garrulous old soul who knew a fighter when he met one. He recruited James into Delta Green.

James had fought a number of strange enemies in his clandestine years of DG service, and emerged from bad-dream scrapes that took the lives of lesser men. He weathered it all with stoic equanimity—except for the memories of that first time, on the deck of the *Santa Cruz* nine hundred feet down. That one came back, again and again, tearing at his sleep. He bore the scars of that attack on his chest and in his mind, a milestone of the first time in his life that he had plumbed the depths of primal fear. It was the legacy of that encounter that had triggered the incident in San Francisco, when a combination of alcohol and stress had sparked a flashback that put an innocent woman in the hospital.

He walked faster and then jogged, crossing the rest of the way across the yard and re-entering the prison. As he moved he tried to leave that memory behind, that sensation of awesome terror and helplessness, of being alone in the wet and the dark and the cold while things with claws tore at his flesh. But it followed him, that memory, shadowing him for all his days, swallowing him for all his nights.

By comparison, life in the Castle was easy. But only by comparison.

Chapter Four: The Profit and Loss

Thursday, February 18–Saturday, March 13, 1999

THURSDAY WAS A VERY long day; for most of it, not a damn thing happened. Vic, Abe, and Stephanie had made their report to Alphonse last night, and Nick had brought the photographs he took of the entrance to the Bountin property. They were hot to make a move, but Alphonse sent them all off to get some rest and said he'd be in touch when he had news.

Wednesday night had not been a problem. Cell T was exhausted from little sleep and much tension, and they crashed as soon as they got back to the motel. But all three were awake at six the next morning, taking turns in the shower and slowly getting their act together. Vic was third in line, and came out of the shower shivering and pissed that the hot water was gone. She glared at Abe and Stephanie darkly and stomped out to get some coffee.

"She always this much fun in the mornings?" Stephanie asked as she toweled her hair.

Abe chuckled and pulled on his socks. "Vic? She's the Queen High Bitch of the Galaxy until she gets her java fix."

"So what about you? What's your jones?"

"Basketball," Abe replied, lacing up his loafers. "I haven't been on the court since Saturday and it's driving me nuts. If we weren't hanging out for Alphonse, I'd find a gym and get a game going."

Stephanie balled up the towel and tossed it at the trash can. It missed and got hung up on the television.

"Brick," Abe said.

Δ

Vic found an espresso stand whose coffee she thought she could stomach and got a grandé triple mocha, plus a cheese-twist pastry. The punky barista boy behind the counter looked her up and down. "That's a lotta coffee for a little lady," he said, smiling.

Vic gave him a withering look. "That's a grandé triple mocha," she said. "Not a grandé triple mocha with a stupid fuck on the side."

The barista scowled and handed her the drink and a sack with the pastry in it. "Bitch," he muttered.

"And loving it," Vic said sweetly, fluttering her eyes.

Heading back to the motel, gulping the drink, her mood was much improved—so much so that she stopped at another stand and bought croissants for Abe and Stephanie.

All told, she was enjoying herself. The unpleasantness with Stephanie in Knoxville was behind them, and they'd just come off an intense but fruitful work cycle. Soon there'd be some action. Some payback.

Vic was grateful. The last thing she wanted to do was go back to work. The park was all well and good, and playing guitar in Seattle on the weekends kept her busy, but this extended op was making it clear how much more she liked doing these things, being with these people, than she did spinning out her carefully humdrum life back home. She wondered if she should make a change, get out of the parks service and the Pacific Northwest, maybe find a job in law enforcement someplace. For a moment her mind got away from her, and she flashed on a fantasy of getting a job with the FBI, maybe in Milwaukee . . . *Stop it,* she thought. *Stupid. Stupid.*

Her mood had soured again. She felt conflicted and confused. She took a gulp of her mocha and wrestled her thoughts back onto the situation at hand.

Now if Alphonse would just call, she thought impatiently.

Joseph Camp sat in his office at the Library of Congress, Federal Research Division. His office was small and tidy, decorated only with some old photographs from his Army days. He liked to regale his assistants with stories of the war, usually bawdy ones involving smuggled liquor shipments and beautiful Chinese whores. He created the impression of a man whose best days were long, long behind him, and who was now content to toil in obscurity and live on his memories.

The truth, of course, was very different. Joe Camp was never really in the Army, though he was given the rank of major for logistical purposes. He was a spy. He joined the Office of Strategic Services—the OSS—in 1942 out of Harvard, and spent the war in China working for the organization's DELTA GREEN operation. They were allegedly conducting psychological warfare using occult folklore against superstitious members of Hitler's elite in Europe and their counterparts in Japan; in reality, Joe and his associates were fighting a shadow war against very real and very inhuman powers that had only tangential connections to the horrors of the Axis or the conflict that had set half the world aflame.

When the war was over, the OSS was disbanded. Joe spent some down time doing research and catching up with family and friends, then signed up with the new Central Intelligence Group (forerunner of the CIA) the following year. The CIG stuck him with mundane analysis work, keeping an eye on post-war Japan, until Delta Green was reconstituted as an independent agency under the Joint Chiefs of Staff in 1947. He worked for DG full-time until it was disbanded again in 1970. Joe then found work with the Library of Congress's Federal Research Division, and he'd been there ever since. He knew he should've retired years ago, according to the rules, but he'd become a resource of such singular value and had so many connections throughout the U.S. intelligence community that he'd held onto the post. Joe was an institution within the FRD, though he made sure to stay a very quiet one; despite his sometimes-dramatic OSS service and his brief affair with fellow OSS agent Julia Child, his name had never cropped up in a single history book or memoir. He liked it that way.

Carssandra Buie, one of Joe's chief researchers, knocked on the open door. "Joe? I've got that file you wanted." She lay a dingy folder down on his desk; it was closed with rubber bands that looked to have been there a long time. "Just get it back to me before I go home so I can drop it back by Frank's office. He'll have to do some paperwork if it's out overnight."

"Thanks," Joe said, smiling at her kindly. "I'll tie a string around my finger."

Carssandra smiled back and left. Joe got up and closed the door.

The file was from the CIA. Carssandra had an old college friend over there in the records division who occasionally slipped her information that the FRD needed. Technically, the FRD was only supposed to use unclassified materials in their analysis work for various federal agencies. They sifted through books, magazines, newspapers, and so forth, reading between the lines and putting together summaries for their "clients." Carssandra's friend wasn't adverse to loaning them CIA files for an afternoon, as long as the documents didn't address current operations. It was a security breach, but Joe was careful to ask only for moldy old stuff that no one else cared about, much of it scheduled for declassification whenever the CIA got around to it.

Here was a case in point. The file Joe had requested contained old contracts and duplicates of analysis documents from a private think tank called OUTLOOK Group. They specialized in global political and military issues—usually one and the same—and had a contract with the CIA in the late 1950s and early 1960s to prepare forecasts, conflict scenarios, and other egghead projects with little day-to-day relevance. OUTLOOK had a minor security clearance, but they didn't appear to have been anything very special. In fact, according to the documents Joe was reading, the CIA had canceled their contract not long after the Bay of Pigs disaster. OUTLOOK was one of several think tanks who had provided data and scenarios on a possible Cuban rebellion, and got a pink slip in the general scape-goating that went on afterwards. A follow-up memo noted that most of the think-tank employees were soon let go by OUTLOOK's founder and owner, a political scientist named Dr. Lewis Strater. A newspaper clipping recorded Strater's death in a household burglary in 1963.

That was the extent of the file. Countless think tanks had come and gone over the years, and OUTLOOK appeared to be little more than a footnote among them.

Joe Camp wrapped the file back up and put it to the side of his desk. He stroked his bearded chin and sat for a moment, lost in thought. Then he picked up some photocopies that had come during lunch from the Prince Georges County Dept. of Records and looked at them again. It showed that the Bountin property at the end of Marginal Way where Agent Susan had been taken was owned by OUTLOOK Group Inc., a privately held company who had purchased the land in 1960 and been there ever since. They always paid their property taxes, and reported annual gross income of about three million dollars to the state of Maryland for 1998. Other documents showed that the company had just two officers and owners, Valentine Krogen and Albert Yrjo. Joe didn't recognize Yrjo, but Krogen's name was unsettlingly familiar—he was the author of the CIA memo describing Dr. Strater's scaling-back of OUTLOOK Group after the Bay of Pigs. Presumably, Krogen had been a CIA employee at that point in time. But now?

Joe felt certain that the CIA had more records on OUTLOOK Group than the one dusty old file Carssandra's friend had sent over. Of course, it was hardly surprising for the CIA to be holding back information.

He got up slowly, joints creaking, and left his office. He padded down the hall, stopping by Carssandra's desk to drop off the file and thank her for getting it for him. Then he made his way through the building to the rare-document storage vault, where the Library kept numerous items too fragile or too important to go in the general collection. He rummaged around for some time before he found what he was looking for: a yellowing box about the size of three thick phone books. Hefting it under one arm, he returned to his office, stopping by the bathroom on the way to relieve himself.

Back at his desk, he opened the box. It contained copies of documents that together comprised a very rare copy of an infamous work, known in the intelligence community as the Family Jewels. Inside were all of the CIA's dirty little secrets—at least, all the old ones. Collation of the document was ordered by Director of Central Intelligence James Schlesinger during his brief 1973 tenure, to provide a full internal accounting of all of the CIA's illegal activities up to that time. It was part of a general housecleaning going on then among U.S. intelligence agencies, signaled by the death of FBI director Hoover in 1972 and the Vietnam-fed recognition that times were changing. In retrospect, the disbandment of Delta Green in 1970 could be seen as a tremor of the earthquake to come.

The Family Jewels documents had eventually been made public in the mid-1970s—at least, *most* of them had. Joe had obtained a complete copy from Bill Casey in 1986 when Casey was the head of the CIA, in return for an old favor from their OSS days, best forgotten. By '86, of course, the Family Jewels were well out of date; they were even moreso now.

This set had an index of sorts, a summary labeled "Potential Flap Activities." It listed OUTLOOK Group.

Joe flipped pages and read. The material he expected on OUTLOOK's role in the Bay of Pigs was there, though it suggested that OUTLOOK had been more significant in the CIA's decision-making process than the file had shown. But the interesting part began where the file had stopped.

OUTLOOK Group's life didn't end with the death of Dr. Strater. Although there was no indication of CIA complicity in Strater's death, the CIA did purchase OUTLOOK from Strater's bereaved wife through a front company. At that point, OUTLOOK had only a dozen employees, and was subsisting on dribs and drabs of analysis assignments from the DIA and the NSA. The CIA's front company immediately sold a controlling interest in OUTLOOK to Valentine Krogen, who had recently been "let go due to budget restraints." This was a ruse, allowing Krogen to run OUTLOOK full-time and distance him from his masters.

The CIA's ownership of OUTLOOK was a secret—a big one.

OUTLOOK's role in the Bay of Pigs ensured that no one else in the intelligence community would suspect that the CIA had anything to do with OUTLOOK anymore. But it did. The CIA supplied selected data to OUTLOOK that made their analysis assignments quite accurate and revealing. Under Krogen's charismatic stewardship and with his secret pipeline of solid-gold CIA data, OUTLOOK expanded dramatically. Its clients included numerous U.S. and allied-nation intelligence agencies as well as corporations with global interests, all of whom drank deep at the OUTLOOK well through the latter half of the 1960s.

In return, the CIA got a very good picture of what its colleagues in both the public and private sectors were doing. The nature of their analysis requests and the raw data they supplied to OUTLOOK for processing were of great interest to the CIA, giving it vast quantities of new information the agency did not otherwise have access to, in exchange for releasing a few careful tidbits to make OUTLOOK's analysis the gold standard of the day.

At the time of the Schlesinger report in 1973, OUTLOOK was a successful corporate double agent, teasing information out of its clients (including numerous groups within the State Department, the Defense Department, and the White House, as well as corporations ranging from McDonnell-Douglas to Coca-Cola) and handing it over to the CIA. Schlesinger and his successor, William Colby, clearly considered OUTLOOK an embarrassment.

Unfortunately, that was as far as the Family Jewels went. Albert Yrjo was not mentioned, and indeed OUTLOOK's public records showed that he didn't get involved until 1978, when Krogen sold him a large portion of his stock. Joe was fairly confident that OUTLOOK's double dealings hadn't lasted long past the drafting of the Family Jewels and the housecleaning that followed, so what had they been up to for all the years since then?

Joe tapped his fingers on the desk. He'd taken his research about as far as he could for the day. There were other sources he could consult, but not without risking attention he didn't want.

He stood up and stretched. It was four o'clock, and he felt like knocking off early today. He'd head for home, get some dinner, and prepare to brief his agents later in the evening. It was time for them to do some good old-fashioned legwork.

VIC, ABE, AND STEPHANIE had spent the day bored out of their skulls. None of them dared leave the motel for more than half an hour or so in case Alphonse called, ready for action. So they moped around the room, eventually settling into an afternoon of pay-per-view movies; Vic and Abe had a lively debate over whether to watch *How Stella Got Her Groove Back* (Vic) or *Blade* (Abe), which Stephanie settled in Abe's favor. Vic sulked unconvincingly; when the movie ended and Alphonse still hadn't called, she got her *Stella.*

Alphonse didn't call. Instead, he just showed up at the door around eight o'clock that night, announcing his arrival with the shave-and-a-haircut knock. Abe checked the peephole and then let the old man in.

"It's about time!" Vic complained. "We've been sitting on our thumbs all damn day."

Alphonse glanced at the television and sighed. "These things don't happen swiftly, agent."

"So what's the deal?" Stephanie asked. "Is Susan back? Do we hit them tonight?"

"No, we don't hit them tonight. And no, Agent Susan is not back. She phoned in sick this morning, presumably from the facility." Alphonse took off his coat and took a chair. Abe sat down on the edge of one of the beds next to Vic, while Stephanie sat cross-legged against the headboard of the other. The room was quiet for a moment as Alphonse sat there and regarded them.

"Well, we're all ears," Abe said helpfully.

Alphonse stared at them a few moments longer before he spoke. "The facility where Agent Susan was taken is a private corporation known as OUTLOOK Group. They were a CIA think-tank until the mid-1970s. I haven't found out what they've been up to since then."

"A think tank?" Stephanie asked. "Are they some kind of CIA front?"

"They were. My suspicion is that they aren't anymore. They may still have some old ties, but I'll wager that they're up to something else these days."

"Any ideas?" Vic said.

Alphonse shook his head. "Not really. That's where you come in. You're going to set up a stakeout on OUTLOOK Group. Tomorrow you'll drive to Bountin and visit that office park you stopped in, Agent Tonya. See if they've got some space to lease, and if not there, find some other useful location. You're looking for an office, preferably on an upper floor, with a view of OUTLOOK Group—or at least of Marginal Way. I'll handle the lease. You just find a place. Once we're in, your first priority is photographic. Get shots of every license plate of every vehicle that enters the facility. Draw up a chart of those vehicles. Description, license plate, times of entry and exit, and anything you can tell about the occupants. Feed me that data and I'll run it through the appropriate DMV so we can identify who works there. Pay special attention to service vehicles. Janitors, office supplies, anything. I want you on surveillance for at least a full week, so we can try and establish as much of their routine as possible. You'll get a motel in Bountin so you can work in shifts. Besides the employees, I want photographs of the facility from your office; you may need to get roof access in your building or another one for the best vantage point. Blanket the lot, zoomed in tight. We need to study those photos for outbuildings, wires, service tunnels, satellite dishes, incinerators, anything. I'll get you a thermal video camera that you'll use on a staggered burst schedule, day and night, to see if they're giving off any unusual heat patterns that might indicate heavy machinery; it also might help spot any exterior features that are visually camouflaged. This all make sense to you?"

Abe and Vic glanced at each other. Stephanie sat quietly.

"Well?"

Abe spoke up first. "I've done a bit of this stuff, Alphonse, but not tons."

"It's Greek to me," Vic said sheepishly.

"Ditto," Stephanie chimed in.

Alphonse shook his head. "Yes, I know. You people are good with witnesses and smash & grabs. It's time for you to learn some patience and some tradecraft."

"Can we get some help?" Vic asked. "What about Cell N?"

"Cell N is off this op for the moment. They don't need to spend the next week pulling shifts with you on surveillance detail. I'll bring them back in when the time is right."

Cell T sat quietly, a little sullen. Vic glanced at Alphonse out of the corners of her eyes.

Finally he relented. "But yes, I will get you some help. We have a friendly in Chicago who's a surveillance expert. I'll get him out here for the first couple days, and hopefully you three will pick up the basics pretty quick. Just don't tell him a damn thing about this op."

"Great!" Vic exclaimed. "You won't regret it. We'll dope this out in no time." Abe and Stephanie looked relieved, but said nothing.

Alphonse nodded. "See that you do. There's no room in this organization for cowboys, not anymore. I expect you to master a variety of skills to do the work effectively." He eyed Stephanie and winked at her. "And try not to shoot anyone."

"Yes, sir," she replied deferentially.

He stood up gingerly and slapped his thighs. "Well. That should do it for tonight. First thing in the morning, go find an office. When you've got something good, PGP me and I'll get right on it." He picked up his coat and glanced at the television set again, which was still on—Abe had muted the sound when the knock at the door came. Angela Bassett frolicked on a beach. Alphonse smiled and arched his eyebrows. "Reminds me of a lady friend of mine. Good night, agents."

By the following afternoon, they were set. Vic had found an upstairs office for lease in a building at the entrance to Marginal Way—not the closest building, but the closest with space available. She PGP'd Alphonse immediately, and he wrote back a few hours later that the office was theirs for three months, under the Memphis Private Investigations front they'd gotten started in Tennessee. Alphonse had been busy. As soon as they'd told him about the front last Sunday, he'd filed for a Delaware corporation under that name and got the paperwork fast-tracked. By the time rush-hour traffic was jamming the Capitol Beltway, Cell T had moved to a motel in Bountin and purchased a cheap desk, some chairs, sleeping bags, a small cube fridge, snacks, and other odds and ends for the office. Abe put the desk together while Stephanie got the door keys duped. The office didn't have an active phone line, but they didn't need one—their encrypted cell phones were safer, anyway.

They also didn't have surveillance gear. Greg Mason took care of that.

Greg showed up at the office that evening, as Cell T was dining on Thai take-out. He gave the shave-and-a-haircut knock and Vic opened the door.

"Hi, I'm Greg," he said. "I'm here about the opera tickets."

Vic smiled. "I'm Tonya. Come on in." Greg had two large shipping cases with him, and he brought them into the office behind Vic.

"This is Terry and Thomas," she said, gesturing to her compatriots as they put down their chopsticks.

"Alphabet city, huh? I must be on Sesame Street."

"Yeah," Abe replied. "But we're sponsored by the letters D and G."

Greg smiled and sat the cases down on the floor. "So Alphonse didn't tell me much about this op. He just said you guys were on surveillance detail and didn't know your asses from your elbows."

Stephanie laughed. "Yeah, that's about right. That your gear?"

"And my silk boxers. What's the target?"

Vic nodded towards the large window in the next room. "See that walled compound down there at the end of the road?"

Greg walked over to the doorway. Memphis Private Investigations' new suite consisted of a small windowless foyer and two larger private offices with big picture windows. Cell T had set up in the foyer for privacy—their surveillance had to be a one-way street. Through the window in the nearest office, Greg could see the compound. It sat on a chunk of property maybe ten acres in size, with a twelve-foot stone wall that enclosed the perimeter. A single gated entrance gave way to a road that ran about a hundred yards to a single-story building without a single window. There was a parking lot large enough to hold dozens of cars, and a small road ran from the parking lot around to the back of the building, presumably for deliveries. He didn't see any phone or power lines—probably buried.

"Binoculars?" he asked.

Abe took his collapsible pair from a drawer of the desk and held them out to Greg, who took them and shook his head. "Got these from a gumball machine, huh?" Abe rolled his eyes.

Greg stepped back into the doorway and sighted on the roof. A moment later, he whistled.

"What is it?" Vic asked.

"These guys are serious. They've got a microwave transmitter and a laser transmitter on the roof, plus whatever phone lines they've got in the dirt."

"Transmitters?" Stephanie asked.

"Yeah, probably redundant communications channels, or else heavily encrypted so they can stay off Ma Bell. No satellite dish, though, which is interesting. They don't trust the eyes in the sky, I guess. I bet their receivers are seriously tricked out."

"You've lost me," Vic said.

Greg lowered the binoculars and closed the door. "Microwave and laser transmitters work on line-of-sight. They have to have receivers someplace nearby, probably on a rooftop of one of these office buildings—maybe even this one. The receivers catch the signals and then either shunt them into land lines, feed them into a satellite dish, or redirect them on to another set of receivers further out. The receivers are vulnerable to tampering, so I bet they're tricked out with alarms up the wazoo. If these guys are smart, they manually inspect the receivers on a regular basis to ensure that no one's bypassed their security. If you wanna listen in on what they're sending out, you'll need a specialist. I'm just a camera boy."

Vic shook her head. "That's all we want. Our first priority is building an employee list."

Greg nodded. "So we're on license plate detail. Gotcha." He gave the binoculars back to Abe and started opening his cases while Cell T watched, curious. As he pulled equipment out, he rattled off brief descriptions, clearly proud of his gear.

"Okay, I got three autowinding Nikon N5s with an assortment of zoom & telephoto lenses, a Sony Hi-8 vidcam, a Palm IR-250 thermal-imaging vidcam, a G3 PowerBook with a FireWire PC card for the video, some tripods, and a shitload of film and tapes. This place got running water?"

Stephanie nodded. "There's a bathroom off the other office."

"Sweet. I'll set up the darkroom there. I need to do some shopping, though. I hope you guys got buckage 'cuz I can't put this on my expense report. Fifteen hundred should do."

"We'll talk to Alphonse," Abe said. "This sumptuous meal represents the last of our petty cash."

"Look out, the big geek's quoting *Ghostbusters*!" Greg

exclaimed, then struck a formal pose. "*Quis custodiet ipsos custodes.*"

Vic smirked. "And that means?"

"Who watches the watchmen?" he replied, fiddling with his equipment.

Abe snorted derisively. "*Ecce dorko.*"

The next morning was Saturday. Over breakfast, Cell T and Greg made plans. The bulk of their license-plate surveillance would start on Monday, when they expected the heaviest employee traffic. This weekend Greg would go shopping, set up the darkroom, and check them out on the still cameras. They'd practice on whatever traffic happened along, in the hopes that Greg would have them ready for the work week. Greg also suggested that they scout around to figure out where the receivers were, for future reference.

Alphonse stopped by briefly to greet Greg and drop off a manila envelope full of cash—about three thousand dollars. He looked at Greg pointedly. "No funnybooks." Greg whistled and stared at a wall. Abe cackled.

That afternoon, they piled into their rental sedan and went shopping. Greg had called around to some camera shops in D.C. after breakfast, and found one that he said had its act together. He spent an hour there, picking through the merchandise. He settled on a Beseler 67 enlarger, easel, five-roll developer tank, 8*10 trays, tongs, thermometer, digital timer, two amber safelights, a grain focuser, film dryer, bolts of darkroom cloth, T-Max developer for the film, Dektol for the paper, stopbath, fixer, hypo, and three boxes of variable-contrast rc paper. He also got another bushel of film, all of it Kodak T-Max P3200, a multi-speed black-and-white film suited to rapid-fire, high-detail surveillance use. All told, they spent almost two grand.

Moving Greg's purchases to the office took two trips. The MPI suite's bathroom was much too small to serve as the entire darkroom, so he'd use the office it was connected to, as well. Whenever it was darkroom time, they'd have to black out the big window and the door in that room. Abe suggested they do this only at night, since the blacked-out window might look suspicious from the street. Greg glanced at Vic archly: "Look—it's trying to think." Abe looked at Stephanie for sympathy, but she was too busy cracking up.

Greg was both tall and scrawny. Next to Abe, he somehow looked like Rumpelstiltskin. He had long brown hair in a ponytail and Buddy Holly glasses, and thus far had showed a predilection for retro bowling shirts, khakis, and dingy canvas basketball shoes. He spoke with a Chicago accent—not too thick, but noticeable—and had an infectious, mocking laugh that suggested everyone was an idiot except for Greg and those in his circle. In the case of Cell T, his circle extended only to Vic and Stephanie, a point that was not lost on Abe. Abe tagged him as a horndog on the make, his technique as old as time: first, cut down the competition. Unfortunately for Abe, Greg had a wit as quick as a shutter.

The rest of the weekend passed quickly. Greg got his darkroom set up and led the Cell in camera lessons. By Sunday night, they were doing a passable job of catching license plates. Tomorrow morning the real work would begin.

MONDAY'S "REAL WORK" HAD mixed results. Three hundred vehicles turned onto Marginal Way over the course of the day, about fifty of whom went to OUTLOOK; the rest were divided among a handful of office parks. Between Cell T and Greg they shot more than four hundred pictures, the quantity owing largely to some heavy-handed operation of the speed-winders by the neophytes. Since they only had three cameras running, they took turns, with the extra Cell member loading film; Greg stayed on his camera nonstop. He worked in the darkroom until very late that night running contact sheets, which they then pored over. Greg scored fifteen useable license plate shots from his rolls; Cell T totaled a collective twelve, from which they had six overlaps with Greg's. Stephanie created a multi-page grid in a spiral-bound notebook and worked until the wee hours transcribing as much information as she could from the contact sheets about the makes of cars, while Greg made fast, grainy prints of the best license-plate candidates. Vic and Abe went back to the motel for some shut-eye.

Tuesday they fared better, despite some snow flurries. Three hundred pictures got them forty license plates, of which twelve were new. They had thirty-three now, plus better makes on a lot of the cars and some useful information on the number, gender, and race of the occupants. Greg was supposed to leave Tuesday night, but he opted to stay on. "You guys are hopeless," was his only explanation.

Wednesday through Thursday were a blur. The office reeked of darkroom chemicals, and Greg was running ragged. He visited a circuit of photo shops and had large prints made of everything they had to date, which Stephanie inspected and logged in the notebook. The work of cross-referencing all the cars, license plates, and occupants to improve her data was exhausting.

Friday morning they assembled in the office before rush hour to check the results. Stephanie's book had forty-six rock-solid license plates and car makes, with another dozen cars made but not plated. She had decent occupant profiles for thirty of the plated cars and six of the unplated ones. When the traffic hit, Stephanie played spotter, pointing out unplated cars she recognized from her book so the others could triple-dog them on the cameras. It was Stephanie who first noticed the truck.

It was a private waste-hauler, different from the utility trucks that came through the neighborhood to pick up the regular garbage on Wednesday. The logo read "Stoli Bros. Medical," and it headed straight to OUTLOOK, staying there twenty minutes. Stephanie made sure they got plenty of shots of the truck. In her job with the EPA she'd become familiar with the intricacies of the medical waste-disposal industry. If OUTLOOK had medical waste, it meant they should have a sheaf of permits and contracts on file; it also suggested that OUTLOOK had, indeed, left its think-tank days behind.

They ran a final barrage of shots during the evening rush-hour exodus. By three o'clock Saturday morning, she and Greg had filled out the book: sixty-two vehicles made, plated, and with at least partial occupant notes, compiled and cross-checked while Abe and Vic puttered and made hot-coffee runs. Before they hit the sack, all four of them pored over Stephanie's meticulous notebook, dozens of photos cropped and glued into the pages within grids of lines and notes. Greg pronounced them honorary Peeping Tom Perv-o's, and for once he and Abe laughed with each other, rather than at each other. They bombed back to the motel and sat up until dawn, trading shots of bourbon and laughing hysterically, winding down from the week. When they finally crashed, they stayed down until two o'clock Saturday afternoon.

Alphonse came by that evening, after the team was cleaned up and fed. He went through the book, nodding pleasantly as they rattled off their observations and anecdotes. Greg played the staggered thermal videos he'd had running on a timer, and Stephanie pointed out the one piece of useful data they contained: very late on Thursday night, there was a protracted discharge of heavy smoke from a vent at the rear of the building, probably coming out of an incinerator. The only tasks remaining were the photographic survey of the facility and locating the two receivers, neither of which the frazzled group had managed to accomplish during the week. They did both of these on a drizzly gray Sunday, after Alphonse had taken the notebook and said he'd be in touch when he had results.

The survey brought few surprises. They made the two building entrances, and got good shots of the transmitters and other rooftop features. The stone walls had coils of concertina wire hanging just inside and below the top, making a climb difficult. The grounds were dotted with trees and even some aging picnic tables, but there were no other discernible structures or features of interest. The photos did show that the two security booths on either side of the gated entrance had what appeared to be thick, bulletproof glass and "murder holes"—slots through which weapons could be fired at attackers. There were no guards roaming the grounds, but they caught one guard taking a smoke break outside the delivery entrance, armed with what Abe recognized as a Heckler & Koch MP5 submachine gun, not exactly standard security-guard issue. They also made a small patch on the guards' shoulders that identified them as employees of a security company named Wackenhut. Greg took the photos and sketched out a somewhat accurate map of the compound, noting features such as clusters of trees and the picnic tables.

As for the receivers, they were mounted on the rooftops of

two different office buildings, blocks apart but still in line-of-sight with the facility. Greg spotted them using Abe's binoculars, since he was the only one who knew what to look for. They considered sneaking up to take a closer look, but ruled that out—they didn't know what security measures OUTLOOK might have in place on the receivers.

Greg was booked on a red-eye flight to Chicago late Sunday night. The team sat up again, drinking and laughing, until the taxi came. Before leaving, Greg attempted to get Vic and Stephanie's phone numbers—and real names—in private, turning on the charm to each in turn. Both were amused but declined, and shared this information with each other shortly after Greg's taxi came. To Abe's horror, they spent a couple minutes trying to sort out who Greg had asked first; the results were inconclusive.

Cell T, alone again, hit the sack. When they rose groggy in the morning, they once more had nothing to do but wait.

MONDAY MOVED ALONG. SINCE action was not imminent, Stephanie suggested that they find a gun range and blow off some steam. Vic and Abe agreed readily, and they found a facility near Andrews Air Force Base that sounded promising. They ended up making a day of it. The range had a variety of firearms available for use, so once the trio had finished squeezing off a couple hundred rounds from their own handguns, they worked their way through the rentals: a Desert Eagle, a Ruger Super Redhawk, an FN FAL, and a few others. Abe, being an FBI field agent up against a park ranger and an EPA scientist, expected to easily ace his companions, but Stephanie handed him his ass on a silver platter. When he boggled at the results of her latest paper target, she smiled and shrugged. "Practice," she said. Vic trailed Abe substantially, but both were well below

Stephanie's results.

After leaving the range that evening, they retired to a bar that turned out to be lounge central for the Andrews flyboys, many of whom gave Vic and Stephanie the once-over—and, in some cases, the thrice-over. The two received several dance invitations from extremely polite Air Force personnel; Abe had made a guy by the bar as a captain keeping an eye on his boys, which perhaps explained their unusually gentlemanly behavior. Stephanie danced briefly with two of the men, but Vic demurred graciously. "My husband," she nodded towards Abe, "would get jealous." Abe grinned and put his arm around Vic, who made a show of scooting closer and batting her eyelashes at him while the flyboys made apologetic exits.

"Rug muncher," Abe whispered.

"Starfucker," Vic replied.

ALPHONSE FINALLY PGP'D THEM on Tuesday afternoon, scheduling a meeting for that evening. It couldn't come soon enough for Stephanie.

She had a hunch. That medical-waste disposal truck and the incinerator discharge had gotten her curious, and she'd made a few phone calls on Tuesday morning while they were killing time. She didn't discuss the hunch with Vic and Abe, brushing off their questioning looks.

Tuesday evening, Alphonse showed up at their motel room. The briefing began. Alphonse looked tired.

"I've got a tentative employee list for OUTLOOK, based on your surveillance work. A lot of them are pretty mundane. Valentine Krogen is still there—that was his gold BMW you spotted. Presumably he's running the place. The big news is that about half the personnel are medical. Doctors, nurses, pharmacists.

They're straight medical private-sector, as far as I could find. None of the people you made had government backgrounds, at least not on casual inspection. And besides Krogen, there isn't a single political scientist or academic among them. I guess they're out of the think-tank business."

"What about the security guards?" Abe asked. "Saturday we made them as Wackenhut personnel."

Alphonse nodded grimly. "Yeah, I found that, too. Something's rotten in Denmark."

"Huh?" Vic said.

"Thomas, what do you know about Wackenhut?"

Abe thought for a moment. "Well, they have a lot of government contracts. The founder was old FBI, one of Hoover's boys way back when. I think they run some prisons in Australia, maybe here, too. They're pretty big."

"That's putting it mildly." Alphonse shook his head. "Wackenhut is bad news. The reason you don't hear much about cowboy operations like Iran-Contra is because they're mostly handled by the private sector these days. Goes back to the Pinkertons, really, though the CIA and the FBI pulled a lot of dirty tricks on their own for a while in the '50s and '60s. Feeling their oats I guess. Anyway, Wackenhut guards nuclear power plants for the Atomic Energy Commission, and they do a lot of perimeter security for the military. Whenever you see those UFO nutjobs getting chased off Area 51 by the guys in white Broncos, that's Wackenhut at work."

"So?" Stephanie asked.

"Companies like Wackenhut are tight with the intelligence community. A lot of them get started by former federal personnel whose political agendas got them in trouble. So they go private, call on their contacts, and do cowboy dirty-tricks work that they couldn't get authority for when they were in the government. The CIA has used Wackenhut as cover for their own personnel at times—agents get contracts as security guards under fake names to provide deniability."

"You think those guards are CIA?" Abe asked.

"Maybe, given Krogen's background. But they could be anyone. A ten spot says they aren't legit Wackenhut hires, though."

Vic looked pensive. "Do you know anybody at Wackenhut? Could you find out?"

Alphonse shook his head ruefully. "I can't go near those people." He sighed. "We were tight with Wackenhut back in the '60s, before the shutdown. Fellow travelers, really. When we went underground in '70, Reggie Fairfield started using them for a lot of ancillary DG work. They never knew what we were really all about. Just thought we were a bunch of frothing Goldwater cowboys out to save the world from Communism. Reggie even served on their board of directors for a few years in the mid-'70s. Then he had some sort of falling-out with them. He didn't tell us the details; he always kept that stuff pretty compartmentalized. Reggie was good at that." He laughed. "Hell, I'm still drawing a pension from Wackenhut under one of my aliases. If you ever wondered where we get our funding from, well, we've juggled a lot of books in our time."

Abe looked incredulous. "Damn."

"There's a lot of water gone under Delta Green's bridge, agents. Most of it doesn't smell too good."

"So what does this mean?" Vic asked. "What's OUTLOOK Group up to?"

"That I don't know, but I can guess. Obviously, they're tied in with the people responsible for what's happened to Cell

S. OUTLOOK and Groversville are just two of their operations. Based on what we learned from Groversville and the personnel list we've assembled, I'd bet that OUTLOOK is conducting medical research for them, probably involving the neo-tissue and God knows what else. There's another thing, too, though I'm not sure how it fits into this. Besides Krogen, OUTLOOK's other owner is someone named Albert Yrjo—Dr. Albert Yrjo, actually. He never turned up in your surveillance photos. I found a book he wrote in the Library of Congress: *The Group Dynamic in a Stress Environment,* from 1966. I've only skimmed it, but it looks like Dr. Yrjo was doing psychological research at NYU, running traumatic simulations to see how people would react. Nasty stuff. How he managed to segue into an ex-CIA think tank that's gone into medical experimentation . . . well, it's not a pretty picture. I'd surmise they're in MKULTRA territory. Brainwashing, programming, and worse."

"Who the hell are these people, Alphonse?" Stephanie asked. "Who's running this show?"

Alphonse sat quietly for a few moments. "They're a lot like us. They know things other people don't know. But their angle is different. It's exploitive. Where we see shadows, they see stealth technology. And unlike us, they've never been shut down."

"It's them, isn't it?" Vic asked. "The ones who killed Fairfield."

Alphonse nodded. "Reggie pushed too hard. They pushed back."

"But that's what we're doing now," Stephanie said. "We're pushing."

"Yes. But so far, we're still within the rules of engagement."

"The *what*?" Abe said. "We have *rules* with these people?"

"Unspoken ones, but yes. They've got dirt on us, but they know we've got dirt on them, too. So we've got a sort of truce. For the most part, our respective agendas rarely overlap. They're very tightly focused."

"What about now?"

"Now? Well, they made the first move. They took Cell S. That gives us certain leeway—they expect us to respond, and they're willing to take the hit we deliver if it still furthers their goals. In this case, I think that goal is Groversville—Promise, I mean. Whatever they're up to there, they want us to stay clear."

"So?" Vic said. "What do we do?"

"We stay the hell out of Promise, that's what we do. That's why I yanked you out of there. But we can still go after our people. That much, I think, they'll be willing to tolerate. And in tolerating us that far, we'll get a little closer, find out a few things—they will, too, of course. Maybe we can teach them a small lesson, discourage them from pulling this kind of crap on us again. But if we push too hard, if we break the rules of engagement, there's no telling what will happen." He looked at each of them. "We're on very dangerous ground, here, agents. We have to be careful."

The room was quiet. Abe pulled out the bottle of bourbon and began passing plastic cups around. Alphonse lit a cigarette and sipped at his drink.

Vic broke the silence. "So we can still go after OUTLOOK. That's where they took Susan and probably Shasta, and that makes it fair game."

Alphonse nodded. "I'd say so."

"So what's the next step?"

"Our only real option is some sort of raid. We have to hit them very fast, find our people, and get the hell out. But that means we need a lot of manpower, and that's not easily done. Ideally, we'd pull a Waco on them—sic somebody like the ATF on OUTLOOK, use them as cover to get inside and do the job, and let them take the fallout. The trick is keeping it low-profile until we're ready to strike. With their connections, they could get wind of a major investigation and get it quashed."

"Then we've got them," Stephanie said. "We can nail them to the wall."

"How?" Alphonse asked, leaning forward in his chair.

"They're doing medical work. We know that from the personnel. We made that medical-waste truck that came through, and I'm betting that discharge we caught on the thermal is them incinerating medical waste that they can't trust to the truck company. I made some calls this morning, and OUTLOOK doesn't have permit one. They don't have any authority to perform medical procedures, dispense drugs, nothing. Between the EPA and OSHA, we can get a warrant from Justice. We could bring the DEA in on it, too, since they probably have controlled drugs on the property, but that's too high-profile. I can contain it to just my guys and OSHA, make it look like a routine violation case, and we'll have Deputy U.S. Marshals kicking down their doors before they know what hit them."

Alphonse cackled. "The EPA and OSHA. Hell, that's the stuff! Keep it beneath their radar, direct your people away from OUTLOOK's CIA roots, and we'll catch them with their pants down."

"Damn," Vic said, looking admiringly at Stephanie. "I knew there was a reason we brought you along."

Stephanie grinned. "It'll work. I know it'll work. But if we've got somebody at Justice, it'll go smoother. Do we?"

"Yeah. We've got a friendly over there who's helped us out before—a deputy U.S. attorney. Funnel it through her and she can keep a lid on it until it's showtime. She'll also know the right judge to sign the warrant. And no, before you ask, we don't have any judges in our pockets."

"Then it's settled," Stephanie said.

Alphonse nodded. "But this is going to take a couple weeks to set up, even on a fast track. Thomas, Tonya, I want you two to go home and get back on the job. We can't keep you out here for this."

Vic got stern. "Damn it, Alphonse, I want a piece of this!" Abe nodded in agreement.

"You'll get it, agent, but not yet. When it's time for the raid we'll bring you back in. You three and Cell N will be our reps on the raid. It'll be up to you to find Susan and Shasta and get them out of there, along with whatever files you can lay your hands on." The pair looked mollified.

"Terry, you're back at work in the morning, too. Play this as an anonymous informant who's ratting out OUTLOOK from the inside. Maybe they're doing illegal organ transplants, or unlicensed cancer therapy. No bioweapons, though. This needs to be as boring as you can make it."

Stephanie nodded. "No problem. I've prosecuted a couple cases like this before, actually."

"All right, then. You two get to the airport and take the next flights home. Terry, let's work out some details and get the story straight. The clock is ticking."

The next two weeks were busy ones for Stephanie. She and Alphonse settled on the illegal organ-transplant scenario, running with the idea that OUTLOOK was buying organs from Mexico and putting them into rich old alcoholics and other well-heeled people who didn't like the risk and the wait of the official transplant channels. Stephanie's "anonymous informant" dropped her the info, and she took it to her superiors. They repeated some of Cell T's surveillance work, making the medical personnel, the waste-disposal company, and the incinerator. EPA scientists took clandestine air samples during the burn periods and found traces of biological matter and pharmaceuticals. EPA researchers checked out Stoli Bros. Medical Waste and found that while they had contracts with a number of area hospitals, they didn't list OUTLOOK as one of their clients. EPA investigators went over the hospitals' paperwork and found that Stoli was disposing of more medical waste than they were picking up—officially, at least. Stephanie called a friend at OSHA and got them involved. An FBI liaison tied Stoli Bros. to one of the five families of the East Coast mafia; the mafia ran a number of garbage-disposal companies, especially in New York, and since the early '90s they'd begun diversifying into the lucrative and growing medical-disposal industry. With the FBI's help, the EPA and OSHA co-opted Stoli Bros. into the investigation. The head of Stoli agreed to testify against OUTLOOK in exchange for immunity for his company—and its owners in New York, whom he was clearly in fear of. Stoli also turned over OUTLOOK's waste from a run in the second week of the investigation, which the EPA and OSHA examined; it confirmed the presence of illegal surgical procedures inside OUTLOOK. Stephanie pushed hard and had her evidence in record time, though it certainly helped that her case was pretty much made before the investigation even started. She also kept tight control on research into OUTLOOK's personnel and history, keeping her colleagues busy with surveillance, physical evidence, and the rather colorful Stoli connection, while she doctored her corporate-research reports to hide any trace of the CIA's involvement. Finally, she took the case to DG's friendly at the Department of Justice and got the warrant started—but just barely, as a major snowstorm hit D.C. and shut down government offices for half a day just after she got things started at Justice. Due process prevailed over the elements, however, and the raid was set for Saturday morning, when the presence of OUTLOOK personnel should be at a minimum. The U.S. Marshals' Special Operations Group would serve the warrant with a dozen deputy marshals in tactical gear, while Stephanie supplied a dozen investigators—including Vic, Abe, and Agent Nancy, who would pose as FBI and DEA reps along for the ride; the rest would be legit EPA and OSHA personnel. Agents Nick and Nolan would miss the raid. They were going to be busy destroying the two microwave and laser receivers OUTLOOK had on nearby buildings. The marshals would take care of the phone lines with the help of the phone company.

A week into the official investigation, Alphonse brought Stephanie some news. Agent Susan had resigned from the ONI—again communicating by fax. She hadn't been seen since they observed her entering OUTLOOK. Much like Shasta, she'd simply gone away. Unlike Shasta, she resigned, staving off any immediate official investigation.

In the evenings, when she wasn't conferring with Alphonse, Stephanie sat in her apartment petting Clotho and thinking. She was sure that this little operation would mark the end of her career with the EPA—Alphonse had warned her that the fallout was likely to be severe. His best-guess scenario was that the CIA or another agency would claim ownership of OUTLOOK and kill the raid-in-progress on national-security grounds. They might have an hour of free access, or more if they succeeded in blocking all the communications lines out of the facility, but soon enough the word would come down and the raid would be cut short. They'd have to move fast to find Susan and Shasta. In the aftermath, Stephanie would almost certainly take the fall for what would be portrayed as a massive cock-up, and her doctored reports on OUTLOOK might well be exposed. The EPA would take it in the shorts, and they'd throw her to the wolves. Alphonse said that if push came to shove, Delta Green would try to extract her and get her a new identity someplace else—but he couldn't make any promises. Events might spiral beyond their ability to modulate.

Stephanie didn't give a damn. Her job, her mundane life, these things no longer mattered. They hadn't mattered for months, maybe years. But Delta Green was different. There were people in trouble, people who desperately needed her and all the courage and talent she could bring to bear. People she cared about. She would not let them down, no matter the cost. This would be her finest hour.

Vic spent the two weeks bored out of her gourd. She was back at Oly Park, walking the trails, helping campers, supervising foresters. She didn't even go to Seattle for the weekend, which prompted a worried call from Sue. Vic had effectively ceded control of the Cell to Stephanie, given the circumstances, and her inactivity drove her up the wall. She spent her free time in her apartment, playing guitar and reading, anything to make the time go faster. She resisted contacting Alphonse, or Stephanie, or Abe. She cleaned her gun. She swept the floors. She vacuumed the curtains. She bought jigsaw puzzles and threw them away. She drank vodka to get to sleep. She waited.

Abe was back at the FBI office in Milwaukee, picking up his case-load from the agents who'd taken it over while he was "consulting with the DEA." Looking over his current projects, Abe came to the conclusion that they collectively inhabited Shit City, U.S.A., and he had to force himself to maintain any interest or focus on the work. He played basketball every evening when he left the office, and spent as little time at home as he could. Carol gave him funny looks and started arguments he refused to finish. He ignored her and read bedtime stories to Eric.

On Saturday, about a week after he returned, he went to the gym for more basketball. The game went poorly, and he left in a foul temper.

Phenomen-X was waiting for him in the parking lot.

It took him a moment to recognize them. He spotted the video camera right off, of course, but he thought they were local journalists. He'd been on Milwaukee TV a few times in the course of his job. Then he recognized the short brunette from Promise, and then the two guys with her, and then his stomach lurched like he was in a falling elevator.

He'd been made.

"Agent Mannen," the young woman called pleasantly as the old fart ran the camera and the balding guy with the bifocals stood behind them with his arms folded, smiling. "We'd like to have a word with you."

Abe jogged down the steps to where the trio were waiting for him in front of his car. He got right up in the small woman's face, leaning over her. "Fuck off," he spat.

The woman was unperturbed. "Just a few questions for our audience. Who do you work for, Agent Mannen?"

"I work for the F–B–fucking–I."

"We know that, Agent Mannen. We mean, who do you *really* work for? Like when you're in Tennessee, for example?"

"That's none of your goddamn business. I'm a federal law-enforcement agent and I cannot discuss current investigations with the press. Or with you people."

"Your superiors believed you were consulting with the DEA, Agent Mannen. I didn't notice any DEA agents in Tennessee."

"That just means they were doing their job, lady."

"Oh, were those DEA agents you were with when you drew your guns on us? Those two attractive young women you shared a single motel room with in Knoxville? Does Carol know about your little girlfriends, Agent Mannen?"

"You leave my family alone!" Abe thundered.

"Leave your family alone? But that's *your* specialty, isn't it?"

Abe snapped. He gave the woman a roundhouse slap that drove her against his car. She folded to the ground. The other two froze in shock. Abe ripped the camera off the old fart's shoulder and hurled it to the pavement. People on the sidewalk nearby were staring in horror. The young woman started yelling for help, her nose gushing blood. Abe shouldered past the trio and got into his car, his face an angry red, sweat pouring off his brow. The two men helped the woman up, and the balding one called out: "Your ass is ours, you MiB fuck! You tell the group we want some answers and we want them now!" Abe burned rubber and sped out of the parking lot.

The Milwaukee Police Department arrested Special Agent Abraham Mannen at his home three hours later.

It was Friday night. The raid was set for eight o'clock tomorrow morning. Stephanie sat in MPI's office in Bountin with Alphonse and Cell N, going over the details one more time. Vic showed up, smiling and jumpy, fresh from the airport taxi. The roads had largely cleared since the snowstorm and flights were once again on track at Ronald Reagan National Airport, though it was still chilly and wet outside.

"We good to go?" Vic asked as she came through the door.

"All set," Stephanie replied cheerfully. "The warrant was signed at five P.M. today. The marshals are assembling."

"Fuckin'-A. Here comes the cavalry!"

Alphonse picked Abe up at the airport five hours after Vic arrived. He'd booked Abe onto a succession of roundabout flights under a false identity so the Milwaukee authorities wouldn't realize he'd left town. They walked to the rental car in silence. Alphonse didn't speak until they were on the road.

"Let's hear it."

Abe sighed and ran his fingers through his hair. "I'm out on bond. The arraignment's in two weeks. I'm under an administrative suspension from the FBI pending an investigation. My wife is filing for divorce and she wants sole custody. That about cover it?"

"I don't suppose you have any idea how they made you?"

"Yeah, I figured it out. When we saw them in Promise, that mouthy reporter shoved a tape recorder in my face. I destroyed the tape. They must've gotten my prints off the recorder, had someone run them and my FBI file came up."

"Idiot."

"Yeah, tell me about it."

"I spoke with Carincola, the producer. They're willing to drop the assault charge. They're also willing to not file a civil suit against you and the FBI, which they're otherwise contemplating. In exchange, they want information."

"What information?"

Alphonse chuckled coldly. " 'The truth,' he said. Whatever

the hell that's supposed to be."

"What are you going to give them?"

"I'm working on that. Right now this raid is our first priority. We're at T minus seven hours."

"Thanks for letting me come."

"We need you. I'm not willing to involve any more of our personnel in this situation. It's too big and too dangerous as it is. If you're going to be compromised anyway, I want to squeeze as much utility out of you as I can before it's too late."

"Thanks a lot."

"Spare me the goddamn sarcasm. You've put us in jeopardy. I back my people up in the line of duty, but you get zero sympathy from me for this cowboy bullshit. I'll help you insofar as it helps Delta Green, but the rest of the mess you've made is yours to clean up."

"Do the others know?"

"No, and you're not going to tell them."

"Compartmentalized," Abe said bitterly. "Got it."

"Damn straight. I'm not going to let you drag your partners into the shitstorm you've unleashed."

They were quiet for a few minutes. The lights of Washington blazed in the night sky all around them as they drove towards Bountin. Alphonse finally broke the silence.

"I'm very disappointed in you, Abraham."

EIGHT O'CLOCK SATURDAY MORNING. Showtime. Stephanie, wearing body armor, spoke into a radio and gave the order to get moving. She was standing upright in the back of a big black panel van the U.S. Marshals had brought, surrounded by six deputy marshals in the SOG. They wore full tac gear and carried M16A2s. The van lurched forward and began driving down

Marginal Way.

Behind Stephanie's lead van there were two more vans containing the rest of the raid party: six more SOG deputy marshals, five EPA investigators, four OSHA investigators, Abe, Vic, and Agent Nancy falsely repping the FBI and DEA, and two Prince Georges County Deputy Sheriffs along so the task force could make nice with the locals. Behind the third van was a huge motor home chock full of Electronic Counter-Measures gear that Alphonse's friendly at Justice had managed to requisition; the independent counsel wasn't using it this weekend. They sped down Marginal Way, making a straight line for the front gate of OUTLOOK Group. As they neared, Stephanie spoke into the radio again.

"Approaching target. Sandman One, Sandman Two, green light, repeat, green light."

Agents Nick and Nolan were inside two different office buildings elsewhere in town, waiting inside stairwells. On Stephanie's signal they each emerged onto the roofs of their respective buildings wielding sledgehammers. Nick reached the microwave receiver perched on an air vent just as Nolan reached the laser receiver mounted on the corner of the roof. Both raised their sledges and brought them down in cruel arcs, smashing the equipment.

"Sandman Three, green light, repeat, green light."

A third deputy sheriff was at an open phone company junction box two blocks away with two company engineers. He nodded at them and they flipped several switches. OUTLOOK's phone lines were deactivated.

"All units, radio silence begins now. You know the drill. Sandman Four, green light, repeat, green light."

In the ECM motor home, a Justice Department technician

started turning his equipment on. Within moments, every form of broadcast signal within a half-mile went to static—car radios, headsets, walkie-talkies, cell phones, and so forth, all neutralized. The technician smiled and ate a butter cookie.

The task force would not be able to communicate except in person. But in return, Stephanie hoped that it would buy them time inside OUTLOOK before the hammer came down.

They were nearing the gate. Stephanie could see the two khaki-clad guards in the booths swapping looks and picking up telephones. A vicious smile stole across her features.

"Eat shit, assholes," she muttered under her breath.

The ECM motor home came to a halt. It didn't need to be any closer. The three vans pulled up to the entrance in a line and stopped.

"Go go go!" Stephanie shouted. The back doors flew open and four marshals in tac gear piled out, followed by Stephanie. Two marshals ran for the left guard booth and two ran for the right. Stephanie on a bullhorn, breathless: "U.S. MARSHALS WE HAVE A FEDERAL SEARCH WARRANT DROP YOUR WEAPONS AND OPEN THE GATE NOW!"

At each booth, a marshal shoved a copy of the warrant against the bulletproof glass while the other poked the end of his rifle through the murder hole. The two guards stood, curiously unruffled, and did nothing.

Stephanie on the bullhorn, catching her breath: "I REPEAT, U.S. MARSHALS, WE HAVE A FEDERAL SEARCH WARRANT. DROP YOUR WEAPONS AND OPEN THE GATE NOW."

One of the guards spoke up, his voice eerily calm through the crackling speaker mounted next to his booth. "I have to talk to my superior before I can comply. The phone isn't working."

The marshal in front of him thumped his fist against the glass. "*I'm* your goddamn superior, son, and you will comply with this warrant or we will take you into custody for contempt of a federal judge and obstruction of justice and then we'll ram your gate down anyway."

The two guards looked at each other again, and one shrugged. They both opened the doors to their booths and tossed out H&K MP5s and Ruger M117 .38 revolvers. The marshals boggled. One guard pressed a button and the gate began to glide open. The marshals picked up the weapons and waved the guards out, then handed them over to the deputy sheriffs who had by now emerged from the second van. Four sheriff's prowlers came around the corner, lights and sirens suddenly blaring, and blocked off the end of the road behind the ECM motor home. They'd be policing up any detainees and keeping the entrance secure.

"LET'S GO!" Stephanie bellowed through the bullhorn. She and the four marshals piled back into the lead van and all three vehicles sped through the gate. They covered the hundred yards to the front door of OUTLOOK Group Inc. in moments.

All twelve marshals came out of the vans at a run and blazed forward. They faced a large metal door with a mail slot and a small window at eye level. Four marshals gathered at the door and then one pulled it open, stepping back so the other three could enter. The lead one yelled: "U.S. MARSHALS! WE HAVE A SEARCH WARRANT!" The building swallowed them up.

Stephanie led the investigative team, all in body armor, and they hurried up behind the rest of the marshals who were already spilling inside. The team followed.

Inside was a small lobby, appointed with prints of country scenes and a large creeping ivy plant that spiraled up one wall, across the ceiling, and down the other side. A matronly woman was standing up behind a desk on the wall opposite the door, holding her empty hands gingerly in front of her. On top of the desk sat an old Selectric typewriter and a fashion magazine. Two guards in khaki stood off to one side with their hands in the air, Ruger revolvers lying on the floor at their feet. They seemed relaxed. The marshals were already dispersing down two hallways. Two marshals remained with the guards, hustling them over to a wall out of the way. They would move all three staffers outside to the deputies once the lobby was cleared.

Stephanie took five investigators with her down one hallway behind the marshals. Another EPA inspector led the rest down the other way. Abe was with Stephanie. Vic and Nancy went with the second team.

The marshals were moving down the halls, checking one room at a time. No one was inside. Stephanie's team checked out the rooms once they were clear: two offices, a supply closet, a small, disorderly library with three desks and chairs, a sterile-looking conference room. They kept moving.

The hall made a turn and came to an end at a door. Two marshals stood guard while three more went inside. Stephanie's team followed them.

They'd entered a plush office. A massive executive desk stood at one end, piled with magazines. The rest of the room contained a small conference table, some chairs, three televisions and VCRs, more country prints, and a desktop computer and printer. A small humidor rested on a corner of the desk. There was another door opposite the one they'd entered, and the marshals were already moving through.

Stephanie directed a lady from OSHA towards the computer, and pointed Abe at the audio/video cabinet where she noticed stacks of tapes. As the remaining two marshals entered and followed their companions, Stephanie turned her attention to the desk. The magazines all appeared to be assorted political-science journals of recent vintage. The labels were addressed to Valentine Krogen, OUTLOOK Group Inc. She flipped open the humidor and found a layer of cigars concealing run-of-the-mill pornographic magazines. Abe pawed through the videotapes, none of which were marked. He popped one into a VCR and got it running. Two blond women with obvious breast implants were having sex with a strikingly hung man in a skull-tight crew cut. It was obviously a porno film. Abe snorted. "Hairless fuck-ape," he muttered, then more loudly: "We got porn!" Two of the investigators laughed.

One of the marshals stepped back through the inner door. "Ms. Park, you should see this." Stephanie hurried forward, followed closely by Abe, who left the video running.

The door led to a very large room. At one time it had been some sort of conference room. There was a massive table, lots of chairs, chalk boards on the walls, and an old overhead projector shoved in a corner. Now, however, it was full of magazines. They were more political-science journals like Stephanie had seen on the desk. But there were hundreds—no, *thousands* of them, piled in haphazard stacks on the floor and table. Some of the stacks reached almost to the ceiling and were supported by the walls and by other adjacent stacks. The room was dusty. Stephanie walked towards the back of the room and picked up a random magazine; it was dated Summer 1961. There was no obvious order to the stacks, except that recent magazines were closer to the door. In the back half of the room there was only enough space between the stacks for one person to walk sideways. It reminded Stephanie of the occasional news reports of little old ladies with sixty cats and a house full of decades-old daily papers, moldering and occasionally toppling fatally over on their owner.

"Dead end," Stephanie called out to her team. "Let's backtrack." She left one marshal behind with the OSHA investigator who was still examining the computer. Then she hurried back into the hallway with four marshals, Abe, and three other investigators. Whatever secrets OUTLOOK might possess, Stephanie figured that Vic and Nancy would find them first. She cursed under her breath and double-timed it back with the others.

IN THE OTHER HALL, the second team found bathrooms, a storeroom with office supplies and a percolating coffeemaker, and a small exercise room with very up-to-date equipment. Rounding the far corner, they came to a stairwell heading down below ground. Another guard stood there, pointing his Ruger straight at them.

"Halt!" he yelled. The marshals froze, M-16s pointing at the guard. The lead marshal spoke up: "We're U.S. Marshals executing a federal search warrant. Lay down your weapon and stand aside."

The guard stood firm, slowly shifting his aim to the lead marshal. "No. This is a national-security facility and you may not progress without authorization from my superiors."

"I don't see your superiors here, son, but I do see this search warrant and you *will* comply or we will place you under arrest for contempt of a federal judge and obstructing justice. If what you say is true, we'll get it sorted out. But right now, you are threatening the lives of federal officers executing a federal warrant and if we have to, we will use deadly force. Five on one, son. Make the smart play."

The guard and the marshal locked eyes. Vic, Nancy, and the rest of the investigative team stood back around the corner, listening intently to the tense exchange.

Seconds ticked by. The marshal held the guard's gaze and nodded slowly, affirming his intent.

The guard lowered his weapon. "Okay, cowboy. It's your funeral, not mine." He placed the Ruger on the floor and raised his hands. Two marshals rushed forward and took him by the arms, then grabbed the weapon and hustled the guard back down the hall. "All clear," the lead marshal called. The investigative team spun around the corner and saw the stairwell. "After you," the lead EPA rep said. The marshal nodded and led his two partners down the stairs.

Stephanie's team arrived in the lobby just as the two marshals who had removed the first three staffers re-entered from outside, having handed their detainees over to the deputies. There was some sort of commotion down the other hallway, and then two marshals double-timed towards the lobby escorting another guard. Stephanie addressed the pair that had just come back in: "With us!" Then the group scurried down the hall, sidling past the latest detainee and his captors.

At the end of the hall they found the second investigative team waiting at the top of the stairs. The lead rep, a middle-aged co-worker of Stephanie's named Archie Sanders, nodded forward. "They just went down. We're waiting for the all-clear." Stephanie turned to look at the six marshals she'd brought, but they were already hustling down the stairs after their colleagues. Vic caught her eye. "So far, so good."

The explosion shook the building like a rag doll.

A blast of wind and smoke blew up the stairs, engulfing the marshals.

At the top of the steps, everyone went down in a confused mass.

On the other side of the building, the marshal and the EPA inspector in the executive suite heard the boom, accompanied by a tremendous crash from the next room. Alarm klaxons began to sound. The marshal raced to the inner door and threw it open. Inside, the back half of the huge conference room had collapsed into a basement—or more accurately, had been blown open from below. Magazine confetti was floating in the air along with a huge ball of smoke. Debris from the conference table, the shattered floor, and whatever had been below was scattered pell-mell amidst the scattered thousands of journals. Fires were everywhere, fires that the marshal knew would engulf the massive piles of combustible magazines in moments and start a blaze that could bring down the whole building.

"Son of a bitch!" he yelled. He turned to the inspector. "Yank that damn thing outta the wall!" The inspector pulled the cords out of the back of the computer while the marshal lifted the monitor off and tossed it to the floor. They picked up the CPU, the inspector bundled it under her arms, and the marshal led her at a full-tilt run back into the hallway. On the television, the women mimed ecstasy.

The pair reached the lobby, where two marshals and two sheriff's deputies were looking back and forth down the hallways, confused. "Fire!" the marshal yelled as he and the inspector rushed in. "Maybe a meth lab! Get the trucks!"

"The radio's out!" one of the deputies replied, panic on his young face.

"Get in your goddamn car and go get us some help! This place is gonna burn!" The deputy sped out the door. The marshal turned to the inspector. "You! Take that thing and get to the street. Stick it in the ECM and stay there!"

She looked confused. "The ECM?"

The marshal sputtered. "The—the damn Winnebago! Take it to the damn winnebago and stay there!" The inspector turned and fled with the computer.

"Christ almighty!" the other deputy said. "What the hell is going on?"

"Find some fire extinguishers! And if you smell chemicals, get the hell out! You guys, follow me." He took off down the hallway where he figured the team had gone, the other two marshals in tow.

Stephanie stood up slowly, her ears ringing slightly. There was no debris or fire, and it didn't look like anyone was hurt. The rest of the team got up gingerly. The six marshals on the stairs had apparently already moved into the basement. Three more marshals were coming down the hall from the lobby. Vic stepped over to Stephanie and spoke quietly between blasts of the klaxon.

"Nancy's gone."

Jean Qualls—Agent Nancy—had recovered from the blast immediately. She saw the marshals piling through the door. From amidst the collapsed agents she leapt up on her powerful, inhuman legs and landed at the base of the stairs in a feral crouch, a momentary growl escaping her throat. A wild mix of smells coursed from the basement, too subtle for a human to decipher. There was a chemical odor she made as some sort of explosive, as well as the fragrance of something on fire. But there was more—a human smell, the pheromone signatures of numerous people, all oozing terror. She didn't recognize the fear-smells as being any of the marshals, all of whom she had instinctively and unconsciously catalogued by odor. There were medical smells, too: disinfectant, pharmaceuticals she didn't know, and the rich odor of the human body lain open, probably from surgery. The human smells were powerful, and fantasy images flashed in her mind's eye of stacks of corpses, bulging with the secret flavors only she could savor. A hungry thought flashed before she could squelch it: *Maybe there's a morgue.* But no. She wasn't picking up anything that reeked of the dead. There was one more smell, a strange one, that at first resembled burning cardboard, presumably from the fire; but somehow, that wasn't right. This was something new, something alive.

Then she was up and through the door.

Stephanie and Vic groggily took the lead and hurried down the stairs, sidearms drawn. The rest of the investigation team and the three marshals followed right behind.

They entered a large room. There was some sort of desk station just inside the door, covered with computers and papers. Security doors lined the walls, twenty of them, each with a small window. A single hallway led left, hazy with smoke. The lights were flickering in that direction.

Stephanie turned to the marshals. "Watch this hall!"

Two of the marshals took up positions at the entrance to the corridor. The third grabbed her shoulder as she started to turn away. "Ms. Park, this building's going up. The explosion went off beneath that big conference room, and all that shit's in flames. I sent a deputy for the fire department."

"Shit!" Stephanie blurted. "Goddamn it! All right, watch that hall. You guys, take all that crap from the desk and get it out of here! The rest of you, with me."

She led Vic and Abe and several agents and they fanned out to check on the doors. They were all the same—cells with bare white walls. All but one contained single occupants, men and women of various ages and races, wearing patient gowns. Some were lying in their bunks, asleep or drugged or dead, but many were up and about. Those that were awake began screaming incoherently and banging at the locked doors as soon as they saw the agents outside.

Cell T ran from door to door. Neither Shasta nor Susan were among the prisoners, but there was the empty cell to consider.

Archie Sanders hurried over to Stephanie. "This must be their organ bank! Forget Mexico, they're harvesting 'em right here! Jesus!"

Stephanie stared at him blankly for a moment, then remembered the cover story. "Yeah, that must be it," she responded coolly. "Look, this place is on fire. You've got to get these people out of here. Check the desk for keys, or maybe the locks are computer-controlled. Send someone up and get ambulances out here. These people may be injured. You don't have much time and there's a lot of people to evacuate." Archie nodded and got busy.

Abe and Vic joined Stephanie and the three exchanged looks. "All right, let's go," Stephanie said. They turned and ran into the smoky corridor, Stephanie yelling "Help them!" to the three marshals.

Δ

Jean entered the large room and saw the desk and the doors. The terror-smells were coming from those doors. But the marshals had headed down the corridor to the left—their scent was fresh and strong. She could hear the footsteps of the second handful of marshals as they ran.

She followed at a sprint. The corridor was hazy and the lights were off and on, flourescent tubes buzzing in her ears. She reached a corner. There was a door directly ahead—lying on the floor. The open doorway past it was belching smoke, and debris partially blocked the entrance. Somewhere beyond, a fire was raging. Whatever the explosion had been, it had happened through there. The marshals, though, had continued down the hall to the right. She ran.

The hall opened up onto a wide ramp leading down into a huge sunken chamber, two stories tall. The ceiling was gridded with metal struts and dotted with black metal cylinders Jean recognized as theatrical lights. The floor was bare cement. Within the chamber were the makings of a Hollywood soundstage: portable walls, backdrops, furniture, props, big speakers, and on and on. In one corner was some sort of control area with electronic equipment, presumably to operate the lights and sound. A huge horizontal mirror—two-way, Jean guessed—was set into the opposite wall next to another ramp that led up to a hallway beyond.

This room was a container of fear. The cement, the props, everything was permeated—*drenched*—with the human odor of stark terror. The power of that fear was almost animate. The hairs on the back of Jean's neck stood up and she shivered, wondering just what the hell went on here. There were a few old smells of blood, but this was no abattoir, unless it could be considered a slaughterhouse of the soul. People came in here and were shattered, leaving shards of fear of every conceivable origin.

The marshals were not here. They'd moved on, down the hall. Jean shivered again, fighting off a panic impulse to drop her human guise, and bolted, wicked fast. There was a fresh odor wafting out of the hallway up ahead. Something was going on.

She moved up the ramp, down the hall, past several doors, then around a corner where she skidded to a stop by a pile of MP5s and Rugers. Three marshals were standing watch on six security guards, all in a knot. The speed of Jean's approach startled them.

Just beyond, six marshals were standing in a rough line, M-16s pointed down the hall. At the end of the hall, maybe thirty feet away, there was a single door before which stood a seventh guard with his MP5 pointed at the marshals. She shot a questioning look at one of the men standing by the Wackenhut guards. "Standoff," he whispered.

"Damnit, I'm not gonna ask you again, son!" the marshal on point was saying. "Now the rest of your boys have done the sensible thing. Just stand down so we can get this business over with!"

"No, sir," the guard replied in a voice like a dead man's. "You and your men must withdraw."

The marshal looked over his shoulder at the guards who had surrendered. "Can't you talk some sense into this fool?"

One of the guards straightened up. "Shane!" he called out. "Stand down, man. These assholes are gonna take it in the shorts soon enough. Let's keep this simple."

“I can’t do that, sir,” the guard called back.

“I mean it, Shane, it’s not worth it! You know as well as I do that this bullshit’s gonna be over any minute now.”

“Sir—” the guard said, then stopped.

“What?”

The guard paused before answering. “We’ve got Visitors, sir.”

The hallway got quiet. It was the calm before the storm.

For much of its history, the National Reconnaissance Office didn’t exist—officially. Founded in 1960, the NRO took the role of operating the network of American spy satellites orbiting the Earth. The government did not publicly acknowledge its existence until a number of leaks finally outed it, after three decades of secrecy. Its staff is recruited primarily from the Air Force, the CIA, and the Navy. Officially, NRO staff are on the payroll of the Air Force Intelligence Agency, which provides them with a layer of cover against exposure.

Being a very secret, very “black” project, details of the NRO’s budget are not available to the public. Given these circumstances, the NRO is a very handy place to hide other, even more secret operations, even those that have no real connection to the NRO’s purpose or operations.

Like SECTION DELTA. Since the mid-1960s, NRO DELTA has gathered together a unique group of people, all of whom have an important unifying trait: they are among the finest, most ruthless, resourceful, and remorseless trained killers in the world—efficient, finely tuned products of the American military and intelligence culture. They provide physical security and wetworks capability to their superiors in the United States government. Although NRO DELTA agents are already hidden behind multiple layers of deniability, sometimes it's necessary for them to use yet another layer, that of the private sector.

Such as Wackenhut Corporation.

—SIX ARMS SNAP SIX knives slip into palms and they are moving these blurs of tan and steel the three marshals next to them turn to respond raise weapons a startled cry then plunge and again and straight through blood arcs spilling onto the tile staining the walls the uniforms the kevlar and these men are hard they are diamond-hard ghosts of motion and fury the other marshals spin and their guns rattle but the ghost at the door erases the old marshal's face with a burst so pure and clean it's like a thought and the five spin back to respond confused another erasure then two gutted from behind and they're in the ghost dance now calling up the spirits of all their secret dead Vietnam Guatemala Chilé Sudan Iraq a mantra of things that will never be known and bodies are hitting the floor and this is their time the dream time of blood lust that they train for that they live for and they are nothing but bespoke death and from their midst then something—something wrong—something wrong ROARS—

CELL T CAME DOWN the ramp into the huge soundstage, guns drawn.

"What the hell is this?" Abe asked.

"Some kind of studio," Vic replied. "I guess. Jesus."

Stephanie shook her head. "It's a funhouse. Let's go."

They started forward, and then halted as the sounds came from somewhere up ahead. Cries, and the *chuk-chuk-chuk* of M-16 fire, mixed with the sleek German working of an MP5. The gunfire stopped almost immediately and then the screaming started, men wailing and the inhuman roar of some enraged animal.

"Shit!" Abe shouted, but Vic and Stephanie were already running to beat the band.

BY THE TIME THEY reached the turn, all was quiet. Bodies of guards and marshals were strewn about the hallway, and the floor was thick with blood and the fluid of human beings ripped wide. Agent Nancy was crouched in the midst of the dead, drenched in blood from head to toe, her blond hair matted and thick. She held a severed human head in her hands, skull cracked open, her face buried in the man's brain as she wolfed down the meat.

Cell T stopped short, stared, uncomprehending. Vic fired and shot Nancy in the shoulder before she knew she'd pulled the trigger. Nancy fell on her back, dropping the half-eaten head, and came up in a menacing crouch. Her features seemed to ripple for a moment, loosely blended with some terrible monstrosity, but then they stabilized. She put one gore-streaked hand over her shoulder.

"Chill out," she said thickly. "It's under control."

Vic, Abe, and Stephanie just stood there in shock. All three lowered their weapons slightly.

"Nancy?" Stephanie asked in a trembling voice.

Nancy nodded towards the door at the end of the hall. "In there," she said. "Something's in there." She picked up the head she'd dropped and resumed eating.

"Wh—what are you doing?" Vic stammered.

Nancy swallowed another chunk of brain and licked her lips. "Debriefing."

The three agents moved slowly over the corpses and past

Nancy, who now ignored them. They backed down the hall towards the far door, their faces pale.

"What do we do?" Abe whispered.

"Let's just leave her the fuck alone," Vic replied shakily. "Check out the door."

Reluctantly turning their back on the carnage—and the feasting—behind them, Cell T opened the door.

Inside was an operating room. A procedure was under way.

Abe immediately flashed on that grainy "Alien Autopsy" video that had been on TV a few years back. This looked like an alien autopsy, all right. But the scalpels were in the wrong hands.

Three short, spindly humanoids with pale skin and huge eyes were gathered around an operating table, oblivious to the commotion outside and the nervous trio who had just entered. Agent Susan was spread out on a gurney. Her body cavity was open, but to their horror the agents realized she was still breathing. The creatures wielded strange instruments expertly, poking and prodding among her living organs. A plethora of state-of-the-art medical equipment was nearby, but it was not in use. These things had everything they needed in their slender, skeletal fingers.

The agents were never sure who fired first.

The blaze of gunfire was deafening, and all they could smell was cordite. The three creatures staggered and spun awkwardly, metal slugs punching through their little childlike bodies. Multicolored fluids spattered the floor. Abe, Vic, and Stephanie kept firing until they were clicking on empty and the three things were sprawled at their feet. Then they just stood there, gasping.

Stephanie recovered first. She holstered her weapon.

"Come on. We've got to get Susan out of here." She strode forward, taking a hard step on the face of one of the creatures. She got to the far side of the gurney and wheeled it around. Vic stepped forward and grabbed the other end, then they lifted it roughly over the bodies and rolled it out the door.

Abe stood staring for a few moments as Vic and Stephanie passed by him with Susan on the gurney. Then he recovered and looked around the room. Among the medical equipment was a small video camera bolted to a cart. A little red light above the lens was glowing. Wires ran to a DVD-RAM unit lower on the cart, beneath a television set that was turned off. Abe ran over and ejected the disk, then stuck it in his jacket and hurried out into the hallway.

His partners were negotiating the gurney over and through the sundered dead. Nancy was on her third severed head, and glanced at them only briefly. "Check these rooms!" Stephanie called out. "Look for Shasta!"

Abe hurried from door to door, looking briefly into each. All were unoccupied. They were additional medical rooms: surgical theaters, pharmacies, storerooms, and so on. He moved as if in a dream, splashing in the congealing fluids as Nancy continued to devour the mind-meat of the security guards.

Finally he was done. Vic and Stephanie were way off down the hallway, racing with the gurney as fast as they dared through the sound-stage. Abe was alone with Nancy, who promptly finished off the last guard's head. She rose and wiped her mouth with her sleeve, which did no good at all. *She looks like that movie* Carrie was all Abe could manage to think coherently, and later he would look back at this moment and feel that that was really doing pretty good. Considering.

"Come on," Nancy said. "We better get out of here." She

turned and ran down the hall, Abe following because he didn't know what the hell else to do.

Chapter Five: The White Road

Sunday, March 14, 1999

JOSEPH CAMP ROSE AT dawn on Sunday morning. He took a shower, got dressed, and made a simple breakfast of English muffins and marmalade with a pot of coffee to wash it down. The morning sun was bright and clear outside on this cool March day. His little house felt stuffy and smelled of cigarettes and old man. He resolved to get the maid service to pay a call sometime this week, get the place freshened up a little.

Breakfast finished, Joe plodded to the front door and opened it, blinking in the light. The *Washington Post* was on his doorstep. He brought it in and spent a few minutes reading and remembering.

Yesterday's incident in Bountin was national news. A joint DEA–Sheriff's Department investigation had uncovered a large methamphetamine manufacturing and distribution facility hidden in an office building. Deputy U.S. Marshals led the raid and the lab had exploded, killing nine marshals and all seven suspects. Troops from Fort Detrick were called in to seal off the area, allowing hazardous-materials specialists from the Army's nearby USAMRIID institute to process and detox those exposed to the large quantity of dangerous chemicals released in the blast. Buildings in the vicinity were evacuated and their occupants treated, as well. President Clinton would hold a brief ceremony in the Rose Garden this afternoon to honor the nine fallen deputy marshals—the largest single loss in the organization's 120-year history. "It is a time of mourning," the President said in a statement late Saturday evening, "but also a time of warning: we have zero tolerance for those who would push drugs on our youth and place the brave men and women of law-enforcement at risk. Illegal methamphetamines are a plague on our nation and we will fight their makers to the bitter end." Flags in the capitol flew at half-mast.

Joe shook his head. "What a crock of shit," he muttered.

On the surface, much of the story was true. Three truckloads of Army troops had, indeed, shown up as the raid was winding down and local emergency crews were fighting the blaze that quickly consumed the OUTLOOK Group building. The troops did seal off the area and USAMRIID was trotted out to show off their Racal suits for the media. There was little or no danger other than the fire, however. No meth lab existed. No dangerous chemicals were released. The show of force had two purposes: to lock down the scene from civilian personnel and to explain why the Army had hauled off everyone who'd been involved in the raid.

It was a shitstorm, but Joe had really expected no less. The good news was that Cell T had gotten away, with Agents Nancy and Susan in tow. They'd stolen one of the dozen ambulances that showed up in response to the explosion and were gone before the Army moved in. It had been a tight escape.

It was true, also, that nine innocent Deputy U.S. Marshals had died, slain by NRO DELTA to protect OUTLOOK's greatest secret: collusion with inhuman creatures, presumably for scientific gain. Their lesser secrets had gone up in flames. The thermite blast set off by the guards destroyed OUTLOOK's paper files and their network database servers, and of course the patients they'd rescued had fallen into USAMRIID's hands, which meant the people who ran OUTLOOK would get them back soon enough. None of the computers and documents seized in the raid had escaped the Army cordon. The surviving non-DG raid personnel would be debriefed and counseled on what to say about the incident in the future. Those who complied would be fine. Those who resisted or leaked information would probably be killed, victims of suicide or car wrecks or a bad case of the flu.

Delta Green had little to show for the disaster they'd unleashed, but it would have to be enough. For starters, Agent Susan was alive—for now. Cell T had rushed her to a small clinic run by a retired Delta Green agent. The incisions made by the inhuman surgeons had closed up by themselves *en route*, to Cell T's considerable distress. At the clinic, they secured her and kept her under with sedatives. She was still there, still unconscious, guarded by Agents Nick and Nolan; they were waiting for the arrival of a DG-friendly medical team from North Carolina. Tonight they'd try the experimental therapy to see if they could purge her body of the neo-tissue. Joe wasn't looking forward to that.

They had Susan, but they didn't have Shasta. Cell T was pretty positive that he hadn't been in the facility at all, though Joe thought it was conceivable that he was simply dead, buried in the smoldering and collapsed basements beneath OUTLOOK.

They also had the videodisc that Agent Thomas had recovered from the operating room. Joe had brought it home and reviewed its contents yesterday afternoon and evening. He then made a videotape dub of selected portions of the disc, digitally blurring out the faces of Agent Susan and Cell T in the process, and took the video to the airport in a small shipping container. It would arrive in Los Angeles this morning, destined for *Phenomen-X*; in exchange, they would drop the charge against Agent Thomas and leave him alone.

Finally, they had Agent Nancy.

That had taken some explaining. Cell T was more than a little paranoid about her. Joe had given them the short version of her story, leaving out details of identity. Agent Terry had ranted at him for sending them into OUTLOOK without knowing Nancy's situation, and Joe's answer hadn't really satisfied her: "Compartmentalization, Agent Terry. Compartmentalization."

"But what if we'd killed her?" Terry demanded. Joe laughed. "Not likely."

It was almost seven o'clock now. Time to go. Joe tossed the newspaper on the floor and rose from his armchair. He put the little videodisc in a pocket of his overcoat and headed outside to drive to the D.C. airport. He had a meeting to attend.

CELL T ROSE AROUND ten, groggy and fitful. They'd gone through most of two bottles of bourbon last night after leaving the clinic, staying in yet another new motel, this time in Seabrook near the Goddard Space Flight Center.

Vic stumbled out of the bathroom, fresh from vomiting. "Anybody get the number of that UFO that hit me?" Stephanie cracked a smile. Abe looked too bleary to comprehend.

They showered and got dressed. Vic went out to get them breakfast and returned with coffee, sandwiches, and Pepto-Bismol.

"So," Abe managed after finishing his sandwich. "Got any bright ideas about what the hell is going on?"

Stephanie shrugged. "I've seen some weird shit with Delta Green. But I didn't expect that. You guys ever seen those things before?"

"Just on TV," Vic replied. "But I've heard they were around."

"Really?" Abe said, surprised. "I thought that UFO stuff was bullshit."

"I don't know about UFOs. But I read Cell S's original report on Groversville, back when this op started. Alphonse PGP'd me a copy for background. At the end of their op, they found a barn up in the hills with a bunch of those things inside, operating on cows or something. That guy with the gold teeth showed up and chased them off, and that's when the Hantavirus struck and it all went to shit."

Abe shook his head. "I guess the neo-tissue had to come from somewhere." A thought occurred to him. "Is this what they killed Fairfield over? This UFO shit?"

It was Vic's turn to shrug. "I guess. I never heard much about that, just that he'd ticked off the wrong people and got wacked. But from what Alphonse has let slip, it all ties together."

"So those geeks are right. Aliens, government conspiracies, all that crap."

Stephanie snorted. "*We're* the government conspiracy, Abe. Those guys are just the government."

They were silent for a minute, sipping their coffee and passing the stomach medicine around.

"It's so strange," Stephanie finally said. "Up till now, I thought we were just hunting monsters, weird old cults, all that hocus-pocus stuff. I never imagined our own government would be collaborating with it all somehow."

"I don't think they're collaborating with all of it," Vic said. "I don't think these people know jack about the things we've faced. Alphonse said they had a really narrow focus, that's why we don't cross paths that often. He said something about stealth fighters, exploiting technology. I think these people have deluded themselves into thinking they're onto some huge secret, but they don't see the big picture. I mean Stephanie, when you were dealing with those things from the ocean, there weren't any sinister cover-ups or secret government projects or anything, right?"

"Just ours," Stephanie replied. Abe chuckled.

"Well we've never come across anything like this before, either. But Cell S has, in Groversville." Vic paused. "I wonder what else Cell A hasn't told us about?"

The plane touched down in Burlington, Vermont, an hour before noon. Joe disembarked without any luggage. He walked to a rental-car desk and got a Volvo. He wanted something sturdy.

From the airport, he drove to an outdoor storage facility and parked the car. It was cold and crisp here, and there was snow on the ground. He was about forty miles from the Canadian border.

Fishing a key out of his pocket, he unlocked one of the storage units and slid the metal door up. The fifteen-by-fifteen area inside was another one of DG's Green Boxes, but this one wasn't for general use. It was just for Alphonse. He walked in, turned on a battery-powered lamp, and pulled the door down behind him.

He undressed methodically. From an old padlocked footlocker he removed a complete suit of body armor, protection against small arms and blades. He put it on, and then got into a winter-camouflage jumpsuit that covered the armor completely. A pair of sturdy hiking boots and a warm fur hat with earflaps finished off the ensemble. He transferred his keys, wallet, and the videodisc into the pockets and then opened another footlocker. From it he removed a fully automatic AK-47 assault rifle, which he placed in a long drawstring bag, and six forty-round magazines, which he stashed in various bellows pockets of the jumpsuit. He also took out a Walther PPK and three seven-round magazines for it and stashed these, as well. Finally he pulled on a thin pair of gloves.

There was a walnut vanity with a large oval mirror in the front of the unit, part of a jumble of furniture that shielded the interior from casual observation while the door was open. He looked at himself in the mirror, and decided that he looked like an idiot. He was a short, portly, eighty-year-old man with snow-white hair and a pugnacious look to his face, wearing winter camouflage bulging with ammunition and topped by a ridiculous hat. The idea that he might be going into some sort of violent action made him laugh out loud. "What the hell are you doing, Joseph?" he asked his reflection. His reflection smiled at him and shook its head. "Taking care of business," it answered.

Returning to the car, he placed the bag with the rifle in it on the passenger seat and hit the road. He took Interstate 89 north to St. Albans, then headed northeast on Highway 105. Exiting on a private rural road, he pulled up to a sturdy metal gate. A heavy chain lay piled on the ground, clipped with bolt cutters. Joe got out and pushed the gate open, drove through, and then closed the gate behind him. Apparently the person he was meeting was already here.

He reached the vicinity of Fairfield Pond half an hour later. It was rather large to be called a pond, but so it was. It had been named by the Fairfield family, who had lived here along the Black River since colonial times. Reggie Fairfield's ancestors were frontiersmen, militiamen, revolutionaries. They raised hell and children with equal fervor. Reggie's kids were aging hippies somewhere in California, the grandkids scattered across the country like so many prosperous American families who had no reason to stick together. No Fairfields still lived in this neck of the woods, but the old family farm remained. Reggie had died here five years ago, though officially he was still alive; he hadn't spoken to any of his family for a decade before his death, and they hadn't ever come looking. There was never an investigation or a death certificate. Reggie's death was a secret that had stayed buried, his pension checks flowing into Delta Green's coffers. Joe still paid the property taxes on the land and came out here once in a while to walk around.

He drove past a barn and into a snowy gravel-covered patch, where there was a black BMW already parked. Fifty yards off were the ruins of the old family cabin. The timbers were charred and collapsed, and now mostly grown over with grass and scrub and blanketed in snow. A flagstone chimney still stood, mostly intact, a comforting presence here for more than two hundred years. The house it served was gone, the family dispersed, and the lord of the land was somewhere in the ground underneath. It made sense, Joe thought, for Reggie to be buried here, beneath a chimney just as proud and stubborn as the man who last used it.

Someone was leaning against the chimney, wearing a long black overcoat. The figure waved congenially.

Joe turned off the car, took the AK-47 from the bag, chambered the first round, and got out. He slung the rifle from his shoulder and gripped the handle, thumbing the safety off and the action to full-auto. Then he started walking across the snowy plain to the ruin, rifle pointing at the ground.

As Joe approached the ruin, the man stood up straight and walked towards him, smiling broadly. His three gold teeth caught the winter sun.

"Why Joseph," he said merrily, eyeing the rifle. "I didn't know you cared."

"Hello, Adolph. I'm glad you could make it."

"Wouldn't miss it for the world. You here to kill me?"

"Not if I can help it."

"Delighted to hear it."

The men began walking slowly side by side, skirting the edge of the ruin.

"I had no idea you were such a sentimentalist, Joseph. I suppose you'd like to atone for old sins?"

"No, I thought I'd commit some new ones."

"Really? How melodramatic. Speaking of melodrama, that was quite the show you folks put on yesterday. I didn't think you had it in you, anymore."

"You know better than to underestimate me, Adolph."

"I would never do that, Joseph. But my superiors did. To be honest, they haven't given you much thought these last couple years. You've had a low profile."

"I'd like to keep it that way."

"So naturally, you blew up OUTLOOK Group."

"*Your* men did that. We just wanted our people back. We were within the rules of engagement."

"So you were. We took your people, you had to do something. I understand perfectly."

"We need to resolve this. We have other priorities, as do you."

"Indeed. Do you have any suggestions?"

"A few. We'll leave Groversville alone."

"You mean Promise."

"Whatever. We'll stay out of there. We're done with that

crap. OUTLOOK, too."

"And in return?"

"Our agents who were in on the raid and Liz Severs. You leave them alone."

Adolph laughed. "All right, we won't kill them, if that'll make you happy. But I don't think Ms. Park has much of a future at the EPA, and that's hardly our doing."

"Understood. Also, let David Nells go."

"That's impossible."

Joe stopped. Adolph turned to face him.

"Really, Joseph, it is. That's not negotiable."

"Is he dead?"

"No, he's quite alive. He's rather a remarkable person, you know. Very interesting to us. We can't let him leave."

Joe stood quietly and considered this for half a minute. Finally he reached a decision. "All right. But don't you pull this shit again. If you take any more of my people, you'll pay a price for it."

"We already have, Joseph. That facility you destroyed was rather important to us."

"You didn't lose anybody you can't replace."

"That's not true, actually. You killed some friends of ours. Foreign dignitaries. We have some explaining to do."

Joe chuckled. "They've really got you by the balls, don't they?"

Adolph turned and began walking again. Joe caught up.

"Speaking of your friends, I have something for you." He reached into a pocket with his free hand and pulled out the videodisc, which he handed to Adolph.

"What's this?"

"My people recovered it from OUTLOOK. It's footage of

your friends, working on Liz Severs."

Adolph arched an eyebrow. "Why the hell are you giving this to me?"

Joe stopped walking again and his features hardened. Adolph stopped, too. "Because I don't *want* the goddamned thing! I don't want anything to *do* with your stupid little conspiracies if I can help it. I've got problems of my own, and the last thing I need is your monkeys on my back. Take it and burn it or shove it up your ass for all I care."

Adolph regarded Joe for a moment, then spoke quietly. "You do have other problems, don't you? I think I understand. There's a lot more in heaven and earth than my superiors dream of, isn't there?"

Joe just stared at him angrily.

"Really, Joseph, you don't have to glare at me like that. I *do* understand." Adolph reached into a pocket and pulled something out, which he handed over.

It was an old, tarnished, metal dogtag, the chain long since lost. The stamped name read WADE, SATCHEL GRANGE. Joe's brow furrowed and he looked up at Adolph.

"I was there, Joe. In Cambodia, '69. I'm the one who killed Wade *and* his gook slash. I saw that thing he called outta the temple and I pissed my pants and ran like a woman. I ain't seen nothing like it since, and I thank my lucky stars." He chuckled with a sound like a death-rattle. "You really do have bigger fish to fry than a bunch of desk jockeys with delusions of grandeur."

Joe handed the dogtag back. "You're full of surprises today, Adolph. I've got one for you. That videodisc? There's a copy."

"I assumed as much."

"We don't have it. *Phenomen-X* does."

Adolph stared for a moment, and then burst out laughing. "Oh, my. My, oh, my. That's the best news I've had this whole rotten weekend."

Joe looked at him oddly. "Really?"

"Oh, yes. My boys are itching for some payback, but they're not going to get it from you. I'll sic them on those fools and we'll have a little fun. Maybe we'll swing by Disneyland on the way back."

"You going to kill them?"

"Eventually. That is why you told me, isn't it? They've crossed you somehow and you want me to make them go away."

"Something like that."

"Well, we're both full of surprises, aren't we, old friend?"

"I'm not your friend, Adolph," Joe said coldly. "We're not married. We're just engaged."

He turned and started walking back to his car. Behind him, Adolph stood, laughing in the snow.

THE OSTERMAN CLINIC WAS a small private affair in Bethesda near the National Naval Medical Center. Dr. Jack Osterman had been a Navy doc and Delta Green agent in the 1970s and '80s, but he retired and went into private practice during the Bush administration. He'd always been a family man, and decided that he wanted to spend his twilight years with his family doing what he loved instead of spending them as one of Reggie Fairfield's catspaws. He still kept in touch with Alphonse, and made his clinic available to Delta Green when duty called, which was rarely. The clinic mostly treated the elderly for the infirmities of age and the facilities were modest, but DG couldn't be picky. Besides, Jack had spent his Naval career treating military injuries in the field, and he liked to say that he could do a heart bypass with a butter knife and a fifth of Wild Turkey if the situation warranted. Jack really knew his way around the human body—or at least he thought he did, until he met Agent Susan.

Susan was resting, sedated, in one of Jack's three examination rooms. Last Friday Alphonse had warned him to be ready for visitors, so he'd given his staff the weekend off and rescheduled his appointments. He also borrowed a vanload of equipment from an old buddy at the Naval Center and converted an exam room into something approximating a crash unit. When the ambulance pulled up Saturday morning, a man and three women piled out in tactical gear with a gurney containing a healthy-looking but unconscious woman in her thirties. Jack was confused at first. One of the women was covered in blood and gore, and he was sure she must be wounded. She shrugged off his entreaties and nodded at the gurney. "She's the one in trouble," the woman said, her breath like a butcher shop. Jack guided them into the exam room and got to work.

The woman they called Susan was fine. She showed no evidence of injuries or illness. He wasn't sure why she was unconscious, but on first inspection she seemed to be in no danger. Then another one of the women, who had introduced herself as Terry, produced a small unmarked plastic bottle with a spray nozzle from one of the bellows pockets on her tac suit. She spritzed the clear fluid on Susan's bare torso, and several purple lines appeared, approximating the Y-incision of an autopsy. "Make a little cut along one of those lines," she ordered. Jack took a scalpel and complied, making a shallow two-inch incision within the purple stain. Susan's skin immediately closed up again, without spilling a drop of blood.

Jack touched himself at the stations of the cross and invoked the blessing of Mary, the mother of God. Then he stood up, put the scalpel down, and demanded an explanation. When Cell T was finished, he took a fifth of Maker's Mark out and had a shot. They had several more. Tonya made a crack about this being better stuff than Thomas usually bought.

He'd stayed at the clinic from then forward, calling his wife to say he was assisting at the Naval Center for the weekend—they called him in to consult sometimes. On Cell T's advice, he kept Susan on sedatives to keep her down. Alphonse came by around noon and they discussed the situation for a while. Cell T watched television—the raid at Bountin was on all the local stations.

It was now Sunday evening. Dr. Grant Emerson and three assistants had flown in from the University of North Carolina, Chapel Hill, to help out; Emerson was the DG-friendly who had first analyzed the "neo-tissue" and developed the leucopararosaniline spray technique. They had some sort of experimental treatment planned that they thought would purge Susan's body of the substance that had wormed its way into her tissues. While Alphonse and the agents stood by, Jack and Dr. Emerson's team went over the plan.

"As near as we can surmise," Grant said, his British accent clipped and studious, "the neo-tissue is inhibiting certain T cells to prevent tissue rejection by the body. Otherwise, it would be unlikely to co-exist as invasively as it does. We don't know which it targets, and we haven't the luxury of finding out. We must activate the entire immune system and pray the neo-tissue withdraws."

"How?"

"Septicemia. We'll give her five milligrams of lipopolysaccharide. Her leukocytes will take up the LPS and flood her bloodstream with cytokines, activating the full spectrum of lymphocytes to reject the neo-tissue."

Jack's brow furrowed. "Five migs sounds like a lot."

"It is. Safe dose is one mike per kilo."

"Couldn't five migs be fatal?"

"That's the idea. She'll go into shock in under an hour and die soon after. We must be prepared to bring the fever down before it kills her."

"Is that really necessary?"

"This neo-tissue is a wily beast. We need Susan to crash, hit her hard so the neo-tissue has no choice but evacuation. If we go with a lower dose, it might fight back, shutting down the process."

"You're sure about this?"

"As sure as we can be, which is a damned sight too little. We've never tried to fight the neo-tissue before. But I think it'll work."

"All right. We'll need an ice tub ready for the fever. But what about those incisions? When it leaves, she's going to open up, isn't she?"

"Yes, she'll start to bleed out. We've brought whole blood and plenty of saline. As long as the neo-tissue hasn't replaced anything critical, we can handle it."

"I hope you know what you're doing."

"I don't. Just hope I've guessed right."

Agent Tonya spoke up. "Wait a second. What's going to happen to the neo-tissue when it leaves? Can it survive outside the body?"

Alphonse nodded. "Yes. It'll coalesce into a single organism and look for a new host. We've got MOPP NBC suits for everyone in the OR and we'll seal the exits to the room. That'll slow it down."

"Then what?" she asked.

"Leave that to me," Alphonse said.

THE MEDICAL TEAM NEEDED a couple hours to prepare everything for the treatment. Cell N showed up and joined Cell T and Alphonse in another exam room to talk. Agent Nancy looked haggard. There were dark patches under her eyes and she was jittery. Vic guessed she hadn't slept since the raid. *At least she got cleaned up,* Vic thought.

Nancy spoke up first. "I've been processing the debriefings I made at OUTLOOK. There's still a lot for me to go over, but I've got some preliminary information about the seven security guards from the hallway."

Abe looked uncomfortable. "How does that work? I mean, do you know all their memories or something? Are they—are they *conscious* inside you? Do you talk to them?"

Nancy shook her head. "It's not like that. It's like . . . well, I have to sort of visualize it. I've got this room in my head, full of boxes. First I have to put each . . . each debriefing into its own box. I have to compartmentalize them."

"There's that word again," Vic said.

"No, I really do. I've never debriefed this many before. It's been really difficult." She paused. "Anyway, those seven guards didn't really work for Wackenhut. You were right about that, Alphonse."

"Let me take a guess," Alphonse said. "They worked for the National Reconnaissance Office, didn't they?"

Nancy nodded. "Yeah. Something called SECTION DELTA."

"What's the National Reconnaissance Office?" Vic asked.

"They run our nation's spy satellites," Alphonse responded. "It's a very quiet outfit. For a while now, the people behind OUTLOOK have hidden DELTA within the NRO's black budget. They don't really have anything to do with satellites. It's just a convenient place to put some very nasty people." He smiled slightly. "Your tax dollars at work."

"Nasty is the word," Nancy said. "They're killers. Ex-military, mostly. Evidently OUTLOOK is some sort of plum assignment for them. Fat pay, easy work. Until we showed up, at least."

"So do they know what's going on?" Abe said. "Do they know about those things working on Susan?"

"Three of them did," replied Nancy. "They've stood guard at some meetings with those things, though they always wait outside so they didn't really know what went on. I also know who their boss is at DELTA. It's the guy you shot in Tennessee, Terry. Word got around that you're quite the hellion."

Stephanie smiled and leaned forward in her seat. "What's his name?"

"Adolph Lepus," Alphonse interjected. "He's the head of security for these people."

"You knew his name!" Stephanie blurted. "Why didn't you tell me?"

"I can guess," Vic said, her voice sardonic. "Compartmentalization."

Alphonse smiled. "Very good, agent. Yes, that's why, Terry. In our line of work, information is not just a commodity, it's a hazardous substance. Knowledge of someone like Lepus is the equivalent of plutonium. You start handing it around willy-nilly and people hurt themselves with it. Continue, Nancy."

"Well, the good news is that David Nells is still alive. He's in Puerto Rico. OUTLOOK has a second facility down there, on Vieques Island. The bad news is that it's OUTLOOK's HQ. It's incredibly secure, way more than the Bountin office was."

"How did the guards know about this?" Alphonse asked.

"Only one did. He'd been working at Vieques for eight months, but he screwed up and they kicked him back to Maryland just last week. He was still at HQ when they brought David in."

"How'd he screw up?" said Vic.

Nancy flinched and was silent. She shut her eyes tightly and clenched her jaw, then gripped her knees with her small hands. A sob escaped her throat and tears ran down her face.

The other agents looked at each other warily. Nick and Nolan shifted in their seats. "Nancy?" Alphonse said quietly.

Finally she opened her eyes and wiped her face. "I'm sorry. It's just . . . you ask a question, and a box opens, and that man's thoughts come spilling out. Sometimes it's hard, it's really hard." She took a deep breath. "He raped and murdered a twelve-year-old girl. She was the daughter of a cleaning woman at the facility. He'd been hitting on her, she told him to get lost, so he got back at her through . . . through her daughter."

"Damn," Abe muttered.

"What happened?" Vic asked.

Nancy wiped her face again, but her voice grew diamond-hard. "They, well, they covered it up of course. Lepus flew in. He was pissed. He had the woman killed, her husband killed, her son killed. They cut up the bodies and threw them in the incinerator. They punished the guard by sending him to Maryland for six weeks. Where, I'm happy to say, I tore his black heart out so fast he got to fucking *watch*."

Nobody spoke. From the next room came the faint sounds

of beeping machines and the medical team talking. Nick and Nolan exchanged inscrutable looks.

"You can't understand," Nancy started again, voice quavering, fresh tears running down her pale cheeks. "Those men, those DELTA agents. I mean, I know this sounds pretty funny coming from me, but they weren't *human*. Not in the ways that count. I know I . . . I may not have the best claim to humanity anymore . . . but those people, those people were *monsters*. And now," she paused and began sobbing, "*now they're in here with me and they're never going to leave!*"

Vic got up and sat down next to Nancy, putting an arm around her shoulders. Nancy hugged her and cried. Vic glared at Alphonse, who lit a cigarette.

"Well," he said after a few moments. "That's that."

"What do you mean?" Stephanie said. "We're going to Puerto Rico, aren't we?"

"No. We've taken this as far as we can."

"But David's still alive! They've got him down there doing God knows what to him!"

"I know that!" Alphonse shouted. "And we can't do a damn thing about it. We're going to cure Susan and then this op is over."

"That's bullshit!" Vic spat, still cradling Nancy in her arms. "We can't stop now!"

"We stop now and that's final!" He lowered his voice. "Right now we're still within the rules of engagement. We're even. We've pushed them as far as we can. If we hit them in Puerto Rico, they'll hit back, and we can't take what they'd dish out. Besides which, do you think we're going to get another warrant? Do you think we're going to sweet-talk another bunch of marshals to fly down there and *die* for us? For our petty little intrigues? We don't have a prayer of getting into that place."

Stephanie was fierce. "David deserves better than this. He deserves a shot."

"We *took* that shot, agent, and we saved Susan. That's it. We can't continue this."

"We can!" she replied. "If you don't want to help, fine, but we're not going to stop!"

"You *will* stop! This isn't about you, agent. If you go down there and pull some cowboy nonsense, they'll smear you across the Caribbean. But they won't stop there. They'll come after the rest of us. Are you going to sign the death warrant on this entire organization for the sake of one man?"

"Do you even *give* a shit about David? Do you give a shit about *any* of us?"

Alphonse jumped to his feet and started yelling. "David's father and I fought side by side in the war! I was in the hospital the night David was born! I've watched him grow into a man I respected and admired! I recruited him into Delta Green, as I did his father before him! Their blood is on *my* hands! But I'm not going to throw away the lives of everyone in this room and who knows how many more besides to save him! *This is not about* you, *goddamnit, this is about* all *of us!*"

He took a step back and sat down again, breathing heavily. Everyone's eyes were locked on Alphonse. When he spoke again, it was almost in a whisper, but he spoke with passion. "We've never come so close to the brink. Believe me. You have no idea of the magnitude of what we did yesterday. You saw those troops come pouring in. This afternoon the President of the United States addressed the nation about those good men who we deceived and delivered into the hands of our enemies for the sake of our private war. These people have the power of the entire government behind them. If they wanted to, they could kill all of us, tonight, and we couldn't stop them. The only reason they don't is because they're afraid of what we know, or what they *think* we know. They're afraid we'd expose them, even in death. But their fear only goes so far. If they decided that the risk of us alive outweighs the risk of us dead, they'd destroy us. It's a simple equation. And may I remind you: as evil as these people are, as terrible as the things are that they've done and will surely do again, ultimately they're small potatoes. You know that. Terry, think of Roscoe, think of Massachusetts. Tonya, Thomas, think of Baltimore, Seattle. If we're gone, who would help *those* people? Who would save *those* lives? Who would push back this darkness? You've all seen it. We *have* to stay alive, we *have* to be here, because if we don't do this work, no one will, and our children will inherit nothing but apocalypse. *Please* understand. This op ends not because we don't care about David, but because we care about all the other lost souls out there who need us, too."

Nancy sniffed and wiped her face with a tissue. Vic stared at the floor. Abe rubbed the back of his head. Nick and Nolan watched Nancy. Stephanie closed her eyes, and when she finally broke the silence it was with a voice laden with sorrow and surrender.

"Okay."

IT WAS TIME FOR the treatment. The medical personnel and Alphonse got into their suits and sealed the room's vents and door with plastic sheeting and duct tape. Cell T hung around the waiting room.

Cell N went home. Nancy hadn't spoken since her last outburst, and Nick and Nolan helped her out to the car and drove off into the night.

After forty-five minutes the treatment kicked in, and the noises from the exam room were terrible. The beeping of the machines grew frantic, and there were shouts and the sounds of people hustling around the room. Cell T listened, pale. Someone screamed.

Then they heard Alphonse speak, shouting at the top of his lungs in a voice that had a strange and awesome power unlike anything they'd felt since they left the womb. The words were unintelligible. They sounded like a command in some strange, alien language. The lights dimmed. A strange gust of wind blew through the clinic. On the little table Cell T was seated around, the magazines fluttered and one shot to the floor and skidded across the tile. Then the lights came back up, and there was more shouting and movement from the exam room. A few minutes later, Cell T heard a wet clattering as the medical team moved Susan into the ice tub. The machines stopped beeping as the leads on Susan pulled free. More time passed. There was a murmur of voices and then more shouting and more noise as they took Susan out and put her back onto the table. The machines began beeping again. It went on and on. Cell T sat and listened and didn't say a word.

Alphonse came out of the room twenty minutes later, plastic and tape ripping as he opened the door. He stepped into the waiting room and pulled the respirator off before dropping it to the floor. He slumped heavily into a chair next to Abe and picked up the bottle of bourbon that Jack had left. He unscrewed the cap and took a slug, then wiped his mouth and set the bottle down.

"She didn't make it."

Δ

Stephanie took Abe and Vic to her apartment in Georgetown. They were sick to death of motels.

Clotho was meowing and scratching at the door as Stephanie unlocked it. She picked up the cat and hugged her as she walked in, Abe and Vic close behind. The answering machine light was flashing, and the readout showed a dozen messages waiting. Stephanie unplugged the phone and fed Clotho.

They spent the evening talking about everything but Delta Green. Abe talked about his son and how the boy's favorite show was *Arthur.* Vic spoke about her music, and her plans to put together a CD, and how beautiful Oly Park was in the spring. Stephanie mused on what she might do now, since her career with the EPA was almost certainly over. She'd always thought about doing some traveling, and had enough money in the bank to make a trip.

They talked in circles, avoiding the things that hurt them, sticking to the shallow end of the pool of their lives lest they drown. They drank nothing but water. Around midnight Stephanie made them cheese toast, and finally they went to sleep on the living room floor, entwined together in blankets, hoping not to dream.

Joseph Camp ordered pizza. As he ate, he thumbed through old photographs of his China days in the war. There was Andrew Nells, smiling and drinking in a Taipei nightclub. The wedding day, Andrew splendid in his uniform, Sarah radiant in her gown. Little David, a flush-faced infant in the little apartment his parents had, "Uncle Joe" holding his tiny hand and smiling.

Joe had never made time for a family. For most of the 1950s, the Nells were his family, him playing the part of the funny and much-loved uncle that visited from time to time. Those were good days.

The 1960s were different. Andrew died in '64, the victim of a DG op that went horribly awry. Joe had been in charge, and he'd roped Andrew into serving as pilot. Two agents were on board the plane, there to assassinate a wealthy occultist with his fingers in all the wrong pies. Joe didn't know what went wrong, but the C-46A went down in the ocean and was never found. At the memorial service, Sarah had taken him aside and said sternly, "Stay away from my son."

He tried to do just that, but he kept tabs on David all the same. David grew into a brave young man, and served in Vietnam. Joe didn't see him in person until 1970, at the Joint Chiefs of Staff inquest into the Cambodia disaster that brought down Delta Green. David had briefly been assigned to do some translation and interrogation work for Colonel Satchel Wade a little while before Wade sent three hundred troops across the border and into a nightmare, and he was called to testify as to Wade's activities in those final months. Joe watched him from the gallery, but didn't introduce himself. He managed to respect Sarah's wishes until 1984, when he desperately needed an agent in China. David was there, a military attaché secretly working for the CIA at the embassy in Beijing. He got in touch, and David was thrilled to see him—Uncle Joe was a connection to his much-loved and much-missed father, dead those twenty years. Joe told him a raft of stories about Andrew, and eventually recruited him into Delta Green. They'd remained friends ever since.

Joe cupped his face in his hands, and a tear ran down his

cheek. *How many?* he wondered. *How many good people have I sent to their graves?*

It was going to be a hard night. Joe didn't want to be alone. Finally he called his friend Carssandra Buie, his assistant at the FRD. They'd grown close over the years. Joe was deeply in love with her, but he refused to do anything about it. Still, he wasn't above calling her sometimes, when the darkness seemed to stand outside his front door, a palpable presence. On the phone, Carssandra was understanding, and said she'd come over with some camomile tea. They'd talk and laugh and chase away the shadows for a while.

Joe got up, wiped his face, and began puttering around, straightening things to get ready for company. Ten minutes later, there was a knock at his door. He brushed his hair back with his thick hands and hurried to the foyer and opened the door.

The woman on the porch wasn't Carssandra. She was gracefully old, with distinguished silver hair and a noble bearing. But she was crying.

Joe looked at her for a moment, confused. Then he remembered the pictures from the good old days.

"Sarah," he said, and then she pulled the gun from her pocket. She looked into his eyes and fresh tears ran down her face, flush with anger and sorrow.

Joe looked back at her and took a breath.

"God bless you," he said quietly.

She pulled the trigger three times, fast. Joe thought of brilliant fireworks, exploding on a Chinese New Year.

David Foster Nells awoke on a gurney. He was in a small, hot room with bare white walls and a concrete ceiling, like a bunker. He couldn't move—not even his eyes, except to blink. In the periphery of his vision he could make out a number of other gurneys with people lying on them in cardboard trays, motionless. There was an odor of putrefaction and bleach.

Then there were voices. Two men had entered the room, somewhere out of sight.

"Ah, hell! There's a half-dozen tonight. This is gonna take hours."

"Well, quit bitchin' and let's get started. Man, they're ripe."

"Which one you wanna do first?"

"Let's get that fat chick over there. She's the biggest. Might as well get her outta the way first."

The men entered David's field of vision. They were in their twenties, dressed in gray jumpsuits. The two made their way through the gurneys until they reached a certain one, which they wheeled away beyond where David could see. The men grunted as they pushed the gurney.

"Get the door."

There was a metal clanging sound and a squeal of old hinges, and then the room blazed with heat from some unseen source. The men grunted some more.

"All right, come on."

There was some more noise.

"Okay, got it."

The metal clanged again and the heat dropped off.

"Damn. Did you see how bloated she was? That shit's gonna stink."

"Let's get outta here. Conan's on."

"*Vaya con dios*, darlin'," one of the men called cheerily. Then both left the room.

David lay still, paralyzed. There was a low whooshing sound

coming from somewhere nearby. Then a crackle.

It was several minutes before the smells began to reach him. Burning cardboard, and then flesh. The sounds he began to pick out were almost worse than the smells—sizzling, and the gust of gasses leaving a body. For a moment he thought of Vietnam.

Realization dawned. He was in a crematorium. These men thought he was dead. They were going to burn him alive.

Dr. Baker yawned and leaned back in his office chair. "You think he's figured it out yet?"

Dr. Strysik was staring at a bank of monitors. "Heart rate's increasing . . . yeah, must be. Yeah. He's racing now. Panic attack at 1846 and twenty seconds."

"What was up with that *vaya con dios* shit? That wasn't in the script."

Strysik shrugged. "Derek must think he's an actor."

"Hah. *Everybody* thinks they're a goddamned actor."

"That guy who played the lawyer was pretty good."

"Which one?"

"The second one. The one that exploded."

"Oh, right. He *was* pretty good. You know, if he hadn't been such a good actor it might not have worked. Poor bastard might still be alive." Baker chuckled.

"Wait a second. Heart rate's dropping."

Baker sat up. "Dropping?"

"Yeah. He's back to normal. 1847 and fifteen seconds."

"That's weird. Hey, is he negating the paralytic?"

"No, the readings are normal. It's like he just calmed down all of a sudden."

"Hmm. You think he's figured it out?"

"This guy? Anything's possible."

Andrew Nells stood in the mock-crematorium, dressed in his pilot's uniform, and took his son's hand. David stared up at him, heart racing, a terrified thirteen-year-old boy.

"Dad?"

"Hello, son."

"I'm scared, dad. I'm gonna die."

Andrew smiled. "No you're not, son. You're not going to die. Not today. Not ever."

"Promise?"

"I promise."

David relaxed. His dad had never told him anything but truth.

"I saw mom. She was crying."

"She missed you, David. She misses both of us."

"I want to see her again, dad."

"You can't do that, David. I'm sorry."

"But why?"

"You've seen her and you've told her what you needed to say. You were a brave boy and I'm proud of you. But you've got to move on now."

"Move on? Where am I going?"

"China clouds, son. Hold onto my hand and make a wish."

They were flying, flying in the clouds. Andrew sat in the pilot's chair, young David in the co-pilot's. The twin-prop C-46A Commando transport lumbered in the sky.

The plane had left Taipei, Taiwan, almost six hours ago. It was a covert charter flight on Civil Air Transport, the CIA front company that provided commercial flights between Taiwan and the rest of Asia. The flight had been booked by a wealthy international businessman with CIA connections who had a private vacation home west of Tsingtao, and evidently didn't want some of its contents to fall into the hands of the Communists. They were traveling to a secret airstrip run by some Nationalist rebels; CAT used it on occasion to move spies and supplies back and forth. From there they'd take a truck up to the businessman's home and empty it out, then return to the plane, refuel, and fly back to Taiwan.

"Isn't this your plane, dad?" David asked.

"Sure is, son. The Bathing Beauty! Besides your mom, she's the only sweetheart I've ever had."

David looked out the windows of the cockpit, catching glimpses of the waves below. "Where are we?"

"We're off the coast of China right now, near Shantung province. That's the Yellow Sea, son."

They flew without speaking for a few minutes. Outside, the two Pratt & Whitney engines thrummed powerfully.

"Dad?"

"Yes, son?"

"Isn't this where you died?"

"Yep. This very flight, in fact."

"But I wasn't here."

"No, but I thought you should be. Don't worry, son. You'll be fine. It's like television."

Just then a Chinese woman in a CAT uniform stepped into the cockpit. "Captain Nells? It's time."

Andrew's face darkened. "All right, Li. We're ready, aren't we David?"

"Sure, dad."

The woman smiled at Andrew and left.

"Now David, I want you to get unbuckled and follow Li. You need to see what happens back there."

"But I want to stay up here with you, dad."

"You'll come back here in a minute, okay? But right now you need to be in the cabin. It's important."

David grumbled as he took off the belts and stood up. "When do I get to come back?"

"I'll give you a shout. Get going, son."

The cabin held a couple dozen plush seats. David stepped in and immediately ducked into the front row, where no one was sitting. He crawled up into the seats and peeked over the top.

There were nine people in the cabin, including Li, who was now serving drinks to two burly caucasian men in Army uniforms. Each carried a book in his lap. Several rows behind them was an olive-skinned man with dark hair, slim and dignified in a new white suit. He was surrounded by five Chinese women in matching saffron robes. They were whispering among themselves. The man caught David's eye and smiled briefly, then returned his attention to his companions.

Li walked to the back of the plane and entered the cargo compartment.

The two Army men looked at each other and nodded. They put the drinks down and opened their books, which were hollow, and removed identical handguns. David's eyes widened. He recognized them as Colt .45s, a weapon his father also owned. The men stood up and spun around, bringing the weapons to bear.

In a fluid motion, the five women stood up as a unit just as the men fired. The shots were deafening in the cramped cabin.

The women staggered, blood splashing across their robes. One of the men stepped into the aisle and advanced, not firing, while his companion continued to take measured shots at the women, who were collapsing into their seats around the man in the white suit.

The Army man hurried down the aisle and reached the carnage in moments. His companion squeezed off one last shot, and the back of a woman's head burst open, spraying blood and brains across the man's white suit. The man looked up at the soldier in the aisle with a bored expression. "*Vaya con dios,*" he said. David shivered.

The soldier fired six times, the impact jerking the man around in his seat. He began gasping and coughing up blood.

The gasping turned to laughter. The man raised his arms out level, and blood dripped from his palms. He gazed at the ceiling of the cabin. "My father, my father, why hast thou forsaken me?" he said in a mock-pleading voice.

The soldier took a step back, frightened now. His companion worked a fresh magazine into his gun and raised it to fire.

Suddenly the man shot him a look. He spun left like a marionette and fired three times into his partner's back, then whipped the gun back under his chin and blew his brains across the ceiling.

Blood dripped onto the seats. Some of the women were still moaning in pain. The man in the white suit stepped unsteadily over the corpses and into the aisle. He looked down at the dead soldier at his feet, then up at David.

"Causality bullshit," the man said.

"David!" Andrew Nells called from the cockpit. "Come back, son! It's time!"

David stared into the man's abyssian eyes.

"David!" his father called again.

This time it worked. David broke the man's gaze and climbed down off the seats, then raced into the cockpit.

They were still in the clouds, but the clouds were dark, like they were in the midst of a thunderhead. Yet the plane was flying as smooth as silk.

"About time!" Andrew said. "Get buckled in, son."

"What's going on, dad?" David's voice was quaking and tears were running down his face as he sat down in the co-pilot's chair. "I'm scared."

"Don't be scared, son, you're safe. I just wanted you to see this. It's important."

The plane lurched for a moment. David's stomach did flip-flops.

"Dad?"

"It's okay, son, it's just the cargo door. Li's bailing out. They'll get her in '69."

A few minutes went by, and then the clouds parted. All around them was the night sky.

All around them. There was no ocean beneath. They were flying in space, in a limitless field of stars.

"Dad? What's going on?"

Andrew Nells was gone. The man in the bloody white suit was seated in the pilot's seat.

"Where's my father?" David demanded, middle-aged again. "What have you done?"

"Relax," the man said. "We're going to see your father now."

The cockpit filled with light. Ahead of them, the star field opened in folds, like a vulva. Light was spilling out. Through the opening were hundreds of terrible creatures, moving in strange patterns, bisected by black geometric shapes that flickered in and out of view at different angles. The dancers parted and the light burned David's eyes, the light of a seething chaos, a thousand stars compacted into something that looked like truth.

"See?" the man said. "There He is."

THE MOCK-CREMATORIUM WAS COLLAPSING. The false walls, the gurneys, the corpses made of latex. It was all pulling together, condensing.

"Shit!" Dr. Baker yelled. "What the hell!"

Dr. Strysik was talking frantically into a microphone. "1847 and thirty seconds subject is exhibiting drastic telekinetic activity heart rate normal brain activity spiking."

On the other side of the large two-way mirror, everything in the huge soundstage was moving. The three-sided crematorium set had imploded, leaving David Nells behind on the gurney, still motionless. Now objects all over the cavernous chamber were sliding forward across the floor, collapsing and bending as they went. Other sets, furniture, speakers, props of every description, all the components of the terrible fantasies OUTLOOK constructed to break and mold the human mind, all were being pulled into the center of the room.

"What's going on?" Baker demanded.

Strysik watched the tumbling detritus as it coalesced in the center of the room. His eyes grew wide. "He's building something."

All the raw material of the room, all the matter at hand, all of it came together, grinding and crackling and snapping. It was gathering into an oblong shape half the length of the soundstage.

Baker was sweating. "What the hell is it?"

Strysik just kept his attention focused. When the long flat shafts began to extrude from the tumbling mass, he knew.

"It's a plane," he said. "He's building a plane."

In moments it was over. Every scrap of material in the sound-stage had been gathered, smashed, and restructured. A patchwork replica of Andrew Nells' C-46A "Bathing Beauty" stood in silence.

David still lay on the gurney near the plane's cargo door, like a patient awaiting transport to a hospital in some far-off land.

Strysik picked up a phone. "Dr. Yrjo? You better come see this."

Interlude: Thirty Three Thirteen and a Wake-Up

Monday, March 15, 1999

The Hollywood actress Meg Ryan was riding a bike along a wooded rural road. Music swelled. She raised her arms, joyous, letting go of the handles and closing her eyes, living in a moment of perfect happiness. A truck hit her.

"Fuck!" an inmate yelled. "What a crocka shit!"

Forty-five prisoners were clustered in chairs in front of a television set that was bolted to the wall. It was movie time. A fire had broken out in the woodshop on Friday, and the work detail on shift had put it out before any serious damage was done. As a reward, they got Monday off.

Each of the four cell wings had four cable televisions. Guards set the channels as they felt prudent, avoiding the likes of *World's Scariest Police Videos.* Home-improvement shows and sitcoms were frequent choices. A regular schedule of movies on videotape was offered, controlled by the guards. This afternoon, the woodshop detail was getting *City of Angels.*

Ex-Captain Forrest James shifted in his seat. The inmates had to bring their own chairs from their cells to watch television, and they weren't very comfortable for lengthy sessions.

"Goddamn chick flicks," another con groused. There was a murmur of assent, modulated by the latest debate over who was foxier, Meg Ryan or Julia Roberts. James fell in the Ryan camp, but he kept his mouth shut.

Within a few more minutes the movie was over. A flurry of conversation bubbled up, convict movie critics weighing in with their opinions. Then the movie cut off and *The Simpsons* came on in mid-episode to general acclaim, despite the fact that it was a syndicated rerun.

James got up and lifted his chair. He'd had enough TV. These sessions reminded him of his days at Annapolis, guys clustered in dorm rooms around a television having the same conversations and arguments he was hearing now. Sometimes life itself felt like a rerun.

Back in his cell, he put the chair by the desk and dropped onto the cot. He picked up the book he'd been reading, *Lonesome Dove* by Larry McMurty, but then put it down again. He didn't feel like reading, though as a rule he liked westerns. He'd gotten on a Louis L'Amour kick the last few months, checking out book after book from the prison library. All were well-thumbed; L'Amour was popular here. Danny Sun, a former Army major two cells down, had been pushing the McMurty book lately and so far, James was liking it. It was shorter on action and longer on introspection than the L'Amour stuff, but then again, that about summed up the change in his life since coming to the Castle: short on action, long on introspection.

He was feeling old, and he was feeling lonely. His two-year anniversary was coming up in a couple months. Not long after he'd turn forty-eight. Like the old Navy saying about battleships went, he was gray and underway. Hitting the stride of middle age behind bars was not a pleasant experience. That mark of a man's life was stormy enough without having all the time in the world to dwell on it, too.

As a young man in Annapolis, he'd seen a bright future ahead of him. He'd come back from the Olympics with a medal and the respect of his peers and instructors alike. A promising career with the Navy was unfolding, coupled with the looming cloud of the Vietnam conflict waiting for him on graduation day. It seemed like a damn stupid war to be fighting, but for a young serviceman wartime meant opportunity, a chance to prove something, to distinguish oneself, to test one's mettle, to advance in the ranks. He'd had a long conversation with his father about the war during a Christmas break. His dad was a retired Navy man who had friends—and had lost friends—in that strange and troubled land. They had argued over the merits of the conflict, groused about how the brass were handling this or that initiative, but in the end his father's words had stuck with him: "If a house is burning and there are people you care about inside, it don't matter whose house it is or how the fire started, you gotta go in there and get them folks out." That was how his dad saw Vietnam, a burning house with good men inside who deserved a shot at getting back home alive, and the politics be damned. You went and you helped out and you prayed some other guy would do the same for you.

The same analogy applied well to Delta Green, James reflected. He didn't know the big picture, didn't understand the source of the strange darkness that stole out of secret spaces to lay claim to the innocent. But he had resolved to fight it all the same.

Of course, he couldn't fight jack all here in the Castle. Out there, he sensed, the whole world was burning down, and everyone out there deserved a shot at living to see another sunrise. But in here—in here there was nothing. He was trapped in a fire department where the alarm never rang, and the trucks sat rusting.

Turning gray.

James thumped his fist against the wall. He'd had the itch the last few days, the itch to get out and do something, make some kind of recompense for what he'd done to that woman in San Francisco. She'd written him a couple weeks back, out of the blue. When he saw the name on the envelope, he thought it was a prank. But it was her.

Her name was Carly Lisle. She wrote because she'd been in therapy for the last year, and was trying to reach some sort of peace with the hell she'd gone through at his hands. She told him how she'd suffered, about the nightmares, about how she hadn't been able to get close to another man since that night, how she'd cursed him a thousand times, how she'd hoped he'd suffer in prison the way she had in the free world. But finally, she was ready to move on. She just wanted to say that she forgave him, that she hoped he would find peace, too, and that he would never hurt anyone ever again. She didn't supply a return address. It was signed, "Yours in Christ."

Jesus, James had thought. The letter was about the last thing he had ever expected to happen.

Then this weekend he'd seen the news, about that raid on the meth lab near D.C. that had gone so wrong. He watched the story carefully, studying the footage of Army troops, the USAMRIID geeks, and he had a feeling. The raid smelled like Delta Green to him. Something was up, out there in the free world. It felt like it was time to get busy, to move on, to do something.

Of course, he couldn't do a damn thing.

He wondered about Stephanie Park. He didn't think about her much because when he did, he felt worse about his life than he usually did. She'd pulled him out of jail just after his arrest and dragged him north to Roscoe for a Delta Green op that was, perhaps, even more hideous than usual. It was especially so because there had been an instant sort of attraction between them, some spark of chemistry that had put them both on edge.

He'd been in a terrible state of mind, grimly determined to exact some final vengeance against the shadows before the Navy threw him overboard. But the price of that vengeance was the dashing of any faint hopes he'd had that the two of them might find each other, fumbling in the dark. They'd embraced at the airport, and he'd slipped a note into her hand. It was a piece of poetry, sort of, a few ragged words that had come to him once while swimming alone in a tropical bay at night, many years ago. A woman he'd been seeing stateside had sent him a Dear John letter, and he'd gone out to drown his sorrows in the warm waters. Emerging from the water, he saw the waves crashing against the shore, and he'd cried a little, something he wouldn't do again until Roscoe.

That was how he'd felt after saying goodbye to Stephanie. Adrift, abandoned, broken and bleeding on the rocks of his life. He'd washed ashore on the shoals of the Castle, crawling from the moat and staggering inside to a little room, a safe haven from the peril of bad choices. Here there were no choices, no choices except to get up every morning and decide you'd live to see sunset. He'd made a virtue of necessity, rebuilding his confidence, rebuilding himself. Life had made him older; prison had made him wiser.

A guard stepped up to the cell door. "James!" he barked. "Wake up! You've got a visitor."

James opened his eyes. If that letter had been *about* the last thing he had ever expected to happen, this was *the* last. He sat up and swung his legs around.

"You sure about that?"

"I'm sure. Come on."

James stood up. The door opened. It felt like *departure.*

Chapter Six: The Expected Guest

Monday, March 15–Tuesday, March 16, 1999

CELL T WAS AWAKENED by a pounding at Stephanie's door. For a moment they thought they were dreaming. They sat up and looked at each other, blinking and confused.

The pounding continued. Abe lurched over to where his jacket lay on the carpet. He retrieved his sidearm and stood up.

Vic and Stephanie got to their feet. Vic hurried over to the couch and began rummaging in her bag. Stephanie advanced cautiously towards the door. She noticed the clock in the kitchenette. It was four in the morning. Clotho looked up from the counter and blinked.

Abe and Vic caught up to Stephanie, guns out, and they reached the door. More pounding. Stephanie looked through the peephole and then looked back at her companions.

"It's Adam," she said, bleary.

They relaxed. Stephanie opened the door.

Agent Adam stood in the hallway, looking hollow. "Are you okay?" he demanded. His suit was rumpled, no tie, collar open, his trim brown hair disheveled.

"We're fine," Stephanie said. "What's wrong?"

He hurried inside as she shut the door and turned on the lights. Vic and Abe looked at Adam, worried.

"It's Alphonse," Adam said. "He's been shot."

"*What?*" Vic said. "What happened?"

"Someone from his office came by tonight. His front door was open and he was lying in the foyer. She called 911. He's in surgery now."

"When?" Abe asked.

"A few hours ago. Ten, I think. I got the call around midnight."

"Jesus," Vic said. "Is he okay?"

"It's not good. Three shots from a .22. Internal bleeding. He's a mess."

"Who did it?" Abe said. "Do we know?"

"Not yet. I guess the cops are investigating."

"Why didn't you call?" Stephanie asked, then she remembered unplugging the phone.

Adam shook his head. "I don't trust the phones. If they got in his house, they may have compromised our security. We have to assume it's all toast. Email, cell phones, our files, the works."

"They?" Stephanie asked. "Oh Jesus, you think Lepus did this?"

"I don't know. But we have to assume the worst until we know different."

"Shit, this is it, isn't it?" Vic said, her voice frantic. "Alphonse said we were on the brink! He said they could kill us all tonight if they wanted. It's happening!"

"We don't know that yet. I'm just trying to play it safe."

"Safe?" Vic replied angrily. "Safe? I thought we were playing by the rules! I thought everything was fine!"

"I know! We all did! Alphonse met Lepus yesterday and it was cool."

"He met Lepus?" Stephanie said, shocked. "When?"

"In the afternoon. Before Susan died."

"Why didn't he tell us?"

"Guess," Vic said, giving Abe a look.

"Well what do we do now?" Stephanie asked.

"Get out of here. If they're cleaning house, they'll come looking for you."

"Where do we go?"

"Cell N is holing up at the Watergate. Room 219."

"Okay, we'll get moving. How do we reach you?"

"I'll be at the hospital here in Georgetown. I'll give you the number." Adam fumbled in his pockets and pulled out a notepad and a pen. He scribbled a number and handed the sheet to Vic. "Don't call from the Watergate. Go out and use a payphone someplace."

He turned to leave, then stopped. "One more thing. If they come for you, don't let them get Nancy. No matter what."

Matthew Carpenter—Adam—drove out of the parking lot as fast as he safely could. He wanted to get back to the hospital, keep watch over Joe in case the shooter came gunning for him again. He was hoping against hope that the old man would pull through.

Matthew was the first agent Joe had consulted after Fairfield's death, when he decided it was time to restructure Delta Green. Matthew was already a deputy director with the FBI, in charge of organizing interagency task forces to fight organized crime. He'd been in DG since 1985, and embodied the new breed of driven professional that Joe saw as the bedrock on which to build the organization's future. Joe wanted to bring DG's history of cowboy ops to a close, and reform it into a focused tool that could get things done quietly. The two men had spent days making plans, combing through lists of agents to sift out the seventy-eight who should be brought into the new order; the rest would be retired, or consigned to the role of consultant friendlies. Matthew took charge of structuring their security protocols, assembling the secure computer databases and encryption systems that would become DG's core communications infrastructure. Using his task-force experience at the FBI, he also laid out the procedures they'd use to cover their bureaucratic tracks. Together they built a new Delta Green, a consummate conspiracy honed to do what no one else could.

Five years into their grand plan, things were going well. Until tonight.

Matthew cursed as he drove through the darkened streets. He'd always known that Joe wouldn't be there for the long haul. The old man didn't have a lot of years left in him, and the experience of Fairfield's death had taught them against relying too heavily on one individual. Matthew had done what he could to prepare. He'd spent his time building the organization's files, tracking down obscure old reports from across the federal government, interviewing retired agents, trying to bring some coherent, tidy order to the mysteries they opposed in hermetic secrecy. He and Joe had passed countless evenings ransacking the old man's memory, trying to extract every detail of every op he'd ever been involved with, filing it all away as best they could. The result of all of Matthew's efforts was, perhaps, the greatest assembly of first-hand reports on the supernatural since the Bible.

Yet the combined files could fit onto a handful of high-density diskettes—with room to spare.

This is too soon, Matthew thought. *I'm not ready. We're not ready.*

They had their contingency plan. It hinged on Agent Nancy. But there was no guarantee it would work, and for that matter, Nancy wasn't the most stable or reliable of individuals. She was a good agent, to be sure, and perhaps Delta Green's greatest resource. Still, she was struggling with the perils of her strange existence, and both Matthew and Joe feared she might eventually lose her fight against the alien mindset that had come with her transformation. If she went, their plan went with her, and then Matthew really would be on his own.

Damn it, Joe, he thought. *You can't die. Yet.*

CELL T'S DRIVE IN to D.C. was nerve-wracking. They'd thrown their belongings together and bolted, Stephanie pausing only to leave several bowls of food and water for Clotho, who acted petulant at all the activity. It took them forty-five minutes to reach the Watergate.

Cell N was wide awake and jumpy as hell when they arrived. Nick and Nolan, imposing in their suits, didn't look pleased to see them.

"What's up?" Nolan asked guardedly, standing with Nick in the doorway, handguns tucked behind them.

"Adam sent us here to hole up," Vic said.

The two men exchanged looks. "Okay, come on in," Nolan said.

Cell T entered the suite. The lights were off. Nancy came out of a bedroom wearing a sweatshirt and jeans and hurried over.

"How's Alphonse?" she asked, her face gaunt.

"Adam said he's in the hospital," Vic replied. "That's all we know."

"Has anything else happened?"

"Nope. We were sound asleep at Steph—at Terry's, when Adam came. If they're after us, they shouldn't have had any trouble finding us over there. But nobody showed up until Adam."

"You weren't followed, were you?" Nolan asked.

Cell T exchanged glances. "I don't think so," Vic said.

"Did you *check*?" Nick demanded. "Or did you just haul ass over here?"

"We didn't check."

"Damnit!" Nolan blurted. "Amateurs! Nick, get to the lobby."

Nick nodded and ran out of the room. Nolan stepped over to a window and looked carefully through a part in the curtain.

Stephanie turned on a lamp. Nolan spun around and glared at her. "Turn it off!" She complied.

"Damn it." Nolan lowered his voice. "Look, if you guys are gonna hole up here, you've gotta do what we say. No lights, no phones, no noise, no room service. Just sit tight and shut up."

Vic glowered. "We could just shoot ourselves if it would be easier on you."

Nolan glared back. "Too noisy. But there's a plastic bag in the trash can if you'd care to try suffocation."

The tension was like another person in the room. Nancy stepped between them. "Enough," she said quietly. "Cut the crap. We're in a lot of trouble and six is better than three."

"That's debatable," Nolan spat.

"Nolan, please! I didn't see *you* putting your ass on the line at OUTLOOK."

Nolan looked at her for a moment, a little wounded, and then backed off with his palms out. "Okay, all right. Point taken. It's just that my first priority is *your* safety, not theirs. I'm sorry." He walked back to the door and stood watch at the peephole.

"Jesus," Abe whispered. "What's with him?"

Nancy sighed. "Nolan's okay. He's just very protective and very jumpy. Look, do you guys want some coffee? We've got a little kitchen here."

"That'd be great," Vic said, smiling a little at Nancy. "How are you doing?"

"Lousy. Par for the course, I guess."

"Come on. I'll help you with the coffee."

Abe watched them leave, then turned to Stephanie. "Nothing like a little drama to liven up the night."

Nick eventually returned, giving Nolan a quick shake of his head. The two men paced around the living room, alternating between checking the peephole and the windows.

Cell T and Nancy gathered in a bedroom with the door closed and the curtains drawn. Abe found a complimentary deck of cards in a little basket on the dresser, and they played poker for an hour. The morning light through the curtains gave the well-appointed room an amber glow.

Eventually they grew tired of the game. Abe kept losing. "The women of the world are against me," he said morosely. Vic snickered and rubbed his head. "Poor Abe."

"You mean Thomas," Stephanie said with a smile.

Nancy cackled. "Security breach."

The room was quiet for a moment. Vic yawned. Stephanie stole glances at everyone.

"So I've been thinking," she finally said. Everyone looked at her. "I think we should go to Puerto Rico."

Vic nodded. "I've been wondering when we'd get around to this."

"They hit us, we hit back. That's the way it works, right? That's the rules."

"Yep," Abe said, nodding.

"For all we know, they're going to kill us anyway. Why

should we sit around here waiting for it? Let's *do* something."

Nancy exhaled slowly. "I have to agree. I was willing to cut our losses yesterday. But after this? You might as well take a shot at getting Shasta back while you still can."

"Aren't you coming with us?" Stephanie asked.

"I can't. I have to stay here."

"Why?" Vic said.

"Adam and I had a long talk. Succession protocols, he calls them. If Alphonse dies—" she stopped.

Abe looked aghast. "They want you to debrief him."

Nancy nodded. "At the very least."

Vic shook her head. "Damn."

"Yeah. I'm not wild about the idea myself."

Stephanie looked anxious. "Well look, maybe you can't come with us. But you know the place, right? I mean, that . . . that guy does. Can you tell us anything? Any way inside?"

Nancy looked at the table. "Well, I've been thinking about that, actually. I've got an idea. The head doctor there, Dr. Yrjo. There's a whorehouse in Luján that he goes to fairly often. He's in charge, so he gets away with it. Two guards go with him. They're bad news. But if you could get to him, maybe he could get Shasta out. It's a longshot, but believe me—that place is a fortress. You guys could never get in on your own."

"Okay," Stephanie said. "That's it, then. You guys with me?"

Vic grinned. "Fuck yeah. Let's stick it to 'em."

Abe nodded. "Anything to avoid going home."

Stephanie looked at both of them, eyes bright. "Well, all right. Let's go."

They had their suitcases packed and were out the door in

ten minutes. Nick and Nolan were glad to see them go. Nancy hugged them all before they left, and gave them several pages of notes she'd made as they packed. There were maps of the facility and parts of the whorehouse, names of people, and so forth.

Stephanie drove them to her bank, where she emptied her account. "I told you I wanted to travel," she joked nervously. They bought a few items and swung by the D.C. Green Box, where they retrieved all their borrowed tac gear from the raid. They left their ammunition there, since they couldn't take it on the plane. Then they drove across the Potomac to the airport. Stephanie was deep in thought.

As they waited in line to buy their tickets, she broke the news. "I'll catch up to you guys in San Juan tomorrow. We'll meet on the steps of city hall, wherever that is. Call it noon, local time."

"Where are you going?" Vic asked.

"I need to go see someone. I'll catch up. Just get down there and start making plans."

"Are you sure about this?" Abe said.

"Positive. I'll see you in sunshine."

Abe and Vic hung around the airport for a couple hours, waiting for their flight. Stephanie's plane had left almost immediately.

"I wonder where she's going?" Abe said.

Vic arched her eyebrows. "I bet I can guess."

Tommy Prendergast was the first to reach the *Phenomen-X* offices on Monday morning, as he was every morning. He wore a *Buffy the Vampire Slayer* t-shirt, a khaki photojournalist's vest, blue jeans, and grimy Converse All-Stars sneakers. He still couldn't believe that he had a key to this place. His job with the show seemed like the high-water mark of his young life, better even than the three years he'd worked at Hi De Ho Comics and Fantasy in Santa Monica. Today he was extra-excited because Monday meant taping day, the day when they'd shoot the show and send it out via satellite to their syndication customer stations across the country. The stations would automatically record the show and air it later in the week, depending on their local schedules.

Most mornings he'd spend an hour straightening up. He'd gather all the coffee cups and run them in the dishwasher, start a fresh pot of coffee, grind the beans for the espresso drinks he'd make to order throughout the day, refill the paper in all the printers and copiers, distribute the faxes that had come in overnight, and make sure the bathrooms had plenty of supplies—even the ladies' room, which he hurried through quickly because it made him blush. This was Tommy's happiest time of the day, the time when he was alone in the office. Sometimes he had fantasies of a big story breaking while he was there in the early morning, but in reality *Phenomen-X* didn't have very many big stories.

This morning was different.

Tommy was still collecting dirty coffee cups when he reached the office of Frank Carincola, the show's news director. He started to open the door but it immediately banged against something inside, opening no more than an inch. Tommy was puzzled, and shoved harder.

Suddenly there was the tremendous roar of a gunshot, and splinters from the door stung Tommy's face. He stumbled backwards and hit the ground on his ample ass. The basket he was carrying fell to the side and coffee cups tumbled onto the carpet. White-faced, he scuttled down the hall on his hands and knees and then rose to a crouch, hurrying around a corner. He huddled there and peeked back down the hall, panting.

There was a noise from inside the office, and then the door swung inwards. Frank Carincola jumped out into the hallway brandishing a silver revolver and checked both directions. He spotted Tommy looking around the corner.

"Jesus, Tommy! What the hell were you doing?" Frank bellowed. Wisps of hair on his balding head were sticking up at every angle, and his clothes looked even grimier than usual. He wasn't wearing shoes.

"Uh . . . I was just gettin' the coffee cups."

Frank lowered the gun and ran his other hand over his head. "Damn! Sorry about that, kid. Good thing I was asleep or I might've been a better shot." He peered through his bifocals at the wall opposite the door. There was a neat hole punched in the plaster where the slug had entered, a foot above Tommy's head. He chuckled. "Good thing you weren't any taller, either."

Tommy got up and came around the corner slowly. "Everything okay, Mr. Carincola?"

Frank grinned slyly. "Well, Tommy, I got good news and bad news."

"What's the good news?"

"I got a videotape yesterday, from a confidential source." He arched his eyebrows. "Aliens, Tommy! Top shit! It's gonna put us on the map. That Santilli prick ain't got squat next to this bad boy."

Tommy's eyes grew wide. "Wow! No way!" Then he paused. "So what's the bad news?"

"The bad news is this is such good shit, they might kill us

before we can air it."

Tommy gulped. "Really?"

"Really, Tommy. We're in the big water now. I been here all night, studying this tape. Fell asleep at my desk. I had the door barred just in case those MiB fucks tried to catch me napping." His eyes narrowed and his face went grave. "Can you bend your little finger for me, Tommy?"

Tommy just boggled. He didn't know what to say.

Frank grinned again. "I'm shittin' you, kid. Ya gotta laugh in the face of death!" He looked at the scattered cups on the floor and grimaced. "Clean this up. I gotta take a crap. Anybody else comes in, you don't say jack. We'll have a news-staff meeting as soon as everybody's here, so don't let any of those slackers go out for donuts. In fact, I want you on the horn as soon as you're done. Make sure they're on their way in. Anybody still asleep, you wake them up and get them on the road, pronto."

"Yes, sir."

Frank locked his office door and gave Tommy a stern look. "No peeking, kid."

The Happy Bear Florist van left the front gates of Edwards Air Force Base at eight o'clock. It took them about an hour to enter the heart of Los Angeles on the San Diego Freeway. They drove steadily through the San Fernando Valley, just another van among the hundreds of thousands of vehicles muscling their way through the extended L.A. sprawl's morning traffic. At 9:20 a.m. they took the Culver Blvd. exit and entered Culver City, northbound. From there it was just a couple miles until the turnoff into a light-industrial area dotted with warehouses. They found the one they wanted quickly, having come here a few hours earlier to get the lay of the land. It was an old two-story sheet-metal warehouse that once served as auxiliary props storage for 20th Century Fox Studios, over on the other side of the Santa Monica Freeway. Since 1990, a small sign by the main entrance had read Haley Productions Studio E. Inside was *Phenomen-X*.

The van came to a stop a block away. A man in a blue jumpsuit got out of the driver's seat with a bouquet of flowers and a clipboard. He set the flowers and clipboard on top of the van, shut the door, and began smoking a cigarette, just another wage slave grabbing a few minutes of slack time on the job.

Inside Studio E, things were revving up. The production staff was down on the show floor, checking lights and cameras. The host, David Carmichael, wouldn't be there for another hour, but the technical crew still had plenty to do. The one thing they *didn't* yet have was the final script and video roster for the show. The news staff was supposed to have this together by now, but they were cloistered in the offices up in the loft overlooking the set. Some big meeting was going on. Rumors were circulating among the crew that they were all going to be fired, that Haley Productions was going out of business and the show was doomed. Only Stuart Prendergast, Tommy's older cousin and an electrician on the show, remained calm. Tommy had slipped him the word that they had some hot video and might be scrapping all the stories for today's taping in favor of the new stuff. But Stuart, unlike Tommy, kept his mouth shut.

Frank Carincola pressed stop on the VCR. He turned to his staff, gathered around a conference table in his office. "So? Whattaya think?"

Sonja Dewey spoke first. "Those three people at the end, with the guns. Is that who I think it is?"

"I'm guessing so. You can't really tell with the blurring they did, but I'm willing to bet it's our MiB friends from Groversville."

Robert Hoggard, their scrawny lead writer, was red-eyed and cranky. "We shouldn't run this today, Frank. It's too damn soon. We need to check this out. Besides, if this is the stuff, we ought to promo it to hell, save it for sweeps. Get Tallent to open the pursestrings for once in his goddamn life. I'm thinking big push, video release, maybe even a two-hour special. But don't run it today, man. Let's stick to the schedule."

The staff was quiet, waiting for Frank's response. He'd been so insistent and excited at the start of the meeting that they expected him to shove the tape down Robert's throat for daring to suggest that they wait. But watching the footage in the cold light of day had calmed him down. Frank looked thoughtful.

"You're right, Robert. Today's too soon."

Sonja snorted. *There's a first,* she thought. She'd come to learn over the last few months that Robert had a major coke habit and was unreliable as hell, though he was a good enough ass-kisser that Frank hadn't caught on. He'd been sliding downwards through the industry for years, and *Phenomen-X* was the bottom rung on the ladder. If he blew this job, his next stop would probably be porno, and they didn't have much call for writers. *He could always be a fluffer,* Sonja thought, and chuckled to herself.

"All right, people. Let's get today's show taken care of. And keep this under wraps—nobody outside of this room needs to know, understand? Anybody comes sniffing around, you tell me. Sonja, call the Milwaukee PD and drop that charge. Our buddy's off the hook."

As the staff stood up and began filing out, Robert sidled over to Frank and spoke quietly. Sonja rustled her papers and eavesdropped.

"Listen, man, that tape is gold. We need to play it safe, make some dupes. And ixnay on the echtays, you know? Start the production meeting and I'll run 'em off while you keep the crew busy."

Frank nodded conspiratorially. "Yeah, yeah, that's a good idea. One of those peons might blab." He popped the tape out of the VCR and handed it to Frank. "Be careful," he said. "Don't let Tommy watch. I shot my mouth off this morning and now he's all over me. He gets ahold of this and that little fuck will have it on the Internet in an hour, I just know it."

"No sweat, boss. I'll keep it on the Q.T."

"See that you do."

Down the street, the delivery man crushed his third cigarette beneath his sneaker and took the flowers and the clipboard down off the roof. He hustled across the road to a metal shop and went in the door. A couple minutes later he came back out shaking his head, still with his possessions, and studied the clipboard some more. He looked up and down the block, checking the street numbers, evidently trying to figure out where the flowers were supposed to go.

Frank called all the techs down to the floor and got the production meeting started. When the first words out of his mouth weren't, "This isn't easy for me to say . . . " they breathed a sigh of relief. Everything was back to normal.

Up in the offices, Robert slipped down the hall and entered the editing room. He took some blank videotapes out of a supply cabinet in the corner and began setting up the gear to run off copies.

Sonja followed him. It was quiet in the office; most of the news staff were down on the floor with Frank and the crew. She walked softly over to the door and took a compact out of her purse. She flipped the lid open and angled the mirror so she could see through the little window in the door.

Robert took the alien-autopsy videotape out of his jacket and pushed it into a deck. He hit the speed-dub button and the machines began whirring. Then he pulled a little vial out of another pocket and began laying down a line of coke on the desk. Sonja's eyes narrowed as she looked closely at the lights on the dub decks. The SOURCE light was lit next to a blank tape.

She threw the door open. Robert jumped, spilling coke on the controls. "Jesus!" he yelled.

Sonja nodded at the decks. "You're erasing the tape."

Robert looked at the decks and back at her, then stood up, blocking her view of the controls.

"No I'm not!"

"Yes you are. You're wiping it. Boom."

"No, I'm just dubbing it! For Frank! You don't know what the hell you're talking about!"

"I know *exactly* what I'm talking about. You're erasing that damn thing." She stepped forward, moving right up against him. He cowered back against the desk, even though he was at least a head taller.

"Got a new sugar daddy, Bobby boy? They got to you, didn't they?"

His voice was frantic. "*What are you talking about?*"

"Paid you off in nose candy. Did they offer you a job, too? A lot of *Phenomen-X* people seem to get a lot of good job offers. Too good. But I bet you never noticed that."

Robert stared, cocaine dusting his face. He was pale.

"Here's the deal. I'll take the fall for this. I hit the wrong buttons and *oops*, silly little Sonja erased the tape." As she spoke she briefly tossed her head from side to side and made a ditzy face, then went back to glaring at him. "Frank needs me too bad to fire me. But *you* give me the phone number."

"Wh—what phone number?"

"The number you're supposed to call to tell them the tape's wiped. So those goons in the florist van don't come in here and shoot every-body."

"*What?*"

"Oh, you didn't notice that, either? Gosh, I guess nobody did but little old me. They've been sitting up the block for over an hour. I took some gear from Allen and made them through the back windows. There's six of them sitting in there. Six people in a florist van, up the street. What do you think they're here for, Robert? That's why I haven't hit STOP, you dumb shit. I don't want to die. But I do want to nail these guys. And you, candyman, are going to help me do it."

"Uh—"

"Shut up. Starting now, you're my bitch. We're gonna erase that tape, then I'll go boo-hooing to Frank while you make the call. You've got to string them out, promise more help in the future so they'll keep in touch with you. Later today I'll run the number and see what it turns up, and try to get a make on that van. It'll take time, months or more, but we'll nail 'em. You and me, Bobby boy. I'll make a reporter out of you yet."

Robert's eyes were huge, his pupils dilated. He was trembling before this elfin little woman.

Sonja gave him a big TV smile as she quoted the show's motto.

"'Can you handle the truth?'"

AN HOUR LATER, THE delivery man finally found the right address. He left the flowers at the front desk in Studio E, with a card addressed to Robert Hoggard. Hidden inside were three more little vials of cocaine.

The man left the studio and headed down the street as Sonja watched from a parked car. He climbed into the van and started the engine.

"Goddamn," Adolph Lepus said from the back. "I hate these goddamn diplomatic solutions."

The five NRO DELTA assassins began putting away their weapons and stripping off their gear, grumbling.

"I know, boys, I know," Lepus said. "But the trip's not a total loss—Club 33's just around the bend and the steaks are on me." He addressed the driver. "Corey, get back on 405 eastbound." He grinned, gold and white. "We're going to Disneyland."

JEAN QUALLS WAS DEEP asleep in one of the bedrooms at Cell N's Watergate suite. She'd finally gone to bed shortly after Cell T left that morning, with Nick and Nolan standing watch in the main room. She dreamed terrible dreams—blood and viscera, swelling bodies leaking sweet smells. When Agent Adam shook her awake, she was ravenously hungry. She spun around and snarled, lips wet.

Adam jumped back, hands up and empty. "Whoa! Whoa! It's okay! It's me!"

In the main room, her handlers shared a knowing laugh. "She's hell in the mornings!" Nolan called cheerfully. It had been a long, tense time and they were grateful for the relief.

Jean sat up and rubbed her face. "Sorry." She looked up sharply. "What's wrong?"

"It's okay. Alphonse is in intensive care. He's not out of the woods yet, but his chances are improving. He's a tough old bird."

She sighed. "That's a relief."

"Where's Cell T?"

Jean looked away and composed herself for a moment. Adam looked at her sharply. "What?"

"They went to Puerto Rico. For Shasta."

"Oh, shit."

"Look, it's the rules. They hit us, we hit back."

"Shit, shit, shit," Adam muttered. "Those *idiots*! Why didn't they tell me?"

"Probably because you wouldn'tve let them go."

"You're damn right! Oh, shit." He sat down heavily in a chair and put his face in his hands for a moment. Then he spoke.

"It wasn't them. It wasn't Lepus."

Jean stared, a cold shiver passing through her body.

"The shooter turned herself in to the cops a couple hours ago. It's Shasta's mother. She blamed Alphonse or something, she was ranting about ghosts. I don't really understand it. But we were wrong. Everything's fine. We're still within the rules of engagement."

"Until Cell T gets to work, you mean."

"Yeah. I've got to call them."

"They left their phones. You said not to trust any of the

protocols."

"Damnit! Do you know where they are?"

"Somewhere in Puerto Rico, I imagine."

Adam rubbed his bloodshot eyes. "This is terrible. This is really bad."

Jean pulled her knees up to her chin and shivered some more. The heat was off in the room and she was cold.

"I'll have to warn them," he said wearily. "I have no choice."

"But how? They could be anywhere."

Adam looked at her gravely. "I don't mean Cell T."

Jean realized who he meant. "You can't *do* that!"

"What else *can* I do? They went down there on their own. They'll have to take their chances. Maybe OUTLOOK will beef up security enough that they'll just come home and forget this crap."

"They're going to a whorehouse," Jean blurted. "In Luján. Yrjo goes there sometimes. They'll grab him and make a play for Shasta. Tell OUTLOOK to keep Yrjo out of that whorehouse and Cell T will be stuck. They'll come back. They'll *have* to." She really wanted to believe what she was saying.

Adam glared at her. "You know, I'm not very happy with your role in this. You had my number at the hospital. You could have gone to a pay phone and warned me. You could have discouraged them from even going."

Jean was angry. "Look, we were all really freaked this morning. So were you! We thought the hammer was coming down and they decided to take their shot. Can you really blame them?"

He looked at the floor for a moment. "No, I can't. But I still have my duties. I have to protect the organization, and that means I have to call Lepus. Maybe you're right. Maybe they'll keep Yrjo's dick in his pants and Cell T will come home."

"Let me go down there. I can find them."

"No. We need you here. Alphonse isn't in the clear."

"Then send someone else!"

"No! This thing is way too big and way too out of control as it is! Anyone we send down there is gonna be a walking target. They're on their own."

Jean shook her head, her voice breaking. "I can't believe this. I can't believe you're going to snitch them."

"It's the only way, Jean. You know it is. We can't risk a war."

Tears welled up in her eyes and she buried her face in her hands. Adam got up and left.

"I hate this world," she whispered, trembling.

Stephanie's plane touched down in Leavenworth, Kansas, around six o'clock that evening. She rented a car and drove swiftly to Fort Leavenworth Army Base. The U.S. Disciplinary Barracks had visiting hours on weeknights from seven until nine-thirty. She drove onto the base and stopped to get directions from a passing MP, then headed for the USDB and parked in the visitor's area. The weather was cold as she walked to the entrance. She spent half an hour waiting in line behind other visitors before she was finally let in.

"I'd like to see Captain Forrest James," she told the admitting guard, a tall, stocky man in uniform.

"Have you been here before, ma'am?"

"No."

"You on the list?"

"List?"

"The list of authorized visitors. If the prisoner hasn't put you on his list, we can't let you in."

"I—I don't know."

"What's your name?"

"Stephanie Park."

"Just a minute, ma'am."

The guard stepped behind a desk and began flipping through some files. Stephanie waited anxiously. She hadn't spoken with James since she put him on a plane after the Roscoe op, almost two years ago, and had no reason to think that she'd be on any list.

"If I'm not on there, could we contact him? Get his permission?"

"Just a minute, ma'am."

He looked through some more files. Stephanie fidgeted.

"You're on the list," he said. "You're the only one *on* the list, in fact."

Stephanie smiled, a glow of happiness stealing over her entire body for the first time in what seemed like forever. There were butterflies in her stomach. *Hello, James,* she thought. *Hello.*

They told her the rules. They emptied her pockets, searched her, and ran her through a metal detector for good measure. Then they escorted her into a large open room with chairs scattered around and vending machines against one wall. Prisoners in brown uniforms and their visitors were everywhere—wives, children. Guards moved here and there amongst the chairs, keeping an eye on the little groups. Stephanie took a seat, her pulse racing.

A buzzer sounded. Two guards brought James in through a

large metal door. He spotted her immediately and winked. They led him over to a chair and he sat down.

"Hello," he said, his voice deep and kind. Prison had agreed with him. He was better-fed than he had been when she'd last seen him, though he was still in good shape, and his blonde hair had mostly turned a very distinguished gray. The mustache was gone, and the sharp angles of his face had softened. It looked good on him. He looked altogether mellow, a word Stephanie would never have thought to apply to him before.

"Hello," she replied with a wide smile. "How are you?"

"I'm pretty good. Nothing a week of blue sky and sunshine wouldn't help."

"You look good."

"So do you."

They sat for a moment.

"You just passing through town?"

She laughed. "Not hardly."

"Still with the EPA?"

"Not anymore."

"What happened?"

"Well, it hasn't happened yet. I guess I should have shown up for work this morning, actually. But there didn't seem to be much point. All they would have done is fired me."

His brow furrowed. "What's up?"

"You watch the news this weekend?"

"Good God," he said. "That *was* DG, wasn't it? I smelled it all the way out here."

"Yeah, it was."

"Damn. So you've signed on to the opera?"

"Yeah. It's been . . . well, it's been interesting."

"That sounds like an understatement."

"Look, I . . . I'm taking a trip. My Cell is. We're being very positive about it, but . . ." Her voice trailed off.

"But you don't think you're coming back."

"No. No, I don't. I think this is a one-way ticket."

"Then don't go. Tell Alphonse to blow."

"We're going on our own. It's kind of a long story. Alphonse is in the hospital. He's been shot."

"Jesus. I go away for a couple years and it all goes down the toilet."

She laughed at that. "Yeah, that's right. Things fall apart."

"The center cannot hold."

"Yeah . . ." She looked at a nearby prisoner, his hand cupping a woman's face. They kissed.

"So where are you going?"

"Puerto Rico. A place called OUTLOOK Group."

A shadow passed over his face. "Don't. Don't go there."

"You know it?"

"I've been there."

"*Really*? When?"

"A few years back. I wasn't supposed to know what it was or where, but I had some buddies on Vieques that filled me in afterward."

"Why were you there?"

"I was being recruited. There's this group of people, called SECTION DELTA."

Stephanie blinked. "The National Reconnaissance Office."

"That's them. They offered me a job with DELTA. Alphonse thought it might be a good idea. Someone on the inside, you know?"

"What happened?"

"I washed out. I didn't make the cut."

"Why?"

He laughed grimly. "I passed the psych eval."

She smiled at him. "You old softie."

"Yeah, that's me. Anyway, that's why I was at OUTLOOK. For the test. That place is bad, bad news. Why do you have to go there?"

"Do you know Agent Shasta?"

"Not well, but yeah."

"He's down there. They've got him. Doing experiments, something with the neo-tissue from Groversville."

James leaned forward and put his hand on her knee for a moment. "Then you *really* can't go there. You don't want to fuck with those people."

"I already have. Last weekend. They got back at us by shooting Alphonse."

"So it's war. Damn it! I can't do any fucking good in this place."

Stephanie shook her head. "It's okay. It's my war now. I'm going to see it through."

He looked at her warily. "So you're in? No hesitation?"

"Nope. I'm in."

"I wish I could say I was glad to hear that."

She smiled and took his hand, holding it tightly in her own. Her eyes were moist. "I need to go. I've got to catch a plane. I wanted to say goodbye. I wanted to say I was sorry."

"You've got nothing to be sorry for."

They stood up, still holding hands, and drew close. They kissed. For a moment, Stephanie's trip to Puerto Rico didn't seem very important—not nearly as important as the prospect of staying here, in this moment, for all time. For infinity.

Then she left.

James stood, watching her leave, as the guards approached to lead him back to his cell. He looked at his hand, the one she'd been holding. There was a piece of paper there. It was dingy, and badly creased from being folded and unfolded a thousand times. He knew what it said, knew it was his own handwriting on the note, but he opened it and read it just the same:

You are the rock and I am the wave—and when I touch you, I break.

VIC AND ABE ARRIVED at Luis Muñoz Marin International Airport in San Juan that evening, just after sunset. They took a meandering *publico* from the airport and a fellow passenger recommended a hotel, Casa del Caribe in the Condado district. They'd decided against renting a car just yet, so they could avoid using credit cards.

The hotel was a renovated old guest house, with just seven rooms. It was a Monday night, though, so one was available. They checked in with cash and fake ID and sprawled on the generous bed, reveling in the welcome warmth of Puerto Rico beneath a slowly oscillating ceiling fan.

"Are we doing the right thing?" Vic finally said.

"If not, it's still a heckuva vacation."

Vic smiled and propped herself up on one elbow to look at Abe. "Well, there's that."

They looked at each other for a while. Eventually, Vic sat up. "So tonight we're on vacation. Mr. & Mrs. Smith. Take me out, Abe. I want wine and food and dancing."

"Dancing? You've gotta be kidding."

"Come on!"

Δ

In five minutes they were changed and out the door. On the desk clerk's advice they took a taxi to Old San Juan, a centuries-old walled neighborhood frequented by tourists. After arriving they wandered on foot, navigating the steep streets of blue adoquine cobblestones and marveling at the Spanish Colonial buildings on every side. Eventually they selected a restaurant more or less at random and ended up with a brilliant meal at Amadeus—and plenty of wine—then left quite tipsy. Passing through the crowded Plaza de San José just afterwards, they drunkenly saluted the huge statue of Ponce de León.

Abe insisted on dropping into a small casino for an hour of blackjack—"For you, we'll dance; for me, we'll gamble"—and Vic hung on his arm, play-acting a smartass gangster's moll from an old movie. She was good at it. They left the casino bright-eyed and happy; Abe had won fifty dollars.

Up the street, Vic spotted a nightclub and dragged Abe inside to dance. He did his best, which was frankly terrible. Eventually, they settled on Abe sort of dancing in place while Vic bounced around him, happy as a lark, to the rhythms of a live salsa band.

They left the club and hailed a cab, which ran them back to Condado and the Casa del Caribe. Vic danced all the way to the door, snapping her fingers as Abe fumbled with the key. Inside, they fell on the bed, laughing—and then Abe kissed her.

She touched his face with one hand, tracing a line with her fingers, and he kissed her again. Vic wrapped her arms around his neck and kissed him back. They made slow, sweet love in the warm and the dark, flush with the aroma of the tropics, as the ceiling fan traced lazy orbits deep into the night.

Δ

San Juan City Hall was beautiful in the noonday sun, a two-hundred-year-old replica of its counterpart in Madrid. Vic and Abe loitered out front, taking in the warmth of the day. They hadn't spoken of what happened in the night, but they hadn't been regretting it, either.

Stephanie got out of a taxi and waved. They walked over to greet her, bringing their bags to join hers in the cab.

"God! It's beautiful here!" she said brightly. "I'd forgotten what the sun looked like."

"Me too," Abe said, glancing at a smiling Vic.

Stephanie cocked a suspicious eyebrow at them. "Well, it's about time," she said, which was the entirety of their discussion on the subject.

Vieques Island was a footprint eight miles off the southeastern coast of Puerto Rico, twenty-five miles wide by four miles deep. It had once been home to Arawaks, and served as a pirate enclave in the 1600s. Today the western and eastern thirds were under the authority of the U.S. Navy and Marines, respectively, who used the land for training exercises, bombardment ranges, and storage. But the center third still boasted a low-key, low-glitz tourist trade and a population below ten thousand. Architectural landmarks were in short supply; Hurricane Hugo had obliterated most of the civilian structures in 1989, and they'd been rebuilt out of modern brick and stone.

Cell T had taken Stephanie's taxi right back to the airport. There was a quick flight to Vieques on Isla Nena Air at half-past noon, and they barely made it. After the flight, they decided to take a chance and rent an SUV on Vic's credit card; of the three of them, she'd left the fewest footprints on the op to date. They found a small pawn shop that also carried ammunition, and they bought plenty. From there, they went to a small tourist store and bought several oversize, floppy outfits—tropical shirts, khaki cargo pants, and the like. At a gas station restroom they put their bulletproof vests on beneath the loose-fitting clothes, and hid their firearms and extra magazines in the bellows pockets of the pants. They were ready as they could be, under the circumstances, though Vic made a point of saying that they looked like geeks. The huge green Island Rent-A-Car logos on the SUV certainly didn't help.

Then they drove to Luján, a small town near the main entrance to the USMC's Camp Garcia. Following Agent Nancy's notes, they found the whorehouse. The neighborhood was quiet and friendly. The building was a private residence, attractive in a bordello sort of way, with no visible security; Nancy had said things were pretty relaxed there, and that most of their clients were wealthy Puerto Ricans. A couple of spit-and-polish men with crew cuts were walking furtively into the front door; military personnel were prohibited from entering the civilian areas of Vieques, but it looked like these two were breaking the rules. Vic snickered. "Sailors. Go figure." Cell T parked up the street and watched for a while. They had a description of Yrjo and his car from Nancy, down to the license plate. Although they didn't really expect to see him today, they figured they might as well start the surveillance immediately and get used to the surroundings.

Dr. Albert Yrjo drove up two hours later.

It was him, all right. They checked the license plate to be sure. He was driven by two men in Wackenhut khaki uniforms, an unsettling sight in this warm and inviting land; the last such uniforms they'd seen had been on dead men.

Yrjo's car came to a stop in front of the whorehouse. The three men inside conferred for a moment, and then Yrjo opened the door and stepped out jauntily.

The spring in his step didn't suit him. Yrjo was a hunched little man, his skin wrinkled and dotted with liver spots. He had a ring of wispy white hair around his head, which fluttered unbecomingly in the breeze and made him look crazed. He wore a floppy tropical shirt and white beachcomber pants, rolled up above the ankles, and sandals.

"Viagra," Abe said. "Gotta love it."

Then the car drove away.

"Jesus!" Stephanie exclaimed. "They're just leaving him!"

"I thought Nancy said they always came inside?" Vic asked.

"Maybe they're going to refill his prescription," Abe replied.

"Fuck it," Stephanie said. "Let's go."

The car was out of sight and Yrjo was inside the whorehouse. Vic cranked the ignition and whipped a u-turn, putting them right at the front door. Stephanie and Abe piled out of the SUV, guns tucked under their shirts, and ran inside. Vic kept the vehicle idling.

The lobby was furnished in Early Cathouse: red plush velvet curtains, red plush velvet furniture, vintage oil paintings of Rubenesque nudes idling on divans, tall floor lamps shaded with gauzy amber fabric, the works. An ornate gilt staircase with red carpet made a graceful arc down to the floor, ending by a massive wooden front desk carved with frolicking nudes. The only people in the lobby were Yrjo and a dusky, voluptuous older woman speaking to him from behind the desk.

She glanced at the harried-looking tourist couple that had just entered, no doubt mistakenly.

"May I help you?" she asked sweetly.

Stephanie and Abe walked swiftly over to either side of Yrjo and took him by the arms. Abe pressed a gun against his stomach.

"You're coming with us, doctor," he said.

"Oh, my," Yrjo replied.

The woman behind the desk raised her hands and stepped back, fearful.

"Have a nice day," Stephanie said. She and Abe wheeled Yrjo around and force-marched him right back out the door and into the sunshine. They climbed into the back seat, putting Yrjo in the middle, and Vic drove off.

"Jesus!" Abe said. "That was easy!"

"What's going on?" Yrjo said in a pleasant voice.

"You've got a friend of ours, doctor," Stephanie said. She had her gun out now as well, likewise pointed at Yrjo. "David Nells. We want him back."

The doctor looked back and forth at the pair with him in the back seat.

"How interesting," he said.

"We're the ones who hit OUTLOOK in Maryland," Abe cut in. "We know what you're up to. We don't care. We just want Nells."

"I see," Yrjo said. "No warrant this time?"

"No warrant," Stephanie replied. "Nells alive or you dead. That's the choice."

"Well," he said. "This is quite the quandary."

"It's no quandary, doctor."

"No, it is," he said, clearly intrigued by the situation.

"You see, there are several possibilities here. First, this might be a stress simulation. Perhaps my own staff has drugged me and arranged this ridiculous scenario to see if I'm still reliable. If so, then I have no intention of complying with you and we can stop this charade right now because I won't tolerate this indignity. Second, it may be that I've had a stroke in Maria's boudoir. This could be some sort of hallucination, in which case I should comply so that I can resolve it successfully and alive, since it could be my mind's way of recovering from the stroke and therefore success could be symbolically therapeutic to my life-threatening condition. Third, it may simply be that this is all real, in which case I should comply because I have every intention of living to an even riper old age than I already have."

Stephanie and Abe looked at each other, baffled.

"Very well, then. I will comply. Under the circumstances, the odds are two to one in favor of compliance. And even if the first scenario is true, they can hardly expect me to play the hero given my present physical faculties."

The agents looked at Yrjo, still boggling at what he was saying.

"Driver?" he asked. "Do you know the way?"

"Sure do," Vic replied.

"Then let's go."

They arrived at OUTLOOK in twenty minutes, Vic driving as fast as she dared. The facility was by itself at the end of a promontory between two bays, Puerto Ferro and Bahía Corcho, within the eastern third of Vieques owned by the U.S. Marines. The promontory was ringed with a thick band of mangrove trees, within which OUTLOOK was nestled.

Just before they entered the boundaries of Camp Garcia,

they'd moved Yrjo to the front passenger seat and Abe had taken over the wheel. Vic and Stephanie sat in the back seat, guns trained on Yrjo from behind. The Marine guard at the checkpoint checked their drivers' licenses and let them through. There were several beaches within the Marine zone that the military allowed public access to, with only a cursory check to verify U.S. citizenship. OUTLOOK was near one such place, known as Red Beach.

OUTLOOK was huge—a walled compound with many buildings, a small town unto itself. An electrified fence surrounded the entire place. At the entrance to OUTLOOK, a Wackenhut guard approached wearing a straw fedora. Yrjo waved merrily through the front window. The guard stopped, nodded, and went back into the sentry post. The gate swung open and Abe pulled forward.

Beyond the fence was another fence, with concrete posts in line with the gate to stop charging vehicles. They turned left and drove fifty yards, then reached a second gate. Once again, Yrjo waved to the guard and they were allowed through. They turned left once again before a twelve-foot stone wall with guard towers at the four corners, drove another fifty yards, and passed through a third and final gate before they were in the compound proper.

Yrjo pointed towards a large building off to one side, a couple hundred yards from the residential areas. "Over there," he said. "We'll take the rear entrance. It leads straight down to the labs, and we'll find your friend there." Abe turned the SUV and advanced.

A very bad feeling was settling over Vic. She'd seen the quick map Nancy had sketched out, but she was unprepared for the size and complexity of this operation. They were in very,

very deep water here. She leaned over to Stephanie.

"I don't like this," she whispered. "This has been way too easy."

Stephanie nodded, anxious. "Well, he *is* the boss," she whispered back. "Maybe he's just getting careless in his old age."

Yrjo sat, patient and smiling, hearing every word. His hearing was as good as it had been in his youth, a fact he credited to a lifetime of despising music and noise of every sort. He preferred silence, silence in which to think, silence in which to plan—and to execute plans already made.

They reached the rear entrance, where there was a small auxiliary parking lot. Cell T climbed out of the car, helping Yrjo out carefully. No one was around.

He led them to the door, and slid a key card through a slot. The door swung open and they walked inside, Abe taking the lead in front of Vic and Stephanie, who walked alongside Yrjo.

"Hello."

Adolph Lepus and a dozen NRO DELTA agents were waiting for them. As the soundproofed door swung silently shut behind them, Abe raised his weapon.

OUTSIDE, THE TROPICAL SUN beat down on the facility. On the far side of the stone wall, beyond the mangroves, the waves crashed against the shore and broke. The cries of sea birds rang across the sky. It was a beautiful, beautiful day.

Chapter Seven: The Sound of Horns and Motors

Wednesday, March 17–Monday, March 22, 1999

Forrest James sat on the cot in his cell at the USDB. Breakfast was in an hour, and then would come his first work detail of the day in the woodshop. An order for sixty-seven plaques had come in from Altus Air Force Base in Oklahoma, needed in a month for some ceremony. It was going to be Lacquer City in the woodshop for the next few weeks. The thought made him gag; he could smell that thick brown syrup just by thinking about it. Woodworking was fine. He liked the precision, the care, the chance to make something with his hands. But treating the wood with rosins and varnishes sucked rocks. It was messy work and invariably he'd get drops on his uniform, which meant laundry time. The guards kept a close eye on the prisoners' appearance, and their clothes had to be crisp and clean. He might be in prison, but he was still in the military. Some things never changed.

James shook his head. It wasn't the work that was pissing him off. It was Stephanie. It was the fact that she believed she was going off to die. It was the fact that he was stuck in here, on the fifth floor of the fourth wing of the Castle. It was the fact that he couldn't do a damn thing to help her.

Even that wasn't the whole truth. There *was* something he could do—maybe. He just didn't like it very much. Since she'd visited him the night before last he'd been thinking. Thinking about a phone call he could make. About a man in New York City who just might be able to give him a Get Out Of Jail Free card.

The problem was, he'd want something in return.

"Fuck it," James said to himself, and thought: *What the hell else am I good for?* He stood up and took three steps to the bars.

"Hey Anderson!" he called out.

Corrections Specialist Donna Anderson snapped her head to the left from where she was standing guard down the hall. "What is it?"

"Got a minute?"

She looked at him for a moment. Ex-Captain Forrest James, USN, had been a model prisoner. There were fewer than fifty ex-officers incarcerated in the entire Castle, and while their rank didn't entitle them to anything special, the staff nonetheless appreciated it when they set a good example for the rest of the inmates. James had done just that. Finally she turned and walked smartly down the row until she stood before his cell.

"Well?"

"I'd really like to make a phone call."

Anderson raised her eyebrows. "This got anything to do with that blond that was here the other day?" she asked with a faintly amused tone. Word of James' visitor had spread among the staff and the population alike; it was the first one he'd ever had, and it was the considered opinion of the male guards and inmates alike that she was a doozy. Within twenty-four hours, you'd have thought that most of the population and a third of the staff was in the visiting room when she was there, given the eloquence—or at least, the enthusiasm—of their descriptions.

"Come on, Anderson."

"You can do it on your own time, after breakfast."

"It's important. Please. When have I ever asked you for

anything?"

Anderson thought for a moment before replying. "All right." She turned towards her partner, watching from the end of the row. "Lewis! Prisoner to the phone."

They led him down to the ground floor and into an open area frequented by prisoners during free time; at the moment, it was empty. There was a low murmur from the tiers of cells around and above them, as cons got up to greet yet another day behind bars. A bank of phones were arrayed on one wall. Lewis and Anderson stood patiently a few feet away.

James picked up a handset and dialed. He also entered his identification number. All calls from the prison had to be collect, and were placed by a prison operator to prevent inmates from lying about who they were. There were a series of clicks as the call went through Delta Green's secure routers.

"Adam," a voice finally said.

"This is the Fort Leavenworth prison operator. Will you accept a collect call from Forrest James?"

A pause. Then, "Yes."

"Thank you." Another click as the inmate phone's receiver was enabled and the operator dropped off the line.

"What the hell do *you* want?" Adam barked.

"The tropical trio. They back yet?"

"I don't know what you're talking about."

"The hell you don't. Are they back yet?"

Another pause. "No. They're not coming back."

"Explain."

"Their hosts called this morning to say they're having a wonderful time together."

"Thanks," James said angrily, and hung up the phone.

Anderson stepped forward. "You done?"

He looked over his shoulder at her and dialed zero. "Not yet. Give me a minute, please."

She stepped back and exchanged a look with her partner, who shrugged.

"Prison operator."

"Please connect me with directory assistance," James asked.

"Hold please."

A recorded voice came on the line. "AT&T directory assistance. What city, please?"

"New York."

"What state?"

"New York."

"What listing?"

"Club Apocalypse."

"Please hold for the number."

James waited. He really didn't want to make this call, but he didn't feel that he had a choice.

"Hello, Captain," a cultured voice said.

He jumped a little. "Hello?"

"I thought I'd cut out the middleman. Or rather, I thought I'd substitute one. Jelly has a message for you."

The line clicked off and there was a dial tone.

James lowered the phone and stared at it. *How the hell did that happen?* he thought, and swallowed nervously. *How'd he do that?*

"All done?" Anderson asked behind him.

"Yeah," he said quickly. "All done." He set the phone down and turned around slowly, his face carefully blank.

The guards led him back to the cell. When they closed and locked the door, it actually made him feel a little better.

Δ

George Rhodes was a big man, three hundred pounds if he was an ounce. He'd come to Fort Leavenworth buff as all get out six years ago, a Marine sergeant who'd raped a woman in Italy and got fifteen years. Two years ago, another inmate stuck a shiv in his brain. George survived, but he wasn't really George anymore. He lumbered where once he strode, and the muscle turned to flab. He sat in his cell as often as he could, staring at the wall. They'd ruled that he was still competent and didn't need special care, which was true, but if he served out his sentence he would be one of the scant 10% of USDB inmates who returned to society worse off than they'd left it. When he came here, people called him Steel and gave him respect. Now they called him Jelly, when they noticed him at all. Rick DuBois, the inmate who'd shivved him, got twelve more years and was bucked back up to the sixth floor, shackled in maximum security like any other new fish; but he walked tall, bragging that he was the man that broke the Steel.

Forrest James didn't know either one of them, except by sight and reputation. The tale of the day the Steel broke was a popular one around the Castle. James had heard it three times in the first six months he was here.

He didn't share a work detail with Jelly, but he found him shuffling around the yard that afternoon. James looked around to make sure no one was giving him the eye and then ambled over to walk alongside the big man.

"Hey," he said cautiously. "Hey man."

Jelly kept walking. James had to move slow to match his pace.

"Rhodes, hey. What's up, bro?"

More walking. James stole a glance and noticed a few inmates watching them.

"Rhodes?"

"Hello again, Captain," the cultured voice said. Jelly's lips were moving, but it wasn't his voice coming out.

James stopped for a second, shocked, and then caught up again.

"Hello?" he said tentatively.

"I'm pleased you called. It's a shame we've never met before."

It was chilly in the yard, but that wasn't why James shivered.

"Yeah, well, I don't get out to the Big Apple much."

"That's all right. I get around."

"No shit."

The voice chuckled. "They record the calls here sometimes. I thought this might be better for our little *tête-a-tête*."

"Whatever floats your boat."

"I take it you're looking for a vacation? A week of blue sky and sunshine, wasn't that it?"

You've gotta be shitting me, James thought. The voice was quoting his conversation with Stephanie from the other night.

"I'd be delighted to help. But my resources are limited. I can arrange for you to have your freedom, but you'll have to get outside the Castle first."

"If I could do that, I wouldn't need you, would I?"

"Oh, I'm not suggesting you make some sort of foolhardy escape. There's an inmate by the name of Dennis Bounds. A serial killer. Tiresome fellow. Murdered some little black girls down in Georgia, at Fort Benning. There's three bodies still missing, one of whom the authorities don't even know about.

He's also got a partner out there who's still killing. John Law knows he exists, but they don't know who he is. If you could fill in this lacunae for them, they'd be most grateful. You could be taken out of the Castle for a deposition and so on, if you ask the right people. That's when I could give you a hand."

"So I ask Bounds and he just spills it, right?"

"Well, you'll need to persuade him. It shouldn't be difficult. He's tough in court, but he's really the weak sister of the pair. The taxpayers provided you with a lot of skills, Captain. Use them."

"This is bullshit," James said.

"Huh?" said Jelly, in a slow, deep voice.

"Hello?"

"What you want, man?"

"Never mind, Jelly," James said, as he turned and strode off across the yard.

He'd heard of Sergeant Dennis Bounds. Bounds showed up at the Castle a month after he had. The guy was a pasty little dude with bad skin, but he had a way of twitching that was unnerving. He'd been an instructor at Fort Benning's School of the Americas before Benning's Criminal Investigation Command caught him in his home on base with the young daughter of a black MP, sawing the hands off the corpse. Within a few weeks of his arrival at Fort Leavenworth he'd hooked up with the prison's chapter of the Aryan Brotherhood, a loose-knit confederation of white supremacists that had spread from prison to prison and throughout the armed forces from the 1970s onward. The Castle held about twenty such people, many from a purge of the Brotherhood the military had undertaken in the last few years. They generally kept a very low profile, but they hung tight and occasionally got in scraps with black inmates. Bounds fit right in. Rick DuBois was with them, too, though it was more in spirit these days since he was still under maximum-security restrictions.

Bounds' alliance with the Aryans made leaning on him a little difficult. Although James hoped to be out of here not long after he got Bounds to spill the beans, there was no guarantee, and the Aryans would want payback. If he was going to make a move on Bounds, he'd need help.

The day after his chat with Jelly, James took a trip to the weight room. Cons pumped iron, sweating and straining and trying to beat their last marks. To one side, the Muslims were hard at it. There were almost fifty Muslims among the Castle's black population, righteous men who followed Allah and didn't take shit from anybody. They tended to keep to themselves, but they weren't spiteful; they just wanted to steer clear of the faithless.

One of the Muslims in the weight room that day was Ex-Major Frank Holmes, a reformed alcoholic who'd killed his wife ten years ago during the last in a long string of booze-fueled slapfests in their little house at Fort Leonard Wood, Missouri. James knew him from anger-management classes. Frank was doing eighty years at the Castle, which meant he'd die here. In class, he'd come across as genuinely reformed, a man who accepted responsibility for the way he'd lived his life and was now committed to a higher path. They hadn't really spoken outside of class before, but if there was anyone in the Muslims James felt he might could turn to, it was him. He strolled over as Frank toweled off his massive chest and watched some of his pumped-up brothers going through their routines.

"Major," James said respectfully, nodding his head as he

stepped up.

Frank looked at him, stone-faced. "The Army doesn't call me that anymore, and I don't either. I'm just a man now, a man on the road."

James shifted uneasily. "What can I call you?"

"That depends on what you want."

"I'm looking for some help. I thought you and your brothers might be the ones to talk to."

"If you're looking for spirits or drugs or tobacco, you have come to the wrong man."

James shook his head. "I know better than that, and I wouldn't be interested anyway. It's the Aryan Brotherhood. They're sheltering someone, someone who did some terrible things. He's not done. He's got a partner on the outside still at work, a guy the cops never found. I'd like to see that justice is done."

Frank nodded. "I know the devil you mean. What do you care?"

James paused, thinking hard of the right words. "On the outside, I fought for a righteous world. But I was weak, and I succumbed. I'm strong again. I'm not willing to stop fighting just because I'm doing my time. This man killed children. He didn't give up all the bodies. There are families out there who have never found their dead. And there's his partner. He's still killing. I want this man to give up his secrets and end this suffering. But to do it, I need your help."

Frank looked at him for a long moment. James felt like his soul was being laid bare before this man's blazing sight. Finally Frank laughed.

"You're a righteous man, Forrest James. I know that. But don't think your newfound hubris excuses your crime."

"I don't."

"So what do you propose?"

"I need to get Bounds alone and make him see the error of his ways. I need you and your brothers to run interference, keep the Aryans at bay, and watch my back for a few weeks afterwards. If Bounds dies, I'll take the fall."

Frank nodded. "An interesting plan. My brothers and I will pray on this matter. Bounds is a devil who slew my little sisters, and Allah is not fond of devils."

"So what do I call you?"

"What?"

"You said what I called you depended on what I wanted. So what do I call you?"

The man laughed. "You can call me Frank."

It went down two days later. Bounds and two of his Aryan buddies were on laundry detail, pushing carts full of linens down the narrow halls. Their route took them past a locked storeroom.

At least, normally it was locked. Jesse Smith, a grizzled little old Muslim who'd been in the Castle for forty years, helped out the cleaning staff and could get the keys when he needed them for work. As the three Aryans pushed the heavy cart, the storeroom door swung open behind them. They turned to look.

Four burly black men poured out the door. Two grabbed Bounds and picked him up like a doll, a powerful hand clamped over his mouth, while the other two faced off with the Aryans.

"We need Mr. Bounds for just a minute," one said, as Bounds was dragged into the storeroom squirming and moaning.

The Aryans gawked for a second. Then one sprinted off down the hall, quick as a rabbit. The other one glanced at his fleeing partner and then looked back at the Muslims, his chin trembling.

"Uh—"

The fists came down like righteous hammers.

Inside the storeroom, the two Muslims held Bounds while Frank Barnes gagged him with a cleaning rag, fastened his wrists behind his back, and tied his ankles together. Little Jesse stood in the corner, grinning and nodding. "Look at that devil kick!" he exclaimed merrily. Forrest James cracked his knuckles and stared into Bounds' eyes with an executioner's cold gaze.

When Frank was done, he shoved Bounds to the floor. "He's all yours." Then the Muslims pulled the laundry cart inside—it now contained a badly battered and thoroughly unconscious Aryan—and went to wait in the hall, closing the storeroom door behind them.

Bounds looked up at James from the floor. He'd pissed himself, and the smell rose off him mixed with sweaty fear.

James hunched down next to Bounds, keeping his gaze fixed. "I'm going to ask you a few questions in a little while. But not right now."

Bounds whimpered.

"Right now, I'm just going to hurt you."

It didn't take long for the Aryans to respond. Within a few minutes, the one who'd rabbited came back with six of his friends. The gang caught sight of the Muslims standing outside the storeroom, arms folded, a formidable wall of black power. One of the Aryans, his sleeves rolled up and his powerful arms covered with blue jailhouse tats, pushed to the front as his buddies slowed. He walked right up to Frank and got in his face.

"What the fuck is going on here, Sambo?"

"We're taking out the trash. Why don't you just run along?"

"I don't think so."

"What do you care for a child molester?"

"Bounds ain't no fuckin' kiddy-raper! Those nigger bitches got what they deserved. Stand aside or get the same." His allies gathered around him, eyeing the Muslims and nodding with determination.

Frank grinned huge. His smile made him look even bigger than he really was.

"You know," he said, "in class I learned how to keep my temper. And I do. I keep it inside, like butane in a blowtorch. I've been saving up."

"Oh yeah?"

"Yeah."

Frank threw his head forward, cracking the Aryan right above the eyes. The man staggered back, dazed, then the rest of his crew leapt into the fray. Black on white, white on black, they fell on each other like jackals, fists flying and blood spattering the walls.

Inside the storeroom, Bounds wasn't doing well. His face was covered in blood, which was streaming out his nostrils from a broken nose. Several ribs were busted, as were several fingers. James stood over him, kicking him in the guts again and again, one arm windmilling like DeNiro in a gangster flick. Bounds was squealing and sobbing. Finally James relented.

He knelt down and took the gag off. Bounds gasped for air,

his face contorted from more pain than he'd ever known.

"*J—Joey!*" he wailed, delirious. "*Joey! Help me!*"

"Who's your partner, Bounds?" James asked, his voice cold. "Who is he?"

"*Joey!*"

"Joey who?"

"*Joey! Joey Carmichael! Joey! He said this wouldn't happen! He said it'd be okay! He said we wouldn't get caught! Joey!*" He trailed this last word out into a wail.

"Where are the bodies, Bounds? What did you do with the bodies?"

Bounds panted. James put his massive hand on Bounds' throat and squeezed.

"*Ahhhk! The range! We dumped 'em on the artillery range!*"

James raised one eyebrow. These guys would have to be crazy to have ventured onto the Fort Benning artillery range, which was littered with spent shells and unexploded munitions; it was virtually a minefield. But on the other hand, no one would go looking for bodies there, either—assuming the bodies hadn't been blown to bits by the shelling. For a psycho, Bounds was pretty clever. Or else this Joey was.

James grabbed Bounds by the back of the neck and pulled him up to his face. Bounds whined, his busted ribs grinding away at his innards. James looked into his eyes.

"You're not lying to me, are you Bounds?"

Bounds stared back, his eyes open doorways into his fearful dark soul. What little truth he had in him was spent.

James nodded. "I believe you." He let go of Bounds, who dropped to the floor and conked his head on the cement. James stood up and went to the door. The sounds of fighting outside had abated. He opened it, ready for anything.

Frank Barnes turned around and grinned. He was missing a tooth, and his face was bloody. "You done in there?" he said, breathing heavily. Four Aryans were piled on the floor, beaten and bleeding. The other three had fled. One Muslim was out cold. Little Jesse, who'd stuck to the sidelines, was dabbing the man's broken nose with a handkerchief.

"All done."

"Then let's go. Allah be praised! It's a glorious day."

SIX HOURS LATER, CAPTAIN Forrest James was in shackles on a military transport plane to Fort Benning, Georgia.

THE MPS LED HIM off the plane at dusk. They were greeted by the Provost Marshal, four CIC investigators, two detectives from Columbus Homicide, and two FBI agents. One of them was Agent Adam.

They led James to the Marshal's office and took him into an interrogation room. A stenographer was there for his deposition. It took two hours. Afterwards, Adam led James to the mess hall with a couple of MPs following them.

"You just don't know when to quit, do you?" Adam said.

"Nope."

"Assuming any of this checks out, you've got your week of R&R. I'll be your chaperone. I can't vouch for the weather here, but we'll get you out and about. You like golf?"

"Can't stand it."

"Well, we'll find something to do."

"How's Alphonse?"

"He's okay. He'll be in the Georgetown hospital for a while, but he pulled through."

"Any word from Puerto Rico?"

"They're gone, Forrest. I'm sorry." He paused. "You know better than to try anything, don't you? If you've got something planned, you're a bigger fool than I thought you were."

"I just wanted out of that damn place for a while."

Adam nodded. "Okay. I trust you. But I can't say I have much hope for you when we ship you back to Leavenworth. The Aryans are going to want revenge."

"I can take care of myself."

"Sure you can." They were outside the mess hall now. "Here we are. I hope you like chipped beef."

James spent the night in a cell. In the morning, Adam showed up. He brought breakfast, a big Southern meal he'd picked up at a restaurant off base. The MPs let him into the cell and James rubbed his face, feeling grimy. The MPs left and shut the door.

"Lieutenant Joey Carmichael went AWOL last night just before you got here," Adam said as he sat down on the opposite bunk. "I think someone called him from Leavenworth. We'll get him, though."

"You been to his house?"

"Last night. He kept trophies."

"Stop. I'm eating." To James, the food tasted like freedom.

"They're going to start checking out the range today. It'll take a while. But you're Benning's new golden boy. The Provost Marshal wants you at his house tonight for dinner. What do you want to do until then?"

James swallowed a mouthful of buttery grits. "I want to get the fuck off this base. I want grass and trees and dirt."

Adam nodded. "Roosevelt State Park is an hour north. I'll

get a couple MPs and we'll make a day of it."

"Sounds good."

"You earned it, you stubborn son of a bitch."

James smiled and took a gulp of coffee. "Just doing my duty, sir."

A couple hours later, they reached the park in a Fort Benning MP sedan. James was shackled and had a tracer on his ankle, but as he stepped out of the vehicle and into the parking lot, surrounded by trees, he felt like a free man.

The two MPs had chatted him up on the drive out. Word had gotten around that Dennis Bounds was in intensive care from the beating he'd gotten, and they wanted to hear the story. James left the Muslims out, referring to them only as "some associates," but besides that he spared no detail. His mimicry of Bounds' whining had them in stitches. Adam kept his mouth shut but couldn't help a smile. He knew that Fort Benning had been badly shamed by Bounds and his accomplice, and across the base men were laughing and telling outrageous stories about this badass Navy SEAL doing ten in the Castle who'd done them all a solid. The MPs who'd pulled this excursion detail knew their buddies would be buying the beer tonight, hot to hear the latest.

The first shot caught the MP square in the face, splattering the back of his head across the hood of the car. The second and third jerked his partner against the vehicle, striking him in the chest, blood pumping from the wounds. Adam whipped out his sidearm and clicked off the safety just as a fourth shot punched through him. He dropped to his knees on the concrete and wheezed, gun tumbling to the cement.

James looked around, frantic. There were a dozen vehicles

in the parking lot. He made the shooters, two men sitting inside a big panel van, the door open, rifles pointing. James hit the ground and fumbled through his chains to reach Adam's gun.

A tall man in a jogging suit and black leather gloves ran over from a different direction and kicked the gun away. James looked up.

"Alzis sent us," the man said in a clipped German accent. He was as big as James was, maybe more so, with short-cropped blond hair and harsh Aryan features. "Get up." He pulled James up with one thick hand as the two shooters and a third man rushed over from the van.

Adam tried to sit up and coughed blood. "*You fuck!*" he screamed. "*How could you fucking do this!*"

James looked down at Adam, incredulous. "I didn't know!" he yelled. "I didn't think it would be like this!"

The blond man drew a Luger and pulled Adam up, gun held against his bleeding chest. "You will have to die," he said. "But I will give you a present first." He nodded at the two shooters, who immediately seized the third man by the arms. The man wriggled. "Hey! What the fuck!"

The German pushed Adam against the car, where he stood, supporting himself on one elbow. Then the man picked up Adam's sidearm, a Colt Delta Elite, and put his Luger away. He ejected the magazine from the Colt and checked the action to make sure there wasn't one in the pipe. One by one, he popped the bullets out of the magazine until only one was left, then slid the magazine back into the gun and chambered the round. He took his Luger out again and held the Colt's handle towards Adam.

"This man is Joseph Carmichael. If you like, you may kill him. But you only get one shot."

"Galt!" Joey screamed. "You son of a bitch! What the fuck are you doing!"

Adam took a ragged, panting breath and glared at the German called Galt, then at James. His eyes were furious with anger.

"Well?"

"Fine," Adam spat. The two shooters dragged Joey over, kicking and screaming, and forced him to his knees. Galt handed Adam the Colt, pressing the Luger against his temple.

Joey wailed. Adam blew his brains across the pavement.

"That felt good, yes?" Galt said, smiling. "Now he will precede your soul into Hell and serve you in the afterlife." The shooters trained their rifles on James.

Adam fixed James with a terrible stare. "Make this right," he said, trembling, blood pouring from his lips. "*Make this right you son of a bitch!*"

James looked back, speechless, his face pale. Galt pulled the trigger.

THEY TOOK THE VAN to a private airfield and hustled James on board a small jet. The plane landed in New York State hours before dawn. Not a word was exchanged during the flight. Galt smoked Turkish cigarettes and read *Entertainment Weekly.*

THE TEESE BUILDING STOOD in the Upper East Side of Manhattan at the intersection of E. 98th and Lexington. It was a huge office building, the headquarters of an international paper-products company. Off to one side, in an alley, was a stairwell that descended thirty-one steps below street level to a pair of unmarked blue-steel doors. The nearby street was full of cars, Monday morning commuters rushing to work. The sidewalk was crowded with pedestrians.

A panel van pulled into the alley. Two men got out of the front seats and opened the big sliding door. Galt stepped out, then the trio took James out by his arms. He was still shackled, but the ankle tracer was gone—they'd destroyed it at the airfield upstate. A few people on the sidewalk gave them funny looks, but this was New York, after all. Anything could happen here.

They led James down the stairs. A slim young blond man in a perfectly tailored gray suit opened one of the doors from inside, and they stepped into Club Apocalypse.

The first room was a small foyer, done up in red velvet with a coat-check counter, presently unstaffed. The blond man led the newcomers through the foyer and into the main room. It was done up in classical style, red velvet and earth tones and subtle lighting, with a row of booths running down one wall. A young redheaded woman in a formal white shirt and black tie stood behind the long mahogany bar opposite the booths, smoking a cigarette.

The procession came to a halt at the bar. "Drinks?" the blond man said.

"*Nein*," Galt replied. "Where is Alzis?"

"He won't be joining us. But I have the item."

He nodded at the woman, who reached under the bar and removed a parcel wrapped in brown paper and tied with black string. The man took it and handed it over to Galt.

"*Danke* . . ." Galt said with a leer. ". . . *Hauptscharfuhrer* Scheel."

The man glowered. "I'm sure I have no idea what you're talking about. The door's over there," he added, nodding.

Galt gave a crisp nod and walked out, trailed by his two associates.

"Well," the man said, turning his attention to James. "A pleasure to meet you, Captain."

James spat in his face.

The man slapped him, hard, but quickly stepped back. He pulled a silk handkerchief from his breast pocket and wiped his face.

"That was hardly necessary, Captain. I'm Belial. Welcome to my club."

"What are you? Alzis's funny sidekick?"

"Hardly. Stephen Alzis is my business associate."

"So where is he?"

Belial turned to look at a doorway filled with a red velvet curtain. Stephen Alzis stepped through jauntily, smiling.

"Hello again, Captain," he called as he strode across the dim room. "I trust you are well?"

"You son of a bitch."

Alzis *tsk-tsked* and leaned against the bar. "Gin and tonic, my dear," he said to the woman. Alzis was a short, trim Arab in his thirties with black hair, the bangs hanging down over his eyes. He wore a clean, attractive white suit that looked to be of several decades' vintage.

"Why did you kill those men? That wasn't part of the agreement."

"I have no idea what you mean, Captain. I sent someone to get you out, just as you asked. How they achieved that goal was their business. I don't do details."

"Don't fuck with me, Alzis. You could have snapped your fingers or waved your magic wand or something."

Alzis sipped his drink. Belial arched an eyebrow and gave a thin smile. "Are you fond of magic wands, Captain?"

James ignored him. "So what now?"

"Now?" Alzis said pleasantly, still smiling. "You're a free man. You can do what you want. I just wanted to make sure you were well. Galt can be a little ferocious."

"He killed a friend of mine."

"That's not my concern. He doesn't work for me. We had a simple agreement, much as you and I do. If you're displeased, take it up with Galt."

"I will."

"Those chains don't really become you, Captain. Take them off."

James looked down at his shackles. They were unlocked—a moment ago they'd been fastened tight. He took them off angrily and threw the chains on the floor.

"Quit fucking with me, Alzis. What do you want?"

"I want the same thing you do, Captain. I want you to go to Vieques Island and find your friends. I want you to rescue David Nells. Surely you can't argue with that."

"That's it?"

"That's it. Go play the hero and we'll be even."

"I don't believe you."

"That's none of my affair. Believe what you want."

"Why?"

"That's none of *your* affair." Alzis reached in his jacket and removed an envelope. He handed it to James, who looked inside. It was bulging with new hundred-dollar bills.

"I'd suggest you make a tailor your first stop. You could use a change of clothes."

"And a shower," Belial added pointedly.

"Goodbye, Captain."

James looked at them both and started to say something,

but thought better of it. He turned and walked swiftly out of the club.

"*Vaya con dios*," Alzis called after him.

Manhattan was oppressively intimidating and noisy as hell. James had only been to New York a handful of times, and he'd never liked it much. He liked it even less now. Standing on the corner at Teese Plaza, he looked around, lost. Alzis was right about one thing: he needed clothes. The brown uniform of the USDB looked decidedly odd in this place.

He spotted a men's store up the street and strode forward through the crowds. Inside he got a shirt, slacks, loafers, and a heavy overcoat. That ran him four hundred dollars. He had about a thousand left from the money Alzis gave him. Without any form of identification, he couldn't get a flight or rent a car. Hailing a cab, he decided to go Greyhound.

It took him seven hours to reach Georgetown. From the bus terminal he fed coins into a pay phone, calling hospitals, until he found the one Joseph Camp was in. He grabbed a taxi and was there in twenty minutes.

Joe was watching TV in a private room. The remains of dinner sat on a cart next to the bed. He was bundled up under blankets, his thick, pale face barely protruding to lie against the pillow. He looked very old. James entered quietly and Joe turned to look at him.

"You son of a bitch," he said groggily. "You've got a lot of damn nerve coming here."

James walked up and stood over the bed. "Hello, Joe," he said guardedly.

"You here to kill me, too?"

James closed his eyes. "I didn't kill Adam."

"Fool," Joe said bitterly. "You made a call, didn't you? You picked up the phone and you called PARIAH to get you out of jail. And you got Adam killed."

He opened his eyes again. "I didn't know, Joe. I didn't think anyone would get hurt."

Joe snorted. "You didn't think anyone would get *hurt*?" He was furious now. "*What part of selling your soul to the devil do you not understand?*"

"I know. I fucked up. I'm sorry. I feel like shit."

"You *are* shit. How could you do this?"

James was quiet for a moment. "I love her, sir. I couldn't just sit there and let her fall into their hands. I had to do something."

Joe stared at him. "Well. So you're a fool for love. I should have guessed. This organization is positively riddled with doomed romantics."

"Do you know anything, sir? About Puerto Rico?"

"Not much. They went down there without permission. Lepus called to say he had them and we wouldn't be seeing them again."

James was surprised. "Why did Lepus call?"

Joe exhaled slowly. "Things have been very dangerous of late. The truce was holding until I got shot. Everyone thought it was them. That's why Cell T went to Puerto Rico, for revenge. But they were wrong."

"Who shot you?"

"Sarah Nells. David's mother. She . . . well, let's just say that I don't blame her."

"So why did Lepus call?"

"Adam warned him. Cell T was incommunicado. We couldn't get in touch. We had to preserve the truce, had to warn Lepus that Cell T was on its way and that they were acting on their own. Agent Nancy knew what they were planning. Adam told Lepus and hoped they'd just beef up security and Cell T would come home empty-handed, or check in with us so we could bring them back."

James shook his head, disgusted. "You bastards."

"What were we supposed to do?" Joe complained. "Start a war because Stephanie Park had a wild hair up her ass? We were trying to stay within the rules of engagement."

"Damn your rules and damn you, Joe. You betrayed your own people."

"Forrest, you have no idea what's been going on! You think I like any of this? I've been doped up on my back for days, out of touch, while you goddamn cowboys run roughshod over everything we've accomplished since Reggie died! And before you accuse me of things I couldn't control, you damn well better not forget that your arrogance got Adam killed."

James nodded. "Okay. You're right. We're both bastards."

"Damn straight," Joe replied. He shook his head, tired now. "I've tried so hard, Forrest. I really have. I've tried to turn this organization into something that would work, something that could survive and maybe even triumph someday. But you cowboys always screw it up."

"Jesus, Joe. What do you expect? You recruit a bunch of people, doomed romantics, cynical idealists, people who are willing to fight authority, break the law, shred the Constitution, all for the sake of some higher purpose, and then you act surprised when they don't play by *your* rules? What part of selling your soul to the devil do *you* not understand?"

Joe laughed. "You're right, Forrest. We're both bastards."

James sighed and looked away. "I need your help, Joe. I need to get to Puerto Rico."

"That won't be easy. You don't know what Alzis has done to you, do you?"

James looked worried. "What do you mean?"

"He's tarred you with your own brush. Informants have told the FBI that you're a leader in the Aryan Brotherhood, that Bounds was your punk in Leavenworth, that he rolled over so your men could free you in Georgia. They found the bodies of those poor girls, but they weren't on the artillery range. They were on a little farm near McRae. They found a damn arsenal there, too, illegal munitions, bunkers, I don't know what all. They're saying it was a militia HQ for the Aryans."

James was pale. "Oh, Christ."

"Yes, I thought as much. It's your farm, isn't it? Some little bolthole you set up years ago?" James nodded. "They'll link you to it. They'll charge you with Adam's murder. They'll implicate you in the killings of those girls. You'll probably be on the ten-most-wanted list by this time next week."

James steadied himself on the railing of Joe's bed. "I can't believe it. That smug fuck. He set all this up to trap me."

"Yes, he did. We can't get you out of this, but he could. Alzis owns you now. The only question is, why?"

"I'm not sure. I asked him what he wanted and he said he just wanted me to go to Puerto Rico, to get Cell T and David."

"Really?" Joe said, sitting up gingerly in bed, his mind working. "How very interesting. I just assumed he wanted you for some other stratagem. My goodness. If Alzis is involved with whatever OUTLOOK wants David for . . . oh, my." He looked thoughtful.

"What is it?"

"Do you know how David's father died?"

"No."

"David's father was CIA, a pilot for Civil Air Transport in Taiwan after the war. He was a friend of mine. I used him for a few DG jobs. In 1964 his plane went down over the Yellow Sea during one of my ops." He thought to himself for a moment. "Stephen Alzis was on that plane. I put two men on board to kill him—foolish, of course, but we didn't really know him then. Anyway, Alzis turned up three months later in Brussels, none the worse for wear. The plane was never found."

"What does it mean?"

Joe shook his head. "Beats the hell out of me. But under the circumstances, I think you're right to go to Puerto Rico. If Alzis is involved, this is bigger than OUTLOOK and Lepus."

"I need help. Money, ID, gear."

"What you need is Agent Nancy. I'll call her and tell her you're on the way."

"I appreciate it, Joe. And I'm sorry."

"We're fighting a very ugly war, Forrest. There are no clear choices, no pure motives. Good people die. Sometimes it's our fault. But follow your heart and I'll trust you'll make it right."

"I'll do my best, Joe."

They shook hands.

"Goodbye, Forrest. I hope I see you again."

James smiled. "Count on it."

Agent Nancy lived in a large, secluded house in Brookmont, just across the river from the CIA. The house was screened by tall hedges on all sides, and the shutters were always kept closed. Inside, she tried her best to live something resembling a normal life. In her old identity as Debra Constance, she'd worked in the field on big cases all over the country for the FBI's Psychological Crimes Unit. Now, as Jean Qualls, she was just a telecommuting PCU paper-pusher, a consultant who reviewed files and commented on the work of others. It wasn't very satisfying, but it paid the bills; Delta Green had supplied the house for security reasons, but she didn't expect or want them to give her a free ride. Her yogurt was her own.

Around the house, she dropped her illusion of humanity. The blond woman vanished, replaced by a grotesque humanoid with distended canine jaws and the grubby, dusky skin of a corpse. Agents Nick and Nolan, her handlers, had slowly gotten acclimated to the surreal sight of a nightmare being watching *Star Trek* in a Temple University sweatshirt and shorts; they'd seen a lot of weird things with Delta Green over the years, and at least Agent Nancy had developed a slight sense of humor about her condition. She still had bad days and worse nights, and the task of bringing her a steady stream of human body parts to feed her alien cravings was unpleasant to say the least, but the trio had come to accept that no matter how terrible and crazy things were at times, life just went inexorably on. You adapted, you found answers to your problems, and every day you got up and decided to live. That was the human—or inhuman—condition.

Alphonse called around seven to say that Agent Darren was on his way over and they should assist him any way they could. Nolan took the call, and he hung up the phone puzzled. Last he'd heard, Darren was in prison for a dime. No word of his escape or the tragedy in Georgia had leaked to the public, and Cell A—or what was left of it—was keeping Adam's death a secret from the ranks for the time being.

"Nancy!" Nolan called out from the bottom of the staircase. She was upstairs, tinkering on her computer. Agent Terry's cat Clotho listened from the couch; Cell N had retrieved her at Alphonse's suggestion, and the cat had taken an immediate liking to Nancy, much to her surprise.

"Yeah?"

"Put your makeup on. Company's coming."

AGENT DARREN SHOWED UP at the door half an hour later. Georgetown was just a few miles from Brookmont. He looked grubby and worn out. On the street, a taxi pulled away and drove off.

"Nolan," he said as they shook hands. "Good to see you, bro."

"Likewise. What the hell you doing outta jail?"

Darren shook his head. "It's a long and shitty story. Where's Nancy?"

Nolan looked around just as Nancy came down the steps. She was in her human guise again, wearing a dark green dress and sneakers. "Darren?" she said, her eyes surprised behind her thick glasses.

"In the flesh," Nolan said. "Can you believe it?"

"What's up?"

Darren stepped inside and closed the door. "I'm going to Puerto Rico. I need your help."

Nancy stopped suddenly on the next-to-last step. "Thank God," she said. "I thought Cell A was writing them off."

"Not anymore. Will you come?"

"Hell yes," she said, reaching the floor and walking towards them.

"Nolan?"

"You kidding? I hafta keep you kids outta trouble."

"I'll call Nick and see if he's free," Nancy said, hurrying to the phone. "Nolan, start packing."

DAVID FOSTER NELLS LAY unconscious in a hospital bed within the basement laboratories of OUTLOOK Group's Facility B on Vieques Island. A rat's nest of wires and tubes ran from his head and arms to a variety of equipment on wheeled carts next to the bed. Drs. Yrjo, Baker, and Strysik stood outside the door, watching him through a window.

"The dampers are working," Strysik said quietly. "His brain activity is normal. We've got him under control."

Yrjo nodded thoughtfully. "Of a sort. Nothing in the other subjects?"

Baker shook his head. "Zip. We duplicated the surgery as close as we could, but they're not showing any unusual abilities. Whatever powers we've unlocked seem unique to Nells."

"RECOIL was on the phone an hour ago," Strysik said. "They're still demanding our data."

"Keep stalling them," Yrjo replied gruffly. "Kroft will back me up. This is our project, and it's far too early to hand anything off to those fools."

"Is there any word from the Others?" Baker asked.

Yrjo frowned. "That bastard Ringwood is stonewalling. He was furious over the Maryland incident, which was hardly our responsibility. He says he's still in negotiations. From the sound of his voice, I'd say he was lying. I surmise he hasn't even gotten a response from them."

Strysik shook his head. "What a mess."

"I quite agree," Yrjo concurred. "But if we can replicate Nells' powers, it will all have been worthwhile."

Baker sighed. "I've been over the red binder a dozen times.

Nothing there suggests that the surgery should have had any results like these. I can't understand it."

Yrjo snorted. "The Cookbook is hardly reliable. The Others have never been straight with us. Perhaps this is another damned test."

"If so," Strysik said, "I think we're failing."

David dreamed. He was floating in a sea of dark clouds, bright points of light like stars swirling through the mist. He knew there was something beyond the clouds, something he needed to see, but he felt weak, unable to pierce the veil.

Occasionally he would glimpse a break in the clouds. For a moment the terrible light would shine through, and he'd see the roiling things that lolled and danced in great arcs around the bright chaotic mass at the center. A distant sound of piping, a weird atonal music, would reach him, only to fade as the cloud bank closed around him again. There would be another sound, too, a familiar sound: a pair of Pratt & Whitneys, thrumming powerfully if improbably in the deeps of space. It was a comforting sound, a sound he associated with his father.

David drifted, lost in dreams of China clouds.

Chapter Eight: The World Pursues

Tuesday, March 23–Wednesday, March 24, 1999

The noonday sun was warm and inviting as the airliner touched down in San Juan. On board, James nudged Nancy awake. Nolan was two rows behind them. Nick hadn't come; he couldn't get away from his day job in time for the op.

They hadn't left D.C. until after midnight. James took them on a whirlwind tour of DG's secondary Green Boxes in the area, securing an impressive array of equipment and firearms. Cell N had never seen these Green Boxes before. "Special gear for special ops," James explained. Nolan suspected that some of these stashes were only known to James; among other things, they contained a variety of forged ID and passports, all with James' picture.

Driving at last to the airport, James directed them to a cargo road and they pulled up to a shipping company he'd used before called Tiger Transit. James shook hands with a man he knew there, who had them pull Nolan's car around into a cargo building. He helped them pack up all of their equipment—including submachineguns, a sniper rifle, explosives, night-vision goggles, and ammunition—into a large cargo crate, which he then topped off with boxes of light bulbs and other innocuous goods. James gave him an address on Vieques Island, and the man began filling out forms. Then they raced to the terminal for the flight south.

At San Juan's Marin Airport they deplaned and immediately booked passage on an Isla Nena Air shuttle. While they waited for the three o'clock flight, Cell N had lunch and James made a phone call. A few hours later, they were on Vieques.

Emerging from the modest terminal, they came into view of

the tropical paradise around them. Vieques was beautiful in the warm afternoon glow. "Blue sky and sunshine," James said to himself.

In the distance they heard whistles and explosions. Nancy and Nolan looked around, surprised. James laughed. "It's the Navy. They do shore-bombardment exercises on the coast."

"Jesus," Nancy said. "It's a hell of a welcome."

James nodded at the street. "Here's the welcome."

A Ford Explorer had just pulled up, and two burly fifty-something men with crew cuts piled out. They grinned and hustled over to meet the group.

"Forrest! You son of a bitch!" one called as they shook hands. "How the hell are ya?"

"Lean and mean, Pete."

The other man slapped James on the stomach. "You been leaner, man!"

James rolled his eyes. "Sure Jason, what's *your* mile at these days?"

"Hah! That's on a need-to-know basis."

"Pete, Jason, I want you to meet Nancy and Nolan." He nodded at the men. "These two old codgers were on my SEAL team years ago, before they retired to paradise."

They all shook hands and exchanged pleasantries.

"So is this business or pleasure?" Pete asked.

"Business. The less you know, the better."

Pete and Jason exchanged looks.

"Well, get in the truck, then," Pete said. "We've got rooms for you at the Sea Gate. Ruth'll take good care of you."

"I've got a shipment coming in later today. It'll show up at the Dive Center."

Jason chuckled. "Lemme guess. Keep it away from open

flame."

"You got it."

Pete shook his head. "I hope you know what the hell you're doing, Forrest. Last we heard you were up for ten at Leavenworth."

"Duty called. Let's go see this roach motel you've got for us."

They piled into the Explorer and headed off.

The Sea Gate Guesthouse was no roach motel. It was a beautiful compound on the bluffs overlooking the port of Isabel Segunda and Fort Conde de Mirasol, an old Spanish fort renovated into a museum of Vieques history and culture. Forrest's SEAL buddies had scored them a two-bedroom bungalow on the grounds of the Sea Gate, and as they got the trio checked in Pete and Jason joked with the owner's daughter, Penny, who doubled as the small island's veterinarian. "Better get some horse tranquilizers," Pete said with a wink. "This guy's trouble."

Pete and Jason ran the Caribbean Blue Dive Center, the finest such facility on the island. James' SEAL team had spent some time on Vieques years ago, running training exercises on the Naval compound, and he and his buddies had fallen in love with the place. In 1989 Pete and Jason resigned and came here to lead tourist dives, rent equipment, and soak in the rays; Hurricane Hugo had just devastated the island, and property was cheap. They'd spent their lives mostly single, driven men committed to the rigors of combat and discipline, but within a few years of their arrival on Vieques both were married and they now had young children. Island life had agreed with them. James had always said he'd join them someday, and in fact he owned a third of the Dive Center, but someday had never come.

Watching his friends now, happy and content in this tropical paradise, he felt like something of a fool for staying away. Then he remembered the *Santa Cruz* and the things that came out of the deeps to tear his teammates into bloody, bubbling shreds, and he shut his eyes tight. Someday was not today.

The two ex-SEALs stood on the grounds, talking and laughing in the sunshine, while the three DG agents got changed and cleaned up inside the bungalow. When they were ready, Pete and Jason walked them down to Isabel Segunda, the fragrant coastal breezes bringing the smells of salt water and mangrove trees. They settled in at Taverna Espanola for beers and, eventually, dinner. For a while they talked about the island, and about their days together in the Navy. Nancy and Nolan smiled and listened but kept quiet. Eventually there was a lull in the conversation, and Pete glanced around them. They were seated in a corner, and Jason had tipped the staff to keep the nearby tables empty. It was a slow night, and they had this end of the tavern to themselves. Pete's expression grew serious.

"All right, Forrest. What's the story?"

James sipped his beer.

"Look man, you know we're here for you," Jason said. "Just tell us what we can do."

James leaned forward and drummed his fingers on the table. "It's about OUTLOOK."

Pete closed his eyes for a moment. "Shit. I knew it."

Jason looked level at Forrest. "You're not here for more tests, are you?"

"No. We're here to hit them. They've got some friends of ours in there. Medical experiments, MKULTRA stuff. They're being held against their will and no one's going to do a damn thing about it if we don't. OUTLOOK's out of control."

"Shit," Pete said. "You don't fuck around, do you?"

"Those guys are bad news," James said. "*You* know that."

"How you getting in?" Jason asked.

James glanced at Nancy, who leaned forward and spoke. "I know their security inside and out. We're going over the wall with Nolan on sniper assist."

"Then I'm looking at three corpses," said Pete. "'Cuz there's no way you're gonna make it out alive. Believe me."

"You got any better ideas?" James asked sarcastically.

Pete and Jason exchanged looks again. "We just might," Pete said.

The three agents leaned forward, all ears.

"See, we've gotten active in the island's environmental movement," Jason began.

James roared with laughter. "You have *got* to be shitting me!"

"No shit, man!" Jason replied. "This place is our home now. And much as I hate to say it, the Navy's screwing it up. All those years of shelling have polluted the water table. I don't let my kids drink nothing that don't come outta bottle or through a filter."

"So what does this have to do with OUTLOOK?"

"They're on a promontory next to Puerto Ferro." Jason looked at Nancy and Nolan. "Ferro and Bahía Mosquito are bioluminescent bays—at least, Mosquito is. Ferro used to be, but it's in decline from pollution. We think OUTLOOK is partly to blame."

"You've lost me," Nolan cut in. "You mean these bays glow in the dark?"

"Sort of," Pete replied. "They'll full of microorganisms called dinoflagellates. *Pyrodinium bahamense*, to be exact.

They live on vitamin B12 runoff from the mangrove trees, decaying leaves, shit like that. The two bays are real shallow, and they've got pretty narrow outlets to the sea, so the B12 builds up, the *Pyrodinium* clusters, and pretty soon you've got bays that glow in the dark when something moves. Fish leave glowing trails, the wake of your boat is a bright blue, it's pretty amazing stuff. Big tourist draw, of course. We run two excursions on Mosquito Bay every night. Eighteen bucks a head! So you'll understand when I say that we've got a stake in this tree-hugger shit."

"And OUTLOOK?" James prompted.

"OUTLOOK's got this waste pipe that empties into the ocean near the inlet to Puerto Ferro. They don't use it often, and there's no schedule we've been able to figure out, but whatever they're dumping can't be good. They've got an incinerator that runs once a week, and if they're dumping shit they don't dare burn . . . well, you see what I mean. But they're part of Camp Garcia, the USMC, and protests just get shrugged off."

"How big is this waste pipe?"

"Exactly. You could get up in there. It's got bars, though. You'd need to cut them. And I can't vouch for what you'll find at the other end. But it's doable. No harder than Montenegro was."

James sat back and thought for a moment. He looked at Nancy and Nolan.

"I'm guessing you two don't know a regulator from a radiator."

"Huh?" said Nolan.

"SCUBA gear. You do any diving?"

Both shook their heads.

"All right. Nolan, you're on getaway detail. But Nancy,

you and me are gonna have to get wet."

He looked at his friends. "You guys think we can get her ready for tomorrow night?"

Pete frowned. "Shit, man, you know better than that."

Jason raised a hand. "Hang on, now. That pipe's not more than fifteen feet down. Ferro doesn't get much past twelve. Pressure's not a problem, and there's jack-all for current. Hell, she could snorkel it until it's time to go in the pipe. But we're still looking at a night dive. You scare easy, little lady?"

Nancy glared. James laughed. "Jason, my man, you may not believe this but she's got more notches on her knife than you do."

Jason made a face. "Ah, that's bullshit!"

James shook his head and held up his right hand. "I'm lyin', I'm dyin'. Nancy's the most badass psycho chick I ever met." He smiled at her and she smiled back, while Nolan grinned and sipped his beer.

Jason shrugged. "If you say so, man. We'll go down to Sun Bay tonight and get a little wet. But tomorrow, my dear, is crash day. If you aren't ready by sundown, you guys will have to postpone your little job until you are."

"She'll be ready," James said.

"Damn straight," Nancy replied.

After dinner they went back up to the Sea Gate and piled into the Explorer. Pete drove them south to Esperanza, where the Dive Center was. James' cargo crate was waiting in a back storeroom. He checked it quickly to make sure it hadn't been searched, and found all was in order.

They spent the next couple hours at the center, picking out gear to fit Nancy and James and showing Nancy how it worked. Just after sunset, they drove down to Sun Bay. Jason watched as Nancy put her gear on over a swimsuit—a BC, tank, dive computer, and regulator—to make sure she made all the connections correctly. Then he and James led her into the water of the shallow bay. They brought some heavy-duty underwater lights and got them set up so Nancy could find her way back to shore if she got separated, then they went under. Nancy practiced equalizing and clearing her mask, then struggled with the trickiness of maintaining proper buoyancy at ten to twelve feet under.

After a little under half an hour, Jason called time and they waded ashore, where Nolan was lying on his back watching the stars. They had an hour to kill before they'd go back in the water, as a safety measure against pressure problems, and Jason left them on the beach to go see how Pete was doing with a tourist run into one of the bio bays. Nancy and James plopped down next to Nolan.

"It's gorgeous out here," Nolan said peacefully. "You don't get this kinda sky in D.C."

James gazed up into the dark above. A feeling of *déjà vu* crept over him. Two years ago, his last night of relative freedom, he'd been on a beach like this, under a starry sky like this. Stephanie had been there, too. It was the conclusion of the Roscoe op, the moment at which she had put a wall between them. That wall was gone now—but so was Stephanie. He wondered what she was doing right now, if she was suffering at OUTLOOK's hands. If she was even still alive.

"What's your story, Darren?" Nancy asked after a while, interrupting his melancholy reverie. "Why are you here, anyway?"

He folded his arms across his chest and sighed. "Something

my dad said once, a long time ago. If a house is burning and there are good people inside, it doesn't matter whose house it is or how it caught fire. You just go in there and you get them out."

She turned her head to look at him. "So it's nothing personal?"

He smiled slightly and continued staring into the night. "Everything's personal."

They lay in silence a while longer until Jason came back from his trip, then they got wet again. This time they left the big lights off and practiced night swimming. James held onto the shoulder strap of Nancy's BC as they moved around the bay, paddling with their fins, finding their way with a flashlight. When they returned to the bach, Jason said class was over for the night. "You did good, babe."

They hauled their gear back to the Dive Center. Pete had held them slots on the evening's second excursion to Bahía Mosquito, and they joined a bunch of tourists on a Caribbean Blue motor launch.

The bay was eerily dark and beautiful. As the boat pulled out into the middle of the calm water, Pete pointed out the bright blue glow in the churning wake. A school of darting sardines passed by, slender silver fish leaving bright trails behind as they swam. The effect was wondrously bizarre, like a strange childhood dream you somehow never forgot. Jason pulled a bucket of water out of the bay and turned off the lights for a couple minutes, passing the bucket around for the tourists to put their hands in and splash around. The sudden glow was stunning, a myriad of sparkling lights.

Several tourists decided to hop in the water for a few minutes and the agents followed, prompted by Jason. The water was warm and still, but as they jumped in it exploded with light. Nolan treaded water in his life jacket, smiling and pointing at a school of snapper fleeing the intruders, streaks of blue marking their passing. Nancy marveled at the beauty of the effect while James dove under, his body outlined in a glorious shimmer. When they all climbed back into the boat, their swimsuits glittered and sparkled for a few moments. It was magical.

Finally the boat returned to shore. Pete drove James and Cell N back to the Sea Gate and they immediately went to bed, exhausted from the day. Nancy was racked with terrible cravings, and she had a strange, extended dream of a shipwreck, the pale bodies of drowned Spanish sailors drifting in the bay, outlined in brilliant azure, lost forever to the surface world of light and life. In her dream she swam in her true flesh, a predator in a dim land feasting on the haloed dead.

WEDNESDAY THEY ROSE EARLY, awakened by Pete's insistent knocking at the door. They got ready and accompanied him back to Sun Bay. They spent the day there, Nancy learning the ropes of shallow diving while Nolan relaxed on shore, getting a tan and studying Nancy's maps of OUTLOOK. In the afternoon he left to rent a getaway vehicle and then drove all around the public part of the island, venturing into the accessible areas of Camp Garcia to scout routes to and from OUTLOOK. The roads were a mixed lot, ranging from two-lane paved highways to narrow dirt tracks.

Meanwhile, the dive team relocated to Puerto Ferro after taking a break for a late lunch and a rest. Nancy and James swam all through the bay and out into the ocean, learning the terrain. They decided to scout the approach to the waste pipe, and Pete led them on the excursion.

The pipe was just a hundred yards or so from the inlet to Ferro. It was about four feet in diameter, a tight fit. When they went in, they'd have to push their tanks in front of them. There were three metal bars welded to the interior of the pipe to prevent access. They examined the bars, and Pete and James talked in hand signals about the time it would take to cut through them with an underwater blowtorch. Nancy swum up to the entrance and grabbed a bar, bracing her feet on the bottom lip of the pipe. She started pulling. Pete and James looked at her, and then Pete tapped James on the shoulder and shook his head. There was no way they could just break the bars loose.

Nancy strained, and suddenly the bar snapped free of the weld. She kept pulling until it was poking out at a right angle. Pete was incredulous. James held up his hands and shrugged, as if to say *I told you so.*

It took another few minutes, but soon enough Nancy had all three bars bent out, and three more located a few feet inside. The way was open.

James made more hand signals to Pete, and then took some preparatory breaths. The pipe was too narrow to get the tank in on his back and he didn't want to fool with pushing it ahead of him at the moment, so he'd decided to leave it behind for a quick look inside. When he was ready, Pete helped him take the tank off. James took one last gulp of air and removed the mouthpiece, then shot into the pipe.

A couple minutes went by. Nancy gave Pete a worried look, but Pete just shook his head.

James blew out of the pipe and took the mouthpiece from Pete. He breathed for a few moments, and then Pete helped him get the tank back on. James pointed at the inlet to the bay and they swum back into Puerto Ferro. They emerged on the beach a few minutes later.

"It's good," James said as they sat down on the warm sand. "Goes about fifty yards inland on an upward gradient, then it makes a turn straight up. When you get above sea level there's open air. I think it's another twenty yards from there to the top, but we can scale that. I could see a little light from above. There's some kind of hatch, but I don't think it's anything we can't get through. This'll work."

"You sure?" Pete asked warily.

"Sure as I can be for now. We'll try it tonight and bail if we can't get through the hatch."

"This is the end of the road for me and Jason," Pete said. "I'm sorry, man, but you're on your own tonight. We can't be getting into this shit."

"I know," James said. "Don't worry." He looked at Nancy reassuringly. "We can handle it."

The sun was low in the west. The mangrove trees cast long shadows on the sand. Across the bay, a vacationing couple with two young children splashed in the waves, their laughter dancing over the water.

It was a beautiful, beautiful day.

An hour after sunset, they were ready. Nolan parked the Range Rover he'd rented at Red Beach, a public area within the confines of Camp Garcia. From there he was three minutes from OUTLOOK. When James and Nancy were ready, they'd send up a flare and Nolan would come, hell-bent for leather—unless shooting started outside before the flare, in which case Nolan would come anyway. He expected that his weeks at the FBI's tactical-driving school would pay off when he made the treacherous run on OUTLOOK's concentric gates. He had two compact Italian M-4 Spectre 9mm submachine guns with fifty-round magazines, night-vision goggles with flash suppression, a Swiss SIG-Sauer SSG2000 bolt-action sniper rifle that took .300 Weatherby Magnum rounds and was equipped with an 8.0 scope, and his personal Colt Delta Elite 10mm handgun. He wore a full tac suit with body armor. The floor was littered with extra magazines for the M-4s and the Colt, and an open shoebox with twenty Weatherby rounds sat in the passenger seat.

Despite the weaponry, Nolan had never been more afraid. He'd come to Puerto Rico because Nancy was his responsibility; truth be told, he was more than a little bit in love with her. He still found her true appearance disconcerting, but over the last year he'd learned to look behind her strange form and see the talented, driven woman within. She was extraordinary, in every sense of the word, and he'd die before he let harm come to her.

But looking at OUTLOOK and weighing their chances of making it out alive, his chivalrous confidence had drained away. This was ugly, desperate business. They were undermanned and underprepared. But James insisted they had to go, and go now, before whatever was going on at OUTLOOK got worse.

Nolan took deep breaths and steadied himself. He was determined not to let Nancy down.

AT PUERTO FERRO, NANCY and James walked to the southeast edge of the bay, just at the start of the outlet to the sea. Besides their SCUBA gear, each carried a bulky waterproof bag with equipment for once they got inside. They got geared up and James led Nancy into the water.

It was warm and welcoming. Although Ferro wasn't nearly as bioluminescent as Bahía Mosquito, they could still see little specks of light here and there, a reminder of the toll civilization had taken on this place. James and Nancy hung close together, James holding onto her shoulder strap as they swam towards the inlet. Although she was new to SCUBA gear, Nancy felt confident as hell. She was ready to feed, and she knew OUTLOOK would be full of fresh meat. They both had small diving lights with blue gels over them, resembling the glow of *Pyrodinium* to casual observers on shore. Within twenty minutes they reached the pipe.

By mutual agreement, Nancy went in first. With her inhuman strength and build she could quickly and silently scale the dry shaft at the end of the pipe and, hopefully, get the hatch open. James helped her take her tank off and she lay it in the mouth of the pipe. She and James shook hands, and then she was in.

The pipe seemed terribly narrow as Nancy swam forward slowly, pushing her tank as she went. But somehow she felt right at home in this subterranean space. Vague inklings of memory teased at her thoughts, telling her that this was where she belonged, underground, in the dark. She shrugged off the murmurings of her strange inner voice and pressed on. Soon she reached the bend where the pipe turned upward.

Here she left her tank and regulator behind and pushed up with her powerful legs. She broke the surface and took a breath, then looked up. There was some light here, as James had said, shining through in a tight but broken circle from the top of the shaft around the hatch. Nancy pulled her watertight bag up to her chest and tightened the cord to hold it there. Then she waited.

A few moments later, James tapped on her ankle from below, signaling his arrival. Then he tapped again. It was time to go.

Nancy reached out and braced her arms across the width of the pipe, then lifted herself up. When her feet were clear she braced her legs, then moved her hands higher. After doing this twice it became second nature, and she scurried up the rest of the shaft in half a minute. Then she was below the hatch.

Keeping herself braced in the shaft, she reached one hand up and pressed against the hatch. It lifted slightly and then stopped. There was some sort of catch keeping it shut.

Nancy paused for a moment. She could hear James beginning to make the climb up the shaft, but she focused and blocked out the sounds he was making. She was interested in what was on the other side of the hatch.

Gradually she could make out a low, rustling hum, and she could detect a faint odor of gas. *The incinerator,* she thought gratefully. From her acquired knowledge of OUTLOOK's floorplan, she'd guessed that this pipe probably came from the incinerator room, where they disposed of their medical waste. Now she was sure she was right. She was sure of something else, too, thanks to the scents she was picking up through the hatch. No one was in the incinerator room.

She clicked her tongue twice. James answered in kind. *Now.*

Nancy braced herself more tightly, got into position, and then slammed the heel of her palm against the underside of the hatch with all of her strength. The force snapped through the catch and the hatch flew open, pivoting back on its hinges until it clanged against the pipe. By the time the sound came Nancy had propelled herself up and out, tucking her legs in and then tumbling to the ground, landing in a feral crouch, one hand raised to strike if she was wrong. The small incinerator room was unoccupied, hot from the heat of the furnace. She looked at the single door. Her eyes narrowed and her nostrils flared.

The door opened. An NRO DELTA agent in Wackenhut apparel stood there with his MP5 at the ready. He let loose a burst on the dripping blond woman crouched on the floor, but by the time the trigger was depressed she had leapt through the air and tackled him, his shots spraying the ceiling of the room. Nancy twisted his head around backwards and pulled him into the room, closing the door behind them.

James emerged from the pipe, his commando knife in one hand and a hard look in his eyes. The sight before him stopped him cold.

Nancy was feeding. She had her face buried in the guard's innards, devouring his flesh and organs, grunting with satisfaction. It had been days since she'd fed, and she couldn't contain her hunger any longer.

James stepped free of the pipe and gingerly hurried around the pair on the floor. He put his shoulder against the door and listened. He heard footsteps. He sheathed his knife and grabbed the guard's MP5, then held it at the door while he opened the waterproof bag hanging from his shoulder with his other hand. From within he pulled an M-4 Spectre with a stubby fifty-round magazine. He swapped the submachine guns and stood to one side, crouching by the door.

The door flew open. James shoved the MP5 in his left hand against the guard's side and tore his insides apart with a ten-round burst. The guard toppled, squeezing off shots that struck the incinerator, and then hit the floor.

Another guard was right behind him. James rolled across the floor as the man fired, trying to track James as he moved faster than anyone the guard had ever seen. Until a moment later, when a blur lurched through the air and sent him sprawling into the hallway, dead before he hit the ground.

James got up and ditched the MP5. He hurried to the doorway.

Nancy was crouched on the body of the third guard, her face, arms, and chest drenched in blood and gore. She whipped her head from side to side, nostrils flaring as she surveyed the scene, and then tore off down the hall.

James followed as fast as he could. They were in a wide, antiseptic hallway with a speckled-white tile floor. An empty gurney was stationed idly against one wall.

Footsteps behind them, coming to a corner. James spun around, going down on one knee, and let loose a careful burst that caught a guard in the chest, his feet going out from under him and dropping him to the floor on his back. Behind him he heard a roar.

Spinning around as he stood up and in forward motion again, James saw Nancy at a T-intersection rip a guard's gun arm off, blood spraying from the severed artery, before she crushed his skull with one hand and dropped his twitching body to the floor. Another guard appeared at the far end, beyond the intersection. James kicked loose a burst that skated across the man's legs and he went down on his knees, firing wildly. James fired again, tracking up his chest and ending with a head shot that exploded his brains spectacularly across the tile.

Nancy was already gone around the corner. James raced forward, heartbeat thumping in his ears.

As he reached the intersection, shots peppered the wall opposite the hallway Nancy had gone down. James went around the corner low.

Five guards had come racing around a far corner and

opened fire on Nancy after pausing for a confused, fatal moment. The little blond woman, bloody from the carnage, launched herself off the ground, her body arcing and twisting over the streams of fire, arms outstretched, before coming down on three of the guards at once. By the time they all hit the floor, her human guise was gone—in its place was a muscular, grave-pallored creature with massive jaws and feral eyes. She rolled onto her back and simultaneously hurled one fallen guard up against a standing one, then lurched off the floor at the other, driving her hands into his guts and ripping out his intestines. The man screamed and fired, bullets thudding into his two companions still getting up from the tackle. She shoved her hands in further and grabbed him by the spine, claws punching through his back, then pulled him off the ground like he was a mop and threw him into the two unhurt guards. As they tumbled back to the floor she pounced on the two who'd been shot. She ripped the head off one and drove it into the face of the other, crushing his skull and sending a spray of brains and bone fragments across the floor. The two surviving guards were fumbling beneath the gutted, flopping man, screaming in blind terror. Nancy stepped over to them and grabbed them by their faces, driving her thumbs into their nasal cavities and plunging her fingers into their eyes. They wailed as blood and pale fluid poured over Nancy's hands, then she raised them up and flattened the back of their skulls against the wall.

James padded up. Nancy was licking her claws greedily as her human guise reasserted itself, transforming her back into a small blond woman again.

"Jesus Fucking Christ!" was the best he could manage. Eleven men were dead—so far. They'd been inside OUTLOOK for less than three minutes.

"No," Nancy corrected him between slurps, her voice a bestial snarl. "Jean Fucking Qualls."

"Which way?" James asked, panting.

Jean turned and ran. James followed.

They made a turn and entered a huge soundstage. In the middle of the room was some sort of enclosed set. The walls were supported with wooden braces. They heard the recorded sound of waves and the cries of birds, issuing from big speakers placed around the outside of the set.

There was a door set into one of the flimsy walls, standing open. They ran for it.

From inside the set they heard a voice cry out: "What are you waiting for! Go ahead, you fucks! Do it!"

James' heart pounded. It was Stephanie.

The set was built to look like a Caribbean courtyard, stone walls and arches on four sides. Against one wall were three eight-foot posts, set into the floor. Vic, Abe, and Stephanie were tied to the posts, blindfolded. The wall behind them was riddled with fake bullet holes and bloodstains. No one else was in the set. Five bolt-action rifles lay on the ground opposite the trio, evidently dropped by the guards they'd just met, the scenario abandoned mid-way.

"Stephanie!" he called as he and Jean hurried over.

Stephanie turned her head towards them. She sputtered. "*J—James?*"

He pulled the blindfold off. She blinked, confused. "Is this real?" she whispered, her eyes hollow and desperate, wanting to believe that this was really happening, that it wasn't another of OUTLOOK's terrible trials.

He kissed her.

Jean ripped the blindfolds from Abe and Vic, who looked

ragged and confused. She sliced through the ropes with her unseen claws, fully camouflaged once more. They staggered forward, blinking, unbelieving.

James looked into Stephanie's eyes as he withdrew from the kiss. "It's real," he whispered, as he pulled out his knife and sliced through the bonds. She fell into his arms and held him tight.

"*Oh fuck,*" Vic was saying. "*Fuck, fuck, fuck.*" Jean hugged her and Abe briefly, staining their clothes with blood.

"Are you hurt?" Abe said, recovering.

Jean shook her head. "You should see the other guys."

Vic whooped, her eyes bright.

"I can't believe you're here," Stephanie said, dazed, stepping back to look at him. "I never thought I'd see you again."

"Shit happens," James said, smiling.

"Is Shasta here?" Jean asked.

"We haven't seen him," Vic said.

"He must be in the cells," she replied. She opened her bag, slick with blood, and handed an M-4 to Abe and a Colt .45 to Vic, plus a couple magazines. "I don't need these." She dropped the empty bag to the floor.

A klaxon sounded.

"Let's go," James said. "Jean, lead the way."

The motley procession fled the soundstage and entered a hallway on the far side. Jean ran, her thoughts racing. Somewhere in her head was a room full of boxes. One was open. From it she pulled a shuddering, weeping man covered in blood, and slapped him across the face. He began babbling, telling her where the cells were in this place. When the group reached an intersection, she skidded to a stop just before the corner.

"Company," she hissed. They crouched and James and Abe brought their M-4s to bear.

Two guards ran into the intersection. They hit the ground, riddled with bullets. Stephanie picked up an MP5 and they took off to the left, passing more doors.

They reached an open area with twenty cells. It was familiar to everyone but James—a similar room had been at the bottom of the stairs in Maryland. Two technicians were standing behind a desk, their faces writ large with fear. Stephanie recognized them immediately: yesterday they'd played the roles of crematorium workers in another horrific scenario designed to test them, to break down their minds and see what made them tick. She squeezed the trigger, rounds tracking up the tile floor as she raised the MP5, bullets punching into the desk, exploding a computer monitor, catching first one and then the other technician, both shrieking as bloody wounds spattered their white lab coats, jerking and staggering, until Stephanie had run through the entire magazine.

"*Burn,*" she whispered, and tossed the spent weapon to the floor. Vic, Abe, and Jean hurried forward and began checking the cells, looking in one window after another while James stood guard and Stephanie rubbed her arms, feeling cold and jittery, but listening with hot satisfaction as the two men on the floor behind the desk panted and cried, the life draining out of them.

"He's not here!" Abe yelled.

"Fuck!" said Vic. "Where is he?"

Jean thought for a moment. The man in the box was weeping. "The exam rooms. Back this way."

They hurried back down the hall. When they reached the intersection with the two corpses, Jean passed by the way they'd come and continued down the hall. She pointed up ahead. "Check those rooms!"

In the third examination room, David Foster Nells lay in a bed, wired to medical equipment. "Shit!" Stephanie cried. "Here!"

She threw open the door and ran in, the others following.

The room was huge, as big as the room with the cells had been. David was the only occupant.

They gathered around the bed. "Is it safe to take this shit off?" Abe asked, worried.

"We don't have any choice," Vic replied, and began disconnecting everything. Everyone else followed suit.

When the last of the wires and tubes were removed, David opened his eyes. He looked at them, smiling tiredly.

"Hello," he said in a quiet voice.

"David?" Stephanie asked. "Are you okay?"

"I'm fine." The expression on his face was beatific.

"We've got to get out of here," Abe said. "Can you walk?"

"Sure. But that won't be necessary."

"What do you mean?" James said, suspicious for some reason he couldn't place. A feeling was stealing over him, a sensation he'd first encountered eighteen years ago on the sunken wreck of the *Santa Cruz*.

Then they all felt it. There was an energy in the air, a weird tingle. The room shimmered slightly, waves like a heat mirage distorting their field of view. They paused, disoriented, their heads reeling from the power that was now emanating from the man in the bed.

"Well looky here," a mocking voice said from behind them. They turned.

Adolph Lepus and six guards brandishing MP5s had entered the room while they were dazed. They were twenty yards away and had the group down cold.

"It was downright foolish of you to come here," Lepus said coolly. "But that don't mean I ain't happy to see ya." Actually, he wasn't happy at all—he was really quite pissed off.

Then the wave of power expanded, washing over Lepus and his men. A faint atonal piping slipped into the room between the cracks of reality. Lepus went pale and his anger drained away. He remembered.

LIEUTENANT ADOLPH LEPUS WAS humping it, forty pounds of gear on his back and an M-16 slung over one shoulder. The foliage was thick, the night moonlit. He wasn't alone. Three hundred men enclosed him, the whole mass double-timing from the drop zone three miles back.

On the other side of the Cambodian border.

The U.S. hadn't invaded Cambodia, though Lepus kept hearing that was in the works. This sure as hell wasn't an invasion—at least, not from the U.S. point of view. This was a covert mission, Operation MONKEY TROUBLE. Most of the grunts here didn't even know where the hell they were; they figured they were still somewhere in the DMZ. Only a handful knew the truth, and those handful had something in common. On each of their military personnel files was a sticker, a tiny green triangle. This little emblem marked them as possessing DELTA GREEN clearance, a very specialized form of access to a very specialized field of knowledge. That clearance was what separated Lepus from the rank-and-file U.S. Army soldiers around him. He had enough status to be briefed a little more fully than the rest—but he sure as heck wasn't in charge.

Colonel Satchel Wade was. Wade was a Delta Green agent,

though Lepus hadn't met him until this op. Delta Green had mostly stayed out of Vietnam, as their particular talents didn't seem to have much use in this land of guerilla fighting and violent futility.

The CIA was suspicious of Delta Green and jealous of its own status in the conflict, and agitated to keep DG's involvement here at a minimum. DG hadn't mounted even a single official operation in Vietnam—until now. God knows how Wade got approval. Three hundred men? Storming across the Cambodian border? It seemed like madness.

Lepus was breathing hard. They were getting close now, at least according to the briefing he'd received. Wade and his freaky "advisor," Li, had set the scene. Lepus had disliked Wade immediately. The man was stout—if he wasn't a superior officer, you'd say "pudgy"—and he conducted the briefing without any sign of emotion or enthusiasm. Lepus guessed that the act was supposed to make Wade seem like Mister Ice, but the result was less dramatic: he just came off like a halfwit.

The advisor was worse. She was maybe thirty years old, skinny and good-looking. Whatever emotions Wade was lacking were close to boiling out of Li. She took the time to methodically stare down everyone at that briefing as she talked, including Lepus. The feel of her eyes on him was so intense, so ferocious, that he couldn't help but glance away even though he'd already clued in to what she was doing a few minutes before. It seemed clear that she was calling the shots here, that she had supplied Wade with the relevant intelligence, that she had him wrapped around her finger. She wanted this mission to happen—and Wade was making it so.

For all its interior drama, the briefing was not very revealing. Delta Green had identified an ancient temple on the wrong side of the Cambodian border where the locals were up to no good; tentative explanations involved some sort of nasty occult shit that would eventually be turned against U.S. troops. The CIA had given the thumbs-up to the op, Wade said, and he was sending three hundred soldiers in a frontal assault on the temple and whoever was operating out of it.

The plan immediately struck Lepus as hinky. For one thing, sending three hundred armed men into a foreign country we weren't officially fighting seemed like a damn foolish thing to do. If the temple were such a threat, why not just let a bomber "accidentally" go off course and blow the fuck out of it? Why this man-to-man approach? For another thing, where was the military brass? An op of this magnitude—hell, from barracks conversations with the men, Lepus had doped out that Wade had pulled people out of units all over the countryside—couldn't be cleared without a lot of Army seat-polishers stamping approvals left and right. Finally, there was Wade himself. Lepus had been brought in early thanks to his clearance, early enough to see that Wade was pulling all the strings personally. Wade was scurrying all over the place, flashing his credentials and invoking national security six ways from Sunday every time some grunt's CO or some requisitions officer or some nosy bureaucrat asked what was going on. There was a complete denial of information to all of these people. Wade had justified it to his inner circle by pointing out that you didn't want to advertise that you were sending three hundred soldiers into a non-enemy nation, but even so, Lepus was unsettled. Not once did he encounter anyone above Wade in the chain of command who knew what the hell was going on.

Lepus had mulled this at length, and finally decided he was just being paranoid. Wade was clearly on top of things, and was working his ass off to keep this mission a secret. But part of Lepus's mind kept poking at the edges of the question that he wouldn't let himself ponder: was this mission authorized, or even known of, by anyone higher than Wade?

The men broke from the foliage. Ahead of them lay the temple: an ancient plaza of jagged and broken stone, surrounded by a zone of grass half a man's height. The temple was a ruin, and showed no signs of habitation.

Lepus got nervous. But he hauled ass with the rest.

As the men mounted the steps of the temple, weapons readied, wondering where the hell the enemy was, a strange, off-key piping sound rose around them. Lepus ducked behind a column and hazarded a quick look around.

His brow furrowed. Around him, the soldiers had stopped running and were milling around the gaping walls and carven obelisks of the obviously uninhabited temple. They were already starting to bitch about the oxymoron known as military intelligence, which had apparently led them to a fight with an enemy who wasn't even there.

During his first tour, Lepus had consistently been point man for the platoon. He could almost smell an ambush, a skill honed from hunting game in the backwoods of Alabama, a skill his platoon prized. He was smelling one now.

He ran across the massive courtyard, shoving his way through the throng, towards the steps on the far side that would take him back into the grass. He could have tried yelling something to his fellow men, something about it being a trap, but they wouldn't have believed him and frankly, he didn't really give a shit. All he thought about was running.

As he leapt down the steps on the other side and hit the grassy ground beyond, he heard the piping sound stop. Lepus spun around to look at the men in the temple, but kept backing away just the same.

The air around the temple shimmered, like waves of gasoline fumes in sunlight. There was a collective gasp from the soldiers as the wind was knocked out of every one—then, to a man, the soldiers rose to the tips of their toes as if lifted, chests buckled up to the night sky, arms and head lolling back. They were a force of rag dolls, quivering in the moonlight. They didn't make a sound, which was perhaps the worst part of it all.

Lepus turned and ran towards the side of the temple, trying to ignore the silent death unfolding on the harsh stone nearby. When he got towards the front of the structure, he dropped and began scurrying low through the grass, staying out of sight. After a stretch he rose slowly, just far enough to see what was going on.

At the temple, there was a clattering, heavy sound as three hundred corpses fell over.

The wind had picked up. There was a rush of air over the plaza. He smelled ozone and then bolted again, heading for the foliage. Behind him, out of sight, there was a low rumble.

As he gained the cover of the overgrowth beyond the grass, he hit the ground and hoped for the best. When he was good and down, he hazarded a glance.

An obelisk fifty feet tall, smack dab in the center of the temple's main concourse, was glowing. Electricity crackled up and down its length. The glow expanded, and began to suggest a form. The outline of the thing was twice the height of the obelisk, with shapes that suggested vast legs and a snaking, twisting appendage that hung from the top. The outline began to fill in with bone and flesh, one gruesome layer at a time.

Lepus turned away, started running once more. He ran and

ran and did not look at the thing on the temple.

Until it roared. Then Lepus looked.

It was huge, its skin little more than blood-red muscle tissue. Where its face might have been there was a hideous, extended organ that might have been a tongue or an arm or something else entirely. The organ flexed freely, like an elephant's trunk, casually smashing portions of the temple. Lepus felt a warm sensation on his legs and was vaguely aware that he'd pissed himself. He thought he might just stand here forever, staring at this awesome God—for if he knew nothing else, he knew he was in the presence of a strange and terrible deity.

Then the world exploded.

The pair of F-4 Phantom jets came by so fast that Lepus didn't even see them, though he heard them wailing through the air perhaps a thousand feet off the ground. He barely caught sight of the whoosh of smoke from the missiles as they deployed and struck the temple.

But the explosion—that he could see just fine.

The fireball was immense; it was given scale by the living, screaming thing that was at the center of it. The temple blew into billions of pieces, rubble and slivers of rock radiating out. Lepus hit the ground. The foliage encircling the grassy clearing was torn to shreds. The grass caught fire as great arcs of flame *whoomped* out from the center of the blast. The heat was incredible. The sound was deafening. The force was staggering.

The beast was still alive.

The missiles must have struck it dead on. It should have been atomized. It was burning, sure, but if the missiles hadn't taken it out right from the start, Lepus felt little hope that fire would do the trick now.

Worse, whatever force had held the beast in check seemed

to have been destroyed by the blast. The thing was free. Its vast legs swung out over the edge of the temple and into the flaming fury of the high grass. It roared and trumpeted, free of its prison.

THE WARM SENSATION ON his legs brought him back to reality. He'd pissed himself, again, standing in an examination room beneath OUTLOOK's Facility B on Vieques Island, Puerto Rico, flanked by his men, thirty years distant from the horror in Cambodia that was somehow just as fresh and as present as it could be. He smelled the ozone, felt the power coming from the man in the bed, heard the strange music whispering at the edges of his hearing.

"Sir?" one of his men said, glancing at the stain on Lepus's pants.

"*Evacuate,*" he whispered, so low no one could hear him.

"Sir?"

"Evacuate," he said, louder now. "Evacuate! *GET THE FUCK OUT OF HERE!*" he screamed, cold sweat pouring over his pale face, spittle flying from his gold-and-white teeth.

"What about them, sir?" the guard said, nodding at the agents clustered around the bed.

"*FUCK THEM! GO! GO! GO!*" Lepus turned and shoved his men forward towards the door, and they ran from the room, hauling ass down the hall.

The agents looked at each other, confused and slightly dazed from the strange sensation pouring off David Nells.

"What the hell was that all about?" Abe said shakily.

"He's got the right idea," James said. "Let's go."

"David?" Stephanie said guardedly to the smiling man in the bed.

He looked up at her. "Go on. You've freed me. Daddy's coming home now."

"Are you sure?" she said, taking his hand for a moment. His skin no longer felt human, and there was a strange pulsing coming from deep within his tissues. He was transforming, being born anew. The man she'd known was fast receding, the evolving look in his eyes chronicling his departure and the arrival of something *else*.

"Go," he said, his voice resonating strangely in the room. The walls shimmered, changing color and composition and dimension, black geometric shapes flickering in and out, the twinkling lights of stars manifesting through the plaster and tile. "Thank you."

"*Come on*," James said fiercely, pulling at her shoulder. Stephanie backed away slowly, the thing that used to be David Foster Nells watching her placidly, and then the group turned and fled.

THEY RAN RIGHT INTO a dream. Emerging from the exam room, they found themselves in the cargo compartment of a large transport plane, mostly empty. The noise of the twin engines was all around them, but it was overpowered by the rush of wind from the open cargo door.

A Chinese woman in an unfamiliar uniform was pulling a parachute pack onto her back. She looked at them and smiled, then jumped out the open door and into the dark clouds beyond.

"What the fuck?" Abe said as they looked around, disoriented.

James spotted a door into the main compartment and hurried towards it. The others followed his lead.

They emerged into the cabin, a scene of carnage. There was a dead and bloody man lying in the aisle, dressed in an Army uniform. A splash of blood and brain on the ceiling towards the front was dripping down onto another soldier, lying sprawled over the cushioned seats. Closer to the rear was a clot of women in saffron robes, dead from gunshot wounds. Standing in their midst was a third man, also bloody, wearing a white suit. He turned to face them.

"Hello again, Captain," Stephen Alzis said. "I didn't expect to see you here, but that's causality for you. Shake it up a little and you surprise even yourself."

"What the hell's going on, Alzis?" James said tensely. The others gathered around him, confused; they had no idea who the man in the white suit was.

"Just a little family reunion. You shouldn't wait around. It takes a lot of energy to birth a God. Tends to be a little destructive."

"Are we even, Alzis?"

"We're even, Captain. You've done remarkably well. Don't worry. I'll take care of your little situation when I'm done here."

"How do we get back?"

Alzis shrugged. "Use the exit, I suppose." He turned away and stepped out to the aisle; as he did, he vanished into thin air.

James thought for a moment, then he spun around. "Go back!" he said. "Find parachutes! Now!"

It was night on Vieques Island. Agent Nolan sat in the driver's seat of the Range Rover, fidgeting. A few minutes ago, klaxons had begun sounding at OUTLOOK Group. He almost started driving then and there, but decided against it. He was waiting for either a flare or the sound of gunshots. If he went too soon, he could end up dead or captured before the team was even outside.

Then he heard a sound, somewhere overhead. It was a low thrumming noise, getting closer. He stepped out of the vehicle for a moment and looked up into the night sky.

The first parachute opened, and then four more over the next minute. Five people were swinging down out of the clouds towards Sun Bay.

What the hell? he thought.

Then he saw the plane.

Andrew Nells' twin-prop C-46A Commando "Bathing Beauty" broke through the clouds, its twin Pratt & Whitney engines whirring into the night. It sped down at a steep angle, and within a minute it reached its destination.

OUTLOOK Group.

The plane slammed sharply into the rear of the main building's roof, erupting in flames, and the wreckage flipped forward, slapping upside-down onto the bulk of the structure. Then there was an explosion and the walls blew out in flaming chunks, mowing down smaller buildings nearby. A massive fireball emerged, smoke and debris billowing upward, and then the basements collapsed and there was a rush of air that fed the flames. Just offshore, a roiling rush of escaping wind vomited up from the waste pipe. On the grounds of OUTLOOK, people were running and vehicles were starting up. Across Camp Garcia, lights went on and emergency vehicles rolled out, lights and sirens blaring.

Nolan stared, incredulous. "*Fuck,*" he whispered.

Δ

In Sun Bay, five parachutes collapsed and spread on the surface of the water. James and Jean freed themselves immediately—James releasing the parachute pack, Jean simply ripping out of it—and swam around, helping to free the others as soon as they could find them.

Within a few minutes, the five agents staggered to shore. James and Stephanie held hands. They stood on the sand and silently watched the inferno, gawking tourists in some strange and alien land.

Epilogue

∞

There's a room as big as all outdoors. I rise from the still body in the bed and stride forward purposefully, embracing my future. As I near the far wall, the plaster ripples and parts like a curtain of obedient water.

Beyond? Beyond is everything. The cosmos in its strange null entirety, the mad planets whirring in space, the expansion and contraction of the universe, the dancers at the soul of time, the lint in the giant's navel.

I step through the wall, and it all starts to happen. This is the end and the beginning.

Acknowledgements

I relied on a number of people and works in the course of this project, and gratefully enumerate them here. Any strengths of verisimilitude this novel achieved is due to them, whilst any failings of same should be chalked up to my authorial hand-waving.

The chapter titles all consist of phrases from T.S. Eliot's *The Waste Land,* a poem of remarkably rich and varied language; flitting through it is rather like casting the *I Ching*. Dennis Detwiller filled the role of first reader and, as always, my invaluable idea sounding board, as well as creating a number of the characters and organizations seen herein: Club Apocalypse, Stephen Alzis, and Belial; OUTLOOK Group, Dr. John Baker, Dr. Bart Strysik, and Dr. Albert Yrjo; and the *Phenomen-X* characters Stuart Prendergast, Tommy Prendergast, Robert Hoggard, David Carmichael, and Allen Eddington; all originally appeared in Pagan Publishing's roleplaying game sourcebooks *Delta Green* and *Delta Green: Countdown*. Scott Glancy, Esq., served as a reservoir of intelligence-community and federal law-enforcement lore, and created the characters Joseph Camp, Matthew Carpenter (referred to herein as Agent Adam), Reinhard Galt, Forrest James, Greg Mason, and Jean Qualls for Pagan's roleplaying game sourcebook *Delta Green*. Robert McLaughlin created the character Harley Patton for *Delta Green*. Dr. Graeme Price hypothesized the lipopolysaccharide neo-tissue treatment, the leucopararosaniline spray technique, and credibility-checked the medical scenes in chapter five; he also created Dr. Grant Emerson for *Delta Green: Countdown*. John H. Crowe, III, provided information on civilian law enforcement, the military, the C-46A Commando, Southeast Asian geography, and firearms. Janet Wray of the Fort Leavenworth Public Affairs Office supplied information on the U.S. Disciplinary Barracks and generously answered many, many questions. Damon Lipinski did the research for Greg Mason's photography equipment and darkroom shopping trip. Shane Ivey and Steve Keck offered information on Wackenhut Corporation. Rebecca Strong and Michael Tice provided some Los Angeles local color. Evan Ferguson kindly supplied first-hand Vieques Island knowledge and photographs (*Viva Vieques Libre*, Evan!). Eleanor (Em) Frothingham, Jenny Scott, Kim Stewart, and Allan & Karen Tynes all gave support and encouragement. Em also explained the difference between a gaffer and an electrician and consulted on SCUBA diving. Melissa Reizian Frank's friendly cat Clotho appeared in the role of Stephanie Park's friendly cat Clotho. The National Weather Service's assorted websites provided meteorological data for the dates and places cited in the story. The websites welcome.topuertorico.org and www.bolack.com offered tourist information for Puerto Rico. The website www.biobay.com provided material on Vieques Island's bioluminescent bays. Brian Appleton, Adam Scott Glancy, Heather Hudson, Shane Ivey, and John Nephew read the manuscript and pro-vided helpful comments. Ted Arlauskas, Rob Heinsoo, and Chris Womack caught some errors in the limited-edition printing that I corrected for this edition. A Rand McNally Atlas was wantonly marked up to determine the fictional locales of the story (Bountin, Maryland and Groversville/Promise, Tennessee). Reference works consulted include *Spy Book: The Encyclopedia of Espionage, Revised Edition,* by Norman Polmar & Thomas B. Allen (New York: Random House, 1998) [useful for all kinds of intelligence research]; *The CIA and the Cult of Intelligence* by Victor Marchetti & John D. Marks (New York: Dell, 1980) [provided information on Civil Air Transport and the CIA's China/Tibet/Taiwan work in the 1950s–60s, and also described the historical incident on which this novel's scene of the botched assassination of PARIAH was loosely based]; *The New York Public Library American History Desk Reference* (New York: Macmillan, 1997); *Bigger Secrets* by William Poundstone (Boston: Houghton Mifflin, 1986) [if you're curious about the reference to Disneyland's Club 33, read this book]; *The Encyclopedia of World Air Power* (New York: Crescent Books, 1986) [consulted for the Commando, naturally]; *You Are Going To Prison* by Jim Hogshire (Port Townsend, Washington: Loompanics, 1994) [could also be called *Prison for Dummies*—it's sort of a user's manual for arrest, sentencing, and incarceration]; *The Hot House: Life Inside Leavenworth Prison* by Pete Earley (New York: Bantam Books, 1993) [Earley's book deals with the federal civilian prison at Leavenworth, Kansas, not the Fort Leavenworth USDB, but it still provided critical insight into life behind bars]; *Military Small Arms of the 20th Century 6th Edition* by Ian V. Hogg and John Weeks (Northbrook, Illinois: DBI Books, Inc.) [guns, guns, guns]; and "Life Inside Leavenworth" by SSgt. Alan Moore in *Soldiers* magazine, September, 1997 [this set of articles dealt directly with the USDB]. The vast majority of this novel was written in February and March of 1999 at the College Inn Pub in Seattle's University District. Much like the narrator's childhood home in Lovecraft's short story "The Outsider," the Pub is dim, subterranean, windowless, and affords no measurable sense of time's passing; unlike its literary counterpart, however, the Pub's incomparable nachos are half price on Mondays. When in Memphis dine at Payne's on Lamar, and try their smoked sausage. If you liked this book, please hand it to a friend; if you really liked this book, write your name in it first.

About the Author

John Scott Tynes is an award-winning game designer and writer in Seattle. He currently designs Xbox 360 videogames for Microsoft Studios. He was the founder and editor-in-chief of Pagan Publishing and Armitage House and his best-known projects include *Unknown Armies, Puppetland, Delta Green, The Unspeakable Oath,* and *Call of Cthulhu D20*. He has served as a film critic, videogame critic, graphic designer, web designer, videographer, and screenwriter. His film *The Yellow Sign* is available on DVD from Lurker Films and his novel *Delta Green: The Rules of Engagement* litters the shelves of used-book stores worldwide. He is very fortunate to have married the love of his life, Jenny, and to have a brilliant daughter, Vivian. He smokes a pipe and drinks brandy from a snifter because by God, someone should.

Made in the USA
Columbia, SC
02 September 2018